The World in an Orange

Creating theatre with Barney Simon

written by
Irene Stephanou & Leila Henriques

edited by
Lionel Abrahams & Jane Fox

SEVEN STORIES

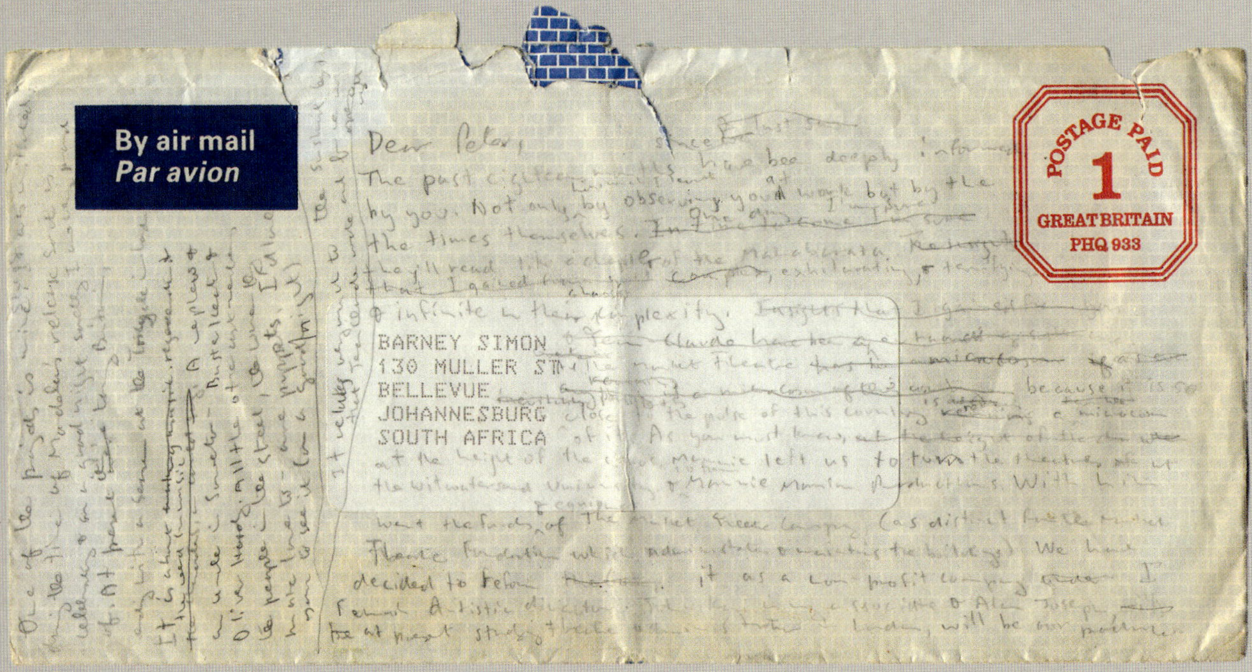

Letter from Peter Brook which Barney covered in writing.

Message from Peter Brook

For Barney

Barney — a book has been made about you and I think you'd like it. It's not been a written book. It's a spoken one. In it, we hear voices. The words flow out, straight from the heart, trying to say what can never be said when the feeling is so strong, but as we listen, we can feel the feeling.

If someone wants to know who you are, you are here. Someone who wants to know how you directed must just listen to the way your friends talk about you — that's the way you first talked and worked with them. That was how you brought them to life out of rehearsals. Touch by touch, with warm and questioning eyes, with your tender, ever-so-vulnerable strength, in your own special way you would draw out the hidden person. And this time it's you, Barney, who rises from the page; you are with us again, a full human being, in all your painful, joyous contradictions. No, not all, because as you insisted there is always a mystery in everything human, something more to find...

I think you'd be pleased with this, Barney, because it's in no way the final homage. You never believed any single person was that important. On every page we can hear you saying: 'It's not over yet. We've hardly begun. We can go on. We must. We will.' And, with one hand on our shoulder you murmur, 'Above all, please, one last note, don't forget — what are we doing it for?'

Peter Brook
Paris
28/06/01

THE ELECTRIC

Contents

Opposite – Aerial view of a William Kentridge fire sculpture in Newtown, Johannesburg.
Photograph by Andrew Meintjes.

Part 1 ◦ Beginnings

Part 2 ◦ A Home

Part 3 ◦ Workshop

Part 4 ◦ New Times

Part 5 ◦ Legacy

Opposite – Barney Simon at home in his garden in Yeoville, Johannesburg.
Photograph by David Goldblatt.

Introduction by Irene Stephanou

I never worked with Barney.

As I began my career in the theatre, however, talk about working with Barney abounded. Phrases like 'Have you worked with Barney?', 'I loved working with Barney', 'I hated working with Barney', 'I once workshopped with Barney – but never again – he did change my life though', were common. They were often underscored by a lamenting chorus of 'Oh, IF ONLY I could work with Barney!' Similar sentiments, with variations of apotheosis, longing, satisfaction, secrecy, anger, inspiration, elitism, hurt, epiphany, desire, rage, relief, joy, delight and catharsis, pervaded rehearsal rooms, theatres, foyers, lounges, streets, cars and many Johannesburg rooms around me. Mystique prevailed. I became terrified of working with Barney.

I had first read about the creation of The Company while working behind the counter in my family's cafe. Barney and The Company became a definition of theatre for me. When I went to drama school, I learnt many things. For the first time, I learnt the value of the Western theatre tradition. As I contemplated university and started acting professionally, I tried to marry my initial vision of theatre at the cafe counter with the fevered talk I'd heard about working with Barney. I wanted to know what exactly this man had given to actors that the rest of us didn't know.

When Barney died in 1995 I was in Cape Town. I attended a hastily organised and well-supported memorial service. I heard Bo Petersen describing the process of working with Barney when she played Vicky, the go-go dancer in "Cincinatti – Scenes from City Life". She said how Barney had always insisted that the character have dirty feet. At this time of mourning the loss and simultaneously celebrating the gift of Barney's life, I realised that all these stories that live in actors who had worked with him MUST be recorded. Why? It is not only the story of a remarkable creative and theatrical process but also a reflection of the legacy of South African life – gleaned from real lives. I believe it is a body of work that marks and mirrors the genesis of a truly South African theatre.

The interviews/stories are often substantial monologues articulated by some of the country's most creative beings. As such they embody motivational lessons about life-generating inspiration and instruction that actors, storytellers, academics – in fact, any soul seeking quality of life – can access. Great actors tell their stories, and in so doing, invite and lead the reader to endless eureka, discovering and rediscovering joys and lessons for life and work. These narrators cut through class and other man-made divisions, and unite humanity as they tell stories of the making of stories.

When I returned to Joburg in 1995, I tested my idea for this book on Vanessa Cooke: a close friend of Barney's and mine, also a Board member of The Market Theatre who subsequently became a member of the Barney Simon Trust. She encouraged me, and reminded me of the people with whom Barney had first begun working. I began with Lionel Abrahams and Sipho Sepamla and also interviewed contemporary theatre people like Doris Sihula and Leila Henriques. I realised the gigantic challenge that lay ahead. I wanted a partner. I approached Leila only after I had interviewed her for the book. She had done both a workshop production and a scripted play with Barney. I had always been aware of her talent and sensitivity. Her account of herself, however, as a young actor who shyly and stealthily avoided impromptu contact with the great director, Barney Simon, after he had expressed an intention of working with her, clinched it for me – I related to her zealous and zany humility. Leila has been an ideal partner. As a team we shared our deep respect for Barney as writer, director and creator, and for the interviewees and their simple and complex processes of work. This approach was encouraged by the Barney Simon Trust. It was also guided by our intellectual angel and editor (now publisher), Maggie Davey.

An important criterion for being an interviewee was having worked with Barney. We needed to bring order into this vast resource of actors' testimonies. We began by using Pat Tucker's invaluable book "The Best of Company" as a cornerstone. We then approached Vanessa Cooke who provided information on the whereabouts and accessibility of actors. Mannie Manim, whom we interviewed twice, offered historic perspectives on his relationship with Barney which led to the creation of The Company and The Market Theatre.

A sense of urgency overcame Leila and I regarding the capturing of these stories. Death had already staked its claim on Barney and others with whom he had worked. We began as actors but soon became authors who fiercely wished to protect, learn, enjoy and always gain strength from the legacy left by Barney Simon. In this spirit, we voraciously began to interview.

Vanessa suggested that we interview at least one actor from every play. Rather idealistically, we were intending to interview all the actors who'd ever worked with Barney. As the project progressed and the volume of the book grew to the size of an encyclopaedia, we realised that this was neither possible nor altogether necessary for the purposes of this book. Our ideal would still have been to be able to interview all the people who worked with Barney because of fresh perspectives and expressions of his process of working. For this reason, we interviewed more than one actor from some plays and in other cases, unfortunately, none. The list of those who could have been interviewed is seemingly endless and the number still increases to this day. After eighty completed interviews, however, we are relying on this mass of testimonies to satisfy the purpose of this book, namely to document Barney's way of working.

Our interview technique was consciously non-directional – we functioned as catalysts, inviting the interviewees to express their stories and experiences as they saw fit. Some interviewees offered their stories as the interview began, while others needed prompting. The three basic questions were:

'Who were you and where were you when you met Barney?'
'What work did you do with him?'
'What did he leave you with?'

These questions were intentionally innocuous, broad and even bland, in order to facilitate the input of the interviewee. All interviewees had our undivided respect and attention, as fundamental and pivotal principles in our communication. The testimonies we share with the reader could not have been gleaned otherwise. Interviewees were assured that they could read their interviews before publication and many altered their input for purposes of clarification, having been reminded that work would still be edited and that our conversational tones must be preserved. We have not attempted a literary documentation of a theatrical process. Many interviewees shared gems of wisdom about the creation of good work as they wrestled with their talents and with a director who was often overwhelming but usually extremely empowering. The interviews are compelling communications of theatre and life as they document discoveries made during and after the process of working with Barney.

Barney's death is a profound loss to the theatre community of South Africa and, indeed, the world's theatrical community. His uniqueness lay in his ability to detect truths and eliminate lies, as he wove stories into exceptional theatre. We believe that our interviews have elicited a unique treasure of evidence, and hope that this book will be a valuable resource. It may function as a handbook with a difference. Ideas, advice and exercises are to be found, but only if one searches for them (as I think Barney would prefer). They are, however, useless if not accompanied by a code of trust and respect in an endless quest for truth. Nothing is judged as trivial, terrible or even tremendous: only its truth is judged. Our mission has always been grounded in this ethos.

Barney was the way he worked. His way of working was inextricably tied up with his person and his sensibility. His love for stories was governed by his meticulous, continuous and unrelenting commitment to a theatre of trust, respect and truth. This sensual, rich, full, unromantic and detailed account of life and work documents an intense and unpredictable living journey with Barney Simon. The book has been a labour of love – please relish these love stories, we have.

Previous page left – Barney Simon.
Photograph by Bruce Davidson, courtesy of NELM.
Overleaf – Lionel Abrahams, Hilary Hamburger and Barney Simon at Clifton Beach, Cape Town.
Photograph by Denis Kuny.

Part 1.
Beginnings

13

Chapter 1. Early Years

Barney Simon was born on 13th April 1932. He lived in Troyeville, a white, working-class suburb. His parents, Lithuanian-born Jews, had started their courtship at the Yiddish theatre in Troyeville (where his father placed chocolates on the seat of Edie, Barney's mother). While pregnant with Barney, her third child, Edie compulsively watched Yiddish theatre and movies at the Regal Cinema in Bez Valley. Sharing her passion, Barney spent many boyhood hours at the Regal, where he joined the Popeye Club – this was only for boys. Girls had the Olive Oyl Club.

However, later he recalled his mother saying, 'You want to be a writer? You want to work in theatre? It's a nice hobby. Tell me how you are going to earn a living?'

Garalt MacLiam – The Star, 1981.

In spite of this, at the age of sixteen Barney got his first theatre job helping Taubie Kushlick with props. A year later he joined an amateur group called the Dramateurs.

After matriculating from Jeppe Boys' High School in the fifties he had a brief stint working in his father's cap and hat factory. About this time he and Lionel Abrahams were meeting and reading each other's stories. Soon afterwards, Barney went to London, where he worked backstage at the Theatre Royal for Joan Littlewood's socialistic theatre company, which was run on a pittance.

Of her he said: 'In her lifestyle, vision and the way she treated people something was confirmed for me. She served the life rather than the literature of the piece, so that the text became a pretext for life on the streets. What happened to her haunts us here... She was one of the greatest geniuses of the theatre. She made theatre from nothing. It was workers' theatre.'

Business Day, November 1986.

And this became integral to Barney's approach. One of his favourite quotes was from Camus: 'A man's work is little more than his journey through life in order to rediscover the two or three great and simple images that first found access to his heart.'

In the remainder of this chapter Barney describes some of the childhood memories that later influenced his work. We also hear from actress Molly Seftel, whose friendship with Barney began in their teen years, as she talks about their world and their initiation into Theatre.

Opposite – The Simons' old home in Magpie Street, Kensington, September 1974.
Photograph by David Goldblatt.

Quotations from interviews with Barney Simon

'I have one very special memory that to me somehow relates to my life, my family, and theatre. That is when I was four or five years old and being in Jeppe Shul during the war years, downstairs with my father, my mother across the way - the most beautiful woman on that side of the balcony - and very proud that this woman was flirting with me, asking me if I was thirsty on Yom Kippur, trying to convince me to eat and showing me great attention. I would sometimes sit upstairs with her. And there was one woman on the same balcony as my mother, in the poorest seat in the synagogue - she had only one leg and a heavy boot on her remaining leg - she was dressed in black, more like a Greek widow than Jewish. When she came up the concrete stairs outside, you could hear the bang of her crutches and her boot, and when she got to the top of the women's balcony and had to walk down, she banged so loud that the service would have to pause. When she prayed, she used to beat herself and wail. To me she resembled a witch, particularly as there she was in a seat from which she couldn't even see the Ark, on the same side where my mother was so resplendent. My mother was a Lithuanian peasant woman, but she had a really natural chic.

'One day a little Rebbe came to the Shul. I didn't know who he was. I remember him being very small and he had a reddish beard. He got up on the podium and started talking in a fast Yiddish, and the whole synagogue, which was this synagogue of landslayt, began to rock and wail. He was describing the slaughter of the Lithuanian Jews by the Lithuanian goyim, not even by the Nazis. From what I understood afterwards years later, he was describing the slaughter of the Jews in the Vilna Ghetto. He was describing bayoneting and rapes and beheadings and God knows what... And I will never forget looking up in the middle of all this chaos in the synagogue - that terrible wail - and seeing my mother beating herself like that old woman in black. That is something that has always remained with me. When I did "Marat/Sade" I used that wail at the moment when Marat fears that he is going blind and is confronted by the fact that he can't see because of the smoke of bodies burning.

'I know that experience somehow made me a Jew. It's something that has always stayed with me and was obviously very important to me in terms of understanding my mother, my family, and the destiny of my people.'

Quote taken from interview with Joseph Sherman, "Rabbi compatriots from Lithuania gentiles", "Cutting Through The Mountain", edited by Immanuel Suttner (Viking, 1997).

Opposite – A Jewish man at a poultry shop in Johannesburg in 1952. Between 1880 and 1910, about 40 000 Jewish immigrants, mostly from Lithuania, arrived in South Africa.
Photograph courtesy of The Star.

SHMUEL
RUBINSKY
טשיקען מארקעט
כשר
KOSHER
COHNS

'I can still remember the click in my life, the turning point, when I must have been five or six, or maybe seven. It was when I went to see a Shirley Temple movie. I was a big fan of Shirley Temple's. I even learnt to tapdance through watching her movies. What happened was this: I went with our maid's son, he was about eleven, to the movie house in Bez Valley, and they wouldn't let him in, they said, because he was black. A shadow, he wasn't seen as a person. I hadn't understood that. We went away and we examined ourselves and saw the palms of our hands were the same colour and the inside of our mouths were the same colour, so we went back to the manager with that as a proposition, but he wasn't interested. Something clicked then. What I try to do in my work always is to give identity to the shadows.'

Interview by Garalt MacLiam, *The Star Weekend*, 1986.

'My sister Celia affected my vision greatly... something to do with her innocent outlook. She used to sit on the verandah and burn in the sun, watching with passion and greed every front door in the street. As soon as someone appeared, she'd call a greeting and invite them to come and chat.'

Sunday Times, March 9, 1986.

'When I went to school there was a plump, ginger kid I knew. We were playing cowboys and crooks – I was a cowboy and he was a crook. We were equally scared. I captured him and kept him in jail, and told him he got sick and then I told him he died and was buried – because that way I could keep him for me, and I could comfort him and he could comfort me. You are scared and in order to protect yourself, you become a jailer.'

New Nation, April 1989.

Opposite – Yeoville Park.
From "Living in Yeoville", an exhibition of photographs by Gideon Mendel at the Market Photo Gallery, 1987.

Lionel Abrahams

'He would draw one into himself and enclose one'

We were close friends for a long, long time, beginning when he was about seventeen and I twenty-two. I recently dug out some very ancient letters to me from Barney on his first trip to London. And they reminded me of just how close we were. It had a lot to do with writing. Barney would turn up at my house late at night and see by the light in the window that I was still up writing. He would call me and I would let him in. My parents were there but asleep. We would talk and talk and read to each other. I hadn't had a friendship like that before and it went on for many years. But somehow it died. In the last dozen years or so of his life I was never alone with Barney – we met as friends but only in other company.

A long time ago I took the image of motherhood to express Barney's way of caring. It was as though he took a person, or the creative possibility of a project, into himself for a long spell of protection and nurturing. In a way I underwent that kind of caring or mothering at some stage too. But his insistence on feeling for me, or for someone I was concerned about, and interpreting my reality, was not always comfortable. At times it seemed presumptuous.

Do you feel that he did that with you, with the writing?

My writing? No, no – or only to a small extent. He sort of protected me and interpreted my work in terms of what was good or bad for me. At a certain time this was very comforting, nurturing, but at other times resistance was required. I don't think that he quite liked the resistance. He wasn't terribly critical. We were simply sharing, more than working together. The first thing that can really count as a sort of working together was when we drew in two other friends in Kensington who also wrote short stories, Peggy Marks and Myrna Blumberg. In 1952 we decided to put together a book of our stories and publish it ourselves. We each contributed five stories and got two artist friends in Kensington, Harold Rubin and my near namesake Lionel Abrams, to illustrate it. We called it "Twenty" because we were all in our early twenties and there were twenty stories.

Barney's own section contained not only five stories but also some powerful prose fragments. The volume was 'Roneoed' in various offices over weekends, and of the four of us Barney, as I remember, was the one who shouldered a lot of the work. He got his hands dirty with the messy business of running off the pages from the inked wax stencils – while I sat by and watched. We ended up with only about two hundred copies. Bookshops agreed to sell some and we sent the thing out to newspapers and were pretty widely reviewed, with Barney's work attracting the highest praises. In those days there wasn't much publishing going on in the country.

Out of "Twenty" grew my first magazine, The Purple Renoster. Barney took a great interest in this plan. But before it took off he went to London for a needed change. I let him know I was placing his story "Fanny Lester" in the first issue of The Purple Renoster. It was a typically tender story taken straight from life. We were about to start the roneo duplicating when I got a telegram from Barney reading 'FANNY BESTER LESTER LIBELLOUS'. It took me quite a while to work out that he was telling me to change the name from Fanny Lester to Fanny Bester because the name Fanny Lester was real and would make the story libellous. We got it sorted out in time. When Barney came back he became my assistant editor. He was a kind of perfectionist and was concerned that the magazine be attractive looking. He wanted it to be right in every respect – whereas I had become urgent to get the next issue out with a minimum of delays and was willing to cut all kinds of corners. We clashed for the first time over that difference.

In one of the early issues of The Classic magazine that Barney edited there is a story called "The Last Leg" about a one-legged man in jail who avoids hard labour by refusing to wear his artificial leg because there was no regulation saying that he had to. Its author was Dugmore Boetie, whom Barney drew into a unique workshop, which he ran at Dorkay House. The idea was to have writers and actors tell stories to each other and then for actors to improvise from the story-situations, and possibly develop new theatre material. So there I witnessed one of the ways in which Barney worked. Everyone learnt something. It was a rich experience. Dugmore Boetie was a total scamp and fantasiser, though he had, in fact, lost a leg. Nat Nakasa, a brilliant journalist with high standards, had a need for order. He listened to Dugmore's yarns very sceptically, while Barney and I were inclined to swallow everything.

In the process of getting a story acted out we discovered interesting facts about the life around us. One story had to do with a man taking leave from his gardening job, where another man temporarily replaces him. While away he is arrested for 'no pass' and imprisoned, so only after a long delay returns and wants his job back. But the new man refuses to let him have it. Barney was puzzled by the obstinacy shown by the actor improvising the replacement. He seemed unbelievably rigid, as though he had no sympathy for one of his own. Eventually Barney asked him what was going on. The answer was, 'Well the other guy is a moegoe.' Barney asked, 'What is a moegoe?' and was told it meant a sort of peasant simpleton not much respected in town. Barney loved learning secrets like that, which complicated our simplistic assumptions about, for example, black people's attitudes to each other.

He was one of those who were taking up the challenge to come together across the racial divisions long before there was a fashionable politically correct consensus. He was looking, identifying possibilities, and nurturing them.

Would you say that his motivation was a love for humanity, a love for people?
That is a complicated one. I remember how much certain people's style of conduct bothered and irritated Barney. He was certainly judgmental, sometimes on grounds that puzzled me. On the other hand, he cared, not only for those with whom he formed his very special protective friendships, but also for humanity in the abstract.

Have you any idea how and why Barney moved from story writing into theatre?
I think Athol would have some interesting ideas on that. We speculated a bit about Barney as a writer. I think that one of us suggested that he didn't really care for the

practice of writing in itself. Barney's writing was always about the life he knew, the truth of things, but I gathered that some part of him didn't want all that to come out. Although he was always urging people he worked with to open and reveal themselves without reserve, he had a certain need to hide, I would guess.

You said that he took people into himself; maybe that was also a way not of hiding but of using himself, living through many different people.
Possibly. Complicated man, mysterious. Passionate about South Africa's particular forms of cruelty, yet not political.

When you say he was unusual and complicated is there anything else that stands out for you about his uniqueness?
Barney decidedly had a strain of the mystical in his nature. His thinking would not be interpreted into logical arguments. He always implied that intuition guided what he had to say. I often couldn't understand what he was getting at and would show my irritation. Through this perhaps I became responsible in a sense for pushing him away. Perhaps he felt he had to hide from me. But if he was guarding his feelings by withdrawing he never acknowledged that that was what he was doing.

So you would say he depended on his instincts?
Very much. At the same time, though, he got an enormous amount out of his reading. He loved books as a source of wisdom, ideas and expressions, which he used in his work. The last two times I saw Barney were, first, at Hilary and Tony Hamburger's wedding, and then, six weeks later, at Joe Slovo's funeral ceremony. And on each of these occasions Barney gave a speech that startled me. I had never thought of him as an orator, but his speech at each of these events was simply beautiful, so telling, so rich, so articulate, so pertinent to the person he was talking about. I had always known there were limits to what I knew about Barney. In fact, he was very nervous before speaking. I think it was a bit of a surprise to him as well that these speeches came out so eloquently. Hilary's wedding was a function for family and friends, but Joe Slovo's funeral event was a big formal ceremony in the City Hall, attended by President Mandela, cabinet ministers, writers – and there was a whole string of speeches. Yet Barney's stood out as something entirely different and especially fine. Nadine Gordimer also remarked on this to me.

Hilary Hamburger, formerly Kuny, played a profound role in Barney's life, as he in hers, from the time I introduced them in 1957 until he died. In his earlier years Molly Seftel was comparably important to him, though in a different way. He had a devotion to Molly which involved a dream of guiding her into a great theatrical career, yet after many years she became one of the many he moved on from, like Maya Kriel and Patrick Cullinan. Hilary was one friend he did not move on from – perhaps the only one apart from Mannie Manim. This might have had to do with her having a profession that did not involve him as director or writer, so their connection was on a different plane. When he was abroad she watched over his sister Celia and his widower father until their deaths. I remember the intensity of her grief at Celia's death. And when he was in

Johannesburg she provided Barney with a virtual surrogate family. During his last illness he lay in her house, begging not to be returned to hospital. And it was at the Hamburgers' that the first mourners gathered, and Barney's nephew from America discussed funeral arrangements, and Mary Benson telephoned abroad the news that Barney had died.

Have you got anything else to say about his tenderness and the perceptiveness that you mentioned earlier, about how he worked with people?

He had a way of perceiving all kinds of sadness in people, vulnerabilities that I usually hadn't seen at all. Of the two of us, Barney was the instinctive one, the subtly perceptive one. Half a year after he died, friends of his, including Nadine Gordimer and me, were at Hilary's to see in the new year. Afterwards I wrote "Ghost" for Barney Simon:

'Half a year you've not been somewhere in the world making
your presence felt. A few of those you taught to need your
caring art then almost taught to let you come and go and
let unfinished business go, tonight are seeing out the year.
Not seen out, you visit us making your absence felt.'

Lionel Abrahams in his Kensington study.
Photograph by John Hogg.

Molly Seftel

'Our parents always told us that we were the most beautiful, most wonderful and the most brilliant, and we should not be afraid of nobody'

There was Barney, his sister-in-law Josephine, Harold her brother, and my younger sister Dolly, who had a great friendship with Barney. We all went to Habonim camp in East London. Do you know what a Habonim camp is? Boy scouts and girl guides – well, the Jews had Habonim, because we had a perception that they wouldn't accept us as Jews. There was a lot of anti-Semitism, latent anti-Semitism, during the war and post war. It was just after the war, about '45 or '46, that we all went to Habonim camp. Now Barney was beautiful. You know I just looked around and everybody was spotty and ugly and not fully developed. Barney was immediately beautiful. He had these wonderful grey-blue eyes and long eyelashes. He looked like Montgomery Clift. And he was always very quiet, very gentle. He would peg somebody to be his friend, and he would edge in. You didn't realise that he was becoming kind of indispensable, because you took no notice of him, and then suddenly, 'Where's Barney?' It was really a very gentle thrusting into our lives. At the camp we always seemed to be together, a crowd of about eight of us. We were great snobbish intellectuals. We had great contempt for anybody who liked jazz or boogie-woogie. We were the classicists.

How old were you?

Fifteen. Barney was fourteen. We came back from Habonim camp and Barney kept phoning. He would say he was coming for lunch. But because he was younger than me, I never took him seriously. I was waiting for a prince to carry me off. Well Barney couldn't even ride a horse.

When did you first work with Barney?

We were doing plays at Jeppe High School, but I first worked with Barney on Sholem Asch's "Night". Barney played the thief and I played the prostitute. We liked it then because there were these extremes. They were all the outsiders: a prostitute, a thief, a drunkard, a fool and other sub-cultural people. They were outcasts of society and we sympathised with them. We all had this socialist dream. We loved and were thrilled by what we thought were the exciting lives these characters led. There was the Federation of Amateur Theatricals. I don't know how it is that we decided to enter the FATSSA festival. Five of us got together, we did it and we won.

And Barney was in it?

Yes he was in it. Then we started to work at the East Rand Theatre Club, where all the big directors used to go at the time. At the time some of the professional theatre companies were those of Marde Vann and Gwynn Frangcon-Davies, Margaret Inglis, Nan Munro, Taubie Kushlick and Leon Gluckman. We were all in love with Leon. Oh,

Opposite – Barney Simon in class portrait at New York University, 1968.
Second row from front, extreme left.
Photograph courtesy of NELM.

he was gorgeous. He did "King Kong", and "Wait a Minim!" He was the Minister of Health's son. We got together with Leon and we worked at the East Rand Theatre Club on James Ambrose Brown's "The Governor of the Black Rock." Barney had one line and had to say, 'Number One.' He was a slave and I was the governor's wife. I loved Leon, but I think Leon preferred Barney.

I was always working. I played opposite Philip Birkinshaw. He was delicious, English and an intellectual giant. He was married and much older than me. Once I bumped into Barney in town. Town was where we went. Nowhere else you could go. Mayfair, you went to the swimming bath and the synagogue, and town was where you met to go to the bioscope. So I was rushing to meet Philip Birkinshaw and I bumped into Barney. I said, 'Walk with me.' He said, 'Where are you going?' I said, 'I'm going to meet someone at the library.' 'Who are you meeting?' I said, 'I'm meeting Philip Birkinshaw.' So he started, 'Don't do it, don't do it.' I said, 'Do what?' 'Don't go, don't go please, please, don't go, it's wrong, it's wrong.' He walked all the way with me. I said, 'I'm going.' He said, 'Please don't go, don't go.' You know how he'd get so intense, but I went. And Philip Birkinshaw took me to tea somewhere, a little café somewhere in the city. Then he said we should go and practise kissing.

Barney's family lived in Magpie Street, Kensington. He had an older brother, Morrie who was also very very beautiful. Their sister was the oldest, but she was crippled and retarded. Celia. But Barney talked about her and her 'lovely wit.' He took delight in things she told him, laughing and giggling. He'd tell us stories about her, and so we discovered her and her world – the world of the mentally retarded and crippled. Barney never viewed her as someone to be ashamed of. In fact, to him she was a storyteller. I remember her with fondness because of what he told us – you couldn't discount her or ignore her. She had a part in our lives because Barney never tried to hide her presence. His relationship with her was sweet, caring, nurturing. His mother was also a storyteller. In fact what also touched us was his delight in telling us about his parents.

One story he told was how his mother kept a chair with its back to the room, facing the window onto Magpie Street. And she'd sit there smoking her cigarette. He'd try and sneak into the house without his mother seeing, because he was always buying books from the second-hand sale tables outside the City Hall. In his room there were books to the ceiling, books on the floor, books under the bed, books, books. Every nook and cranny was covered with books. His mother would say, 'Don't buy books, Barna. No more books!' Can you imagine a mother saying that? But she said it in desperation because the house was small and he was drowning it out with books. So one day she is sitting there, and Barney sneaks in, hardly breathing, and he thinks she's not even looking. But she says, 'Barna! Again the bledda books!' Okay, then Barney went to London.

Is that when he went to Joan Littlewood?

Yes. He went to London and said I should come. Harold Rubin was there. A lot of us South Africans were there. You know you matriculated and then you went to London. I and a group of friends bought an old taxi and travelled the continent. So I did that first. Barney was in London. All his friends were there, a whole lot of us, and we all lived in the same area near Keats's Cottage in Hampstead. And Barney of course had his brother and sister-in-law who were living there as well. Barney made contacts very easily. I was always amazed that he didn't have to put on posh. He didn't have to do anything except be Barney. In fact I think he knew that. He very cleverly became a unique communicator, a unique presence everywhere. That was something we recognised early. We all tried to emulate the English. We were intimidated by their accents, even though we were very positive and confident about ourselves and our South Africanism.

He had this wonderful relationship with Lionel Abrahams. All of our backgrounds were the same – Jewish, Lithuanian, leftist. We ate the same foods and we had the same aspirations. Our parents were hard working and gave us the work ethic: 'There are no stupid jobs, only stupid people.' You just worked, there was no alternative. You couldn't be lazy. When you got leisure, it was so nice. You got an hour, you got some time. We had the Jewish holidays, Rosh Hashanah, Yom Kippur, when the shops would close, or Shabbat, Saturday, when you really rested and slept in the afternoon. But Barney left us Jews and went on to embrace everybody with the same kind of democratic appreciation. He would see things in people that we couldn't see – because people became indispensable to him. But then he would drop one, and go on to the next – then on to the next – group of people. Delight and charm them – then move on.

How much do you think he was influenced by what he learned in London with Joan Littlewood?

Joan Littlewood, let me tell you about her. He was going to get me a job with Joan Littlewood. So he said we must do an audition. He was coaching me and we did a piece from a Lorca play. I had to say, 'My heart's bitter bursting like a pomegranate.' We get on the stage, Barney leading me in: he's playing the other character. When I come to 'my heart's bursting like a pomegranate' Barney starts to giggle. All my concentration was gone and I started to giggle. As we walked away Joan Littlewood came up to us, and he got the job. His job was sweeping the theatre and just sort of generally being a dogsbody and watching. But you know how Barney was a master at getting to know you?

When I was stage-managing for Barney, he was very fussy about the tinkling sound of the glasses. I didn't realise then what I realise now – that God is in the detail.

Chapter 2. South African Stories

On returning from London, Barney Simon saw Athol Fugard's "No Good Friday". Of it he said, 'It changed my life.'

Newsweek, August 22, 1983.

He met Fugard after a performance of his next play, "Nongogo". Fugard was running the Rehearsal Room for AMDA, the African Music and Drama Association, a cultural workshop founded in the 1950s to meet the needs of black artists. It had been developed by Father Trevor Huddleston, Ian Bernhardt and the Union of South African Artists. AMDA's home was Dorkay House, an industrial building at the south end of Eloff Street, next door to the Bantu Men's Social Centre.

Fugard asked Barney to be part of AMDA, and in 1961, when he was directing "The Blood Knot", Barney sat in on rehearsals as a 'third eye'. Barney's involvement with productions at Dorkay House led to the formation of his company, Mirror One: 'a reflecting surface in which we might find an image of ourselves'.

Surface Reflecting Still Looking – quote found amongst Barney Simon's papers.

Mirror One performed "Cayenne Pepper", a play by Diobaldi, and "The Death of Bessie Smith" by Edward Albee. With a group of writers Barney workshopped the musical "Phiri", his adaptation of Ben Jonson's "Volpone" set in Soweto. Fats Dibeco describes how they played at Dorkay House and anywhere else they could — a dining hall in a commune in Parktown, in backyards so that people under house-arrest could watch over the fence. In this way mixed-race casts could perform for mixed-race audiences. Although Barney directed from written texts, he attributed the beginning of his workshop approach to this time at Dorkay House.

In this chapter we read how Athol Fugard and Barney united in a vision of theatre that would be, as Fugard termed it, 'free and fearless'. Fats Dibeco, Vanessa Cooke, Sophie Mgcina, Joyce Sikhakhane-Rankin and Sam Williams reveal Barney's commitment to unearthing real South African stories, at a time when, apart from Fugard, the rest of South African theatre was largely imitating Europe.

Opposite – Dancing in the garden in Parktown: Barney Simon, Athol Fugard and friends, 1978.
Photograph by Rodney Barnett / South Photos.

Barney Simon remembers Dorkay House

'Theatre in South Africa has always been a humbling experience for me. I began in the early sixties working with Athol Fugard and a group of actors in the rehearsal room at Dorkay House. The work we did was sometimes wonderful but always private because that was the only way to do multiracial theatre in those days. We invited our initial audiences and then gathered the rest by word of mouth. We played on Sundays, late afternoons, competing with Eloff Street traffic to the east and mine compound dancers to the west.'

Barney in rehearsal at Dorkay House, for the musical "Phiri". Some of the cast include from left to right, Cyril Magubane, Sophie Mgcina, Mackay Davashe, Felicia Mabuza and Sam Williams.
Photograph courtesy of NELM.

'I wouldn't know how many of you knew or remember the Rehearsal Room. It was on the third floor of a very ramshackle warehouse. Athol and I used to stand at the broken window at the top of the staircase watching to see if any cars were doing u-turns. That meant that somebody was coming to see our work for free. And when a strange old lady – I mean unknown to us – puffed up those dusty concrete stairs, I was prepared – even at the risk of embarrassing her – to dance ahead, strewing rose petals as I led her to the best plastic seat in the house.'

Dorkay House.
Photograph by David Goldblatt.

Athol Fugard, March 1983.
Photograph by Ruphin Coudyzer.

Athol Fugard

'A theatre that would be free and fearless'

It was after a performance of my play "Nongogo" at Darragh Hall that my wife Sheila and I met Barney at a small gathering of kindred souls in the apartment of Benedicta Bonnacorsi, an extraordinary lady who took Sheila and me and our attempts at starting a new theatre under her wing. Bonnacorsi deserves a special mention for her role in theatre in Johannesburg during those early years. Barney had had just returned from overseas where he had been fired-up by the work of Joan Littlewood. He immediately realised that his vision of a new South African theatre – a theatre that broke all the taboos of the then theatrical establishment as regards what theatre should be about and look like – coincided with ours.

When I think back on just how momentous that first meeting with Barney turned out to be in our lives, I must smile now at its very tentative nature. I was the one that held back and the reason for that is that I am essentially a loner and it is this quality more than anything else that went on to complicate my relationship with that beautiful man. Anyway there were the three of us, sitting on the floor of a Johannesburg flat, talking excitedly about the theatre begging to be born in South Africa – a theatre that would be free and fearless. Shortly after that first meeting Sheila and I packed our bags and went over to London in much the same way that Barney had and with the same wild hope of gatecrashing the theatrical party that has been on the go in London for several centuries.

The next and decisive meeting with Barney was when Sheila and I and our baby daughter Lisa moved up to Johannesburg from Port Elizabeth to work with Union Artists (Ian Bernhardt and Bob Leshoai) and for the first production of my play "The Blood Knot", which I had just completed. I can't remember the precise circumstances of our reconnecting with Barney, but what I do remember is the wholehearted enthusiasm and energy with which he threw himself into the creation of The Rehearsal Room. This was the large top-floor room in Dorkay House that we converted into a small theatre. "Blood Knot" was its first production. Barney was simply magnificent, pasting egg-crates on the walls as soundproofing. We had tribal dancing and drumming in one of the mine hostels on one side. He was ushering the audience in and scrambling around for extra chairs and benches when our seventy-seater theatre ended up accommodating one hundred and twenty bodies. He was going to the aid of fainting ladies and elderly gentlemen when the heat and lack of fresh air overcame them. But most important of all he was pooling his limited knowledge and theatre experience with our even more limited knowledge and theatre experience in order to make the play work. He was our 'third eye'.

That experience revealed to me the essential Barney – a soul of extraordinary generosity and talent. He gave of himself in a way that no other man I have known has done. His obsession was with theatre – good theatre, good South African theatre – and I truly believe he would have sacrificed himself in that cause. He certainly gave his whole life to it. I can name four people whom I regard as the true pioneers of our theatre, Brian Astbury and Yvonne Bryceland, Mannie Manim and Barney Simon. Without them we would still be back in the dark ages. The Rehearsal Room went on to be the venue of several other team efforts from Barney and myself.

When Mary Benson phoned me in the middle of the night to tell me that Barney had died, my initial shock and disbelief gave way very quickly to a wave of anger at the loss of that huge fund of creativity at a time when we most needed it. Barney himself was included in that anger because he had neglected himself physically. If he had made only a moderate effort in those last few years to exercise, stop smoking, and eat properly, he would most probably still be with us.

We have to acknowledge now that no one has been able to step into his shoes and give to South African theatre the new direction and purpose which I believe it is still trying to find. Barney had the vision to do that. But what I, as a writer, find most painful to dwell on is my very strong belief that Barney had arrived at a point in his life when he was going to deliver on his huge promise of his own creativity as a writer. And if he had done that, how immeasurably our literature and theatre would have been enriched. If... If... If...

There should have been no ifs in the life of that beautiful man. His destiny was thwarted. Sheila remembers with gratitude beyond words his generosity to the Fugards at a time when we were struggling to make ends meet. Time and time again it was a gift from him of hard and desperately needed cash that helped us through a crisis.

I had four experiences with Barney as a director. The first three were very happy and successful, beginning with his direction of Molly Seftel and myself in "Hello and Goodbye". His understanding and penetration of my still virginal text was extraordinary and revealed his unique gift of giving a vivid flesh and blood reality to a dry text, of mixing laughter and tears and creating a character. He was wonderfully inventive and imaginative in leading me to the seemingly trivial, but in reality all-important, bits of stage business that help an actor arrive at as truthful a performance as possible.

We followed this up with a production of Beckett's "Krapps Last Tape" (in a double-bill with Molly in Barney's own one-act play "Anna"). There again Barney was in total empathy with both the play's mordant humour and its pathos.

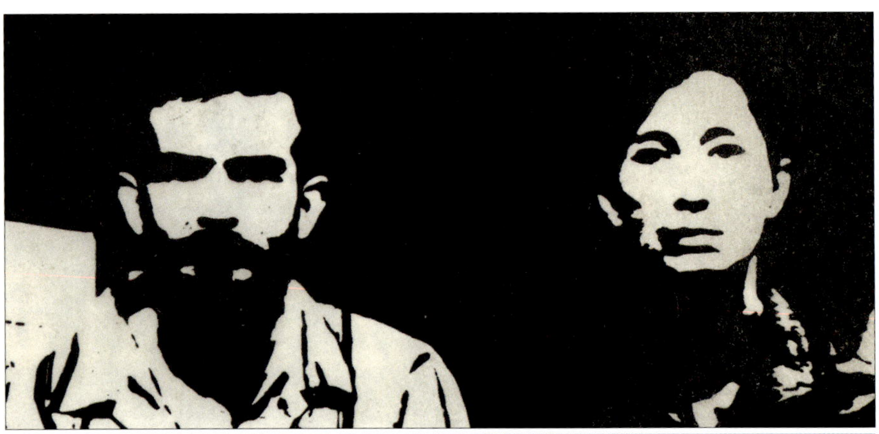

Detail from poster for "Hello and Goodbye", Athol Fugard and Molly Seftel, 1974.

My third satisfying experience was when he directed me in "An Evening of Brecht's Poetry". The less than happy experience was when he joined Yvonne Bryceland and myself in Cape Town for the first production of "Statements After an Arrest Under the Immorality Act" performed at The Space in 1972. The egos and insecurities of the three of us, Yvonne, Barney and myself, proved to be too much and I asked Barney to leave the production. This was deeply hurtful to Barney and I don't think he ever really forgave me for that.

Our last meeting was after the launch of my memoir "Cousins" at The Market Theatre. Once again Barney's extraordinary generosity and his desire to just be of use in making good things happen, was there in the way he took over at the last moment and organised. He staged my reading and book signing on the set of his production of "Hedda Gabler", which was running at the time. It all went off very well thanks to him. After a few minutes at a crowded reception afterwards, Sheila, Barney and I escaped to have a quiet time together. We chose an Indian restaurant and it was from that long, memory-filled meal that I have my last images of that dear friend and remarkable man and artist. He was, as ever, dressed in his impeccably put-together casual style. I can remember seeing Barney standing for quite a long time in front of a mirror before venturing out to face the world. During that meal Sheila and I recall him talking with great passion about his work, particularly with young actors, and his many ideas for future projects at The Market. He was just as eager to hear from us about our plans.

Like everybody else he was very caught-up in the huge political drama that was taking place in the country and I remember his insistence that all artists should recognise their responsibility at that moment in our history, which was every bit as great as during the dark years of apartheid. Sheila and I parted from Barney that night with a very exciting sense of the work that still had to be done. From Barney himself there wasn't any hint of the disastrous health crisis that lay just around the corner.

Athol Fugard and Molly Seftel.
Photograph courtesy of NELM.

Fats Dibeco

'Do you think I can't be without my emotions?'

I met Barney at Dorkay house. He was there with his short back and sides and small glasses and a dark slick. And we didn't know whether he worked or where he worked. A long time after Ian Bernhardt said, 'No, this guy, his father is rich, he owns flats and things.' I said, 'Wow, is that a fact.' He said, 'Yeah.' I said, 'Man, I wouldn't have thought it.'

Was the first play you worked on with Barney "Cayenne Pepper"?

Ja, "Cayenne Pepper" by Diobaldi, set in that jail. It's only two guys. One is a big tall guy, but not there at all, a simpleton. And then Zakes Mofokeng was playing a short guy. Athol started The Rehearsal Room with other guys, David Phetoe and Corney Mabaso. They were the first ones who worked with Athol Fugard – "Wedding Forgotten" in 1963. If there were awards then, I think they would have won an award, because they did it so well. They did it so well, even Oliver Walker had to agree. He used to say he will eat his hat or words, if the Bantu can do a thing right. Then they did it. We started a group called Mirror One.

Who was Oliver Walker?

A newspaper critic. In the Rehearsal Room we did Edward Albee's "The Death of Bessie Smith". From The Rehearsal Room we went to Durban and Swaziland.

Did you enjoy working with Barney then?

I enjoy myself with anybody who directs us, as long as he directs me. I always fight with my director, we have problems. They say, 'It's not like this.' I say, 'Give me a reason why?'

Did you and Barney fight about that?

The fact was if he had a problem, he would say, 'It must taste like this...' I would say, 'No Barney, just get to the core of the thing. Why do you feel I must be like this chocolate, melted down? Do you think I can't be without my emotions?' He says, 'No, but in that way you will get to where I want to get to.' I say, 'No but...' He says, 'Come on.' And we argue straight. We come at last together, compromise, or I do it that way. Or he says, 'Okay, do it your way.' That's how we used to work with him. He was very finicky. Details, details, all the time he wanted details. Sometimes, you know, I just get tired. 'Barney! Can we just break?' He'd just say, 'Look we just getting there.' 'Barney look, I am not getting there, you are seeing it getting there.' But no break. We used to work, work and work. We did well with the thing ("Cayenne Pepper") but in fact it was not played in professional places. One time we just packed, no props, no nothing, just costumes. We went to Jewish friends (they call themselves Habonims) and performed in a courtyard, like this place. We performed one and a half hour's drama.

Opposite – Fats Dibeco in Dorkay House.
Photograph by David Goldblatt.

Where?

Anywhere we could, any corner. Here just here, where all the people were. Just take costumes, put them in a paper bag, get onto the train, and get onto the bus. Phone those people at such and such a place, and they come and collect us. We get a train back home, one and a half hours. And then when we were in Swaziland performing, the same "Cayenne Pepper" and "Bessie Smith", we had some goodies, some Scotch, some brandies and things, and we started singing. And Barney had in his mind the whole time, that he must do "Volpone", but using all those bird things and animal vernacular. But the fact is we started singing a cappella, no accompaniment, just singing, just singing ourselves. We were singing in harmony. Barney says, 'No, I think we must rather make this a musical, because it will just be a comedy without the music.'

So we started on "Phiri". We worked with the late Mackay Davashe. We were planning the music and Barney would come in. I was always better than others, because I was sort of a professional without money. I was there all the time.

Fats Dibeco

Vanessa Cooke

'He auditioned me for about two hours, and then he called me back again. I had two lines'

I had started acting when I was four in "Madame Butterfly" at His Majesty's Theatre, and by the age of twenty-two I had given up the theatre. I had done a play at the Alexander Theatre called "Fanny". I really, really hated it because of the way it was directed and the whole experience. It was very unpleasant. I thought, no, this kind of theatre is dead. I went to work in an art gallery in town called Gallery 101. Then a guy I'd been in the drama society with at Wits, Andrew Cuthbert, said he was working on a play. It wasn't a strictly professional outfit, and there was a very small part and they couldn't find anyone. Would I like to do it? And I said, 'Ja.' That was at Dorkay House. So I went to Dorkay House, and there was Barney. This was in 1971.

I thought he was very strange. He auditioned me for about two hours, and then he called me back again. I had two lines. He made me say them in different ways. Like underwater. Then he asked me why I thought I wanted to be in the play. I had no idea. We used to rehearse about twice a week from five to eight in the evening.

The play was "The Death of Bessie Smith". It was the first South African production, with Barbara Itzler, David Phetoe, Corney Mabaso, Andrew Cuthbert and me. It was done as a double bill. The other play was "Cayenne Pepper" and Fats Dibeco was in that one. So we'd rehearse in the evening at Dorkay House. We rehearsed for six months. Dorkay House was a whole different experience. There would be people playing jazz in the next room, and drunk people and stoned people. Wonderful people. I'd never experienced anything like that really properly before. I knew Wally Serote so I'd kind of known what Alex was like, but I didn't know about that kind of theatre.

There was a lot of sitting around, especially for me. I had to be there at all the rehearsals. So I watched the whole process of how Barney worked. And David and Corney seemed to like the way he worked. He was very slowly finding textures and getting people to do it different ways. Andrew hated that process. It drove him crazy. Because it was like massage. I don't think he ever did it right in all that time. Barney would keep saying it hasn't got the right sensuality. Of course he never used words like that. It would be like: 'Can't you do it as though she was like a soft cuddly toy.' And 'Do it like you're under water.' He always used stories and different visual pictures. It wasn't like working with him later, though, because we only worked together twice a week. It was a nice kind of break from the art gallery. It was quite pure work.

We performed the play at Dorkay House and at people's houses. Then we took it on a tour to Durban and played it at the Gandhi Hall. And that was for the South African Student Organisation guys – Strini Moodley and Benji Francis, Saths Cooper. They were heavy Black Consciousness guys. It was a big hall, I remember. We went to a party and the police came because it was a multi-racial party in a Durban flat. They wanted to know where everyone's passes were. Barney said he was American and that

---

Opposite – Vanessa Cooke.
Photograph by Rodney Barnett, courtesy of Vanessa Cooke.

he lived in New York. He had his green card. They didn't arrest us in the end. They klapped Fats, if I remember, because Fats was drunk and was getting a bit out of control. It was very new, that sort of thing, for me.

Then we tentatively started working on "Miss South Africa (6)", which took a long time. We'd meet every now and then. Barney had written certain things. He'd ask me things about my childhood. It took a long time, about two years altogether, for him to write it down. At the same time he had this big idea for "Phiri", the musical.

Plus he started doing the work with the nurses. He took me with him. It was all around that time, 1971, that I started realising what other work he did. I went with him to Nqutu and met Dr Barker who was doing amazing work at the hospital there – health education, and Barney sidled into it through drama. And then he started writing "Phiri" with these other guys, Wally Serote, Stanley Modjwadi, Oswald Mtshali. It was rehearsed in the Bantu Men's Social Centre, which was next door to Dorkay. I got all the props and had to do whatever anyone wanted me to do. "Phiri" toured to all the townships. I used to make the banners. Then I left the gallery and worked at Phoenix Players for part of that time. "Phiri" was produced for the Phoenix Players – for Ian Bernhardt. I was also involved in Workshop 71.

Sophie Mgcina

'Barney was colourless, he was Barney and that's it'

Barney was walking down from upstairs and I was walking up. I didn't know him. I just knew he was Barney, the director. And he was working with Corney Mabaso. I said to him, 'If you have another play, I would like to work with you.' He said, 'Oh well, okay.' The next day I was his leading lady. And the play was "Phiri" – the Wolf. It was an adaptation of Ben Johnson's "Volpone" or "The Fox". Ja. I worked with these musicians. Mackay Davashe and Cyril Magubane. They are both late. Cyril was a guitarist. I sang every song that was composed before we taught the cast, to see if they worked. I did the translations and I had a hand in composing some of the songs in "Phiri".

I had worked with other directors before him who were very good. Barney was different. Barney had a talent of making you understand text, the written word. He made you own it. So that when I sang the music in "Phiri" I actually wasn't acting. I was story-telling but also living the character, respecting the person I was portraying. If she was a weakling, that would come out. If she was strong, that would come out. I used to hear after performances how touching my work was. How true some of the stuff was that I said on stage. When Barney talked sometimes he just wanted to find out who you were, where you were from. He was political, subtle. He would ask very intimate things about people. And if you were not strong he would pull your soul out.

If you weren't strong he would pull your soul out?

Yeah. You know, Barney would sit there and smile and smoke. Just easy. And just throw a question, and unguardedly you would answer it truthfully. He used to catch me. Sometimes I used to scold him and say, 'There are things I don't want to say to you. I am a private person.' He was that kind of person. He allowed me to show my progress as a composer. He respected my voice – no song was performed without me singing it. He taught me to respect the stage. I owe my acting strength and discipline to him. He said to me, 'You people have a tendency of apologising all the time, even if it is uncalled for. If you believe what you say and you have not done any wrong, do not apologise.' It helped me because I'm straightforward. If I don't like a thing I just say it. I have many enemies because of that. I lifted my shoulders. I stopped stooping.

I did "Brecht on Brecht" with him at The Market. When I heard "Pirate Jenny" it was this German woman singing it, and I thought, 'No, what's this? I don't understand this.' I said, 'It's a speaking voice and she's telling a story. It doesn't touch me. What's happening?' And he said, 'Find the beauty. Find the anger of this maid.' And I did. My anger wasn't beating people over the head, but it was concentrated. I mention "Pirate Jenny" and "Madam Please" because sometimes when I used to sing them, even there at The Market, white women used to walk out.

Opposite – Sophie Mgcina during rehearsals for "Inyanga", June 1989.
Photograph by Ruphin Coudyzer.

Those songs touched you?

Ja, they told of my discomfort as a second grade non-person who needs to be understood as a human being. And that's what he taught me. He said, 'Find the good and the bad in your text.'

And how did you find it?

It was easy. I'm black.

So in other words you looked at your life?

Yes. He told me never to fake tears. He said you have to be moved to a point. The text is not going to tell you to cry. He said, find things that will make your text move off the paper. Somehow I think I got that and I can do that. I do not fake tears on stage. I cry generally. And if I laugh, I laugh. But everything is controlled. I did "The Lion and the Lamb" with him and John Kani. I still look at it and think this guy is Jewish and here he is explaining the Bible to people who are supposed to know it. Barney was easy about it. And again he respected my other life as a composer so that we actually put the music to "The Lion and the Lamb" with Sibongile Khumalo's beautiful voice.

see your skin becom
shades lighter
at once...

One of my songs which is "The Prayer" is actually now used in "Mandela's Story". What can I say about Barney? He made you feel special. He made you valuable. So Barney actually made it whole and holy for me to be on that stage performing.

If you say he made it whole and holy for you, what was it like before?
The director would walk in and do his job, give you the script and say, this is the character. You walk ten paces front, back and to the sides, and that's it. If you made sense that was okay. The accent is all right. But Barney did correct here. So that was important for me. That made me also decide later to go and study. I decided there is more I can do. Not only for myself but for the masses. If I am going to make sense I have to clean up my act. So I went to study.

What did you study?
The voice. My passion. I went to study the voice. I went and studied at the Central School of Speech and Drama and graduated. I just needed to know where the voice was from, so I studied a little of the physiology of the voice. I came back a voice teacher. And all that is thanks to this man saying, 'Respect what you do.' He gave me life, not gold, because I use my voice for everything I do. I do not use my hands like my mum did. I use my voice, the gift that God gave me.

I want to know about the history and how you worked on "Madam Please"?
There was a song "Madam Please" that was written for me by Mackay Davashe and Barney Simon. He had journalists on Drum who gave him stories. They wrote some of the text. "Madam Please" is actually also my story and Rosie's story about the good madams and the bad madams. It was about maids. My mother had an English madam, Mrs Bean. And Mrs Bean worked in some factory with Afrikaners. And they used to call her a rooinek. She used to come back from work and say to my mother, 'Chrissie, you know they're calling me a rooinek. What's a rooinek? And my mother said, 'Ah no, it's nothing. They said you've got a nice neck.'

And your mother knew?
My mother spoke Afrikaans. She'd say, 'Don't worry Madam, they say you've got a nice neck.' It's little stories like that. I'd tell Barney a story about my aunt who couldn't even write her name but could speak English. "Madam Please" is also because as a black person my aunt is my mother. If she's got four sisters, I've got four mothers. My mother doesn't come to work because her sister had died. Meaning maybe the second sister. I say to my madam, my mother has died. I mean my mother's sister. And then she lets me go for a week. I come back and then maybe in two months time: Madam, my mother has died. Which one? So it's those kind of stories. And he writes:

Madam please,
before you ask me if your children are fine,
ask me when last I saw mine.

Opposite – Women shopping in Diagonal Street, Johannesburg – early 1970s.
Photograph courtesy of The Star.

```
Madam please.
before you say the funeral is a lie,
ask me why my people die.
```

It was a political statement but it is also the simple culture that the black woman has. Four uncles. They're all my fathers. I do not lie when I say my father died. You see if my mother sleeps in, I do not stay with her. She will see me maybe once a week, or if it's too far, once a month. I grow up without my mother. If I am lucky, I have my granny bring me up. What my granny teaches me will live with me forever. But I still miss what my mother would have taught me. It is important to have both. "Madam Please" is from those little stories which he put together.

Do you remember any of the stories he told you?
We just talked about things. He would talk about Rose Maseko [Barney's housekeeper] and her children and her husband. He would say, 'Where did you go to school? What were you like there? Your teachers?' I would talk about these teachers. 'When did you start singing?' Whatever I said to him would sort of merge with...

With his script?
Ja. What he's already written or what he is intending to write. But already he knows what he wants. First he wants your character to come out. He worked better if he knew how to write for you. I think he really worked very, very hard. I would say it's a combination of finding stories in you plus the discipline. Barney was honest. Barney was humble enough to say, 'I am white, privileged, educated, I must give something back.' He was giving back. Barney worked with people he respected.

I want to know about Dorkay House and what it was like at that time in South Africa?
Dorkay House was founded in 1955. We had something there. We used to say, 'There's no colour bar at Dorkay House.' Dorkay House was run by whites, people we called angels, the late Ian Bernhardt, Andrew Watson, Arthur Goldreich. We had Guy Routh, Clive Menell and Father Trevor Huddleston. The place was a clothes factory first. Barney used the left wing for rehearsals. Yesterday I heard we were paying thirty-five pounds for that room. Dorkay House inside was also thirty-five pounds. And it was called The Union of SA Artists. Ian Bernhardt was like the administrator there. I joined in '57. I won a talent contest run by them. I won first prize and I never looked back. The musicians there were Mackay Davashe and Kippie Moeketsi. It was like an agency. They were auditioning people. We had these musicals that were going all over, playing at the Selborne Hall, City Hall, The Great Hall. So Ian was like an impresario. Jonas Gwangwa and Hugh Masekela were working there after they left school. Those were amazing times, exciting times, bad times, good times. We were actually arrested walking out of Dorkay House because there was a curfew. Nine o'clock, no blacks in the streets.

Opposite – The Balcony Tea Room at Anstey's building in central Johannesburg. 'White's Only' admission.
Photograph courtesy of the Transnet Heritage Foundation – SAR & H Collection.

```
MADAM PLEASE

Madam please
Before you shout
about your broken plate
ask about the meal
her family ate

Madam please
Before you laugh
at the watchman's English
try to answer
in his Zulu language

Madam please
Before you call a man
a stupid fool
ask him where he spent
his days in school.

Madam please
before you say
that the driver stinks
come take a bath
in a Soweto zinc.

Madam please
before you ask me
if your children are fine
ask me when
ask me when, I last saw mine.

Madam please
before you call
today's funeral a lie
ask me why
my people die
ask me why my people die.

Madam please
ask about my sisters
what they wait for
how we played
if we cried
if we laughed
what we saw.

Madam please
ask about my brothers
if they're hungry
if they work
what they want
what they earn.

Madam please
ask if my mother lives
if she smiles
if she's sad if she's old
if she cooks if she sews.

Madam please
ask about my father
if he sings if he's sick
if he still looks for work.

Madam please
before you call today's
funeral a lie
ask me why my people die
ask me why my people die
ask me why my people die

Madam please
before you ask me
if your children are fine
ask me when
ask me when, I last saw mine

Ask now, what we want
ask now, what we eat
ask now, where we live
ask now, if we dream
ask now, ask now, ask now
Madam Please!

Composer: M.Davashe
Lyrics: B.Simon
```

So how did you juggle that?

We lived. It was beautiful. What they didn't want was mixing. And there we mixed. There was no colour. So Ian was Ian. And Ricky was Ricky. And I was Sophie. But we used to call him Mr Bernhardt because we were young. We didn't understand this thing of calling an older man by his first name. My first wages there was a guinea which he paid to me. I met him going downstairs and I said, 'Mr Bernhardt I sang at the Great Hall at Wits and you didn't pay me.' And he paid me out of his front pocket right there. My first professional payment.

So Sophie, did you and Barney ever talk of the changes since you've lived through an amazing historical time in South Africa?

We were in the struggle and he was part of that struggle. That made things a little bit easier for people he worked with. But no, no politics with Barney. Even with Mannie Manim. It never occurred to us to say, 'Did you see the paper?' Even with things hotting up we used to sit there and have a smoke. I've never discussed politics with that man except in his work. He wrote about politics. So his understanding about politics is the way people's lives are determined.

Opposite – Ndebele women in Hillbrow, Johannesburg.
Photograph courtesy of the Transnet Heritage Foundation – SAR & H Collection.

Joyce Sikhakhane-Rankin

'It wasn't easy for Barney working in 1971'

How did you start working with Barney?

I met Barney when I was banned and restricted, in 1971. I hadn't been getting any jobs. I don't know how Barney got to know where I lived. He sent a message that I should come and see him at Dorkay House. So I went and he said he is offering a job to transcribe scripts for the musical "Phiri". He would work with the artists and there would be a question of language and because I had writing and translation skills he thought that I could do that. So they decided to partition a large office to make an office for me. They put a typewriter and a chair and desk, so that is where I worked from.

What did being banned mean?

Well, it meant that I lost my job as a journalist at the Rand Daily Mail. I had to stay at home. I had to ask permission to take up any job. So also you are restricted to what type of job you could take. I got this offer after nobody wanted me. We didn't tell Barney to go to the Magistrate to tell them I had found another job. I just continued working.

The apartheid police came to Barney and said, 'If you don't fire that woman we will take away the privilege for you to stage this play.' So it really raised a hell of a thing. It was whether I continued working there or the actors earning a living. That was the message. I decided, 'Well I think the play is larger than me, you should continue the production at Dorkay House.' But the association with Barney continued. Before I left South Africa I had been to Barney's house once or twice to meet a contact who had been planning my escape. Then I left.

It wasn't easy for Barney working in 1971. He was white and a lot of us were black and very radical, okay. Extremely radical. You would find that sometimes an actor would refuse to do what he said. And he would say, 'Of course, I am not your boss!' A lot of actors or actresses would be broke because they drank. They didn't know how to budget. Barney would go a long way to understand those issues. He would insist that the actor came back and acted. I mean like Fats liked his bottle and because of that he became a very difficult person to work with. But he did his work and performed at the end of the day. So Barney really had a very good skill of working with really difficult people. I think he worked with any good actor irrespective of colour – but at that time in South Africa the colour was added. So he was a very deep person. Barney didn't engage in the politics. He was more into that inside of a human being, human values and how you expressed them in an art form, which is another way of expressing politics.

Sam Williams

'Little things like that hurt'

I first worked with Barney when I was doing "Phiri". That's way back. Barney wanted somebody to take the part of Ngwane – the owl in the play. Barney added parts into it to make it more exciting, with of course some writers who are African. People writing for Drum. He involved these guys to write this play. We just like increased its intensity.

How did you hear of him?

I was told they were auditioning for parts for a play at Dorkay House, and I just went as an interested spectator. Somebody said, 'Why the hell don't you try him?' And he tried me out and liked me. Next was "Cincinatti". I was a night watchman. That was also workshopped. This one particularly because it involved what was going on in those days. There were nightclubs where white skins mixed with black skins – a thing that was never allowed. I was supposed to be the night watchman of the nightclub. There was a black prostitute who I was fighting with.

Tell us about how you did the workshop?

Well, we just sat down and talked and Barney had a machine on. We talked every rubbish in the world we could think of. Barney would pull out what he thought made more sense in the theatre, and then he would play it back to us and we would do it. There was a theme. Make some kind of history for myself. Where do I come from? Who am I? Who is my father? What area did I grow up in? Things like that. And every character had to have a background, must know who he is. So you forget about yourself, forget that you are Sam Williams. You are just this character. And you begin to really be that character. And you find you can act like him, because you already imagined who he is and what he is.

What was your background before? What kind of shows did you do?

I started off as a singer. I had a musical group in Alexandra. Then from there I moved to the teachers' college and did a teachers' course.

So what about this man called Barney?

The best word I have for Barney is calling him the gentle giant. We had our fights. Sometimes I got so fed up with him I never talked to him for a long time, and then we'd talk again.

Did it strike you as unusual that a white person was directing?

Maybe sometimes that is what we fought about because you get to doubt a white man. He gets fed up that you doubt him. And it's this clash that happens. I had a crazy temper too. I couldn't stand being bullied. Sometimes I felt he was bullying me. I just thought, 'fuck no.' I don't remember. It was things between friends. Remembered, then forgotten because he was that kind of guy. He could forgive very quickly. Yes, Barney stands out.

What was going on at Dorkay House at the time?
It was special because we could meet with friends of any colour. Ja, we were hassled, but we just kept on. People met and talked about their culture. Our people would go and listen to people rehearsing music or bands playing. For us it was nice because you could go next door to the Bantu Mens Social Centre (BMSC) and play games of pool. Yes, the BMSC was for men and women.

What year was that?
It was the '60s. I used to write music for groups and rehearse there. People used to get together, just talk and talk about the state of the country. It was this apartheid. We used to do things at the back, so nobody knew. We used to help people get out of the country if they were wanted by the police and things like that. If they were going to kill us, it was okay, we'd just fire on. Our kids were in that mood too. As a matter of fact they used to say, 'Come on, come on, it can't happen like this, like a white man calls your father boy.' Our sons used to hate it. They used to say, 'Fuck that! Are you a boy? What am I, dad?'

An old man, I think he was going to Natalspruit. We were standing there just chatting. He was smoking a cigar with a cigar holder. Suddenly the cops came and we vanished. We had a place where we could see what was happening. They were talking to the old man saying, 'Where is your pass?' He was confident he had his pass. One Boer was saying, 'Fuck, haal die kak uit jou mond uit...' – this cigar holder. He just couldn't get it right. And they pulled him to the ground. I hated that. We really hated it, but what the hell could we do? Little things like that hurt.

Did you use those kind of stories in the creation of "Cincinatti"?
Yes, yeah I used those kind of stories, mostly in "Cincinatti", when I had to do my dialogue. I was talking about the 16th of June, for instance, and what happened. I think we started quarrelling with Barney and Mannie over that 16th of June. I said, 'But it's against my principles, I cannot sit there and talk in the play. I'm serious about June the 16th.' We didn't get on too well after that, because everybody in the cast said we are not going to perform. So nobody performed on June 16th. In "Cincinatti" I felt good because here was somebody creating something about where I come from. Who I am.

Sam Williams.
Photograph courtesy of The Star.

Barry Ronge, in a newspaper tribute after Barney Simon's death, recalls his work:
'At the Arena Theatre in Doornfontein where he began his remarkable professional association with Mannie Manim, he blazed like a comet. Plays from Europe, America and Africa emerged in intriguing new forms incorporating the techniques of Grotowski and Peter Brook that were revolutionising British theatre. For once South African theatre was on the same cutting edge as international theatre. And it was Barney Simon who took it there.'

The Sunday Times

Chapter 3. The Arena

In 1968, Barney visited America where he worked as an editor on The New American Review. He was fascinated by the work of the Young Lords, the Puerto Rican equivalents of the Black Panthers. 'I saw street theatre, raw, alive and naïve. It inspired me enormously.'

Business Day, November 2, 1986.

In 1970, Barney's father died and he returned home. He started running communication workshops based on those he had attended in America, and he devised and directed health-education projects in what were then Zululand and the Transkei. 'In the early seventies it was Biko and Black Consciousness. It hurt me badly that dear friends that I worked with, like Strini Moodley, decided that they could no longer associate with whites – with me. Joyce Sikhakhane suggested I play white venues for a while, to educate, so I worked at the Arena...'

Business Day, November 2, 1986.

'It took a lot to make me do that work and it was a conscious, political decision. It was out of despair, not with any pleasure that I went to work at the Arena and I specifically chose plays that I thought were relevant.'

"The Best Of Company" – Pat Tucker.

The Arena was a new informal venue launched by Mannie Manim and Francois Swart. Francois Swart was the artistic director of the Performing Arts Council of the Transvaal's Drama Department (PACT) and Mannie Manim was the administrative head. PACT was a state-subsidised theatre. Although there were two PACT companies with permanent actors, Barney mainly used his own actors. As Mannie remembers, 'Barney always used the actors he wanted to work with.' This chapter describes the auspicious meeting of Mannie Manim and Barney Simon. Vanessa Cooke, Paul Slabolepszy, Danny Keogh, Dale Cutts, and Patrick Mynhardt were among the actors whom he worked with at this time.

Opposite – Portrait of Barney Simon.
Photograph courtesy of The Market Theatre.

Barney on *Harold Wolpe & Arthur Goldreich*

interviewed by Joseph Sherman

I did a lot of things in the sixties. I had friends who were political and in danger, and in those years I helped people like Harold Wolpe and Arthur Goldreich to escape. A very, very dear friend of mine was Ruth First. I became friendly with her in the sixties when Joe Slovo (her husband) was in exile, and subsequently when they were both in exile I became friendly with both of them.

Would you talk a bit about that friendship?

I came to know Ruth First just before Rivonia, when a lot of people had gone underground. Joe Slovo, for instance, was out of the country on a mission for the ANC. While he was away the resistance movement collapsed after the Rivonia arrests, and he couldn't come back and Ruth was banned. She was, as you know, a brilliant editor and journalist and writer, and she wasn't permitted to function as such under her ban. She was also not permitted to communicate with anybody else who was banned, and that was the majority of her friends. On Sunday nights there used to be a film club in Johannesburg, and she used to sit alone. I didn't know her well, but began to sit with her at the film club and we became good friends.

You mentioned that you helped Wolpe and Goldreich. Could you tell us something about that?

I gave Ruth the key to my apartment to do what she liked. She just had to warn me not to come there when there were very important meetings happening there. So there were people like Bram Fischer, maybe Mandela, I don't know. I never asked because it was better not to know. I never asked questions. Ruth had my total faith and I was certainly supportive of the struggle against apartheid.

From "Cutting Through The Mountain" edited by Immanuel Suttner (Viking, 1997).

Opposite – Joe Slovo and Ruth First, at court during the Treason Trial.
Photography courtesy of MuseuMAfricA.

"I was a young liberal white English-speaking South African with a Jewish-sounding name"

Mannie Manim

Mannie Manim

'He could actually care in a real way about the functioning of a venue'

I met Barney through Athol. Athol was doing "Boesman and Lena" and "People are Living There" for PACT. I was the managing director for PACT Drama with Francois Swart as artistic director. This is from 1967 to 1973. I don't know which particular year it was. Francois and I went to the Grahamstown festival and we met Athol there and saw a dress rehearsal of "Boesman and Lena". We didn't tell him we were in the theatre. We crept in the back. And then after the show we went on stage and met him. Athol thought that both of us needed to meet this Barney Simon character who came to the plays. So we met him. He obviously had a big friendship with Athol. And so a dialogue started with Barney and me.

I was a young liberal white English-speaking South African with a Jewish sounding name, and Barney was this boy from Jeppe. I'd grown up in Fairview in Johannesburg, which is the sort of poorer part of Jeppe. We realised that we grew up a couple of blocks from each other. We went to the same cinema that Barney always talked about taking his black friend to. I immediately liked Barney. To this day I don't really know what he thought about me. He was very interesting and he spoke in a very different way.

I suppose we clicked in that I kind of had a sniff about South African theatre through the Afrikaans company of PACT. Those were the days of Marius Weyers, Sandra Prinsloo, Tine Balder, Katinka Heyns, Louis van Niekerk, Carel Trichardt, Petru Wessels, George Ballot, Wilna Snyman, Sandra Kotze, Don Lamprecht, Dawid van der Merwe, Grethe Fox and Annelisa Weiland. I can't remember all the people, but it was very strong. They did extraordinary stuff including classics and new South African plays. They did Barto Smit. PG du Plessis was kind of just arriving on the scene with "Nag van Legio" and "Siener in die Suburbs". Chris Barnard was writing strange and wonderful things. André P Brink was doing a lot of translation for us and writing new plays. The Afrikaans company was everything that a drama company should be.

There was a star system in the English company of PACT. People who were stars in their own right and who didn't really become an ensemble. The Afrikaans company was very different. They were an ensemble from the start. They used to support each other. Two hours before a performance the dressing rooms were like a sacred space. Those actors were incredibly committed. It was the kind of stuff you would see in the better happenings later on at The Market.

Somewhere in there Athol came into my life and Athol brought Barney. So I met this funny, grey-bearded character whose comments on the work were always incredibly interesting. He too had a special love for that Afrikaans company. Those were the actors that he liked to work with. This was a guy who did plays in a house in Parktown. I think the first production of Barney's I saw was "The Death of Bessie Smith" and "Cayenne Pepper". "The Death of Bessie Smith" had Vanessa Cooke,

Opposite – Portrait of Mannie Manim.
Photograph courtesy of The Market Theatre.

Barbara Itzler, David Phetoe, Corney Mabaso and a couple of others. "Cayenne Pepper" had Zakes Mofekeng and Fats Dibeco. They performed in Dorkay House on the top floor, which was to become a special space for me in different ways. So I saw this work by Barney with black actors and racially mixed casts. Edward Albee's "Bessie Smith" was an extraordinary play for South Africa when he did it.

Was it the content that blew you away?
It was the content. It was nearer to the cutting edge. Because we could only do plays with white people about white problems with PACT. So when Barney and I started to talk, I would go to see his work in Dorkay House. He was mostly more interested to see that Afrikaans work rather than the English plays we were doing at the time. Also, around the same time, the idea for The Arena started growing with Francois Swart and me. That was the theatre that PACT eventually established in Doornfontein. It was an old house. We took out the insides of the house and made a foyer and a theatre that seated a hundred people. Out of that house we also got two dressing rooms and a rehearsal room that we sometimes used as an art gallery.

I used to go and visit Barney and sit in his kitchen. Rose and Barney would cook and then we'd sit and chew the fat. And it was wonderful for me because it was a different head. I'm not putting Francois's head down, but it was another head. It was Barney. We had sixty-five actors in the PACT drama company, I am proud to tell you, and we had each of the actors' years planned when Francois and I ran PACT drama. So it was a very different scene to what goes on these days. With Barney there was nothing. There were no plays. This was just what theatre should be about, and what people were thinking about at the time. It was like reading a philosophy book, except I had it live in Barney's kitchen. I did a lot of listening, hearing what he thought, what he'd done. He'd done nothing that I would ever have done, you know, and yet it was totally valid. And I'd see this production of "Bessie Smith". Barney slightly changed the ending of the play, where it was over to us to make all the hospitals open to all people. So there was that sort of real background and this wonderful Barney philosophy.

Athol, when he introduced me to Barney, described Barney as one of the twelve wise men of the age. And it was in the area and way that I communicated with Barney. Obviously I was also trying to make PACT the place for everybody to be at the time. I wanted to make it the most successful company. So I wanted this mal oke to come and direct at PACT too. I wanted our actors to work with him.

"The Maids" was the first play that he directed in The Arena. Molly Seftel and Barbara Itzler were in it, and Carolyn Sacks, a wonderful woman who later gave us a grand piano for The Market. Barney did that, it was a fantastic success. Also, at the time in The Arena, we did "Sizwe Banzi is Dead", privately. We were sold out. The people were hanging from the rafters literally every night. We put the show on at midnight, because my Board would have died of heart attacks if they realised that I was having black actors on the stage in that play. I had met John Kani and Winston Ntshona at Athol's house in Port Elizabeth. So we'd become friends. But the only place I had was The Arena, and so they came and performed there for a week, late at night.

Opposite – Barney Simon working with actor.
Photograph courtesy of The Market Theatre.

The Arena manager just phoned people and said, 'Tell your friends to come, you'll get in, no booking. You've just got to come and we'll do the show.' Barney was party to all this. He wasn't a part of PACT but I was talking with him every day.
We started a system of the first dress rehearsal being open to people of all races at The Arena, so that everyone could come and see our work. Dealing with Barney, I started meeting more black actors and directors. And they couldn't come and see the work. Or they would have to stand in the lighting box.

Anyway, these late night dress rehearsals became more and more popular. The kind of people that used to come initially were other actors, Workshop '71, Robert McLaren, Arthur Molepo and so on. Then, as the demand grew, we added more open previews and we ended up doing three. I don't know whether Pretoria really knew what was going on, because we used to say, 'No, no, no, we're setting up and we need to do quite a lot of rehearsals', and then we could do our previews. So there were all kinds of schemes going on. This helped to make more people of all races understand what we were doing. And there was a lot of dialogue. Also there was a lot of friction. We always used to have discussions afterwards. People who didn't have access to all that lekker money and everything used to get up and talk and say, 'This play is kak, why are you doing this? Why aren't you guys doing something that's really meaningful?' It was lekker.

We also started doing open previews at the Alexander Theatre. Towards the end of my time at PACT there was a terrible night when the manager of the Alex freaked out.

The Alexander Theatre sign.
Photograph courtesy of The Star.

He found out what we were getting up to at these open previews and that it was illegal, and he locked the theatre. I had to stand outside the theatre and explain to all the black people that were coming, because they'd always come, why they couldn't get in that night. He was threatening to phone the police if I let anybody in. It was terrible. People arrived with their families. I couldn't go on like that. Stuff like that eventually led to The Company and The Market.

So Barney was this guy who never spoke dates. "The Maids" finally happened. I remember, it was miraculous that he was going to do this play. One day I went to The Arena, and there he was rehearsing on the grass outside the theatre in the afternoon. I said, 'Why are you rehearsing here, Barney?' He said, 'Well, there is no space inside.' I said, 'Ja well, we didn't know you're starting.' He said, 'Ja well, I have to start because the opening is so and so.' So I learnt one of my lessons about Barney. Whenever I used to introduce him to stage management I used to say, you have to be careful with Barney, there is a moment between 'Have you done so and so?' and 'Why haven't you done so and so?' And you have to find that. Because before that he's always, 'So, why haven't you put up the posters yet?' You say, 'Well Barney, we didn't know the name of the play', to which Barney would reply, 'Why didn't you phone me?' Then you have to be careful. So, the moment between was the deadline. But he could be very difficult to handle in the third moment, of 'Why haven't you?' Because then you haven't done it. So "The Maids" was rehearsing. We organised and it happened, and we contracted the actresses and it went on.

The next wonderful moment with Barney and me was after the premature closure of "Ten Bulls". I had something that I've never liked in my life – dark space. I went home via Barney's kitchen and said, 'Ah, Barney, The Arena is going to be dark.' Barney said, 'Ooh, I think I can do something.' I said, 'What? You know if we've only got three weeks to the end of the slot then you have to rehearse something in a week.' So he said, 'Just let me try and think...' So suddenly Barney could. He, who would never decide on what he was going to do, was telling me he could fill an empty space. You know, this was the most wonderful thing. About three days later, we had an appointment, and I watched the first rehearsal of "Miss South Africa (6)" with Vanessa, in Barney's lounge. When it was finished they said, 'Do you want it?' I was jumping over the furniture and going wild. They did "Miss South Africa (6)" in The Arena and solved my problem in the most wonderful way. That was like another cementing: Barney was not just a man of ideas, but he could actually care in a real way about the functioning of a venue, and understood the importance of the life of the venue, and that if you're dark you're dead. People must have something to go and see. Barney did that for me. It was Vanessa and it was new South African work.

The next thing he did in The Arena was one of the happiest productions we ever did together. It was an extraordinary combination of circumstances and people. It was Büchner's "Woyzeck", starring Marius Weyers and Aletta Bezuidenhout and others. "Woyzeck" was the happiest production because everybody was working in the same way and because I think it was Barney's first meeting with Marius. This extraordinary actor and this extraordinary director. I did the lighting. It opened new things in lighting between Barney and me. That was another area in which we could communicate. There was a sequence in which Danny Keogh as the Sergeant Major beat Marius. Some of these things make me emotional: Danny used to hit Marius every night. [Mannie Manim cries] Sorry. You might find this at first with a lot of people when they talk about Barney.

Marius didn't want Danny to know that he was hurting him?

I think only Barney and I knew how Marius was being hurt. Marius wore a shirt so that you couldn't see his body. And he always changed out of the dressing room, which other guys just thought was guys not wanting to change in front of guys. On the last night of the show we had a party and Marius finally took off his shirt in front of Danny. [Mannie becomes very emotional at this point] It just illustrates to what extent people were prepared to go for Barney. Marius was black and blue. I'll never forget it. And also Danny having to cope with that. Barney was wonderful as well, trying to sort of take everybody through it because it was a terrible, wonderful moment, if you know what I mean. We just realised then that every night, this guy who was full of bruises got hit again on those bruises, for a run of four or six weeks. It was absolutely frightening, because he got hit with a riding crop. And Marius wanted Danny to hit him. And Danny wanted to hit. Anyway, I suppose it started the relationship with Marius. It cemented the relationship with Aletta at also round about the same time. We'd also become aware of holy actors and holy theatre.

Barney and I were talking more and more about, 'We can't go on like this. This is not a nice way to do it. We're cheating.' Barney said it in a number of our programmes, and I'm sure that there are other writings where he said he was into white consciousness at the time. He'd come back from England or America, and he'd spoken with his black friends. They'd said, 'We're not really too interested in this crossover stuff. You must sort out whitey's head because he's in a mess and he better start to pull himself together, or else.' We were doing the township tours. I suppose in a way it was Barney and I getting together. We needed a catalyst. I don't know where it happened for Barney, and I don't know if he ever told anybody where it happened, or if he just kept on going. I said, 'Let's start The Company.' And he said, 'Well okay.' He was in right from the beginning. He was the centre of the thing.

What happened for me was, PACT was doing "A Macbeth" written and directed by Charles Marowitz, and we were taking it on tour. During the township tour I got a call one afternoon from a guy who later on became one of The Market Trustees, Cassim Saloojee, whom I knew from Dorkay House and who was my contact in Lenasia theatre. Cassim phoned me and said, 'Hey Mannie, there is real trouble about the performance of "A Macbeth" tonight. They don't want it.' (He meant that they were not prepared to invite PACT.) And I said, 'Oh my God, we're setting up, as I speak to you the whole thing is happening.' So he said, 'Well listen, you'd better come across and I'll arrange a meeting with these people.'

On the day before, the bloody Administrator of the Transvaal, who was the Chairman of the Board of PACT, Sybrandt van Niekerk, had said in the newspaper, 'We will only go to the townships if we're invited. We won't go if we're not invited.' These people in Lenasia had freaked out at that and said, 'Rubbish, we don't invite these people. If they want to come and bring their stuff they bring it. It's no hassle for us if it comes or doesn't come and we're not inviting it.' I went out there with Ian Bernhardt, a big shot in Phoenix Players at the time. He'd also helped me to organise these township tours. I remember being in a room full of men I didn't know. All the women were in another room. These men took me on. 'What are you doing? Why are you doing this?' From about seven o'clock to about nine o'clock I was making excuses. I was saying, 'Well, this is what we're trying to do. We like to bring the theatre because you don't get it and I want everybody to get all kinds of theatre.' At nine o'clock I gave up and I lost it. I said, 'Do you guys want to really know what's going on? Okay well, I'll tell you.' I just poured it out. I said, 'This is a cheat, this is a big cheat and I'm not supposed to be doing this at all. Actually if my boss knew what I was doing, I would be fired tomorrow. I'm doing this, and if you don't want it, well then you won't get it.' I spoke like this for half an hour. They all looked at me. Then there was silence. The chairman and the older guys said, 'Will you please wait outside.' I went outside and I stood on the verandah, and I said, 'I can't go on like this. I'm sweating blood to do this, but actually it's dirty. It's a hand me down. Actually it's not a nice thing for them to accept or for me to give. If I'm discovered then we'll all be in trouble. This can't go on. There's got to be some other way to do this.'

To this day I can remember my feeling that night when I just said, 'Okay, cut loose!' [from PACT] I started talks with Barney, real talks, about how I'm going to leave, and he said: 'you must be with me.' He'd been a freelance director, so he asked, 'What are we going to do about actors?' Then we called together all the people we liked as actors and people, and who we thought had the same view.

Vanessa Cooke

'He had a very good nose for what was truth and what wasn't'

I think he'd learnt the term 'workshop' in America. When I met him he'd just come back from America because his dad had died. "Phiri" was workshopped, but with writers. "People" was the first of his plays workshopped with actors.

For my monologue, I live in a building and he just said to me, tell me about your block of flats, just imagine you're this girl who lives on her own, and tell me about what happens in your building. I told him and he wrote everything down. We'd meet again and add things or take things away. The more uninteresting, the better he liked it. He didn't like dramatic things about people, say, with one leg. That never changed with Barney. He wouldn't be interested in something like a huge shooting that happened outside. He was never interested in that.

With "Miss South Africa (6)", I had a hard time when we were rehearsing that. You'd think maybe you're cracking it and then it would be completely not what he wanted. He thought my voice was terrible because I'd done elocution. He wanted me to speak like a normal person. One part, Aunty Glenda, was based on his aunt. I remember his saying, 'I think we'd better cut it, because, you know, Aunty Glenda's too special. If you're not going to commit yourself to it then...' And I just remember bursting into tears.

I stayed with Barney because I found him fascinating. He was giving me things that I'd never had before. He gave me a whole new life. It was about doing theatre, not British theatre like I had grown up with, with my father Roy Cooke. Somewhere at the back of my brain it made sense. It made sense with my political feelings as well. And the fact that whatever money was made was shared out. I was at the age where it was fantastic, you know. There wasn't somebody making a lot of money out of it. We were doing everything ourselves as well. So it was very, very exciting. During "Phiri" I met the most amazing people, Sophie Mgcina, Sam Williams, Mackay Davashe and Caroline Maudling. It wasn't ever easy. But that was the challenge.

The idea for "Miss South Africa (6)" came from a newspaper. I can't remember if she was Miss Springs, or Miss Alberton, or something like that. There was this article about this beauty queen who had had a nervous breakdown because she couldn't take the pressure of being questioned. They had those interviews for when you are going to be Miss South Africa. It's not only putting a bathing costume on! She cracked under the pressure of being interviewed. That was the gist of it.

Barney was fascinated by this beauty queen who could not cope with the political questions that were asked. He was sure that it was political questions that got her.

It took her back into her childhood, but it was related to my childhood and his childhood as well. He'd go away and write. He told Mannie about it and Mannie said, 'Sandra Prinsloo must do it.' Because no one had ever heard of me. Barney made me do "Miss South Africa (6)" for Mannie, in his lounge in Kensington.

Mannie liked it. It needed work, obviously. At the time Barney already had the short story of "Joburg, Sis!" He then decided with Mannie that the two must be a double bill.

We got it together in a week. We were going to do it in people's houses like we always did. I think a lot of people worked that way with Barney as we did on "Miss South Africa (6)". Barney had projects with different people that went on and on and on. I think it was also a case of, if he liked you, he wanted to find something for you. It was like exploring stories about your life. This could happen having tea and bee-sting cake, chatting, and with other people there. That's the way he put it together.

So there would always be people sitting in a passage, or outside, writing. He'd make you write something. You'd have a very big biography which you'd feed him. Some people wrote songs, lyrics. Barney wrote some lyrics. He wrote a song for me, "Hey do you remember Louie?" John Oakley-Smith wrote the music and we would rehearse it in my bathroom in Braamfontein 'for the echo.' If you said anything negative, Barney would make you do it. Like I said, 'I can't sing.' You'd end up singing. I'd never written before, just romantic poems and shit rubbish like that. Somewhere along the line we trusted him, for some odd reason, this crazy person. We were all young and obviously thought we had a lot to express, which often was of no interest whatsoever to Barney. He'd always find something within what you gave. He'd wait until you gave something, which was often very hard for some people. Some people couldn't do that process. You never knew at the beginning who would, who could, and who couldn't.

For "People" we worked mostly in twos to improvise. We did duologues using tape recorders. A monologue is very difficult really to improvise. So that was mostly written and then given to him. Then there were chats and chats and chats. Then according to what he'd give you, you'd either write or rewrite. Some people couldn't write, so he would write, finally. But it would always contain you. It would always contain the actor and what experience the actor had had. He was very much opposed to creating any kind of fictional character that had no basis in your experience.

Hence even later, for "Outers", he couldn't stand your imagination of what a poor white is like. He absolutely refused to accept that, because it wasn't the truth about that person. You could fictionalise it after you'd found the truth. He had a very good nose for what was truth and what wasn't. You could make something up if your knowledge of that thing was good enough, or if it was something real from your past or from your mother's past that you were putting onto that other person. That was okay, wherever you got it from. As long as it was feasible.

"People" was the basis for "Cincinatti" and for everything else. He was very much in a period of discovery. He'd had all this input from America and he didn't know how to place it. Then he came up with his own thing. "Cincinatti" was very much Barney's own thing. I don't think he'd seen anything like that, exactly like that, in America, or copied something.

"People" was still at The Arena, as well as "Woyzeck". After "Woyzeck" came The Company. In The Company we did "Hey Listen" again, "Lysistrata" and "Adventures of a Merry Madcap". We did three shows at once. That's how mad it was. We were doing two shows in the afternoon and one late night. We were being paid just a little bit. And then we didn't want to be at The Arena anymore because it belonged to PACT. which was not open to a black audience. "Lysistrata" was very physical. The public was

very excited. I don't think that people had seen anything like that. We were all mountains. And there were balloons for penises, salt cellars and mugs, jugs on our heads as helmets. It was fun. For this production we did not go and research people.

Barney had different ways for each thing that he did, except for the workshop stuff. And when he was working on a script he'd work how that script told him to work. So it's specifically the workshop stuff that he had a method for, which he didn't explain terribly clearly, except that you had to come up with something that he'd imagine would be truthful.

Vanessa Cooke in "Miss South Africa (6)".
Photograph courtesy of Vanessa Cooke.

'I stayed with Barney because I found him fascinating'

Vanessa Cooke

Vanessa Cooke in "Miss South Africa (6)".
Photograph courtesy of NELM.

Paul Slabolepszy

'Barney wanted to work with good actors who joined the journey with him'

1972, for me, that was the beginning. Whatever anybody tells you – South Africa's first genuine, non-racial theatre was The Space in Cape Town. Founded by Brian Astbury, Yvonne Bryceland and Athol Fugard. What Barney used to do in Jo'burg with Athol, in the early days, was to grab a bunch of people together and do stuff in houses or at Dorkay House. They were one-off situations. Barney would say, 'Listen we are going to do plays for anybody, anytime, anywhere.' They were in sitting rooms, they were in Dorkay House, they were in anonymous environments, in the sense that no one, except invited guests, knew where, what was happening.

The Space was advertised from day one as a theatre. Athol had a lot to do with that because he got together with Yvonne and they wanted to create an alternative theatre and theatre company. Barney came from Jo'burg to Cape Town to see one of our productions there. Bill Flynn and I and Yvonne were working with Athol. Everyone said, 'Barney Simon's here!' The only thing we knew about Barney was that he had worked with Athol. Barney really put his finger on things. He was known as somebody special in theatre because he had done an outstanding "Hello and Goodbye" with Athol and Molly Seftel. We knew of his work, but it was very much an alternative thing. It wasn't so-called straight theatre, CAPAB and PACT, old vrot white actors doing very traditional British stuff and not doing South African stuff. Barney was this kind of a guru figure even for Athol. We would be in rehearsals doing "People are Living There" and Athol would say, 'Ja, well Barney would do this and Barney would say that.' That's how we kind of knew already that he was obviously something special in the theatre.

Then Mannie Manim arrived on the scene. Mannie was still with PACT and he and Barney had been talking about establishing something. Coming to Cape Town kind of inspired them. They said, 'Gee, look at this Space Theatre Company, playing to all races, mixed casts, zero apartheid.' I remember Mannie came to me saying, 'Listen, would you come up to Jo'burg if we established a company like this one?' I said, 'Yes', and headed north. The Company had not yet formed but I made contact with Barney who was doing stuff in Doornfontein, his late night shows. It was '73 and I was cast in a commercial venture, "Second Edition" at the President Hotel. This wasn't Barney's thing. It was 'frothy' theatre on the other side of town. I remember dashing late at night after the show to Doornfontein to do "Hey Listen" which was me, Marius Weyers and Vanessa Cooke. There were amusing stories in the paper about how I used to run from one side of town to the other to get there in time for my show – '5 minutes – you're on.' Vanessa started first so that I could get there to do "Men Should Cry More Often". Marius was doing "Joburg, Sis". We got a lot of accolades for those three monologues. Vanessa was doing "Miss South Africa (6)".

It was soul food for me to work with Barney. There is no question that my best work was done with Barney. I grew hugely as an actor. I have never ceased drawing on what Barney has given me. It was never 'the easy option' and I have learnt this through my writing as well as my acting. A lot of people go for the short-hand thing, go for

the first thing that comes up. Whereas Barney said, 'Go for that first thing and peel away that layer – then the next, then the next...' You'd do little random things, like take a coin and put a piece of paper over the coin and take a pencil and rub it. You'd have to keep rubbing away until Van Riebeeck emerges. (Those were the days when Van Riebeeck was on the coins). In "Cold Stone Jug" I was playing a jailer. We spent a long time trying to find where this person was coming from. We took all these journeys and they were never the same. That was exciting. That's why it is so hard to put a finger on the way Barney used to work, because there was never a formula. I used to work with guys like Dieter Reible, who always had a formula.

Barney was frustrating because he was never quite satisfied. It always had to come from another source. All you had to do when working with Barney was open up, make yourself available for the exceptional, or the out-of-the-ordinary, and then sometimes accept the deadly frustrating. You couldn't be uptight about it or have any preconceived ideas. You had to go with the flow. Going with the flow was a very Barney experience. Barney gave very short shrift to people who didn't enter into the spirit of the process. Barney did not have a great deal of respect for local directors because he felt they didn't respect the work enough. I used to have lots of fights with him because I would want to work with other people and he would say, 'You will be wasting your time.' Barney wanted to work with good actors who joined the journey with him. He wouldn't always shy away from working with people who wouldn't. I think about Patrick Mynhardt as an example. A real actor of the old school doing "The Crucible".

Then we did "Fortune and Men's Eyes". The Company had just secured The Market building. It was the first play to rehearse in The Market. I remember there were all these walls that needed to be knocked down. Barney says, 'Okay, work detail.' In the play we were prisoners in a kind of reformatory type prison in Canada. These guys were made to work in prison in order to become proper members of society. So Barney gets these huge eighteen-pound, twenty-pound hammers and we had to knock walls down...

Athol Fugard and Yvonne Bryceland in Cape Town, 1972.
Photograph courtesy of Brian Astbury from his book "The Space / Die Ruimte / Indawo – March 1972 – September 1979".

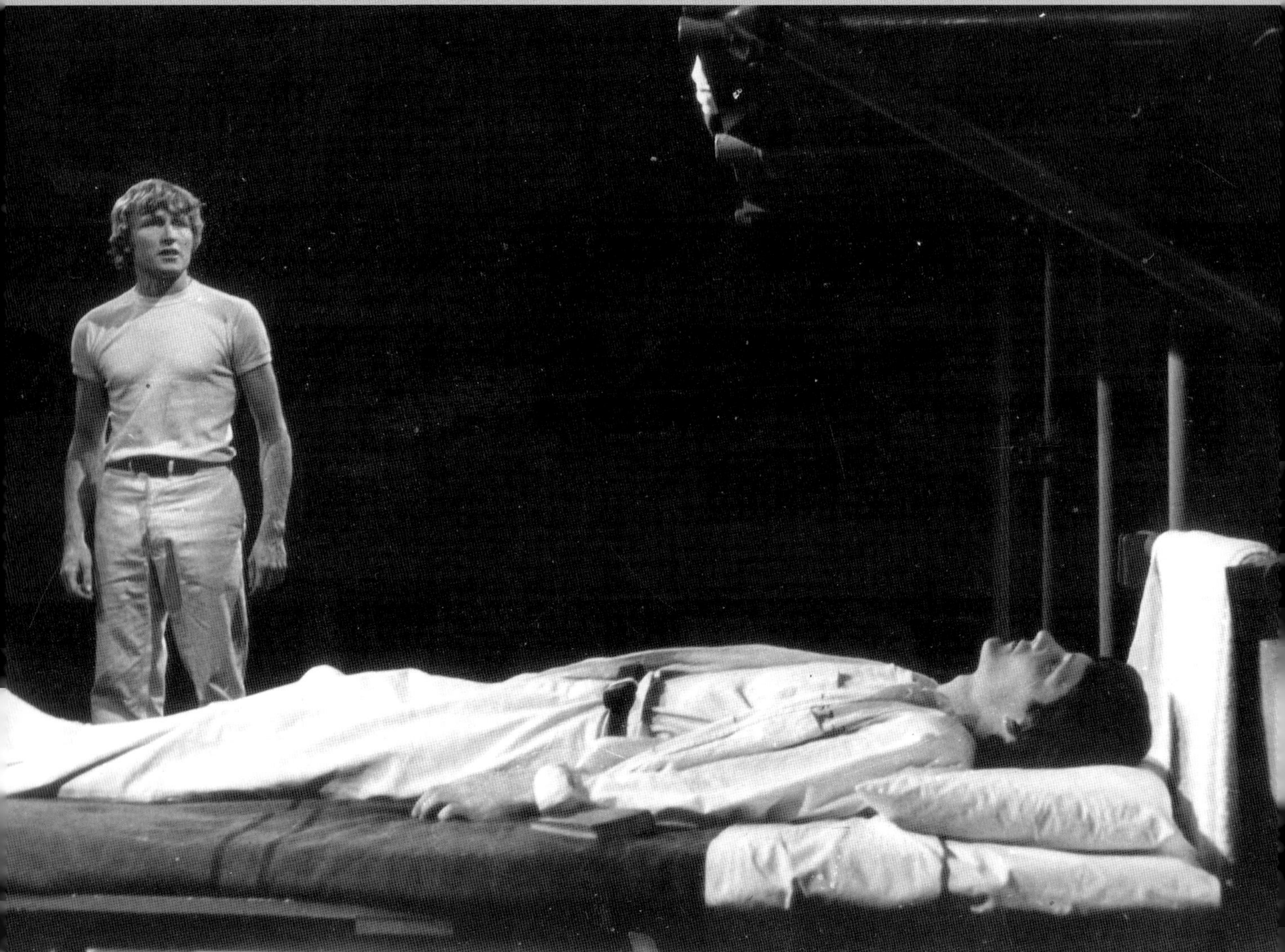

Danny Keogh

'It is almost as though he decided that he was going to make me an actor'

When I first met Barney I was a stage manager and I would have remained a stage manager, but I saw a production that he did of "Begeerte" (the Afrikaans version of Eugene O'Neill's "Desire Under the Elms") that just blew me away. I hadn't seen that type of concentration in actors, and I was working closely with actors as a stage manager on a nightly basis. I couldn't believe that he could draw those performances out of people, so I asked Mannie if I could work for him.

Barney's next show was monologues, and songs with John Oakley-Smith. Barney had a whole lot of young people that had just come out of varsity, a year or two out of varsity. The work started, we played games a lot of the time, which was very confusing for me. What's that game where you go 1-2-3 and you turn around and catch everybody moving? I suppose it was just to get people to relax, and then getting us to start writing. He started 'pick up a story'. You invent your character and somebody else has to take it, and the next, take it, and take it.

He would tell us what he would like us to do, and say to us, 'Be free and don't try and think anything out, just let it come naturally, bounce off the other people.' That's what a lot of the exercises were about, making us respond to the fellow performer. In the long run, eventually, I can see the picture, because that's what you end up doing on stage, please God, if you root yourself in this. Instead of acting you are reacting, which is what good performance is really about, because it changes on a nightly basis.

Then the word games... Why are you doing this? Why are you doing this? Why are you doing this? Why are you doing this?... You would work your way through an entire script like this with other people in the cast, doing exactly the same thing. So you sit with a base of comfort. It just made one very comfortable with the whole process. And also the reactive thing... once you have done all these exercises, once you get into the run of the play, if the emphasis changed from a fellow performer, then you were receptive to it, because somewhere it rang a bell from the first week of rehearsal... you were doing this kind of thing. A lot of the games were trust games as well. Learn to trust your other performers. I never read Grotowski, or any of those books. Barney was obviously very into those things. Like 'stand on a table and close your eyes and just let yourself fall and have the other actors catch you' and things like that.

And so the story telling... He would send us out onto the street: 'Go and find people, bring something back, what you see. The way they walk, the way they talk, something interesting.' Which we did. Then we invented characters. Either characters from our heads or people we knew, or something you got out of the newspaper. Then it was, sit down with a pen and paper and write, and then Barney would edit. Now I was kind of passive in this. I was kind of watching people. Then Barney drew me into the story-telling. Someone would be half-way through the story, then I took over, and I actually found it hell of an easy. I was their stage manager, just making sure everybody had their tea and coffee and behaved and came on time. I just found it

Opposite – Paul Slabolepszy and Danny Keogh in "Fortune and Men's Eyes".
Photograph courtesy of NELM.

incredibly easy and did a lot better than some of the actors. I was writing a monologue as well, and Barney worked very closely with me and very carefully. The monologue that I ended up writing was the closing monologue for the show and it was eventually a fifteen-minute monologue. So I had a cream piece of the thing, and I was the stage manager!

Then Mannie came to see it with Francois Swart, and said, 'This is all fantastic but now we have got to get somebody to do the monologue that Danny's doing. So should we look at Paul Slab or Billy Flynn or somebody?' And Barney said, 'No, I want Danny to do it.' And they said, 'He's a stage manager, he isn't an actor.' And Barney said, 'No, I want Danny to do it, otherwise no more play.' So that's what happened. I ended up acting with Barney, and from there I went on to Barney's next thing. It's almost as though he decided that he was going to make me an actor. I went into "Six Characters in Search of an Author" for Barney. I played the son. What happened to me is that I didn't know I would get the kind of response that I got as a performer. I thought this was actually quite nice, instead of running around looking after other people's business all the time, and pushing buttons on tape recorders.

Then we got The Company going. Driving around with Barney looking for something that could possibly be a theatre-warehouse and all that... We went into "Fortune and Men's Eyes". This was before we got The Market. That was with Paul and Billy and Ron Smerczak. There I had my first fight with Barney. It was an amazing play. I knew nothing about it and when I read it there was my part for me. But my part went to Paul Slabolepszy and I ended up having to play Mona, and that upset me terribly. I didn't want to play a camp guy. I didn't want to play a queen. I was still deeply rooted in my stage management and heterosexuality, and homophobic like you can't believe. I had to play Mona. Barney took me through that and in the end I think it was some of the best work I ever did.

Barney worked differently with different people. He worked very closely with me on that thing. I didn't realise the depths that I had got into it. I mean, Jo'burg's gay community came in droves to see it. And I got people who supported me for the rest of my life as an actor and saw me as this very close friend of theirs, you know... He obviously recognised that I was pretty homophobic. He had to get me out of that. He just talked about how things change and things are different. And how even though I feel like I feel now at the age of twenty-three/twenty-four, just because I had a bad come-on from a guy, not everybody was like that. He helped me through that barrier by talking to me. I knew it was a case of sink or swim. I couldn't walk out of a production so I had to do the best I could with it. And in my head I just turned it around so it doesn't matter whether they are male or female. Basically if you are in love with somebody they work the same way. So I just tried to get myself into a female head, I suppose. And I had to say a poem. Barney made me do in that production what I hadn't done before. Where everything had been stories and part of my personality, now it was try and discover something new every night. He said, 'Don't worry about giving a great performance. Just do the best you can, and it doesn't have to be the same every night.' That helped me to keep things alive, and that is something that stayed with me through all my work.

So what would you draw on?

I think the spontaneity, that reactive thing I mentioned in the beginning. 'You know this is the first time you've heard it!' The other thing Barney would say to me is 'I want to see that light bulb flash, I want to see you get that idea, I want to see you take it in and transform it, and then answer.' Transformation means to take the knowledge you have been given. You are saying something to me, I'm listening to what you are saying, I am receiving what you are saying, now I am transforming this into an answer, which I now give back to you. But actors don't do that because they start learning lines. You say your line and I say my line. That's not what it's about. You are telling me something, and I am listening to what you are saying, and I am now telling something to you, about something that happened to me.

How do you stop that from becoming a set thing in itself?

I don't know how you do it. You just have to try and keep fresh with it. You have to listen and be there. It's not always possible. There are certain things that interfere with every performance. Even if you can do that for only fifty percent of your performance, you are going to give a good performance. It's got to have the life, and that's it. I think that's really all, besides the obvious things of one's voice and articulating, being heard and all those technical aspects. The only other thing you have to do is listen to the information, light bulb goes on, and be true to what the author – you know, the play – is saying, and you have a performance. So, if you have a lazy actor working with you one night, don't just slip into the groove, but take that and do something with it. Make it move, make it change.

Actual changes every night?

Well, it depended on the mood of the play, of course. You have your parameters on which you have got to work. But you know anger can come a little bit stronger, you can come a little bit faster. It's all those things so that you don't get set in a rhythm. The line only works when it is alive. And the life of it can change, according to what your life is. As long as you are centred, doing your work, and you're not dealing with outside problems. If you are just sitting there and doing the work and not reacting to outside problems, if you are reacting and being honest, then it's got a life of its own.

Doing your work?

Doing your work is being true to your character, being true to the work process you have gone through, being true to the decisions that have been made about that production. And also what Barney said: 'A play is teamwork. There are no individuals out there, you are working together, working as a whole.' Sure, you are individuals within the whole, but you are part of the group, it's a team thing and everybody has to hold their end of the workload. Barney also had it in his mind that what you were writing was going to be performed, not just going to be words on paper that would make interesting reading. There had to be a whole different way of writing there, and that's what he had to teach all of us. That you are writing performance pieces, you are not writing to read it. I think he helped all of us tremendously in learning to understand the dynamics of writing these performance pieces, because when we went on to do "Storytime 2" those monologues came a lot faster and quicker and had more depth to them. We created wonderful monologues. Fantastic monologues.

What was the way of writing them?

Well, that is hard because it varied from person to person. With this person he had to have that approach, with that person that approach. Some people couldn't do it. That first monologue that I wrote for him appeared in a book, it was called "Monologue for Danny", with no acknowledgement that it was my story, my concept. All Barney did really was edit and change. And now it was suddenly Barney's monologue, which was very upsetting. Even when it got to "Cincinatti", the actors were saying 'Percentage please... Acknowledge... Written with not by...' Barney took those things and just blandly said that they were his. I mean he did that to Mannie all the time. Then it was, just go with it. But it got a bit more dodgy when I was saying, 'Barney, do you want to publish it? I want a percentage.' He was very upset. None of those monologues ever got anything done with them. Nothing. They just died. There is one other thing that I think was tremendously good for me as a performer, and that was playing Medviedenko, a lonely school teacher in Barney's production of "Seagull". This was our first production Upstairs. It was a tiny part but Barney swung the focus somehow in that I spent a lot of time just being there, seeing my old relationship going away from me. That production is the closest I came to doing what "Begeerte" did. Here what you were thinking was important. That was a tremendous vision of Barney's. Barney had that ability to give characters and the audience another way of looking at somebody. So sometimes I think Barney had this tremendous insight. Anybody who paid attention to what Barney taught them would come out of it a bit better for it. If they paid attention.

How did Barney put the focus on Medviedenko?

Barney emphasised an undercurrent of what was happening. Medviedenko had his scene with his wife when he was treated badly. You had that scene, then it was gone. But what Barney allowed to happen was for Medviedenko to continue to be present and for you to understand that he was absolutely going through hell. It was just a little shift in focus, it didn't change anything. The character was going through that journey. Whereas that character didn't get that focus, that attention, within the structure of the play, Barney just did the shift and said, 'Just look at this for a moment.' So Medviedenko just became a rounder person. Rather like the movies. Take Steve McQueen in "Magnificent Seven". When they offered him the part he had nothing to say, nothing to do. But the director really wanted him, saying, 'You've got nothing to say and nothing to do, but I will give you screen time.' And that's what he did. Steve McQueen hardly said a word in that movie, but if you watch it, he's there, he's one of the guys. You walk away remembering. Barney did that, screen time where you don't have anything to say, you get your close-up. That's what he was doing, giving me close-up. They used to call him the Guru of Doornfontein. Barney had a lot of baggage that he had to wade through before he even began a production. People had put him on a pedestal that I don't think he should have been on and that I don't think he wanted to be on.

Dale Cutts

'He was like a drop of water on a stone'

In "The Crucible", a PACT drama in 1975, I found myself in this funny position, sharing a dressing room with people who were finding Barney's style of direction so funny. I mean, the idea of taking the girls out at night, you know. Having these kind of little covens and rituals. Slaughtering chickens and spraying each other with chicken blood and running naked in the koppies. You can imagine the effect this had on people like Kerry Jordan and Michael McCabe. They were the antics of complete lunatics as far as they were concerned.

Barney attracted different people. He had very erratic friendships. I think that's the right word. Years later, when I was talking to Barney about something else entirely, we talked about the night that Arthur Goldreich and Harold Wolpe escaped from Marshall Square. I was in Johannesburg making a documentary movie. What I hadn't realised was that they were hiding in Barney's flat that very night, while I was in Johannesburg reading all these headlines about Arthur Goldreich and being terrified because Arthur Goldreich was somebody that I knew. I knew he had my name and telephone number in his little black book.

I was really politically neutral at the time, I was really a scaredy cat. We were filming in Johannesburg from the roof of the Quirinal Hotel, which was in those days, well before it was a whorehouse, quite a posh hotel. We were on the roof of this bloody hotel shooting the sunset. But what we didn't realise was that from the Quirinal looking directly west you looked straight down into the Fort. Suddenly we were surrounded on the roof by all these policemen with guns. One by one we had to take these policemen and show them the view finder from the camera to prove that we were actually shooting the sunset. They were paranoid about Arthur Goldreich and Harold Wolpe. All this time they were hiding in Barney's flat [laughter].

I leaned a helluva lot. Whether it was particularly from "Marat/Sade" or whether it was just the process I was going through at the time. While we were playing "Marat/Sade" we were also filming "The Villagers", because you know we all had to have some other source of income. The Market Theatre paid forty rand a week to all its actors, because that was the least that they could pay. They weren't allowed to pay less, so that is what they paid and went on paying for quite some time. Mannie said a lot of things about, 'We are not a subsidised theatre.' I said, 'You lie – the actors have been subsidising you for years.' We were rushing out and doing things like "The Villagers" and making soap operas, in order to feed our families and work at The Market Theatre.

Somehow it was essential. I don't want that to sound too pathetic, but it was the essence of what we were doing. We had acquired a facility which was all radio acting and television acting, which was facile. It involved a facility that we had acquired, but somehow that was fuelled by an essence that I suppose The Market provided. We all got together and hung out. I mean it was a bit of a clubhouse in a way, wasn't it? Barney was... one sort of hesitates to say things like a guru and master.

There was certainly that quality about him. He had this extraordinary theatrical naiveté. He just believed things would happen. This is what he wanted and you had to expose yourself to this vision, I mean literally. He had a concept of some sort. He wouldn't share it with you but you kind of trusted that he had it. He didn't compromise on his way to that concept. It was always in this sort of quiet, patient, Jewish long-suffering way that he had which could be misinterpreted in many ways. It was a vulnerable quality. He was showing you his pain so why can't you show him yours? He was so ridiculously naive and ridiculously honest. In a sense I think we did give him a lot of respect, but I think we were quite demanding in a way: 'Show us, our master...' you know. But I mean Barney was also quite crafty in his way. He had his little way of making you get to where he wanted you to be.

How was he crafty?
'How many Jewish mothers does it take to change a light bulb?' 'Don't you vorry about me, I vill sit here in the dark, you go out and hev a good time.' Barney had a chicken soup way of manoeuvring people into those situations. Exploiting people's guilt a little bit. Exactly the way a Jewish mother does. So when I say crafty I mean that in quite an innocent sense, I don't think there was anything malevolent about it. And he was persistent. Mannie would come out of his office saying, 'Oh for God's sake, somebody save me from forty-year-old hippies.' Mannie was the businessman, the entrepreneur.

Sounds like you were strong enough in what you knew about your work to do it, but also to go on an intriguing journey with someone?
Ja, I think, perhaps to my regret, I never really committed myself enough. I was always sort of rushing back to the lifeboat facility. There are times that I think, perhaps if I had been a little more daring, committed to it... He was like a drop of water on a stone. He kept coming back. If he had this idea of something, you thought somewhere in the process it had been lost, but he would come back to it... Oh God!

I did "Play it Again Sam" which is not really much more than a slick Woody Allen type farce. It wasn't a very deep play at all. It required ability to understand farce and timing. I was quite horrified when I heard that Barney was going to direct it. We can't go through the painful process of Barney's style of directing to get to where we need to be. Barney made a quantum leap. He suddenly accepted that there were certain theatrical conventions that you had to actually embrace in order to get to the end of that particular road. To actually say, 'Okay this is how we time a gag.' Not, why does your character choose to do this rather than that!

And did he go along with that?
He certainly did. In fact he had a lot of fun. Barney laughed a lot in rehearsals. He fell out of his chair.

Opposite – "Play it again Sam."
Photograph courtesy of The Market Theatre.

Because there was that incredible frivolous sort of side to Barney?

I walked into Bev Melnick's kitchen one day. Barney was sitting round the table with Vanessa and various other people and passing round a joint. Barney was smoking dope, I couldn't believe it. I hadn't known that part of Barney. When he got stoned he was absolutely wonderful. He just drifted into a corner and giggled.

And when he did "Play it Again Sam" you suddenly saw a whole other aspect?

Ja, "Play it again Sam" was a huge success, we packed them out. The Market Theatre hired the Intimate Theatre so we could actually keep the show on while something else was coming into The Market. The Market was actually in the business of hiring commercial theatres to transfer a show in order to keep on making money. I don't think many people realise what a brilliant eye Barney had for just looking at the stage and making something look right. He was very accurate.

When you say 'look right' you obviously don't just mean visually?

I mean pretty much visually. He had a brilliant eye for the way something should look. As an artistic director he was involved in everybody's work, so he had come to rehearsals and taken notes and he would give these most stunning notes. He would just sort of pick up on things. It wasn't always obvious but he was very practical in his own way. And I think that was very much more obvious when he was looking at somebody else's work. When he was involved in his own work he sort of lost sight of his practicality.

Billy Flynn was playing the Woody Allen character. He couldn't look like Woody Allen, but that didn't matter. But all the other characters had to look like who they were. I was Bogart and Barney was very helpful. We had this beautiful picture of Bogart laughing with his mouth open and you could see all his teeth. The dental school made me a plate and copied his slightly buck teeth perfectly. They built in a slight whistle as well. It helped the character so much. It was Barney's concept.

Patrick Mynhardt

'I wasn't all that bloody overawed working with Barney Simon'

I warned you that I wasn't going to be kind. I am going to tell you the truth. I'm not going to, you know, because Barney's dead, be kind. I'm not going to be unkind either. I'm just going to tell the truth.

Well, the very first time I ever came across or met Barney Simon, I was sitting sort of halfway down the aisle of the Wits Great Hall. Janet Suzman was out here doing her one-lady show. The man came up to me and gently tapped me on the shoulder – he had a bit of a beard and a bit of dandruff – and he said, 'I'm Barney Simon. I know you're Patrick Mynhardt. Would you just move more forward because Janet Suzman has come from London to do the show and we don't want empty seats in the front.' And I said, 'With pleasure.'

That was the first time I met Barney Simon. I'd heard about him. I knew that he was a kind, gentle man. I knew that he did a great deal of good work, particularly for black theatre and amongst Africans at Dorkay House. I never socialised with him. I was a bloody stoere boer who'd spent six years in London, and who'd come back to this country because Verwoerd had been shot at the Rand Easter Show and there had been a state of emergency. I was crying for the beloved country. I wasn't all that in with the Dorkay crowd or set-up. I was trying to make a living, so I never really had much to do with Barney Simon in those early days, or Athol Fugard, although I'd met Athol once. But I knew that they were doing great work. What I did see of course, and I don't know if Barney directed it, was "The Blood Knot" at the YMCA's little Intimate Theatre, Fugard's play. I was absolutely knocked out by it. What was very upsetting was this Afrikaans sogenaamde 'racist boer' adoring this play which was getting a message across. I had taken the most beautiful girl called Anne Klinglund who was the Swedish Ambassador's daughter and a liberal anti-white lady, and she hated the play. She yawned and laughed in all the wrong places and didn't even clap at the end. There I was going, 'Bravo, bravo!'

Then at some stage there was a phone call. Would I go to his house? He lived near Parktown. Would I do an audition for the part of Danforth in "The Crucible"? I felt, 'Ag shit, you don't expect me to audition at this stage of my life.' It's not that I was big-headed, hell, I'd done some marvellous things in 1975. I'd had my one-man show success. I'd done the "Dance of Death". I'd done "The Cherry Orchard". I had done Shakespeare. But anyway, I sat in this little sort of semi-attic place and I read and read and re-read and I was awful. I thought, well I won't get this bloody part anyway. And I didn't click with Barney. He was very, very terug getrokke, very withdrawn. I'm an effusive person. I want to be loved or hated. I don't like not knowing where the hell I stand with people. And then I was in Durban when Mannie Manim phoned and said, 'Yes, would I play the part?' Barney wanted me. I didn't want to do it, but my wife said, 'Take it, take it. You can't just do one-man shows.' And I agreed with her. So came rehearsals. Now my marriage was in a dicey position at the time. One minute she wanted to leave me and the next minute she wanted to be with me – post-natal depression and all that. So I was in a very mixed up toestand. So I went into rehearsals in a bad frame of mind, to play the part of Danforth. I never liked "The Crucible". I liked the message. I loved what Arthur Miller did in the play. But to me it was so awful. Witch hunting is just such an awful thing. The first time around I thought, 'He's a good man, Judge Danforth, doing his job.'

So what did you feel as an actor, about going to work with this man Barney?
I wasn't all that bloody overawed working with Barney Simon. I mean, I'd seen a few productions – actors desperately need direction. An actor without a director is nothing. So we read through this and that. Then one day Barney said, 'I want...' You know he always scratched, he had a bit of psoriasis... 'Can you come in early tomorrow, before the others, I want to talk to you very confidentially?' I said, 'Of course Barney, I'm delighted you can give me the extra time.'

We sat down and he said, 'Now listen, I want to talk to you very confidentially about Danforth.' Then he'd jump up and go to the door and peep to see if there was anybody around the corner. Then he'd come and sit down again and he'd say, 'Now you see, I want you to...' And he would look under the chair and he would look around and would be very suspicious. And I thought, 'My God, you know, are we being bugged? Is this the CIA? Is it the bossgedoente with General van den Berg? Are we being watched? Is he a communist? Is he a liberal? Is he a links gesinder? Wat is dit? Why all the jumping up and koekeloering round the corners and the doors, and gaaning tekere like this?' And I got more and more nervous. And he said, 'I want to...' and he'd lick his lips and he'd scratch. I say this with love. This is not being shit towards Barney. And he'd scratch. He had a sort of skin infection because he was bald. And he'd say, 'I want you to realise, just think of this play, "The Crucible" as being... do you read me?'

He'd go off and then he'd come back again and he'd say now I want you to think of "The Crucible" as being a (shouting and hitting the table) pit, a pit filled with piss and slime, piss and slime, piss and slime! And I said, 'Ah, ja, ja, thank you Barney, ja, ja, now I understand.'

I didn't know what he was talking about. I was bewildered. I was fucked out of my mind. I couldn't understand a word. I learnt the lines and that was it. It was an awfully difficult experience for me. And I'm not being disloyal – the man was a lovely, gentle, wonderful man – but old actors... Thank God I'm not the only one, apparently, who had trouble working with Barney. They couldn't quite correlate with him. He left us at rehearsal. He put us in a room. He just said, 'Stand there.' We did not know where the set was or anything. I had a little friend Frank Douglas who, bless his heart, battled terribly, didn't have many lines. But as Frank Douglas would say, 'I know my lines, but I don't know where the fuck they come in.' Because they were interspersed. Hier a sinnetjie, and there a sentence.

But one day he left Frank and us in his room and he said, 'I just want you to do what you like.' Well, you know old actors just can't do those things we did at drama school. We did mime, we improvised, but old Frank and I were totally bewildered.

In the middle of "The Crucible" rehearsals madam-wife buggers off with the little baby. I was forty-two years old, the father of a little baby named after my father whom I adored. And I was demented. I couldn't learn lines and it was most peculiar. I started fancying one of the lovely young actresses. I am anti-adultery and yet here I'm jags for a young actress playing a little girl. Ja, so I'm having an affair with her then, just before the divorce came through and walking up and down on stage every night. I wore a bald wig. I wanted it to age me and give me a hawk-like appearance. This little girl would say to me the next day, 'Why do you never look at me?' I'd say, 'I couldn't look at you in the eye because of guilt...' If the public knew what we were up to in bed it would be awful. Imagine this old man Danforth steeking this little girl with a little kappie. The first night we went to bed she left her contact lenses on the table next to the bed in a tissue. When I tidied up I flushed them down the kakhuis. That might have been the most expensive bit of adultery that any man has ever committed. But fortunately for me the tissue paper with the lenses was still bobbing up and down and I was able to retrieve them.

Patrick Mynhardt, May 1990.
Photograph by Ruphin Coudyzer.

Part 2.
A Home

Chapter 4. Texture

It had become impossible for Mannie Manim to continue working at PACT. The work he and Barney had done at The Arena was cutting edge. They knew this work had to continue but with new rules. In 1974 they formed The Company. The Company was a group of like-minded actors who were prepared to move away from the mainstream support system and work with Barney Simon's alternative methods of direction. They were willing to do anything from ushering or building to acting. The Company's founder members were Barney Simon (art director) Mannie Manim (administrative director), Vanessa Cooke, Janice Honeyman, David Eppel, Judith Cornell, Aletta Bezuidenhout, Leonie Hofmeyr, Danny Keogh, Sue Kiel, Lindsay Reardon and John Oakley-Smith. They searched for a venue for two years, performing in various ad hoc spaces, such as the Oxford Hotel, a shop-front in Orange Grove, The Nunnery and the Chelsea Hotel. In 1976 they finally found their home in the old produce market in Newtown. The Market Theatre was born.

'We began by opening our doors in June 1976 to all the people of South Africa and inviting black and white to sit together and watch black and white perform together, when this simple sanity was deemed a criminal act.'

Mannie Manim, The Market Theatre Annual Report, March1992.

In this chapter we learn more about the unique relationship that Barney had with his actors. Marius Weyers, Marcel van Heerden, Wilson Dunster and Aletta Bezuidenhout recall how Barney created texture and detail. An exercise many actors remember is the 'orange exercise' recorded in the following chapter.

'If there are twenty people and you give each one an orange, it can be something different to each person: a baseball, a planet, it can be its biography since it was joined to a tree. They can peel it; they can eat it. By the end of an hour I can tell different things about different people... There's a theatre of possibilities.'

Barney Simon, Business Day, November 1986.

Previous page – Construction on the interior of the Market Rotunda.
Photograph courtesy of The Market Theatre.
Opposite above – The contruction of The Market Building, 1913.
Photograph courtesy of MuseuMAfricA.
Opposite below – Market Square, Johannesburg, 1914.

Mannie Manim

'Overseas they were saying this guy is really something'

In the early days of The Market, people were so supportive, apart from what happened when I went to City Council type people, and so on. The building took about a year and we had a volunteer thing from the beginning. Whether it was folding and putting things into envelopes to send out, or whether it was painting, or washing the dishes: 'Please come and help.' That was the message we put out. Once the building started we had an agreement with the builder, Gary Zulberg. On Saturday mornings he would give me a list of jobs: 'We need that swept out over there, and we need windows taken out over there, and we need this wall painted white.' I'd go there eight o'clock and then a lot of actors and other people would rock up.

The fact that there was a Space Theatre in Cape Town doing what we did gave us strength. The Space was the only theatre that we had a direct equal relationship with. We did have a relationship with the Baxter, but there was always a sense that the Baxter was slightly more comfortable. We were like the poor cousins from up country, but we did the real work. They had a nice venue, we had the nice work, and we could meet somewhere in the middle. John Slemon was very supportive of Barney and The Market. Students were doing theses on Barney. Barney was being celebrated overseas long before he was being recognised here. He was still the weird, strange guy. Overseas they were saying this guy is really something. Then Barney would come back to South Africa where people were saying, 'No, Barney Simon, he doesn't do commercial theatre.' They didn't really like his methods. He was coming from a different angle.

What do you mean by strange?

By strange I mean interesting, skeef, which I found a complimentary term. I don't particularly like straight people. I like people who are interesting because they are different. Okay, so let's get to Barney, what made him different? First of all the care, the kindness, the interest, and the compassion. Auditions with ninety percent of the other directors I've ever worked with, you get, 'Thank you. Your name? Here's your form. Got a photograph, address? What are you going to do?' And afterwards they say, 'OK, thank you'. With Barney I very quickly learnt that wasn't an audition process. We would stop with the actress who was doing something totally incorrect, the actress least likely to be judged right for the part that we wanted her to do. Barney would stop everything and say, 'Do you understand what the scene is about? Have you thought about what's actually happening here?' And then he'd start teaching this person about what she was doing. The minutes would tick away, and it would be half an hour, and the queue would be going round down to Bree Street. Barney finishes and the person goes out, and you say, 'Barney, you can't do that, you know, there's forty-five minutes with a person that's definitely not going to be in the play.' He says, 'Ja, but she didn't understand what she was talking about, I had to explain so that she understands what the play was about.'

Opposite – Barney Simon and Mannie Manim, 1980.
Photograph, Ruphin Coudyzer.

No other director is going to stop and care enough about the person's understanding of the play. Barney would almost do the inverse: 'I don't need to see that person because I know she's good, so thank you very much for coming, we'll be in touch.' Then this other person comes in... I don't know if she ever did another play, or another audition even, in her life, but she gets the forty-five minutes. So that's different for a start. Barney came to a play, not like most other directors. They read it because it was a success somewhere else, other people who liked it think they should do it. Barney came to a play from deep inside his own self and his understanding of the needs of what was going on around him. So Barney's centre for doing a play was somewhere totally else again. He never said, 'There's a West End success, Mannie, can you get me the rights of that play?' It was: 'I was talking with a group of people and I think it's time we did a play that spoke about this.'

He was doing his own work, the work that started for me with "Miss South Africa (6)", "Men Should Cry More Often", "Hey Listen", "People", "Storytime", "People Too", culminating in "Cincinatti" which was the beginning of a new cycle: "Black Dog Inj'emnyama", "Born in the RSA", "Outers" and "Score Me the Ages". They were plays where the characters met, or clashed, or threaded through each other's lives, whereas the previous things were monologues. "Cincinatti" started with an idea to do Arthur Schnitzler's "La Ronde". "La Ronde" was taken into another dimension about what was going on right then in Johannesburg, When we were doing "Cincinatti", discotheques were systematically being closed down by the police because they were breaking the race laws. So we did "La Ronde", South Africa, happening around the last night of the last club, which we called "Cincinatti", wrongly spelt.

So how did he get from "La Ronde" to there?

Woody Allen's "Play it Again Sam", was a massive hit at the time. I said; 'Okay Barney, now we've got some money, now you can do anything you like.' And he said, 'Okay, well I've got this idea about "La Ronde". Off he went, and two or three weeks later I was asked to come to the putting together of bits and pieces, which I think was in Mike Goldberg's flat, somewhere in Yeoville. I realised that there were nine people in this play. I said, 'Barney, what are your intentions, there are three more people than on the budget?' He said, 'Well, why you don't know about it is because I've been paying the extra people out of my pocket, so they can come to rehearsals.' Typical Barney. So of course I said, 'No, you can't do that, we have to take the whole thing on, they've all got to be treated the same.' No director would do such a thing. You need bus money, and lunch money. And so he got these extra people. All he understood was that the play needed it. In Barney's vision he needed more people to get the circle better. He was absolutely right artistically.

We did "Cincinatti" in the Upstairs Theatre, and it was a total smash. When Barney had his way he made a wonderful success. It was a new South African play, and it was a wonderful racially mixed company. It was talking about exactly what we wanted to talk about. It went on tour and played in the Baxter Studio. It was such a hit that it just extended and extended. Then we brought it back and played on the main stage at The Market. After playing everywhere else we ended up playing in the Brooke

Theatre. It was totally commercial theatre, running for a year. It was invited to the National Theatre in London. Three weeks before we left they phoned us and said, 'Only, you can't have the disco music because we have to have live music in the National.' We had to have a disco band. That pushed the budget through the roof. We came back with hundreds of other suggestions but none of them would work. We needed the discotheque songs as Barney used them throughout the play in different sequences.

We started to make friends abroad, and they valued what we did, but from the time that we went abroad there was no doubt that we were the normal ones, and everybody else were the freaks. There was no doubt. When we got into the bigger world, Barney, Mannie and all The Market team could suddenly feel normal and relaxed. No one was saying, 'Why are you doing this? Why don't you just take the government subsidy and get some more money for everybody? You think you're clever to starve like this? What's this liberal pose?'

The context really was that were fighting for our lives. We were without subsidy but making friends. There's no doubt liberal business was on our side. Doing what we did we were then considered to be this more special theatre. Friends coming out after opening nights would say, 'This is my number, phone me when they take you to jail.' It never happened. To this day I don't know why it never happened. Barney and I, we weren't thrown in jail. We were investigated and we were watched. We knew there were people, sometimes amongst our staff. We got tip-offs. Everybody was suspicious in those days. You had to be careful. So-and-so was a police informant. We'd be careful when we were around so-and-so, that's all.

Barney was about understanding needs. We were so together on a lot of things. When we were opening The Market, we came to the idea of "Marat/Sade" together. I said: 'You're never going to be able to do a big show again, so think of the biggest show you can think of.' And Barney said, '"Marat/Sade", this is the moment to do "Marat/Sade". Let's phone Peter Weiss and see if he'll give us the rights.' And that's what happened. We did a play with thirty-two in the cast on the main stage of The Market, with the most wonderful actors all working for nothing, for forty rand a week, I think that was the pay.

We'd seen the movie of the British National Theatre's production, directed by Peter Brook. I remember that we had determined that the Sunday night before The Market opened would be for the theatre community of Johannesburg, and of course, all our volunteers, all the Friends of The Market. At seven o'clock, we did "Marat/Sade" free to all the people of Jo'burg that wanted to come. I remember all the theatre people really raving off about it and saying, this is the national theatre, this is the level, the standard. So, that was Barney with the bunch of actors drawn from all different walks of South Africa. There was a growing sense that: 'Hey wait a bit, this guy is not just good, he's actually world class.'

With Barney, there was also touring abroad with him. There was a wonderful thing of seeing Barney, who in South Africa was this other sort of person – this person that people thought was the weirdo, and strange, and gave actors exercises in the first week of rehearsal, didn't plot moves until they were on the stage in costume. When we went abroad we rated with the work that was happening there. The wannabes used to say;

'Well they only get good reviews because of the politics of the production that they're talking.' Well, you can read all the reviews we've ever got over the years, and it was not about the politics of the play, it was about the dynamism of the performances, or the wonderful production qualities that Barney brought in, or the beautiful play that we were presenting. It was about those things.

Were there any phases in Barney's work?

Certainly. There was the first stuff that we did – "The Maids", "Woyzeck", "People", "Six Characters in Search of an Author", "The Crucible", "Antigone". This was all before The Market, and then work like "Storytime" and "People Too" in the Nunnery where we also did "Fortune and Men's Eyes". Those plays were about white consciousness. He still did the stuff at Dorkay House. I told you about "Cayenne Pepper", "The Death of Bessie Smith" and "Phiri" that happened at the Wits Great Hall.

We got every inch of mileage we could out of every play that we did. If there was life left in the play we never closed early. Life could be described as 'was there a real exchange happening?' The Market was about shared experience. The Market was about how we wanted people to be enriched by their visits. We wanted people to be changed, if possible. We didn't want you to come to The Market and leave feeling the same about everything. We wanted you to come to The Market and leave having experienced something that made you say, 'Hey, I've got to go away and think about this.'

I think the next phase was Barney really getting a sense of himself as a theatre writer. He could create plays. We didn't necessarily always have to look for scripts. We were also looking for groups of people that liked to work with us. He would put a group of people in a room and I wouldn't know what was coming out the other end. I would just have to give him as long a time as possible. It was never long enough for Barney. He always wanted more rehearsal time. What do you mean eight weeks? I can remember these conversations. I said, 'Barney, man, everybody else does plays in four weeks, man. Pieter Dirk Uys does them in three weeks, man.' 'Yes, but I'm trying to make a new one.' 'Yes, but rehearsals cost money.' In that tension creativity happened and Barney sensed himself as a writer I think. The arc went through all the way to "Born in the RSA" and "Outers" as well.

We opened "Woza Albert!" in The Laager to fifty people a night, because our thinking was that if you open in smaller venues you draw less attention from the censor-type people. Then you slowly move into the bigger theatres. We did that with "Cincinatti" and "Woza Albert!" and so on. We started in a smaller venue, and then, as the word got out, and the reviews got out, we'd transfer them. A certain publisher always wanted Barney to be writing stories. And I always used to say, Barney must work in the theatre. More people come to the theatre, and we can publish the plays that he writes afterwards. Anyway, Barney, through those productions in the Upstairs Theatre, like "Cincinatti" and "Black Dog Inj'emnyama", started to have a sense of himself as a writer/editor. You know how those plays were workshopped – people did their own writing, people did improvisations. Then those improvisations were scripted. Then the

---

Opposite – The cast of "Mother Courage", from left – Ron Smerczak, Vanessa Cooke, Yvonne Bryceland and Danny Keogh.
Photograph courtesy of The Market Theatre.

scripts were edited. So Barney's skill was somewhere between a writer and an editor, and of course always a director, controlling all aspects of the play.

And where did we go from there? Barney was beginning to understand that internationally he was being recognised. He was being invited to those workshop festivals in Ireland, or somewhere. He was being asked to talk. He went over and directed Yvonne Bryceland at the Riverside Studios in London. He did "Born in the RSA" in America.

The third phase, Barney becoming an artist who really is aware of his value. He wasn't fighting for his rights anymore. He understood his value and spoke with a maturity of the kind of experience of having gone through all those various phases. A nice thing that threaded through Barney and my being together was that Barney also loved to do the classics. Whenever we made money there were a lot of plays we would then think of doing. We did "Mother Courage" and "Long Day's Journey into Night" in that way. I think the only Shakespeare play he ever wanted to do was "Hamlet" and he never got around to doing it. Shakespeare didn't get to him that much. But he always wanted to do the great plays.

I think that's what might well have happened at The Market now if Barney had been alive, maybe more of those great plays getting fresh stagings by Barney. For me, if anything, that was another phase. They don't all happen one after the other. Some of them thread through because of Barney wanting to deliver those great plays that he always admired but never did because we didn't have the money or whatever it was. He'd never been in a situation that had money before the time with us, never had the possibility to do the great plays, to do the great themes. I think that was important to him and growing in importance. And, of course, there was the new South Africa that we'd only just started to talk about – about what the plays were going to be, what was going to be done. How we were going to meet this new thing of celebrating. In that wonderful "Silent Movie" and also "Starbrites" Barney was saying, 'Now we celebrate, now we jol.' He was moving into trying to let everybody understand that this was the time for the party. That we'd done the serious stuff. I think he would have done more and more jols in this new South Africa and celebrated it. Where other people already started to whinge about crime, Barney would have found a sense of celebration.

'Barney came to a play from deep inside his own self and his understanding of the needs of what was going on around him' Mannie Manim

Marius Weyers

'I growled, "Fuck off. I'm working with Barney!"'

By the time I met Barney I had come to a point in my career where I felt drained. I had done of a lot of wonderful parts in very exciting plays. I had worked with brilliant directors and actors, but I felt that I couldn't find anything new anymore. I was repeating myself, regurgitating past performances. Then I met Barney through Mannie Manim.

Our first collaboration was a short play by Barney, "Joburg, Sis!" and I discovered a new actor in myself. I worked as I always had, only with Barney it became more in focus, more detailed. He led me through questions of what smells mean to the character. What the texture of his life was. Very sensual, very aware of the smallest thing. It was an exciting new way of exposing a character. He never stopped questioning. He was bloody relentless.

We did "Woyzeck" with Barney. We went in search of characters and their worlds by doing exercises and looking at pictures in his vast library of books. One exercise consisted of the group lying on the floor each with an orange. We had to smell it, feel it, with closed eyes. We rolled it over our faces, and eventually peeled it and ate it in a variety of ways. This kind of sensual awareness added so much colour to one's acting.

There was a point in "Woyzeck" where the man made a huge transition. He was delirious and yet also in a state of heightened consciousness. It was like he was falling through space. Barney decided words weren't enough, we needed something more. So one morning, just the two of us went to work on the stage at the Alexander Theatre. After a couple of hours and countless ways of contorting my body we discovered something. It was so simple, yet so powerful. I somersaulted in slow motion and landed on my back. I fell slowly through space, arms and legs flailing, in slow motion, with the head and face presenting a sense of no sound, only this enormous silence. The whole movement took several minutes and it was one of the most satisfying bits of acting I had ever done. Francois Swart commented, after seeing it, that it was almost like watching a ballet performance.

In "Hello and Goodbye" Barney had me walking blindfolded, sometimes with a bucket on my head, on an imaginary tight rope, for what felt like hours. You had to be wide open for any kind of craziness with him. It was hard but it helped. You see, I always believe that we know so much more than we think we know, as humans. So with acting one sometimes just has to get out of one's own way in order to find the knowledge of humans. In just talking about it you prevent yourself from accidental discovery of that knowledge. That's where Barney was good – leading one to discoveries. He questioned, he taunted, he excited, he joined the journey. He was there all the time for you. He made it dangerous but he kept you safe.

During rehearsals of "Outers" we dressed like tramps and joined the homeless in Joubert Park or wherever we could meet up with them. Every day for two weeks we spent time with them and then reported back to Barney late afternoons. We would discuss our experiences and gradually Barney made a play out of it.

We all had painful and sometimes hilarious experiences. Barney enjoyed an altercation I had with another actor not involved in our play. This poor guy walked up to me one day while I was disguised as an outer (a tramp) and I was poking in a trash can. In all innocence he asked me, quite shocked, 'Marius, what happened to you?' I growled, 'Fuck off, I'm working with Barney.'

And that would've explained it all, any madness, weirdness, yes, anyone who's ever heard of Barney, would've understood that. Doing "Outers" we felt a little guilty at times, getting people to expose their lives so that we could make a play. But what was very intrinsic of Barney's character was his respect for people, and that's how we went about it, with respect. And that's how we played the people on stage, with respect, humour and lots of love. I dread to think what I would've missed in life as an actor, and as a human being, had I not met up with Barn.

'He led me through questions of what smells mean to the character, what the texture of his life was'
Marius Weyers

Opposite – Marius Weyers.
Photograph by Ruphin Coudyzer.

The world in an orange

1. A disc on floor.
2. A ball on floor.
3. Watch ball move on floor.
4. Watch floor with ball moving across it.
5. Throw ball in air.
6. Watch ball in room.
7. Watch room with ball in.
8. Examine biography of orange. Joint to tree. Dye. Birds. Bruise.
9. Let orange explore your face.
10. Let it cool your face.
11. Stand. Place on collar bone. Walk in circle, clockwise.
12. Place between knees, walk in circle anti-clockwise.
13. Outstretched arm. Bring orange like planet.
14. Move orange out, stretching arm. Circle orange. The Sun.
15. Use as rock to...?, each other.
16. Sit. Use as cushion to rest.
17. Lie on back. Hold orange in mouth. Gag.
18. Bite only skin. Bitter.
19. Sit.
20. Bite piece of skin off.
21. Look at wonderful orange.
22. Look at piece of skin. Squeeze for sweat.
23. Begin to peel. Careful of flesh.

23(a) Watch others peel.

24. Listen to sound.
25. Look at nude orange.

25(a) Look at pile of peels.

26. Remove one section intact.
27. Peel section without wounding.
28. Remove globule.
29. Taste globule.
30. Eat whole section.
31. Eat orange.
32. Feel life of orange in mouth.
33. Watch others eat orange.
34. Place peels, waste, in centre of room.
35. Look at pile.
36. Someone collect pile. Remove.
37. Look at empty centre.
38. Be aware of mouth, body that has experienced orange.

Barney Simon.
Photograph courtesy of NELM.

'There is this one picture that David took, our heads are cut off, and you just see our hands close together like that, and she is sitting like this, and I'm sitting like this. But the hand is just there' Marcel van Heerden

Marcel van Heerden

'... seeing the light and seeing the lightness'

One of his favourite things was to challenge people to try and go further, to see, to go in, to go into yourself and your own biography. That's what I really respected about him, that he was interested in people, in people's lives. I think he had real respect from actors, which is a rare thing. So I don't want to sit here and weep, but I do miss him. I miss him.

In "Die Verlate Skoolmeisie", which we performed in the restaurant area at the Baxter, people were invited to participate on different nights. It was open for them to do. And I remember there was this one scene where I had to do this very sexual thing with a frozen chicken. It was a whole comedy thing that I did. It would slip out of my hands and fall, and I would try and pick it up and it kept slipping, because it was frozen. There was an aisle between the seats. I was on the ground trying to catch this chicken, and then I sensed something coming from the audience, and it was Barney walking with a portable typewriter. He just like stepped over me and into the acting area and sat down and put down his typewriter and started working, writing. So it was part of the play. And another time it was Richard E. Grant – he is now a movie star – who came on stage. One night he came with Fiona Ramsay, and they were both on roller-skates. I think it was he who took a piece of cotton and wound it around Barney and the typewriter until Barney was completely tied up, couldn't move, was like spun into the typewriter. He just sat like that and at a certain point just dropped his head, and that was his acting, you know, acting his death. He was quite amazing.

I am missing him more than ever, because of that humour, because of that seeing the light and seeing the lightness. Maybe all of us who have worked in South Africa all these years have seen all this death and destruction. But we've dealt with it. If we haven't actually seen it and acted it, we've dealt with it in some way. I've got to the point where I now need more life-affirming stuff and more of that Yiddish wisdom. Barney accessed every kind of almost subliminal personal stuff. Stuff that you didn't know you had inside you. That is why some actors couldn't stand him, because of his psychoanalytical way of finding things in people. People would think, no, he's a wanker, or he's wasting time.

And did he do that?

I remember with "Begeerte" specifically. It happens in America in a rural area. We placed it in Afrikaans. It's this patriarchal figure and he's in his third or fourth marriage or something. And then he takes another young wife. There is just this incredible desire between the son and the mother, the stepmother. It's like fate, they just have to be together. Then she becomes pregnant with his child, and the old man thinks it's his child. And it's this terrible tragedy because of a misunderstanding. She thinks that Eben, the son, doesn't want the child anymore, so she kills the child. At the end the two of them are taken off to get hanged, or whatever, and the old man keeps living.

Opposite – Marcel van Heerden and Aletta Bezuidenhout in "Begeerte".
Photograph by David Goldblatt.

I grew up in the Cape but my grandmother and my mother are people from the Southern Kalahari area, North Western Cape. As a child I used to go to the farm and walk, look after the sheep. I used to spend a lot of time just walking around the veld, dreaming really, when I was about nine, ten years old. He dragged these things out of me. All these stories and all these people. And it became the landscape. There was no doubt. That's where I was. I was back there where I was as a child walking bare-foot on those rocks, and it became very real, and very sensual, very textured. And full of real experience. When Aletta was sitting on the stoep staring, according to the play, I remember him using images like lizards. She knew what she was looking at and she knew what she was feeling. We both knew how the sun felt that we were sitting in. It was just endless texture and detail, and specifics to concentrate on.

There was never a moment where you were floating. You were always focused on something specific. It stayed with me. He would take every word and he'd say, 'What is that word? Let me see what your mouth does when it says that word. I want to hear every syllable. I want to hear every sound. Find that thing. Where does it come from? Where does it start? Where does it end? What does it mean? How does it feel? Where is the life inside?'

So, right from that early stage he was doing that?

Oh, yes, ja. He was very influenced by the Living Theatre people. Barney had a big knowledge of the American writers – Arthur Miller, Eugene O'Neill, Tennessee Williams. All those people. I think in the fifties there was a lot of that influence in the South African culture.

"Marat/Sade" was a very, very exhausting process because we were all on stage all the time. The show was about two and a half hours long. We were all psychiatric cases. He believed in doing dangerous stuff, taking risks creatively. It was during Soweto '76, and there was the whole atmosphere of the country. When we were singing the song, we wanted a revolution... Stuff like that felt like it was really happening. He challenged me. I had two parts in one. One was a religious fanatic who had gone insane. He does that famous prayer to Satan. It's the reversal of the Lord's Prayer. I did that. On the opening night the chairman of the city council walked out and there were banner headlines in the newspapers about blasphemy. Barney sent us into the streets to go and look at people, find people, and at that stage the abattoir had been freshly closed down. The smell of blood, the smell of meat was always around here where we're sitting now.

What was the context of the time politically? We all know '76, but how did it feel for you, what was going on in the country, and what you were doing with this man?

Barney never really spoke politics. Like he said, politics is obvious. And I agree with that. All he said about his relationship with Joe Slovo is they were friends. I don't know what they did together, maybe watch movies together, or have coffee or eat cake. Always bloody eating cake. Sweet things. But not talk politics. I have done a lot of stuff that had political overtones or whatever, but it was never really about talking politics. If you go and dissect "Marat/Sade" it's a kind of dialogue between the classical Marxist and the extreme individuals. Marat is this classical Marxist. Down the line De Sade is the extreme individualist – that's his crime. That's really what the bulk of the play is about. This conversation. So we weren't dealing with that. We were dealing with what does it feel like to step on the corpse. My character is talking about a landscape of bones and flesh and hair. Walking on that. Treading on eyes. That's what I was dealing with, not a communist manifesto, or anything like that. He was always about people and not ideas. And I think that is what I'm missing about him now, what did he call it, 'gift of life.' It was a gift. Just to approach life in that way, you know – how can you throw it away, being given this thing?

Next was "East". That was difficult. I could hardly speak English, never mind copy an accent. We performed it in The Market Theatre Café that faced out on the railway lines. Censorship was so bad in South Africa that you couldn't say fuck or anything on the stage, and East is peppered with that. We couldn't perform it to the public.

You couldn't perform it?

No, because it was illegal to speak like that on a stage. So it really was wild. It was really wild. We performed on these long tables that were stacked into the invited audience. We got five performances or something. But we worked like crazy. It was '78, the stirrings of punk. The hippie thing was over. We shaved our heads. My hair was very short. Ron Smerczak shaved his head. And I remember I put a dog collar on Ron's neck. It was completely different. There was nothing gentle about it. I was reading this book on the Hell's Angels and I said to Barney, 'You know, the Hell's Angels kiss one another just for shock value, because people think that they're closet faggots.' He said, 'Great,' and I thought, 'Fuck, I should never have said that.' Every night a big open

Marcel van Heerden and Ron Smerczak in "East".
Photograph courtesy of NELM.

mouth kiss, me and Ron. I remember Ron getting carried away. I've never kissed a man open mouthed like that on stage. And this audience gasped.
"Cincinatti" and "Cold Stone Jug" were major, major influences on my work. For my work in "Cincinatti" I based my character on somebody I knew. My grandmother had this little plot on the Orange River. It came from the days of the Depression. They gave the poor white people bits of land on the Orange River to go and farm. As a child I used to go there. The people I met there were the people who were running the place. My grandmother wasn't living there anymore. They were the foreman, his wife and the children. One of the children was a guy called Koos Erasmus. Then he went to De Aar to work for the railways. This was all guided by Barney. My character was based mostly on what I imagined because I was about nine, ten years old when I knew Koos Erasmus.

What I imagined was what his life would be like. How they would see a big city like Johannesburg. So we imagined that my character came from Boegoeberg, and some people around here still call me 'ou Boegoeberg'. He was about twenty. He arrived in Johannesburg at the station, which is racially divided – blacks and whites. He has got a little suitcase. And he's got a tie and a jacket on. He's been sent from De Aar. He happens to come to the wrong side of the station, and there's the night watchman, Sam Williams, and this woman Thoko Ntshinga. There's this dialogue between them. The night watchman chases him away. It's his job to keep it segregated. He then bumps into Vanessa's character. They all go and dance at "Cincinatti", you see, which is this club. So really it was about this guy who is completely innocent, but completely racist, and that's all he knows. He ends up at the station and then with this girl who takes him home and makes love to him. So he loses his innocence in a sense, but also it's the beginning of the country's loss of innocence. In "Mapanstula" the film, I played this policeman who is interrogating a guy, and to me it was almost the same guy, twenty years on. So it's haunting, it's quite haunting because it comes from a very real place.

And the writing aspect of "Cincinatti", you would go out and research?
For "Cincinatti" we did a lot of the writing, you know. It was led by Barney. It was written, directed, conceived, blah, blah by Barney Simon. But I've got the original in my handwriting. I don't care where the copyright goes, but I'm just saying that it was a mixture of people. He was leading the process but the stuff came out of us. And it's quite amazing actually. Once we worked for weeks and weeks, and then one day I just wrote this whole speech, it's in the play. I said to him, 'Fuck, Barney, I don't understand this, because we've been working all this time and I wrote this in five minutes.' And he said, 'No, you wrote it in three weeks.' That was a major commercial success. "Cincinatti" ran for nine months. It played all over the country.

And why do you think it was such a success?
It was unique. Never before had you seen an Asian girl, two blacks, a black woman and a black man, an Afrikaans boy, an English immigrant, an ex-hippie who is now looking for some other direction and who is kind of half-Greek South African. There was this incredible mixture. It's like the cross-section of a country. And it was humorous. People died laughing...

Barney had incredible curiosity and tenacity. He would fucking go for something and not let go until he had it. And not take easy answers. You'd say to him, 'Well, I was wearing this T-shirt.' And he'd say, 'No, what colour was the T-shirt?' And you'd say, 'It was blue.' And he'd say, 'What kind of blue? Light blue, dark blue, what kind of blue? Describe the blue.' And you'd describe the blue and he'd say 'Well, what did it feel like on the skin? What did it feel like on your arms? What did it feel like on your chest? What did it feel like on your back? Was it tucked in?' Unbelievable detail. Every little thing. It had to be that. You had to know. Then he also wanted to know where things came from in people's lives. The scripts that we wrote together, a lot of them definitely had this type of stuff that he was interested in.

It's not just the detail; it's the kind of detail. I remember that in "Begeerte" we had this one scene, the first time that they touch. He said to Aletta and me, 'Go and find a church. Go and sit in the church. I want you to find that feeling sitting in a church and wanting to touch.' We walked around and couldn't find a church and finally we found this Shul. So we went into the Shul and it was weird because women had to be upstairs and men downstairs, but it's the only church we could find. So we sat there for a while. David Goldblatt took some wonderful pictures of that show. He did almost a photo story of the whole show. There is this one picture that David took, our heads are cut off, and you just see our hands close together like that, and she is sitting like this, and I'm sitting like this. But the hand is just there. When I see that picture, I feel that church. There is no way you can escape this. It's informed with that privacy.

Privacy?
Yeah, but also that holiness. That kind of silence, stillness of the spaar kamer on the farm. The old man is gone and... that moment, you know. There is no other way that it could have been played like that, not without that improvisation.

What flaws did Barney have?
I think in the same way that, for instance, Jimi Hendrix was a genius guitar player, but responsible for guitarists doing endless solos which brought a lot of shit music... In the same way I think that Barney, always working through a process and not, often not, plotting moves beforehand, gave birth to some endless aimless improvisation by some of his – shall we say? – disciples. That's one of my criticisms. I've experienced it. Some actors simply didn't connect with him. I think the way that he dealt with them and handled them was sometimes very cruel. If I think of some people who are trained in a very formal British school of acting and now had to fit in. Sometimes people couldn't adapt. And there was like an inflexibility on both sides.

You said that "Cincinatti" and "Cold Stone Jug" were very, very important for you?
Ja. I knew that I was having a wonderful time but I didn't know how important it was in shaping my whole psyche. He made me aware of that. I mean, not being aware of colour and stuff like that. There were class differences, but we're all Africans. With "Cold Stone Jug" I played two characters, a condemned prisoner and a transvestite. For me it was a fantastic experience because I'd never dealt with my female side inside

myself to that extent. Not just wearing a dress. He gave me a very important part. The character was not in Bosman's book, the transvestite. It was someone we created between the two of us – a character called Jakes. It was a side, a kind of a side of Barney that was never really shown. If Barney had gay affiliations with people, he preferred not to have to show this publicly. Maybe it's the generation he came from, I don't know. But he certainly knew what he was talking about.

Jakes was a prison rabbit. Which is a kind of a pathetic character, but at the same time a very powerful character, because he's a pathetic creature dressing up for the men to want him. That's his part, but they're always putting him down. And then there's one scene... It's hard to talk about. I think it's New Year's Eve or Christmas Eve in prison. All the prisoners are lying down to sleep, but they're talking through the walls, and Jakes is made to stand up. I actually can't talk about, it's so strong. But I will tell you about it. Okay. He said to me, 'That scene is a gift to all the gay men in South Africa.' He made me stand, and I think I just took my shirt off or something. Mannie did this wonderful lighting. There was nothing on stage, nothing. We just had illuminated areas with blocks of light. And he made me stand, and then the other prisoners, they sing and they joke and they carry on, and then the lights start fading, and then Jakes is just standing there, touching himself. I think it was something like, 'What are you wearing? Hey Jakes, what are you wearing?' and Jakes says, 'The white dress.' He describes what he's wearing, how it feels, and all the men are lying there in prison and imagining it. So he takes everyone on this journey, on this trip. And the audience sees that he's actually got nothing. And then he starts to sing. And he sings "Wanner kom ons trou dag Gertjie?" an Afrikaans folk song. I'd stand and sing this song and then the lights faded to the end of the first half.

It was that time that Mandela was still in prison. Breytenbach was in prison. There were a lot of people still in prison. They were all still in prison. And it almost felt like connecting with people inside from outside. For me as an actor it kind of accessed something that I never knew was inside me. Because Jakes is a transvestite. He is not a gay guy or queen. He's a man.

Opposite – Marcel van Heerden.
Photograph by Ruphin Coudyzer.

Wilson Dunster

'Barney was the toughest man I ever met'

I met Barney in 1971, when i was doing "Orestes" in Cape Town at CAPAB with Athol Fugard. Everything was going just fine for me. I was an established leading man at CAPAB. I was winning awards. Everyone was slapping me on the back. I was involved in elitist exclusive theatre that was viewed by 'whites only.' And then Athol came and shook everything up. It was a different kind of theatre. The performances were real, were raw. In the most wonderful way he disturbed my equilibrium. He did a production of "Boesman and Lena". Athol played Boesman and Yvonne Bryceland played Lena. They turned the South African theatre upside down. It was a revelation. It was unique. And critically reviewed. And all of a sudden Athol Fugard, quite rightly so, was the man in theatre.

I was in my twenties. It was the most important time of my life. Athol opened my mind and made me look at my work completely differently. He made me look at South Africa and the political situation. I was naive, totally indifferent. 'Listen,' he said, 'A very dear friend of mine, and a man I respect enormously, is coming to see "Orestes" – and it was Barney. Barney came to us afterwards, and you know how people kind of gush and say things to you after a performance. Well, Barney didn't. He just indicated that he thought it was good work. He invited me to stay with him in Kensington while I was doing "Orestes" in Johannesburg.

I spent a lot of time with him over those weeks. And I must say, I felt kind of removed in a sense, because he was just so different. He used the anecdote and he used the metaphor an awful lot. And I liked that – I understood. I related to it immediately. Don't always look directly at something. Look at it in a different way. I spent hours talking to this oke. I read some of his short stories – "Men Should Cry More Often", "Miss South Africa (6)" and "The Sixth Day of Christmas" – and they blew my mind. Barney embraced me in the same way that he embraced many people. And in a funny kind of way, when Barney died I felt as if my friend had died. I was kind of amazed that people weren't phoning in and saying how sorry they were that my friend had died. I realise that in actual fact he touched many people's lives. Not only people in the theatre. He influenced people. He has influenced my life to this day. I was young. I was vulnerable. This was before The Space and before The Market Theatre. He said to me, 'Any time you want to work in Johannesburg, you stay here, this is your home.' I realised many years later that he said that to many, many people. But I do believe that I was special to Barney.

The only important thing that the actor ever has to do is to speak the truth. It's a simple philosophy. But it's actually difficult to do. Barney's work was pure, simple, uncluttered and direct. He had his books, his friends, and he was always busy. But men that speak that sort of language and work in that kind of way isolate themselves. They make themselves open to criticism. There was a lot of resentment towards Barney by people in the business because he was doing things that were not conventional. It was not always easily understood. It was his method of working, his process, the way he arrived at things that was criticised. He dressed Vanessa Cooke and myself up as Sissy and Shorty in "People are Living There". He dropped us off in Hillbrow and said, 'Go and find accommodation.' There was little Vanessa next to me as Sissy. We walked into some tatty place in Hillbrow and asked if they had a room. The way these people looked at us. First of all they kept us standing there for ages and we just stood and waited. Finally they turned away to conceal their amusement, and then asked, 'Can we help you?' I said, 'Have you got a room?' They said they didn't have any accommodation, which was a lie. They could see that we had no money. It gave us a real insight into what Shorty and Sissy had to deal with in society. Barney put us in a situation which made us see things and experience emotions which completely changed our perspective.

When we were rehearsing "Marat/Sade", the smell from the abattoir which was still in operation and very close to The Market Theatre, was intolerable. And Barney kept saying, 'Work with the smell, don't try and push it away. Stop gagging, you schmuck.' He was enormously patient, but I think sometimes he forgot that to work with him you also had to be patient. I did "Statements After an Arrest Under the Immorality Act" overseas with Ben Kingsley and Yvonne Bryceland, and Athol directed. Then I came back to this country and I moved to Johannesburg. It was a tough time for me because there wasn't a lot of work around. And there were a lot of actors that I think Barney felt were good actors that weren't working, like Vanessa Cooke, Danny Keogh, Aletta Bezuidenhout and Marcel van Heerden, talented people who needed a home. And Mannie Manim and Barney said, 'Right, let's form a company. let's find a home.' This was in '74. And that really was the beginning of The Market Theatre. We did "Storytime". I wrote a monologue with Barney called "No Extras". I had just spent time in London, and Barney said to me, 'So tell me about it?' I'd never been overseas before. I didn't want to see theatre, I just wanted to go to a strip show and see a woman take all her clothes off in front of me, and pay money for that. 'Well,' he said, 'That's interesting.' And I told him the story of my first visit to a strip joint. That was my twenty-minute monologue. Aletta told another story. Danny Keogh told another. We did it at the Village Theatre on Louis Botha.

So, when you told him a story, how did it move and develop?
Did Barney take it and write it, or did you write it?

He would say, 'You've got a story, now sit down and write. Write it,' and would go away. I would bring it back to him. We would have many gruelling long sessions together. He would write. I would write. He would cut, he would change, he would take it to pieces and turn it upside down. It was an incredibly personal and painful process because of his demanding requirement of detail and truth. All the texture, all the character, was Barney. He dragged it out of you. There was no story without Barney.

Barney's sister was in a wheelchair. It was almost as if she had made him a richer person. His mother sounded like the most beautiful, wonderful woman and he adored his father. After his mother died he used to share a room with his father. It was mid-winter. Barney was working for an advertising agency and drove an Alfa Romeo, can you believe it? He used to have to get up at seven o'clock in the morning to go to work. It was freezing. And he said he'd glance over to his father. His father would have the blankets just below his eyes – covering his nostrils all snug and warm with a little cap on his head. The old man would say, 'Come on Barney, get out of bed, be a man, get out of bed, be a man.' And the old man would lie there very warm and Barney would have to get out of bed.

The Kensington house was full of family photographs. Barney, his mother, his father. It was his parents' space. He wanted to break with that. He furnished his own house in Loch Avenue in Parktown and started a new Barney life – always black people coming and going. Musicians, actors, people from Dorkay House. The neighbours didn't dig it. He didn't stay long. Loch Avenue was too smart for him. So Barney said, 'Well, fuck, bugger this, I'm going to leave.' And he left. He went to Yeoville. Those were heavy times in this country. If a black man walked into your front door a phone call was made. The next thing people were visiting your house and asking you why. He just wanted to avoid all that rubbish.

One day I got a message from Mannie saying, 'Barney wants you to play Marat, but he wants to see you first.' Barney looked at me and said, 'Wilson, you're too fat.' And he starved me. He said, 'Marat cannot have any fat on him. You're naked most of the time.' He needn't have put me on a diet because the rehearsal period was so excruciating – the whole cast got thin. We were working in rubble. They hadn't finished The Market Theatre yet.

It was one of the happiest times with Barney because it was a big cast and he couldn't focus all his attention on me all the time. Barney never praised. He never ever praised me. Actors tend to feel very insecure if they're not praised, and I think it's actually bullshit. That never bothered me. That shouldn't be the centre of your strength. That shouldn't be your main space. So praise, with Barney and Athol, wasn't in the vocabulary. Grotowski, Towards a Poor Theatre, Peter Brook and The Open Space was. He'd say, 'That's good work, that's honest work.' I got used to that. I didn't need or want their praise, but that bothered a lot of actors. The point is that he always told you when something was wrong. "Marat/Sade" was the opening of The Market Theatre and it was wonderful to be part of it.

You know, every time I worked with Barney I hurt myself. I physically did something to myself. When I did "Luv" I had to slide down a pole and swing my leg over a banister. It was excruciatingly hot. Perspiration on my hands, I couldn't always control the move. One night I swung my leg over at the wrong angle and I snapped my cartilage. For the rest of the run I couldn't straighten the leg. We went straight into rehearsals for "People are Living There" and I was in hospital having a cartilage operation. In those days they used to prise the knee open and take out the cartilage, and your leg used to swell up and get very thin at the same time. And it was terribly, terribly sore.

Mannie and Barney came to see me. Mannie walked in, and his mouth dropped open and he went pale. 'We've got to replace this guy,' he said to Barney. And Barney looked at me, and he said, 'Listen, you've got to get out of this bed now and you've got to start rehearsing now. Be a man, be a man.' And I said, 'Barney, if I was a top athlete, it would take me ten days before I'm walking. For a guy like me it's months of recuperation.' He said, 'We need you at rehearsals, that's all. Work through it, work through the pain. I want you to play Shorty.' Barney was a gentle lamb. He had enormous humour. He had enormous intellect. Barney is the toughest man I have ever met, the toughest man I ever worked for. He was ruthless but he had this soft way about him. He was just like a teddy bear. He was beautiful. He said, 'I want you out of that bed.' I said, 'Get an understudy.' He said, 'No understudy, you're doing Shorty.' He came and saw me the next day and said, 'Mannie has talked me into an understudy. You schmuck.' I did get out of bed and I did play Shorty. Barney was right. He gave me absolutely no choice. Vanessa was told to look after me. She drove my car. I was staying in the most dreadful flat in Hillbrow up on the tenth floor. The first day we went to rehearsals I was on painkillers. She parked the car and as we crossed the street I just felt Vanessa tugging at me. I was walking straight into an oncoming truck. I hadn't seen it. She saved my life. I was stoned on those painkillers.

No, Barney didn't always do good work. It was always unique but it was not always right. That had to do with the chemistry, the people he was working with. It had to do with circumstances. But every production I did with him was one hundred percent worthwhile. I reaped the rewards of working with Barney when I wasn't actually working with him. Every production I did with him was a kind of hell. But when I worked with another director Barney came back to me. I tried to challenge myself in the same way that Barney challenged me. Barney got me through those difficult times. But when I was with him he nearly killed me.

I loved him and I hated him. There were times when it was just heavy. It was claustrophobic. We used to fight terribly. He used to say, 'This is a play. I will interpret it the way I want to interpret it. I'm directing this play, so you will do this play the way I want you to do it.' I used to say, 'Barney, I am an actor, I also interpret, we've got to come together.' He would say, 'You tell the story the way I want you to tell the story, no other way.' It came up time and time again. There is a point where I become quite flowery and phoney, and awful things happen to me. And really I'm just trying to get the lines together. It's just a process I go through which is awful, and I would hate anybody to witness it. Barney would say, 'I don't care. Don't give me that bullshit. It's rubbish. Get rid of it.' Barney introduced me to photographs as a way of working, for example by David Goldblatt, Diane Arbus and Bruce Davidson. He would show me a photograph and say, 'What does this mean to you?' When we were working on a production he would find photographs that he felt were pertinent, that were relevant, that could help me. He wanted the truth and nothing but the truth at all times. He wouldn't allow me to crook at any point. He wasn't interested in technique. He said my technique was very often my way of avoiding the real truth, by applying a technique that I'd been taught. He said it was bullshit. He had such a strong personality. He used to reduce me to tears on some occasions. Barney would rehearse the play. We would open. You'd get fantastic notices. The next night he would be back saying, 'Listen, this is not right'. And you'd say, 'We've opened! We've been through six weeks of rehearsal!' 'No, I want this and this and this right.' He picked and picked all the time. That's how he worked, with that unrelenting detail.

Now we talk about me always hurting myself. In "Mother Courage" I played the cook. A little part. Yvonne played Mother Courage. These guys are all dirty and they're hungry, they're at war and they've got nothing. And Barney says, 'Now listen to me, the cook is not dirty enough. You must put bandages around your legs.' I put bandages around my legs and we had notes after the first dress rehearsal. He says, 'Wilson, those bandages are too clean, dirty them up.' And he says, 'By the way, you're not cold enough, you've got to really be cold.' I said, 'Barney I'm being cold.' He says, 'You've got to be colder.' We did it again. He said, 'Wilson, those bandages are too clean. I want you to be really cold in that scene. In fact let's work on it now.' It was after the show. He put me on the stage and we went through the scene again and again. And I was busy being so cold that I popped a hernia. A few months later I was having a hernia operation. Anyway, the next night he gave me the note, 'Not cold enough'. And he says, 'Wilson, if you want me to, I'll tell you what I feel about those bandages. I look at you, I look at the cook, it looks as if you've just stepped out of a fucken Radox bath.' Well, after that I just covered myself in everything, and I've never been so cold in all my life. But he would never let go.

Barney liked doing Athol's plays, but very often he'd change the writing a little bit. And I would say, 'I can understand you doing this with Shakespeare. but how can you tamper with Fugard's text? He's your buddy, at least phone him and say you want to say it this way.' But Barney was a great one for cutting and rephrasing things. He did this with all playwrights – the tweaks and cuts – nothing major. It was a kind of an arrogance but at the same time I think he was right.

And what would possess you to continue when you hurt yourself every time?
I didn't realise it was happening. But if ever I was given a chance between Barney Simon doing this and somebody else doing whatever, I wanted to work with Barney. He just ruffled me to such an extent and the challenge interested me. Do I want to take the easy route or do I want to take the Barney route? I always decided to take the Barney route. I never turned him down. He had such a wonderful sense of humour. I got over the fact that he was such a clever man, and that he was so well read. I was never threatened by him. I was happy to take him on. I wasn't scared of him. He told me 'people are scared of me'. People used to interpret everything he said with some deep intellectual significance. He was simple. He wasn't pretentious. He was just a very sharp guy with an enormous knowledge of life and theatre. He was a giant.

The last time I worked with him was in 1983 when he did Emily Mann's "Still Life". It was Fiona Ramsay, Aletta Bezuidenhout and myself. On the day of the opening night Barney and I were going through every line in the play. 'Say that again. I don't understand. Give it to me straight.' He reduced me to tears. He'd reduced me to tears at a very significant point in the script. And he said 'That's what I want.' In the first moments of the opening night I cut my finger. I'd grabbed onto the set, which was made of steel and they hadn't filed the edges. I just ripped this finger. Do you see the scar here? Aletta left the stage. Nobody is allowed to leave the stage. I thought, what is she doing? I was starting to lose consciousness because I was bleeding so heavily,

---

Opposite above – Wilson Dunster, Aletta Bezuidenhout and Fiona Ramsay, in Emily Mann's "Still Life". Photograph by Ruphin Coudyzer.

Opposite below – Wilson Dunster in "Still Life", December 1982. Photograph by Ruphin Coudyzer.

and the blood was going into the lights. We were lit from underneath. I carried on with my dialogue. And she came back and gave me a handful of tissues which she stuffed into my hand, and I did the rest of the show holding these tissues. It was about seventy-five minutes long. Barney was up there in the lighting box. Afterwards he said 'That's the best you've ever done.' I was half conscious, and he says, 'That's the best you've ever done.'

I was feeling depressed one day. Somehow I landed up with Barney in a restaurant in Hillbrow. All of a sudden there was a noise. The man sitting at the table opposite me suddenly stood up and then fell down stone dead. Barney and I ran to him, and he'd shattered his glasses. We took the glasses off his face. He had a little packet with him, and Barney opened it. Among other things we found a pair of brand new children's slippers. Barney took the slippers and wove a story around them, with so much texture and detail that I felt I knew the dead man. He said, 'Shit man, you're feeling bad? Look what's happened here! You've got a problem? Live through it. Life's a process.'

Just after Barney died I went to his house to see Rosie. Did you ever see the movie of Rosie peeling the orange and eating it? Barney filmed it with his tatty old camera. 'I want to show you this as an example of focus, and honesty, and truth, and it tells a story. It's not just a woman peeling an orange. It's a childlike woman, it's a sensual woman. Nothing is ever one thing.'

When Barney did "Medea" at The Space, Yvonne Bryceland played Medea and I played Jason. I was staying in a flat in Sea Point and Barney came to visit me one night. I was in the bedroom and Barney was in the dining room. At about three o'clock in the morning, there was a knock on the door. It was somebody to come and see me. Barney opened the door and this person saw Barney and saw me and said; 'Ag, I'm sorry to interrupt you,' and left. I said to Barney, you know that person thinks we're having a scene. And he said, 'Well, we are having a scene. There are no cocks involved. It's not the physical thing but we are having a scene. Let them think what they like.'

"Medea" - Based on a text by Franz Grillparzer, adapted and directed by Barney Simon - Cast: Yvonne Bryceland, Charles Comyn, Wilson Dunster, Chris Galloway, Brendan King, Clinton King, Joel Maister, Michale Maister, Monhle Nkonyeni, Jacqui Singer. Designer: John Nankin. Costumes: Zauzaanna Kovaos, Danny Malan. Lighting: Dimitri Nicolas-Fanourakis. Stage Manager: Arthur Benjamin.

Photograph by Brian Astbury, from his book "The Space / Die Ruimte / Indawo – March 1972 – September 1979".

'Barney often reminded us that a performance should have privacy, as if the audience were eavesdropping'
Aletta Bezuidenhout

Aletta Bezuidenhout

'I felt he was always spying on my privacy, my relationships, my sexuality'

It was the Afrikaner, the raw quality in me that Barney wanted for the part of Abbie in "Begeerte". I remember very consciously making a decision that I was going to go completely for this character, with everything. My whole heart and soul. Even if I had to wear cheap plastic belts and stupid-looking high heels. It turned out to be completely the opposite – barefoot and rustic. It was 1975 and I was twenty-four.

I gave up everything. I was with CAPAB at the time and went to Jo'burg on the strength of that production. The other two actors were Carel Trichardt and Marcel van Heerden. That was the beginning of a time of magic for many of us. "Begeerte" had such intensity and passion that I believe it affected people like Mannie Manim, who was managing PACT at the time. David Goldblatt did the photography – that was the collage of photos which Barney had in the entrance hall of his house in Bellevue.

We performed in an old house which had been converted into a theatre, in Doornfontein. "Begeerte" was very simple, very stark. Barney's work had been mainly with black actors and writers at Dorkay House. When he got to the 'Afrikaner thing' in "Begeerte", a lot of issues seemed to surface. The 'Golden Era' of Afrikaans theatre in Pretoria had been very successful, but there was a need for change – to a more real, a more comprehensive kind of theatre – there were still no black actors appearing on South African stages. It was in this atmosphere that Barney and Mannie made a creative connection, and The Company was established and the first steps towards the birth of The Market Theatre were taken.

It was an incredibly exciting time – learning how to script our own experiences, under Barney's guidance, for "People" and "Storytime". Barney often cut dialogue out of a play and replaced it with his own writing, he took a lot of license. He wrote an entire monologue for me at the end of "Six Characters". It began:

'... careful... careful... careful when you think of giving, careful when you talk of caring' and '... if you come to me, I cannot promise that I won't kill you and if I do, forgive me but I cannot promise you that the alternative will be any kinder... but come, come slowly as you like, gently as you can... come, I beg you, I dare you... come.'

During rehearsals of "Begeerte" I broke through as an actress – for the first time. I only realised then what being an actress really meant. Many illusions vanished. After a relentless six days of rehearsing an angry scene with Carel and Barney consistently saying 'You're over-acting, you're not direct. Speak stones...', something broke, and these growls came from somewhere in my belly – I began to speak Afrikaans like I remembered my Ouma speaking it. Everything felt connected in me – I was Aletta Johanna and not an Anglicised product of colonial schooling. I made connection with

Opposite – Barney Simon and Aletta Bezuidenhout in a publicity photograph for "Klaaglied vir Koos", August 1986.
Photograph courtesy of The Market Theatre.

Postcard of Greta Garbo, 1931

an anger I had as a child of Afrikaner parents who, among other things, were discriminated against in British circles in Kenya. Creating Abbie sometimes felt like a Caesarean instead of birth. I was so frightened. I'd drive home in my little white beetle to Barney's house – 13 Magpie Street, Kensington – where I was staying, and I'd hear this wailing in my car, and eventually realise that it was coming from me. When I got home, I'd switch on every single light in Barney's house, open all the doors and windows, take off all my clothes and, covering myself with a black shawl, walk from room to room trying to figure out whatever it was that was happening to me.

In rehearsals I became aware of doing work very carefully and in great detail. For instance a smile became very particular, a single gesture had much more meaning. I became aware of 'opening up' moments. Everything I did had to be specific. He often said, 'God is in the specifics.' He launched me into doing very careful work in "Six Characters". Pirandello's play is about this family who breaks into rehearsal and decides to perform its own bit of reality. Barney said, 'Just go into the PACT rehearsal like you are those people.' Danny Keogh and I had to go into a PACT rehearsal at the Alhambra. I just didn't have the courage. But often, that's the kind of thing he demanded.

He gave me a book called "The Yellow Star" which contained a picture of a young, naked Jewish woman at Auschwitz – he said it reminded him of me. An entire monologue transpired from this photograph, about my personal experiences of apartheid, being harassed by an Afrikaans cop, our farmhouse being ransacked by Mozambican rebel soldiers. Barney often worked from pictures. During "Begeerte" we worked from Munch's "The Scream". During "Woyzeck" we worked from Goya's paintings. He took me to see specific movies, for example "The Garden of the Finzi Continis", because he thought I'd identify and learn from the way in which Dominique Sande related to her grandmother, or we'd look at "The Great Dictator" with Charlie Chaplin. He gave me photos of Marilyn Monroe or Greta Garbo... some of his favourites. He tried to give me a paradigm from where I could play peasant or princess. How a character was alive, was the thing.

'We used to grill chicken livers on paper on a hot stove and talk about a movie star like Elizabeth Taylor...'
Aletta Bezuidenhout

One afternoon he marched me round and round the lake in Rhodes Park, carrying my heavy weekend bag, and talked to me about Abbie. Everything had to be textured, hair, skin and eyes. He hated make-up or what he called 'radical chic'. He had a thing about a woman smoking a cigarette, a 1940s thing. His mother smoked when he was a teenager. His room was crammed with books and manuscripts... just that smell... his home... the 'Hebrew thing'... something ancient and something New York at the same time... I can't explain it. We used to grill chicken livers on paper on a hot stove, and talk about a movie star like Elizabeth Taylor, and Barney would say, 'She got fat and I got bald.' I remember the day he stopped combing the few strands of hair over his baldness – he was radiant.

For "Woyzeck" (Marius Weyers played Franz and I played Maria), we did extraordinary improvs. There was one where Franz is about to stab Maria to death, and I realised that the only way she could get through was to make love to Franz, to embrace and kiss him, feel some sort of passion for him while he killed her. It was inspired by Marius and Barney and the big, old emptiness of the Alex rehearsal room. It remains as one of the most powerful memories of that time, the level of connection the actors achieved.

Postcard of Marilyn Monroe ©1986 ESTATE OF MARILYN MONROE, Represented by the Roger Richman Agency, Beverly Hills, CA Ludlow Sales, Box 554, Chelsea Station, New York, NY. 10011

Postcard of Elizabeth Taylor, 1948 Photograph by Philippe Halsman © 1983 Fotofolio, Box 661 CANAL STA.NY.NY 10013 PH21

We performed "Storytime" in a shop on Louis Botha Avenue, and then moved on to the Blue Fox in the Oxford Hotel – did a couple of plays there. We had to sound-proof the place with egg boxes. Late one night I heard Danny at my window saying, 'Alet, we got the Indian Market.' I was ecstatic – a very true dream came alive... I was so, so, so happy. When my first child was born, The Market Theatre came into being. The night before Hamilton's birth, Barney sat with me for hours hoping for some real action – i.e. the actual birth. I was very restless and we decided to drive around from roadhouse to roadhouse – Benoni, Springs... I was driving very fast and Barney was very quiet, he'd run out of cigarettes and was smoking stompies. Hamilton was born the following morning at the Marymount. When Barney came to visit they refused to let him in as he wasn't family – he said his name was Barney Bezuidenhout – the nuns were not convinced. I was upstairs in Antigone's gown covered with sea-shells.

The Market Theatre opened with "The Seagull" and then "Marat/Sade". Barney spent many hours talking through how I could play Masha and Charlotte Corday with a new-born baby – but I just couldn't. Those were terrible losses for me. When we did "Vroue van Troje" about a year later, Barney and I had become alienated. I played Andromache. Barney had become very harsh towards me. I felt as if he was putting salt on wounds. He exposed intimate details of my life, stories of my mother and father, to facilitate performances from other actors. I wasn't respected enough. I felt that he used a lot of me. In later years, he did not give me a chance. I was a founder-member of The Market which became part of this country's history. But, ironically, I only did six plays in the twenty-four years of The Market's life. I was blocked by whoever was running The Market Theatre at that time, and Barney was part of that.

I accept all the pain that went with knowing and working with Barney – he carried a tremendous amount of pain himself. He had a loneliness and often exposed a cruel cynicism, especially when he was in that lonely space, because those who worked with him eventually got married, had children and all that. And yet he hated familiarity. We had been friends for seventeen years and were sitting on the back steps of his house in Bellevue... He said, in such a surprised way, that he and I had known each other for seventeen years – I can't explain the exasperation and the paradox I felt. All the things we really knew about one another, yet he'd block me off at some point. As the Afrikaners say: 'Tot hier toe en nie verder nie.' He knew so much.

Barney would baby-sit for me sometimes when I had to do filming in the early hours of the morning. He did amazing things for people sometimes – especially if they were experiencing a traumatic crisis in their lives. He was intense in a way that affected his health. I remember being at some open-air fleamarket, sitting in that hot sun, Barney standing over me for an hour, so that I could have some shade. Or driving across town with a bowl of strawberries for a depressed friend, or bringing back a fragile antique lace dress from New York for me.

Barney 'romanced' people. Mostly people wanted his acknowledgement. He appreciated beauty in men and women. He'd let a stray stay at his home, and say something like, 'She needs a resting place'. He did that for many people. I liked his feminine side. He was a nurturer. He had deep admiration and love for Athol Fugard, and tremendous respect for Yvonne Bryceland's work. With Jennifer Ferguson he was almost territorial. He had a strong 'private' affinity with Megan Kruskal, and liked Sandra Prinsloo's beauty and logic, Gcina Mhlope's energy.

While we were rehearsing "Mother Courage", I couldn't get a monologue right. I remember standing in his lounge – I knew the patterns on his carpet off by heart. I'd created quite a few characters looking at them, and I broke down and cried looking at those patterns. He kept on saying, 'Just do it, you bitch.' I just didn't want to do the character. I just didn't want to get in there. It was some block inside me, and he wanted to break through. It was the older version of the prostitute, and I couldn't do that. She comes back as a rich widow with a black veil, and he said, 'I want you to be like PW Botha's widow.' On another level our relationship shifted – neither of us really coped in that session. I think Barney was mastered by his p.o.v. of reality. I felt almost edited out – he wouldn't permit a certain kind sexiness or funniness or a certain loudness. I began rebelling against what he called 'real'. Anyone else's reality was unacceptable.

Okay, he was intensely curious about intimacy – other people's – but he loathed familiarity. I resented the stamp of his reality on my life. I felt trapped in what I felt was a voyeuristic vision of reality. But then, Barney often reminded us that a performance should have privacy, as if the audience were eavesdropping. But still, I questioned his 'truth'. Though I liked being compared to Garbo and Monroe. He gave me a photo-graph of Marilyn Monroe before she went blonde. You know that beautiful classic picture where she is sitting on her hands with this very natural auburn brown hair, that freshness. He gave me the photo and said, 'God, she is so healthy.' I would look at it and say, 'I understand what you mean.'

We were sitting in a restaurant and I said, 'You know I am real but sometimes I pretend not to be real.' And he said, 'Write that down. It's a contract.' So I would write it down on a serviette and he'd keep it and put it in his pocket like a contract. Sometimes I would refuse to be real and he always wanted realism. So when he said that's a contract, he was saying, 'I know that you know what I want. I want you to be real.' Often when I freaked out or something he'd chuckle, pluck at his beard and nod his head up and down. I'd ask, 'Why are you laughing?' He'd say, 'If I nod my head up and down it means I am trying not to drown,' or 'You don't always understand what's really happening to someone.' I am describing a complex friendship.

In "Begeerte" I had to try and cut Marcel's long hair. I had a pair of scissors. Marcel never showed anger or violence but in that improv he scared me. I did not manage to cut his hair but something very steely surfaced in him. Barney did not stop me. He really went for those moments – he'd get quite twitchy. Just before we started rehearsals for "Klaaglied vir Koos" he took me for a walk at the back of The Market, and we saw a plastic bag that flew up in the air. He said, 'Now look at that plastic bag. It has got a history. It has been somewhere. It was made. It carried things, now it is empty and because it is empty, it is just blowing around.' The penny dropped. I understood. You had to face things inside yourself. That was quite scary. He made you feel sick with fear.

Sometimes you'd think, 'Why?' On opening night you'd think, 'Oh God, I would do anything not to be in this play with Barney right now.' It was just so sickening and horrifying. A lot of actors have said that. He wasn't easy, but incredibly passionate. He was like a mother – sometimes he breast-fed you, and then slapped the shit out of you – made you walk on glass. He taught me how to find the reality of the moment. But I was still a very young actress. I didn't know how to sustain the discipline night after night. Sometimes I'd fall flat and he'd make bitchy comments. But he helped me to access those places and then to sustain them. By becoming familiar with the sounds and what sounds work and knowing how to hit those notes. How to find my tears. How to find my anger and just go back to that place. How to use energy.

I felt a strange numbness, 'unrealness', when Barney died, because we hadn't spoken for two years. And then I felt a terrible, terrible sadness. His death was like an expression of the most extraordinary vulnerability. So often, to me, it felt as if he was in danger. But I don't know what was happening in those two years, we didn't speak to each other. We couldn't.

There were the earlier times when he didn't really take care of himself, and one couldn't always get close to him, to care for him. Also, most of us got involved in other relationships, got married and had children. In my relationship with Barney I often felt helpless, mute. He had terrible curiosity, quite voyeuristic! I felt he was always spying on my privacy, my relationships and my sexuality. I was helpless. I used to tell him everything. I was fighting to get out of giving Barney so much. I was too open with him. I opened up my whole private life to him and I am sorry about that. I think he had as much from me as anybody in his life. Not many actors gave that much to Barney about their privacy, not many were as open to him. That's why I had to withdraw, it weakened me. Actors have poor boundaries as it is. I was always an outsider and he connected with that outsider-thing in me. He understood things about people. That's why actors liked him, because he had a place of receptivity inside him.

I sometimes wished that he hadn't happened to me. Often my gay friends have made me feel that way – I just never have what they really want. When I started doing my own work, it was very abstract. People called me weird and crazy. Barney was a haven for my madness. I was fragmented and he helped me channel the bits and pieces.

I hear my students say, 'But Barney Simon and Athol Fugard just had too many issues.' And I give them stories of that time. When we drove around Hillbrow during apartheid time and saw rows and rows of black people waiting, or two black whores in a vicious fist fight, Barney said things like, 'You girls with your radical chic and diets, check! Those guys are dying for a piece of bread.' Drama schools incubate and don't make kids aware enough, aware of themselves and their perspectives. The present 'young' generation needs to work at that and get their heads out of the box/web/windows/net.

To me Barney is master of his realism in the way Chekhov is of his naturalism. He taught me how to be conscious of living history in a person's performance and how to be a spiral instead of a box... magical things and really terrible things. From chicken livers and Rose eating 'putu pap' in Soweto, to Mrs Cataneo's parsley soup and Nadine Gordimer placing another log on the fire... so many people! Oh yes, he quoted this sometimes:

'Life is little more than a journey through the detours of art, to the two or three great and simple images that first found access to your heart.'

Opposite – At the time of his death, Barney had a torn print of this photograph, lying amongst his writing papers on his desk. It is titled "Boss Boy", Battery Reef, Randfontein Estates Gold Mine, 1966.
Photograph by David Goldblatt.

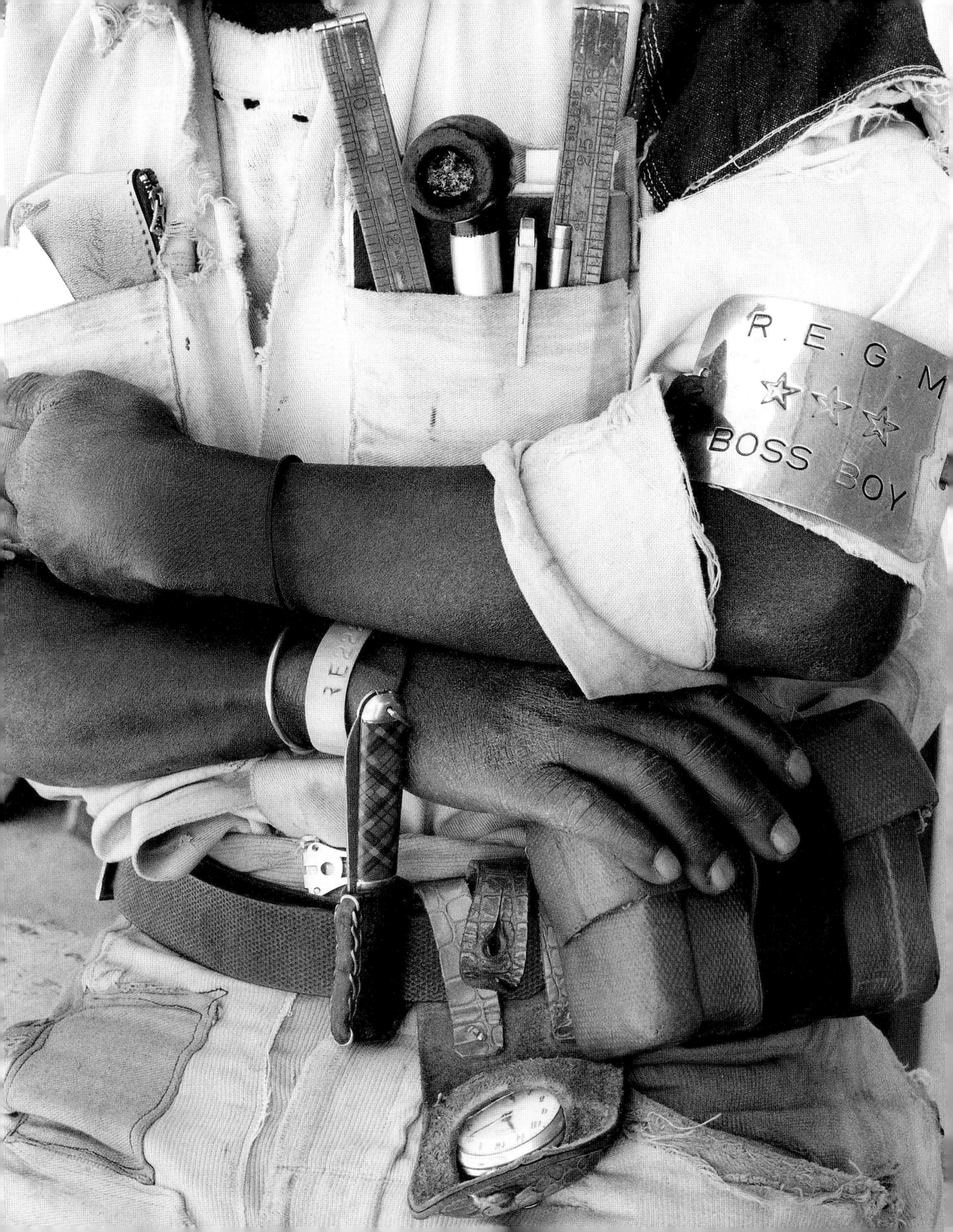
R.E.G.M
BOSS BOY

Chapter 5. Specifics

The Market Theatre opened with "The Seagull" and "Marat/Sade". Ron Smerczak, Janice Honeyman and Sandra Prinsloo speak of how, no matter how big or small the part, Barney worked relentlessly on specifics, and they describe some excercises he developed in order to achieve this.

'That's the wisdom I try to encourage in actors. To use what they know as human beings, as opposed to using what they've learnt as performers. I have terrible times with technical actors: those who insist on doing what worked in the last play or last performance. When they come up with this technical thing, which to me is no communication, I've nothing to say in return. And they think I've nothing to say. There is nothing to say in the face of a lie except to call it what it is. They are not using themselves at all, and what is not personal is fatal. I don't ask for indulgence but danger. Some people call the danger that I demand darkness. That depends on the aspiration of the actor. But basically the darkness comes from hiding yourself. Fear is the cloak people put on themselves. It's not a fearful world. I think we live in fearful cloaks, in shadows. It's how it is done that matters. It's the vision of what it is.'

Barney Simon, from "Conversations" by Avril Herber.

Opposite – Children climbing up sand dune – Transkei, 1967.
Photograph by Rodney Barnett / South Photos.

Ron Smerczak

'A continuation of three, four, very good teachers I had at the Royal Academy of Dramatic Art'

I was brought out here by Pieter Toerien from Britain. I decided to stay in South Africa. I went to work for The Company, as it was known then, in "Twelfth Night". I think I was on sixty rand a week. But in those days you could still live on that. What I particularly remember about "Fortune and Men's Eyes" in The Market Theatre, was that there was like a spark. Aletta Bezuidenhout was around then, Danny Keogh, Vanessa Cooke. It was like a new group of friends.

We used to rehearse in The Market Theatre. Barney locked us in a cupboard for three hours to deal with the motivations of claustrophobic space. Poor Nigel Vermaas was the warden walking up and down, screaming and shouting at us. The cupboard was, I suppose about three metres in length and one and a half metres wide, and about as high as three metres, as well. And there were shelves on the side, little shelves about fifty, sixty centimetres wide on the wall. And four of us lay on them and told jokes, to pass our three hours while we understood what it was like to be confined. Anyway we got through it. And of course the play was a huge success. Barney had an expression for that. It was 'finding the inner life'. Then it was "Marat/Sade". And in that production I played the man who spent three hours in a strait jacket, while they had me running, screaming around the stage.

I loved working with Barney. I don't know who he bonked. There was no delving into his personal history. All that was important were the words on the page and the actors. Occasionally he asked, delved into your own personal life. I never got near to understanding his personal life. I don't think he understood mine. But as a working relationship it was a beautiful, wonderful relationship. Barney as a person was totally asexual. That was the impression I got. Yet when he made you work, when you worked with him, he drew the sexuality out of you. I remember when Marcel and I had to kiss one another in "East". It was vomit for both of us.

But you don't remember how he did that?

No. I have no idea. He just worked with people. He made me feel relaxed and I trusted him. In "Cincinatti" I developed this character who to me was like in his mid-forties, because we discovered a hell of a lot while we were locked in the cupboard. We had five or six sessions in the cupboard. You see he was trying to find out the difference between prisoners and warders. That was the question we were asking. What is the relationship between the prisoner and the warder? Because the warder is also locked away inside the prison. Now the warder in "Fortune and Men's Eyes" only appears on stage for I think five or six minutes in the last act. The warder becomes our friend. And you began to understand why, because when we're locked in the cupboard Nigel is outside. We would bang on the door and say, 'Nigel, get us a drink, we need water.' And you would find out why you have a relationship.

I think it was in "Cincinatti" Barney said to me, 'Ron, you must just let yourself go, you must trust your instinct.' I am paraphrasing. He said, 'You are very knowledgeable for your age, highly knowledgeable.' But he said, 'Knowledge doesn't make you the actor, it's your instinctive use of that knowledge that makes you an actor.' The only time I let my emotions go is when I'm on stage. And that's my release, you know. And that's what I gained from Barney. He taught me a way to channel my knowledge to release emotions. Barney would keep pushing with emotions and want you to discover, explore, and maybe freak out. He would never force me to. I have heard of other actors that he broke down. But for me I only broke down within the character. Once I was acting, something would click instinctively within me and release it. Barney then said, 'Beautiful, thank you. What did you do?' I'd say, 'I don't fucking know.'

As a very accomplished, experienced actor, after so many years what do you feel you gained from him specifically, that you still use?

He was like a continuation of three, four very good teachers I had at the Royal Academy of Dramatic Art. There was a similar wavelength to the way in which he talked to you. Barney had knowledge, in my eyes, of everything that those four people taught me. He had a classicism in him. Knowledge of what I call classical theatre. He had experimentation in him. And he respected what I call technical training – voice production and things. In other words, he, to me, joined those four RADA teachers' work together in what I did. When I do have the privilege to work on a decent stage play, what he did with me in those early days comes back to me.

Ron Smerczak in "Brecht on Brecht".
Photograph by Ruphin Coudyzer.

'All he said to me in the whole of that time, about that part in "Marat/Sade" was "You are an out-of-focus green balloon"'

Janice Honeyman

Janice Honeyman

'I wish he was here to give me all that stuff in person'

Barney used to make us improvise when we were doing "Marat/Sade". We spent a lot of time in some dreadful room doing sound and gesture exercises, which Barney made us do relentlessly. All the time we didn't really understand what it was about. In the end it made sense, I suppose, in the outcome of the production. Eventually we were allowed out of the room and Barney said, 'Now think about what you really loathe, and find it.'

Now in those days The Market Theatre was right next to the abattoir. Further down towards the Diggers Inn was the offal pool. I had been a confirmed vegetarian for seven years. I hated everything that meat-eating stood for. So I wandered off on my own to the abattoir. You could smell the animals. You could hear the tension, the waiting for death. It was too awful. Then I went through these huge gates into a place that was white-tiled, dirty, with lots of guys walking around with white boots and white plastic outfits. In front of me was what looked like an Olympic size swimming pool full to the brim with derms of offal. I got the images into my head, which was too horrific for words. When I walked out onto the street I saw people, heard clattering on the railway line with the animals moo-ing and baa-ing. I saw people carrying dead carcasses around and loading them into huge trucks.

Then I came back and used those images in the moments of horror that Barney then made us improvise on. I told him what happened and he laughed and laughed. Do you know how Barney used to giggle? He just went completely red and his face crumpled into a sort of evil gnome. I didn't get cross at the time, because the one thing Barney and I had in common was the same sense of humour. When I acted for him he did make me do some pretty terrible things. The laughter took the curse out of it in some ways.

Barney never used to give notes as noted. He didn't sit down with a pad. He used to talk. And you used to have to listen like crazy and be like a sponge. All he said to me in the whole of that time about that part in "Marat/Sade" was, 'You are an out-of-focus green balloon.' And I thought, 'Okay, well I've got to get this character somehow.' So I played her very roundish and quite light, not heavy round, light round. And I thought, 'What's out of focus?' So I squinted. In fact for the whole run I never actually saw anything in focus on stage. I would bind the bandages around Marat, squint my eyes and never see what I was doing. Everything that I looked at was completely out of focus, including the lights, the other people on stage, the props and the audience. I didn't know what to do about the green part so I just went up to the wardrobe for the biggest green skirt I could find and wore this over my mental asylum outfit. In the end it made absolute sense. The out-of-focus-ness with everything else was because of this complete focus on Marat. That was the brilliant thing about Barney. As obscure as he seemed to be he always actually made sense. If you cared to listen, you would get a wealth of stuff for your character from him. He had an

Opposite – "Marat/Sade".
Photograph courtesy of Vanessa Cooke.

absolutely alternative perspective on life. I believe Barney taught me to act and to direct. I didn't always act the way Barney had taught me to act. And I certainly don't direct the way Barney taught me to direct, in the exact style. But the basic principle of it is there. He taught me not to go for the obvious, what is easiest. He forced you always to look for another way. Sometimes it was very difficult to construct that and put it into form. He would tell you one thing one day and another thing another day. But if you actually used it properly you could put all of that together and it would give you a take on your part which was certainly different to the way you originally saw it when you read it. He taught me to look at things differently. He would argue about everything you gave. In the end you didn't have to do it Barney's way, but he was extremely particular about what he wanted from you.

For instance, when I played in Marsha Norman's "Night Mother" he made me start smoking again, which was terrible. It was only an excuse so that he could smoke as well. I said to him, 'Barney, please, man, I managed to give up smoking two years ago. I don't want to smoke, I don't care how fat I get. Can't this character eat chocolate right the way through?' He made me smoke. As I would light up, Barney would too. He used to sit there coughing like mad while we were doing hell of a sensitive scenes. "Night Mother" was hell of a difficult. As much as Barney gave me, in that particular instance I still don't think he was entirely right. Because one believed in him strongly, you tried what he meant. It was an extremely heavy play but I believe that the conflict between mother and daughter has a lot of comedy in it. It was the last two hours of this woman's life. She then goes off stage and commits suicide. Barney wouldn't allow Julie Folensby, who played the mother, and I to put any comedy into it at all. And on the last night he came backstage and shouted at me and said, 'It is cheap to get laughs.'

There were two things about "Hello and Goodbye" that were freaky. I was living in a truly grotty little flat in Fortesque Street, Yeoville. Vanessa Cooke was living two or three roads away. It was cold. We were earning something like thirty-two rand a week. I had no furniture. I had a bed on the floor, a mattress. I had an electric frying pan and a hot-plate. And that was it. We did "Hello and Goodbye" in the middle of winter. Barney asked me, 'Do you understand loneliness?' I was young. I said, 'Ja.' But I didn't really understand loneliness at that point. He said, 'Okay, you. This woman is alone and you are going to be alone. You are going to come to rehearsals. You have to go straight home and the next time you talk to another soul is at rehearsals again.'

This was for the whole rehearsal period. I was having a most terrible time trying to learn the words. I didn't have any money. I used to buy a few onions or maybe a potato. I remember one night I was having trouble with words. I said to Vanessa, 'Please you've got to listen to my words.' And she was fantastic. She used to park her car not exactly outside, so if Barney drove past her car wouldn't be seen there. She used to creep into this flat and we used to sit freezing to death around this electric frying pan with two solitary onions in it. We used to have these little onions for supper at about half past nine at night. But listen, the improv worked. Being on my own was quite freaky in this terrible place. There was a guy who used to come and wee under my door.

Opposite – Janice Honeyman in conversation with Barney Simon, November 1981.
Photograph by Ruphin Coudyzer.

It was just one of those sordid Jo'burg scenes. Then there was the improvisation he sent me out on. I had to dress up like a whore because Hester is a whore. I wore stockings and sandals and a straight skirt, tarty make-up and a duffel coat. It was so weird because my mother would never let me wear a duffel coat and now I know why. It was in the afternoon. I had to go to the Bio-Café. It was a black and white film and it was violent. And the next thing this guy shifted. There I was improvising being a whore. He moved one seat and I thought, 'Uh, Janice, Hester, you don't want to be with this guy.' But it was terrible because there was a great conflict between Janice and Hester, I must tell you. Then suddenly – now this is the sordid bit – the whole row started shaking. This guy was wanking. And I thought, 'I don't believe this, what has this got to do with playing Hester in the Blue Fox?' Anyway, suddenly he grabbed my hand and put my hand on him. I got the fright of my life. Well, I jumped up and in my pommiest voice I said, 'I beg your pardon! Please move!' Ugh, it was just too awful for words. I felt a fool. Stormed up the bloody aisle, tripped over those disgusting carpets, in these stupid sandals. I went back to the theatre, to the Blue Fox where Barney was working with Marius Weyers. I was beside myself. I walked in looking like a whore, and said, 'Barney, how could you do this to me? How dare you!' And he just laughed. I was cross. I thought, honestly this is not worth it. In the end everything was worth it if you used it. He was very good on that level. He used to focus you onto parts of the role that you would never have thought of. I certainly hadn't had the experience and Barney probably knew that.

I remember another story. Sarah NcNair and I had been to a show at the Alhambra. It was a Sunday evening. I was in a high-necked granny-print floral dress with a little yellow collar. Sarah was in this hippie kaftan. We were walking back to the house we lived in on Saratoga Avenue, right on the corner opposite the church which used to be a home for tramps before we lived there. So we had an endless stream of these guys, and it was in a grotty area as well. We were walking from Beit Street, where there were lots of prostitutes, up to Saratoga, and we felt this car behind us creeping. I said to Sarah, 'There is somebody trying to pick us up.' And Sarah said, 'We'll just keep walking.' This car never came next to us. It just stayed behind us. So if we turned around it would look as if we were interested. So we walked on, up straight, faster. As we were just getting to the corner of Saratoga this car pulled up next to us and the window opened. The driver pretended he was going to pick us up. It was Barney. And he laughed because, he said, what was so funny was that our noses went higher and higher in the air. These two straight-up women in these long dresses absolutely refusing to look at this little bastard who was actually playing a trick on us. His humour was great.

When I became the Executive Artistic Director of the Johannesburg Civic Theatre and moved into the somewhat intimidating 'corner office', I immediately put up two pictures of Barney – one of him dancing like a mad, naughty dybbuk, above my computer, and one staring at me from alongside my planning board. I was never out of his eyeline! Sometimes he was saying, 'Do it Janice!' And other times chuckling mockingly and saying, 'Ja, jy wil mos!!!' He never failed to make some comment, and he always had some influence on my decisions. I wish he was here to give me all that stuff in person.

Sandra Prinsloo

'Play the struggle, not the pain'

I went to see a production of "Woyzeck", which had Danny and Vanessa, and I was terribly impressed. I think it was the first time I met Barney.

Why were you impressed ?

I had never seen theatre like that. It was, for me, completely innovative. I was a young Afrikaans actress in a permanent Afrikaans company. I hadn't actually done any English work. Then one day I got a call from Barney, saying he was doing "The Seagull". I met him in Johannesburg and he was a fascinating man. When he spoke he used these wonderful metaphors. He decided I should play Masha and I was thrilled. I always loved that part. The work process with Barney on "The Seagull" was probably the most fantastic experience for me then, and even now. He had such a wonderful vision of Masha. I had worked with other directors who had a much more traditional approach to Chekhov. Barney said to me, Masha is a vodka-swigging drug-taking hippie. I said, Oh, okay... Wow! And all preconceived notions on Chekhov were swept out the door. I worked so well with Barney on that production. He was wonderful. My eyes had opened and I saw a whole new world through Barney's eyes, in terms of acting and an inner world to be explored. And the exercises he made us do.

Do you remember any of them?

I remember one specific one. He said to me, 'Masha has a cold front but a warm back.' And he made Danny and me lie together like spoons – we lay there for a long time. So I got this warm back. It was winter. It was cold. My front was really cold.

And how did that help?

Well, it helped because I suddenly physically understood where this woman was coming from. It was not just an intellectual kind of understanding. It was a very physical integration as well. Barney worked a lot like that. Barney had a lekker sense of humour. He'd suddenly come up with something so modern that he would bring to a classical part and just lift the whole thing. I remember the scene when Masha comes to say goodbye. I think he made me play it like no one has ever played Masha. She was completely pissed on vodka, taking snuff and smoking away, with grass in her hair, crying, laughing, dancing and doing things that you wouldn't really think of doing. Normally Masha comes in and she is quite quiet and sad and does her goodbye. I also remember another moment, such a small moment in the play, but Barney understood it so perfectly. I have seen many productions after that and don't think any of the directors grasped that moment the way Barney did. It's the moment when Masha gets up in the middle of company. She starts walking off but she cannot go off. She says, 'My leg is asleep.' Normally it is just a laugh, but Barney saw this deep embarrassment that you get when you are that age and you are so uncomfortable that you are not in your skin. So in Masha I had to laugh and cry and die of embarrassment. It's a moment we worked and worked on until I got it. There are very few directors who give that texture to a script, who work so intensely. It's a moment that everybody remembered. It's just such a heartbreakingly funny moment. Barney was good at doing that sort of thing, where it is funny but is also bloody sore. He was very good at getting that mix, that blend. I never found him a heavy-handed director who would indulge in emotion. He'd always work away from it. What was wonderful was the night before we opened. He said to me after the session, 'We've ended up with something totally different.' And I said, 'Oh my God, I am sorry.' And he said, 'No, it is wonderful, because it was such a journey, such a process.'

I was still with PACT when I was offered the role of Charlotte Corday in "Marat/Sade". I don't know why he offered it to me because I can't sing a bloody note. But I read the script and I was bowled over by this play. I resigned from PACT, because they didn't want to give me time off. They were furious with me. I really wanted to do it because I wanted to work with Barney again, firstly. Secondly, because it was such a marvellous play. We worked with a psychologist for a week and I was flung in the deep end. All these actors had got into their characters and all their madness. That is where Barney was brilliant: even the smallest walk-on with no words, each of those mad people, was accommodated and thoroughly worked. I joined in and was terribly upset after the first day. I just sat there and cried for half an hour. And Barney said, 'Oh shit, I forgot you haven't been here.'

It was 1976. It was the height of the riots, especially in town. The Market was in a very hectic area of unrest and violence. And he sent me into the streets as Charlotte Corday, this woman who falls asleep all the time, who can't stay awake. I thought, well if ever there is a war I am going to pretend I am mad. People just parted in front of me. They were so kind. They said, 'Ag, mummy, are you all right? Are you okay?' There was an awful abattoir next to The Market. It used to stink. It was the smell of blood that really made me freak. This guy came running over and said, 'Are you alright? Can I help? What are you doing wandering around here?' I just didn't want him near me because he had this blood splattered overall on. You go so deeply into these things with Barney, and it was, for me, incredibly important to have gone to those areas, to understand what the character was about. The singing was a huge problem. I was really scared. But Barney was great. He brought in Irene Frangs, and Michele Maxwell baby-sitted me through the horror of singing on stage.

When we did "Vroue van Troje", the Afrikaans Trojan Women, my God, he tried to break us. It was amazing. We were treated like prisoners. And the men did all the tactics that they learnt in the army. I remember Wilna Snyman breaking down and crying, saying, 'I can't do this. I am too old.' It was tough. I mean, they screamed at us. They marched us. They made us do exercises. They locked us up. I remember Aletta and I were the two rebellious ones. We never wanted to listen. We were always out of line. We always got into big shit and had to carry bricks up and down staircases. It was always a fantastic process with Barney. I threw myself into it because I really felt that even if I couldn't use it for the specific character it added so much to my emotional vocabulary as an actress that could always be accessed again, instantly.

You know, Barney didn't just give you a part. He really enriched your life. He was quite extraordinary that way. I just loved working with him. I remember him saying to me, 'Play the struggle, not the pain.' That was one of the most important things a director could have told me. In other words, play the struggle against the pain, get over the pain. Play hiding the pain, and then you really get the audience's empathy. It's one the most important lessons I have learnt as an actress.

"Vroue Van Troje" was real physical stuff, the breaking down until you feel you cannot take anymore. I think it is important to know how women feel in situations before you can start working on the play. If you do not understand your environment and what you have been through... I think we have been living too comfortably to understand what the situation was about. I was battling with one speech. I really battled with Helen.

Sandra Prinsloo and Wilson Dunster in "Marat/Sade".
Photograph courtesy of NELM.

I remember doing the speech and knowing it is not right, it's not gelling. Poor Barney said to me, 'Aah, I've had an idea.' And I said, 'I'm glad, because I haven't had one.' I wanted to smack him, I was cross with him simply because he challenged me. He'd never just let go and say she can't do better than that. In the end you had to get it.

Do you remember what the idea was?

No. I had to climb up the back of his wall and... I've blocked it out of my mind. I do remember him saying though that Helen of Troy's great legend, that men would go to war for her, was so unfair. Women are always being given these labels. She was probably a very nice girl next door. Men made her hateable when she was probably a sweet old pumpkin. So that was quite an interesting approach to Helen, that she was actually not the great virago superstar who caused wars. She just inspired love, and was carried off. I did "Six Feet of the Country", the film of Nadine Gordimer's short story. Lynston Stephenson directed and Barney directed the acting. It was marvellous working with him in the film medium. I found it extremely helpful. It was not easy with two directors on set. Barney eventually withdrew because he felt he was crowding. There was a big fight scene between Wilson Dunster and me. I remember Barney saying, 'No. Play it really very softly, very quietly.' This was very powerful on film, because I never raised my voice. The marriage breaks down between the two characters, and Barney said, 'Don't be sad when you look at him, just look, the camera will do the rest.' And it was absolutely true. I just stood there and looked at him. He was big on that just looking, and it always worked. You do not need to do more than that. We don't in life really do more than that. He was amazing. And we had lots of fun on Nadine's farm for weeks. Not everyone liked Barney. Kenneth Hendel once screamed at him, 'You're an evil man.' It was hectic. Vanessa started swearing at Kenneth to protect Barney. And Barney turned around and said, 'Thank you Vanessa, but that is not necessary.' Vanessa was upset, but I think she understood that what Barney meant was that it didn't mean anything to him. He could absorb it in a way. There were actors who just could not work with him because he had a very demanding and very specific way of working. He asked everything of you as an actor. There was no kind of fiddling around the edges. You were there or you were not. I always loved working that way. I love it when directors challenge you and stretch you and make impossible demands of you. It's what the job is about for me.

What do you feel he left you?

Aah, an enormous amount. One discovers a sense of wonder in the theatre again when you work with Barney. Your eyes really open. He makes you fall in love with theatre all over again. That's what he left me. He would never see a play like most people. He would somehow see it, read it, and understand it differently, which made it terribly exciting. The first reading was always like a telephone directory. You just read the lines. Some older English actors found that hard because they had come prepared. He wanted a clean slate. We would all start from scratch, from nothing, and build from there, which I am all for. There isn't always time to do that, nowadays especially, but we had more time in those days, like five weeks of rehearsals. Barney demanded that we chuck out everything and start all over again.

Frantz Dobrowsky

'It was the imparting of the image'

We did "Rosenkrantz and Guildenstern are Dead" with Richard Haines in 1978. We got together on stage the very first day, just Richard and myself. Obviously there was a lot of work to be done with us before the other people joined. On either side of the stage there was a curtain blocking off the whole corner where the spare chairs were packed. Barney took us through, and I thought now he is going to show us some sort of elaborate entrance/exit thing that he has got in mind. But he took us through, plonked us on the spare chairs that were behind those curtains in the pitch dark and said, 'Oh, just hang around here. I'll be back soon.' He disappeared into the foyer and left us sitting there in the dark. As first we said, 'What rubbish is this?'

"Rosenkrantz and Guildenstern", if you know the play, are with each other and isolated. He wanted, without saying it in words, to give us that sensation. For me that sums up a lot of what Barney is about. You can talk about it forever but until you feel something, unless you get an image in your mind that is beyond words, you don't quite know exactly what you are doing. Now Rosenkrantz and Guildenstern are in limbo. Then fate pricks them into action and the play develops. So that first image, of the two of us, even though we were saying what the hell is this rubbish, and chatting to each other as Richard and Frantz, still left us in exactly the situation that Barney wanted us to somehow get to grips with. And that's exactly what did happen. He must have left us for about twenty-five minutes. Then he came peeping through, and we said, 'Okay Barney we've done enough of this now. There is a lot of work to be done on the actual text.' And he laughed and took us onto the stage and on we went.

That sums up a lot for me. There was a script that you could analyse and look at from a certain point of view, but always, with Barney, it was looked at from a different point of view. It was the imparting of the image. It wasn't like an improvisation. He didn't set us any kind of task. He just gave us an experience that was central to what we should feel, at least to launch the play. The thing is not to take things for granted, but to find the human, to find the heart behind the stories. Even in a brilliant script, you've got to still find that.

I saw his contribution in the way you look at theatre. Now that's a legacy that you have forever. If you give somebody the hint of some new way of looking at something, then everything that they come across for the next ten, fifteen, twenty, forty years is going to be coloured slightly by that. You couldn't go back to doing it the way you would always do it after you had worked with Barney, or seen Barney's work. So that is a legacy.

Patrick Mynhardt

'I knelt in front of him and cried like a bloody baby'

In 1978, I don't remember quite who phoned me, but the next thing is The Market Theatre was now going to do "Rosenkrantz and Guildenstern are Dead". The first reading was at Barney's house. He'd now moved to Yeoville. There was his little secretary lady and this wonderful black African housekeeper lady, and Richard Haines, Dobrowsky and myself. They were Rosenkrantz and Guildenstern, and then I think the next sort of 'importantish' part was the old Player King, my part.

Well, we sat down and we read this bloody play, and I didn't understand a word of what I was saying. I didn't know what was going on between Rosenkrantz and Guildenstern. I didn't know what to do. I hated that read-through. When I left I did something unforgivable, unprofessional. I left my script behind. I didn't want to do the play but I didn't have the guts to say to Barney, 'Barney I don't want to do this play.' We were to meet the next day but I didn't pitch up. Richard phoned and he said, 'Aren't you coming to the rehearsal? You left your script here.' And I said, 'Ja, I'll pitch.' I just didn't want to do that play. Then both Richard Haines and Frantz Dobrowsky and, God forgive me if I'm misquoting, said, 'Patrick you'll be brilliant!' Anyway, to cut a long story short, I rehearsed the play. I do not think I'm a difficult person. I think I'm a neurotic, terrified, frightened, insecure actor. I've always have been. But I don't think I'm difficult.

Well, one morning we were at The Market Theatre, we were rehearsing and I was so confused. There was a counter with cups and saucers, and I didn't understand what Barney wanted from me. Barney would say, 'You are the funniest man I know. I want you to be funny as the Player King. I want you to do what you do in your living room.' I'd gone to see him one Sunday. I was just talking, and I had a hap of cake and Barney fell off his chair. He said, 'You see, you're so funny.' I said, 'Why?' He said, 'The way you happed that cake and talked kak to us.' He rolled on the floor and said, 'That's what I want you to do when you're the Player King.'

Well, I could not do this with the Player King. I could not relate the Player King to Patrick Mynhardt eating Barney's gebakte koek on a Sunday afternoon in his Yeoville house with him rolling on the floor. I couldn't get the two together. I drove Barney mad. I drove myself mad. After that morning of rehearsals when we broke for tea, there was Richard, and there was Frantz, and Barney and myself. I went to the counter and I broke every cup and fucking saucer in The Market Theatre. Then I felt so ashamed. And Haines and Dobrowsky came to me afterwards and they said, 'Thank you for doing that.' I said, 'What do you mean?' And they said, 'It's an unbearable situation we're all in.' Now, this wasn't being disloyal to Barney. We were all floundering because we hadn't found it. I think the fact that I went berserk and broke cups, snapped something and broke the tension, and then things seemed to happen.

But I still could not get the part right. Barney was not happy with me. Barney didn't tell you much. He just sat and scratched his beard. Now I saw this Player King who enters with his troupe of players, and he sees Rosenkrantz and he says, 'Halt'.

And I had this earring. I decided to play him as a sort of big butch bi-sexual, with eye shadow and a beauty spot, here, and this earring. He probably hadn't washed for a week or two, but was proud of himself. At the dress rehearsal Barney came to the dressing room at The Market and gave everybody notes, but not me. I felt terribly hurt. I said, 'Barney, you know, you didn't give me notes.' He said, 'I couldn't give you notes. When you came on I couldn't recognise you, I was overpowered. I was so stunned by your appearance that I just kept looking at you and I can't tell you about your performance. I was totally obsessed with what you looked like, rather than what you were doing.' So I had no notes at the dress rehearsal. Maybe he didn't expect that make-up, but he never made me change it. And of course, opening night, trust Mynhardt... I entered and as I turned, the earring, an enormous curtain ring, flung off and hit a woman in the front row on the voorkop. The day of the opening night I was in the back room and he tried to rehearse me. There was one long speech I couldn't get right for Barney, no matter what I did. Now this is not an indictment of Barney. This is an indictment of me. He was in that room and he'd worked on the speech with me, and I knelt in front of him and cried like a bloody baby. I was just desperate. He was probably very embarrassed. He couldn't cope with me.

You know I always had a loyalty and admiration for Barney and what he's done for theatre. But the youngsters adored Barney. They could understand him. I couldn't. I don't hold back compliments. But I'm called a bitch also. I tell the truth. One day I tackled Barney. I said, 'Do you know, I love you and I respect you.' I said, 'When you see me can't you fucken light up your eyes a little bit and, you know, shake your head and let the dandruff do a snow storm and let us be united in holy matrimony, instead of this fucking deadpan besigheid – jy weet?' Socially, he never looked glad to see me. It was always the deadpan thing. Barney confused me. He was like a maths teacher. He would give me things and say things to me. It didn't help me. And it didn't help him. Maybe in the subconscious it sunk in. And of course, years later, Adrian Steed interviewed me. He said, 'You were so brilliant as the Player King.' I said, 'Why in the shit didn't you tell me in 1978 that I was brilliant? I wanted to commit suicide every night!'

'... I went to the counter and I broke every cup and fucking saucer in The Market Theatre'

Patrick Mynhardt

Part 3.
Workshop

'This is my favourite-ever photograph of South Africa' Barney Simon

Chapter 6. Identity

The focus of this chapter is on Barney Simon's big ensemble workshop plays, "Cincinatti", "Black Dog Inj'emnyama" and "Born in the RSA". We find out how a workshop play was created. "Cincinatti" was based on short-lived multi-racial clubs near The Market Theatre. Actors Bo Petersen and Lesley Nott illustrate how Barney gave them a sense of themselves as South Africans.

When Barney and his actors created "Black Dog Inj'emnyama" they followed the biographies of a black freedom fighter and a white paratrooper. Actors John Ledwaba, Marie Human, Neil McCarthy and Gcina Mhlope describe their very different experiences of creating "Black Dog". Barney had wanted to do a play about solitary confinement. Actors Vanessa Cooke, Thoko Ntshinga, Neil McCarthy, Terry Norton and Fiona Ramsay explore their identity against an apartheid backdrop.

Barney used the image on the opposite page to inspire his actors for "Born in the RSA", he commented:

'This is my favourite-ever photograph of South Africa. Look at the woman's hand behind the boy's heel. That's what I think is part of the passion of South Africa; if it has any kind of passion it's got to do with that. We begin with that knowledge and intimacy, and later it's called not only a crime but also a sin. That's what's mad - the whites, anyway. What I'm trying to do (in "Born in the RSA") is show blacks and whites in a common predicament. Although such is the society that we can never really have a common predicament. We'll always be punished in different ways.'

Quote from The Star, Adrienne Sichel, May 1985.

Previous page overleaf – Sam Williams and Thoko Ntshinga in "Cincinatti".
Photograph by Trevor Matterson, courtesy of Wits Historical Papers.
Opposite – Photograph by David Goldblatt.

Quotations from interviews with Barney Simon

'In starting "Mirror One", I tried to create a reflecting surface in which we'd find an image of ourselves. I would say, when apartheid was reflected in that mirror what else could you write about? In other words, as Brecht says, "Sometimes it's a crime to write a poem about a tree."'

Quote from "Cutting Through the Mountain".

'It's the waste that I was talking about, the terrible waste of human beings who are potentially so valuable... I tried to point to the freedom fighter, to the man, actually a person, not just a shadow or a number or a statistic...'

Quote from The Star Weekend, Garalt MacLiam, March 8, 1986.

'But it was the time, just pre-Rubicon speech, when it seemed Mandela's release was imminent. We didn't know what was happening. And then it was like walking on a beach where a wave came across the beach and began to recede very fast. You had to stand very still otherwise you would have fallen into the water. That was the energy that was around, and so I abandoned the idea of solitary confinement. I had seven actors, and I sent them out and the result was "Born in the RSA".'

Quote from Vrye Weekblad, Charl Blignaut, May 14, 1993.

Opposite – Soweto, June 1976.
Photograph by Bongani Mnguni.

Bo Petersen

'Barney, being a Jewish white man, gave South Africa back to us in a way that could make us feel sorry for ourselves, hate ourselves, love ourselves and laugh at ourselves'

I was actually a go-go dancer at the time, and I used a go-go dancer as my character in "Cincinatti". Barney obviously had something in his head, which I realise now because of how carefully he put us together. We would improvise and he would go away with the tape and come back with a scene. He was fascinated with the go-go dancer. He came to see me dance once and was horrified because it was a brutal place. I would finish dancing and rush to The Market just in time for the half hour call. One evening Barney came in to give us notes. He got very excited that my feet were then actually texturally correct. 'Keep your feet dirty,' he said, 'even if you're not dancing before the show.' And I did. It was an intense period. Rehearsal was six to seven weeks. And then we did our first run-through. Mannie stormed out asking whether Barney wanted to bankrupt The Market. So when we went into our first night we were astonished, because we thought we had rubbish on our hands.

Barney gave you a sense of who you were. I had a huge hang-up, coming from Carltonville, but basically he taught us that everyone has a story. Barney was always there for you as a performer and as a person. He was always interested in the details and textures. That's what made him unusual. He had a big space that normal people could not give, and his sense of humour... He was a wonderful storyteller. I remember him telling things about his hair. He would stick his finger out of the car window before he got out to see which way the wind was blowing because he used to comb his hair over his bald patch. His fear was that that was the way he would die, that he would get chopped on his bald patch by some crazy person.

He gave me a sense of myself, and for me as a young South African actress, it was really important. It really gave me courage to be that, that is who I am. It gave me courage to explore, do many different things in my life, and they are often with Barney in mind. Also the way that I relate to people I have learnt from Barney. Sometimes judgements need to be made, but I think if you make a judgement without really understanding the situation it really cuts you off from a whole life. We are brought up in a society that has forced us to make those judgements, but despite that, a unique country has been created. Barney was witness to that. Barney, being a Jewish white man, gave South Africa back to us in a way that could make us feel sorry for ourselves, hate ourselves, love ourselves and laugh at ourselves. He really gave us back a picture that was not simple. I mean "Joburg, Sis!" – just the title sums that up. I think that is what frees us.

Barney pushed a lot of us into real situations. So people came up with their own stories. What was vital about Barney was the kind of self he instilled in you. If I think of myself at university, my accent was knocked out of me – I had a good South African accent but we were all meant to speak like the Queen. I loved drama school because I never had a sense of me. The 'me' was something I was embarrassed about.

I came from Carltonville. I was ashamed of the fact that my brother was a miner, my parents did not have a big fancy house. In my head I wanted a very middle-class WASP background, and that would make me feel better. We did not travel. I had never been in a restaurant. Socially I was gormless and gauche. I tried to make excuses so that people would not meet my brothers. I was making judgements. Now if I had not met Barney I would probably have spent my whole life apologising. Barney saw something in me that I wasn't aware of. He said that I was important and my life was important. The fact that I had grown up in Carltonville made me unique. No-one had ever said that to me. I now realise all those Carltonville things are worthwhile, and it's what makes me. Barney just gave it back. I was lucky that he was one of the first people I worked with.

Barney performed a vital role in the sense that he presented us with pictures of ourselves. We were in the most awful situation and it felt at times that there was very little hope. It was through theatre that you understood black people and the situation. Throughout the darkest times, Barney's plays were telling what was going on. In terms of what Barney and Mannie were doing, The Market was a very subversive place. They were essential to South Africa and to our psyche. It is inexcusable when people say they did not know. It was there for them to know. Barney gave many actors who came across him a way to work and a sense of self as a South African. He has left us with a fantastic legacy, and I know I am imbued with that. In my work I cannot do anything less than that. I look at others who have been under his wing and I can see the same in them.

'... the process of creating and rehearsing "Cincinatti" was quite fascinating... I remember hunting around Newtown with Sam Williams who played the black night watchman. We were watching faces, eyes, clothes. We watched a group of men pulling a wagon, the different ways in which they were pulling. Some were pulling and some actually weren't. Some were dreaming while they walked... Opening the actors to this fantastic kaleidoscope that surrounds us and getting them to almost wallow in it and begin to find their own emblems as opposed to mine, I think, is... really a celebration of the world that surrounds us. And in as much as possible, I do two things. One is to point out to them the infinity of detail that surrounds us, of fascination, of cause and effect, of decision, of aspiration. And then to find out, help them find out, what matters to them - which are their emblems and what they mean to their lives. It's quite important. It strikes you because it reflects inside you. If you take from outside what you've observed carefully, feed and filter through the emblems of your life, then you can make wonderful things. That's the work I do in creation of text with actors, and in a way,that's what my writing is about...' Barney Simon in "Conversations" - Avril Herber

Lesley Nott

'Someone who saw me'

There were three things that Barney taught me, gave me. The first one was, always stay in the present moment. Secondly, take the line of greatest risk. Don't take the easy way, take the thing that's going to take you to the edge. And thirdly, don't be afraid to fail. That's what I learnt from him, although we never actually articulated it in those words. That's why I loved working with him and why we worked together well.

I found it totally exhilarating that he could come, like when we were doing "Cincinatti", five minutes before a performance and give you three paragraphs and say: 'Learn this and put it in there.' For me that was invigorating. I didn't find it threatening or irresponsible. I loved that way of working. I think about all the productions that I did with him, and other productions of his that I saw, those things were like the cornerstones that he used in his work. Staying in the present moment has to do with not ever commenting on what you are doing. It's about finding out what the essence of that sentence, or that particular word at that moment in time, what the essence of that word is and only allowing that. So you never move ahead of yourself... If you stay in the present moment consistently, the audience has to join you in an experience. You're not telling them what they have to get from you, or what you are, the message that you're intending. In that way there's a kind of broader communal experience, because each person in the audience responds from her own centre to what's happening on the stage, as opposed to you making a comment that you want them to learn. Or giving them a message that you want them to learn. And it is an incredibly risky way of working because you don't have a safety net. But it makes you feel so alive when you're doing it.

He had an extraordinary understanding of a woman's psyche which a lot of men directors don't have. Maybe it was to do with his own ambivalence. Barney's sexuality was a complete mystery to me. He just needed to be a mystery. That's the other thing that I think he liked – mystery. For "East", which we did late at night because we couldn't get the Berkoff rights, we spent a lot of time rehearsing in his house. For that monologue, 'For once I would like to be a feller,' we felt that Sylv's character had to be stripped as far as possible, to make it completely naked. Not in the sense of portraying nakedness, but taking away any kind of performance factor that could enable me to feel safe. I remember going through that speech a number of times. We went through incredibly slowly, and I said each word internally, and then the next one. It took hours to do, but at the end of it I really understood the speech. That was something that I went back to afterwards, and it's a method I use often in the work that I do now. It's a very good way of connecting really strongly with what the speech means, with the whole shape of it as well as the theme involved. On top of that there was this other strange thing – he decided that my breasts were too small and I really needed to have big knockers. So I had to go out and buy this huge bra, and stick lots of socks and stuff inside, and wear this tight black top. And he was absolutely right, because with that kind of strange nakedness of the words, and this person with these

'We did "Brecht on Brecht."
And I don't know why, but it was very controversial'
Lesley Nott

big breasts there must have been an odd kind of disjunction or fracturedness to the character. There's one scene where the character that Marcel was playing and Sylv are discussing making love. I remember our session working on that became completely acrobatic. We had to think of every possible position that you might be able to have sex in. Barney would say, 'Ja no, but now what about if you lifted your leg up there?' It was bizarre. And when we actually did it in the play, it was like a gymnastics performance. He used to go off on these strange tangents.

We did "Brecht on Brecht". And I don't know why but it was very controversial. But that's what I liked about working with Barney. And that's the way I still choose to work. I don't mean it to sound like method acting, because it's not really. It's being prepared to allow a text to access you, and then resonate out. As opposed to imposing your idea on a text and performing it, you allow it to resonate in you and find the places in you, and then you give it back. It's much more personal, because now you allow the words to live through you and your experience. But it's also much more dangerous, because you're putting yourself there every time you do it. You're not putting on a character or a performance. That's the difference also between your focus being on success or on your passion. If you're doing theatre because it's your passion, then you work from a very different centre than if you're concerned about being accepted or not accepted. I often got incredibly conflicting reviews, both from critics and from other people, including friends. But it was okay because I was with Barney and connected with somebody who approached things the same way that I did. Someone who saw me. And I loved him.

The Company

PRESENTS

BRECHT ON BRECHT

an improvisation by George Tabori
adapted and directed by Barney Simon
Music by Kurt Weil
Music directed and arranged by John Oakley Smith
choreography by Bo Petersen
designed by Wilhelm Hahn
lighting design by Mannie Manim

with

Vanessa Cooke
Nomsa Nene
Sophie Mgcina
Lesley Nott
Bo Petersen
Peter Se-Puma
Barrie Shah
Ron Snerczak
Marcel van Heerden
John Oakley Smith

FOR THE COMPANY:
Artistic Director – Barney Simon
Administrative Director – Mannie Manim

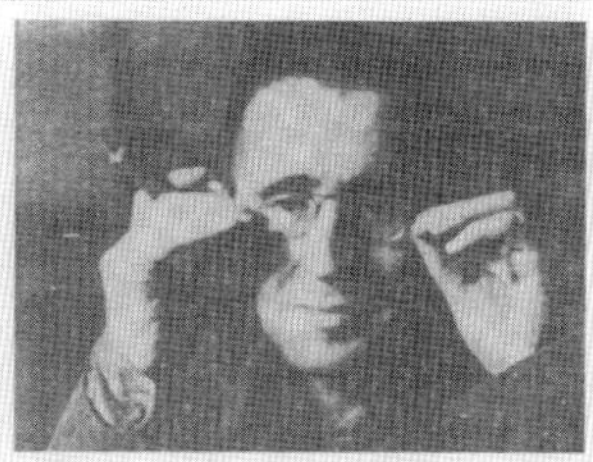

BERTOLT BRECHT

Born in Augsberg, 1898. Died in East Berlin, 1956. Earlier than most of his compatriots – in the early 1920's – Brecht recognised the dangers of Hitlerism. He went from one European country to another and even living in Soviet Russia before he went to the United States in 1941. America also proved a difficult haven for the committed individualist and he decided to return to Europe when caught up in the McCarthy witchhunts of the late 1940's. He finally settled in East Berlin where he created the outstanding Berliner Ensemble Theatre Company together with his wife, Helene Weigel.

BARNEY SIMON

He began his theatrical career working with Athol Fugard in the Dorkay House rehearsal room in 1961.

Is three-time winner of the Breytenbach Epathlon for Best Director. He last won it in 1979 for CINCINATTI-SCENES FROM CITY LIFE, which he scripted with cast.

His productions at the Market include THE SEAGULL, MARAT/SADE, THE SACRIFICE OF KRELI, LUV, MOTHER COURAGE, PEOPLE ARE LIVING THERE, VROUE VAN TROJE, THE DEATH OF BESSIE SMITH, LONG DAYS JOURNEY INTO NIGHT, ROSENCRANTZ AND GUILDENSTERN ARE DEAD, PLAY IT AGAIN, SAM, CALL ME WOMAN, Sam Shepard's SAVAGE LOVE, and COLD STONE JUG.

Programme for "Brecht on Brecht", 1981.

John Ledwaba

'Check, a person is not just a bunch of flesh walking'

I met Barney in the late '70s. He came to see our show, Matsemela Manaka's "Egoli – City of Gold" and we went out on a Saturday jol. We started talking. He asked what we were doing? How we see ourselves in relation to the situation? What was our sense of the future? Then, ja, we struck a relationship. After that I had to work with him on "Black Dog". He also assisted us with "Township Boy". The last production with him was "Jozi Jozi". Ja, he was a fun character. He would go into a jol and encourage you to have fun. Meanwhile he gets you to do what he wants you to do. You know, he'd ask you to come over to his place and you'd start working with him. Twelve o'clock at night – you're still working. The man had passion for work. You see, Barney tried very hard to help whomever he worked with, the actors, to find the central point of the story that he wanted to tell. You had to just look into yourself and find the real core of the information that we were working on. If we didn't have the information he would send you out on the streets. 'Go and find similar people, with a similar problem, and find out about them, their biographies, what they're all about.'

Did you talk about '76?

I was still at school in '76. We met with the police, and firing took place, and the whole situation turned into a real mess. The '76 students were highly influenced by the Black Consciousness Movement, and so was I. You know the Steve Biko philosophy of 'Black man, you are on your own', and the 'I'm black and proud' outlook. This came about because black people needed a combat outlook to counter the system. But by 1984, I had developed politically, even if I was still very angry. And so the coming together of the "Black Dog" cast was to me not a black and white occasion, even if the stakes at that time were high. But work like that enabled me to discover other people. To realise that they also bled, that they also have been affected by the situation. Because of the division of society, one might end up believing that it was only young people in Soweto who were suffering. South Africa was so divided that it was difficult for me to know about people who are in Noordgesig while I'm in Diepkloof. So that gave me the chance to know about other people – people who might want to love their country, but apartheid was saying 'No!' So it was educational, but it also created an element of youthful comradeship. Before that I saw white people as white people, on the side of the oppressor. We, black people, were receiving it, period.

So how did you feel when you first met this old white man and he was asking you about your life?

There was something special about Barney. How he would make you unlock your stereotypes and then you would come out. He did this by insisting on first being able

Opposite – John Ledwaba, publicity for the play "Black Dog Inj'emnyama".
Photographs by Ruphin Coudyzer.

to tell the truth to yourself. Write it inside. Tell yourself it's correct before you can tell it to somebody else. And don't try and tint your life with glorious things. He would insist that you become as brutal as possible with yourself, which is the highest thing anybody can ask you. But in a workshop you have to deal with that. I found that after you have told your piece you find a great relief. You discover that you have let loose on certain things that have been inside you and they are gone, which was good. He did that with all of us. So even when he came to help with my musical, "Township Boy", we basically concentrated on the same effort.

There was an interview Barney gave after "Black Dog". He said there were riots after "Black Dog". And he said it wasn't surprising because of the things that people were dealing with. Were you surprised?

No, I was not surprised that there were riots after "Black Dog". It was just painful because it was about people you knew. I suppose it is in dealing with the pain that one can contend with reality. We actually need a group in South Africa, a group of therapists who go and treat people's emotions, continue doing work like we did before. Work like "Black Dog", but that relates to now. We still need a lot of material in that direction. The material need not necessarily address the violence, but it would address the new order. How do people come to terms with who they are? The young boy who has burned somebody, and here he is assigned to be a responsible grown up, but the tortured image of him burning someone is still with him. He is afraid maybe to even talk to anybody. He keeps it to himself. It chows him day in and day out.

A lot of people, especially young people of that time, are still suffering from the impact of what they saw. They did things that were out of this world, and need to reconcile, to heal. Now they say, 'Ag, it's all over now'. But as individuals it comes back to them. It's all over when you're together, but when you are alone in your own little corner it

African National Congress supporting resident takes body parts from the burning body of an abducted Inkatha Freedom Party female leader, for muti or traditional medicine, Tokoza May 24, 1993.
Photograph by Greg Marinovich / South Photos.

comes back. It can't be all over unless you deal with it, unless you get some distance. You get some help. If you don't get that, it will stay with you. You don't just burn a person with a tyre and become nice.

Barney was gifted in knowing how to talk with people coming from different positions. He wanted to communicate with people and be understood. He would sit for hours talking to you, trying to get himself understood and to understand you. That's why he could give artists the courage to go outside and find stories from strangers, from people they hardly knew. For you to be able to do that, you need to have this 'people-ness' attitude, because people in the street have nothing to do with The Market Theatre. If you don't have a way of approaching them they won't talk to you.

He had a special interest and love for people as individuals with their stories. You know, the way people's faces are shaped. You would be sitting with Barney having tea, a character would walk in and he'd say, 'Oh John, check, check, look at that guy, look at the features, look at his face, his eyes. What do you think his story could be? What do you think is the information he has behind him? Who is this man, where does he come from?' Sometimes those fantasies, those exercises wouldn't make sense, but he'd make you engage in that direction. Especially me, because he knew I have this fancy of wanting to write, so he used to play such games with me, that 'Check! A person is not just a bunch of flesh walking'. The face tells the story. The eyes, the demeanour. The character is the way they carry themselves. I found that it also gives you a discipline, a respect for human beings. The exercise of fantasising. Who could this person be? Where does he come from? Who is his wife, his relative, his brother? What is the most serious thing that has ever happened to him? How does he react to it? Is he angry about it? It gave me a sense of interest in people. I ceased taking people for granted. You look at a person, you ask yourself a lot of questions. I never heard Barney getting into rhetorical political discussions. He was interested in human beings, in life, life above or beyond politics. He wanted to know the human inside of that. That's what I liked about him.

So when he first met you and asked how you feel about the future and where you're going, and even about '76, wasn't that politics?

Barney was not into giving a political analysis of things. He would find solutions through telling stories. For instance we'd come from the situation of black consciousness after '76, and we were angry. Barney wouldn't make you feel that black consciousness hasn't a place. He'd say, 'No, you're fine. But within your belief, within whatever you are understanding, understand the bigger picture of humanity too.' Barney wouldn't really delve into stuff like black consciousness. He would never try and influence anyone's political outlook. He'd rather let the information, the situation, whatever you're working on, influence your decision. But not he himself influencing you. He'd give people a chance to evolve. And I like him a lot for that.

So you were in the black consciousness phase when you met him?

When I did "Black Dog" I was still coming out of it. You must also understand '76 when it erupted, young people were highly influenced by black consciousness. And the situation was that the apartheid system did look like it was succeeding. Jimmy Kruger

(Minister of Justice and Police) on hearing about Steve Biko's death said, 'It leaves me cold'. Those were the cold-hearted kind of chaps we were dealing with. It was very, very tough. But I liked Barney from the way he worked. And to me he will always represent the complete human being who was there for other people. You know, he really didn't place a lot of importance on himself.

What do you think he left you with?

He took out the idea that theatre is a political mouth-piece or an entertainment for theatre's sake. He said to me, 'At the centre of theatre is an individual, and that individual might be an actor, but he's also a human being. His job is to be there on stage and tell a story.' Do we take the stage as some holy kind of place where human stories have to be told? Maybe not everybody does that. But Barney believed in that. He believed that the stage is a temple. Once you hit that place you take responsibility. You're telling somebody a story, but with responsibility. He used to say things like: 'You are directly responsible, so own the story. If that person laughed at the show, if it has advanced his life, his human spirit, you are responsible for it.' And if it had taken him down, you are still responsible for it. So, as an actor, when you go on stage you must walk onto that space with a serious sense of responsibility. It's not the place just to go and play, you know.

So if you had to compare him with other directors what would you say?

I would say he was in the league of guys like Peter Brook, even the legendary Brecht. His influence has gone beyond the frontiers of Africa. It influenced European societies, American societies. He was a specialist of human conflict. And people like that don't just get born every day.

So do you think he was born with this gift?

I like to think so. Look at what he did. I saw "Woza Albert!" before Barney worked on it. It had no discipline of thought, it was just a lot of sketches. Barney put flesh to the bones that was "Woza". He gave structure to "Woza", he made it a walking human being. Barney explored so much in theatre. He didn't only explore technique. He had his own technique. He had a way of designing stories. People's combined biographies give you an idea of the whole world. He was almost like a surgeon when he was dealing with a piece of work. He would carefully work through the material that you're working on until this material gains shape and form. He was a master of his craft.

So what was his technique?

I think Barney's technique was that he didn't want style. He wanted the actor to own whatever material he dealt with, almost like tongue to saliva. Then he'd come through from the inside. So if you're a stylistic actor, you wouldn't come right with Barney. You would have a problem, because he'd wear you out, he'd tear you down until he reached your vulnerable point as an actor, and say: 'That's the part I wanted, give me that, your vulnerable self.' He would talk about a lot of things. He said, 'When you work you must be able to create a little distance between yourself and the theme that you're working with.' And he made an example like this: 'If you bring your

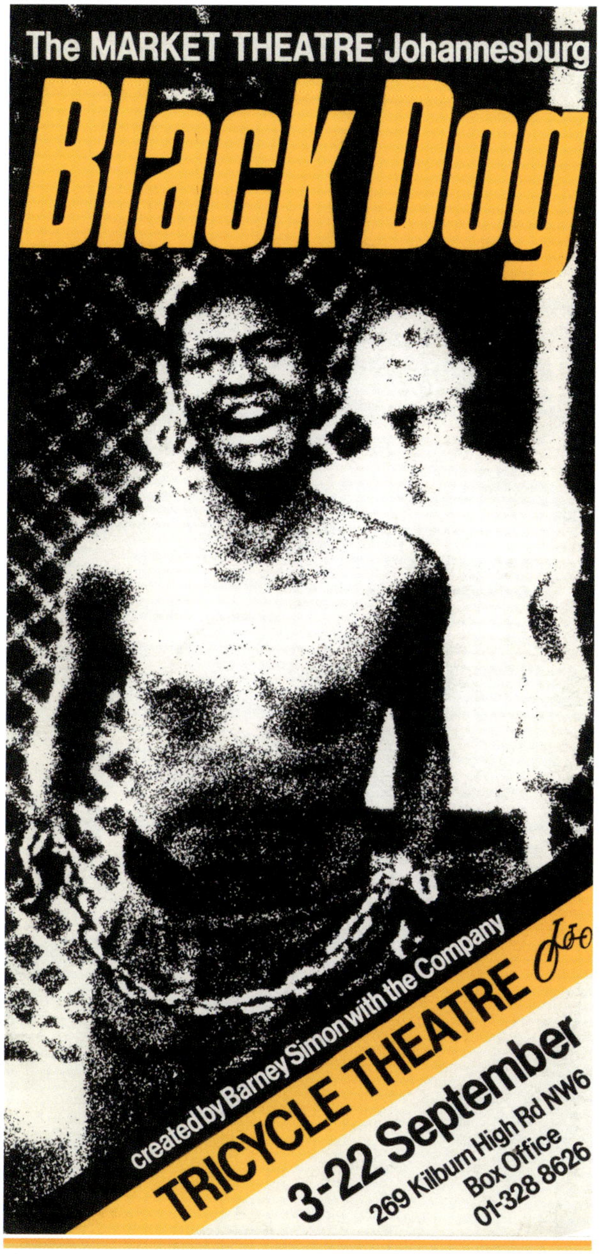

"Black Dog – Inj'emnyama" at the Tricycle Theatre, London.

hand close-up to your eyes, you cannot see it.' But when you hold your hand further away you're able to focus. You're able to see your hand and you know what to do. Simple children's stuff, but important. He said a lot of people, especially some of my contemporaries, when they work they are so passionate about their work, but they work from here [holding hand in front of his face]. So the problem is once you are here, you won't be able to address the work you're dealing with.

You talk about how Barney loved humanity. What if you don't love humanity?

It's almost like if you go to church for the first time and you find this one who has really got it. He will make you fall in love with religion. I think the influence from Barney was also coming from that direction. You never brushed shoulders with him without it making an impact. You wouldn't just bump into Barney without something brushing off.

'I don't think it was coincidence that "Inj'emnyama" was followed by riots. We didn't cause them but merely smelled them coming. It's there in the tone of the play, and I think that's an extraordinary indication of theatre as a sensor'

John Ledwaba

Marie Human

'I prayed a lot at some point in my life that Russia must just vanish'

I went to Afrikaans schools, an Afrikaans university and Afrikaans theatre companies. So I was living in a very closed Afrikaner world, and ja, it was very protected. At Bloemfontein University, where I studied, we had Afrikaans textbooks and we weren't really encouraged to read wider. Somebody once mentioned Sartre to me and I went and read Sartre in English. That formed a whole life philosophy for me, just by being opened, somebody telling me there's another world out there. The little bit that I got stimulated me a lot.

I used my experiences from the Angolan border in Barney's play "Black Dog Inj'emnyama". I worked for SWAPAC (South West African Performing Arts Council). We toured as a theatre group all over Namibia into the Kalahari, to places like Aranos or Kois. In the Kalahari there are villages with a population of eight hundred people and we had to perform in the school hostels. We tied dining room tables together to make a stage. The audiences were mostly farmers. It was all Afrikaans, Boer. They would drive two hundred kilometres from their farms to the nearest town to come see the play. We did French farces translated into Afrikaans. Like "Boeing Boeing". You know, where the one door goes out and the other goes in. And then we also did shows for the boys on the Border. This was 1979 and 1980, the Angolan war was heavy then. We would travel by ourselves up to Etosha Pan, the army would meet us, and then we would travel up to Oshakati and to Rundu in convoy.

I came from a history where all the boys went to the Border. Where mothers sent their children to the Border. I've got three brothers. They all went. And it was a thing to be proud of. To protect your country. I never gave it a lot of thought. But going to the Border, actually going to the places and dealing with the soldiers, I sensed that it was something terrible. You know, they had too much energy. You could basically read it in their eyes – the madness in the eyes. We were right on the Border. We heard the mortars. A thing that shocked me a lot was how many people died not in combat. Because we never heard how many guys died shot by the enemy. It worried me how many Casspir accidents there were. How many guys shot their own friends. Just wildness. The other thing was the arrogance of the civilians in those towns. They were too relaxed. You know, like 'Aha, that's nothing, let's braai, let's enjoy ourselves.' And they kept on talking about the beauty of the place, but it wasn't to me. It was just this road and basically a camp where people lived, with high wires around it with watchtowers on the corners. That was their town.

So we're sitting, I think it was in Oshakati, and we've got to wait for a convoy, at an army gate. I suppose we were six actors in a kombi, and we had to wait, wait, wait, and we're watching the army guys. And then I saw a road roller, those big things that they compress the tar with, coming very slowly. And there is this donkey. I saw the donkey is going to walk in front of this roller. Okay, so the roller is going to stop and then the donkey will pass. The roller didn't stop – it just went over that donkey.

Opposite – Dusty road in the arid landscape of the Richtersveld, Northern Cape.
Photograph by Paul Weinberg / South Photos.

That freaked me because that was what was happening there. Then later on while we were sitting there, this army truck came past with guys saying, 'Do you want to see terrorists?' And they lifted the canvas off the back of the truck, and there were corpses. Just red blood and black skin – I used that in the play. Or Barney used that. The enemy was black. What I mentioned in "Black Dog" is that as a little child I prayed a lot. I was very religious and I liked the idea of having this friend that I can't see. I was very open. I prayed a lot at some point in my life that Russia must just vanish. It was such a threat to me when I was very young. But now the enemy was black. Just the enemy was black. I can't remember that I ever connected the war to communism – the threat was 'die swart gevaar'.

Tell us about your audition for "Black Dog"?
Barney phoned. He said he's thinking of using me in a part and would I audition for him? I did one audition and he was not happy with what I did. I can't remember whether I read or improvised. Then he phoned again and said, would I come in for another audition? And again he said no. He phoned me for a third audition. I just byt vas. He pushed me to a point where I must have done a brilliant audition, because right after the audition he said, 'You've got the part.'

Then we started rehearsing. There were no scripts. We were a cast of black people, white people and a coloured person. I believe Barney wanted to say something about compassion. It was a time of revolution and war. We did all these army exercises, marching and things like that for a few days. We improvised jumping out of a plane. I couldn't understand how this could become a play. Then Barney sent us out into the streets to observe. We came back, told the group what we saw and experienced just being out in the streets. We created our own characters from our own knowledge – the way we see the world – and innocence – so that, perhaps, the theatre would mirror life closest to the truth. Barney did this simple improvisation exercise with us. You sit on the grass, you look at it, the closer you look, the more you see. With your nose in the grass you can see a whole life happening inside the lawn and, you can smell it.

Through the work I slowly started realising the reality of the political situation during the early '80s in full. That protected society I grew up in... I'd always had a sense that all people have compassion for one another because of our common humanity. I could take this for granted. Actually I came from a society which had no compassion but for their own – that is evil. You know that was a big discovery.

I don't know how Barney coped with that. All I know is that he gave me time to speak. He made people listen to me. He was very soft. And that made me very honest. I never tried to be liberal. I never tried to be on their side, to be like them. I've always stayed true to what I know, and he helped me do that, in his embracing sort of way. I can remember thinking: 'Wow! This is nice.' Because sometimes I wanted to say something and I couldn't wait to say it. I would say it, just to him. He could listen to two people at once. I would just say it, directly to him, and he would still be listening to somebody else, and recognise what I said.

One of the older black actors once said to me, when we were in London, 'Marie, you cannot take the Boer out of you.' He said, 'You cannot do that. Just listen to the way you say "John" when you speak to an African.' It was a lot about soul-searching. I suppose workshop theatre, especially in the '70s and '80s, had to do that. Well, I sure did a lot of that. One of the black actresses and myself sat here on the stoep at the rehearsal room. She had this girl-talk with me about, 'I hated you but now I see I can like you.' I didn't see it as a political thing. I saw it as personal. It must have meant a lot to me. I always remember that. What we discovered in the play is that we do not talk and we do not communicate and we're not in contact with one another in this country. And if there's no contact there's no hope. We wrote that. Apart from growing as a person I was growing tremendously as an actress. We first wrote my part as a very urban Afrikaans girl. Rita was my character's name. In the suburbs we used to throw eggs at black people passing on their bicycles, even old men. My brothers did it. All children, all white children did those kinds of things, playing tricks on black people. We were kind of allowed to do that! That was my character.

During our first preview I came in on the wrong cue and cut out half the play. Afterwards I felt terrible. Barney told me about double injuries. If you've injured yourself don't judge yourself, you will just injure yourself again. And then he said, 'Come, we're going to re-work your character.' That's when we started getting to the broader things, that night. It was again the whole process. Finding stories. The next morning my character was re-written for the second preview. And somehow, through all the soul searching and personal discoveries, my character became someone I myself never was, but a fictional character like in any other play. People always thought that Barney just made you be yourself on stage, but it was more about working with yourself to find the humanity of your character. So you can have empathy with any character.

The process of "Outers" was different from "Black Dog" because one of the actors came with a play, a written thing. Barney decided to workshop around it. So we had definite characters. The part in "Outers" was also a very young girl. It was one of those girls that come from nowhere into this nowhere life. She was a prostitute, a down-and-out streetwalker. When I worked on "Outers" I fought Barney a lot. That was the progression of working with Barney. He digs and he digs and you get a feeling of, 'Am I ever going to get anywhere this man wants me to go?' Ah, but once you got there, you were making pure theatre. It was such a pleasure and a privilege as an actor to work with a director like Barney Simon.

'Through the work I slowly started realising the reality of the political situation during the early eighties in full'

Marie Human

Overleaf – Marie Human and Neil McCarthy in "Black Dog Inj'emnyama", April 1984.
Photograph by Ruphin Coudyzer.

Neil McCarthy

'We've got to be able to find what is fresh and magical in whatever circumstances we find ourselves'

My background was so different from Barney's background. The world I came from was so comfortable, complete. And yet I'm not very comfortable and complete. And I think that that was quite intriguing to Barney. And that things always have come pretty easily to me. That I can come up with effective things very easily, but that there is something more that I'm sometimes unaware of: I could come up with something that's more than just effective. But I think that there's something in me that does allow me to be lazy and be quite mediocre, but there's a possibility of moving beyond that. Barney took me to see "Woza Albert!", which was running at the Baxter. It was an incredible experience. I found the play so deeply moving.

Why?

Well, because I think it was so uncompromising in the way that it reflected the pain and the confusion of being here, but at the same time it was so joyous and so incredibly celebratory. And I found that combination just irresistible. It resonated so much with what I'd always felt about being here, and what I'd aspired to reflect in the work that I'd made at that stage. I felt enormously moved to be sitting with him. You know, he'd gone out of his way to bring me along. That was always what was amazing about Barney. I saw it happen many times in the years to come, that he'd just sort of latch on to some sort of energy that he'd feel from somebody. It didn't matter that they came from an entirely different world, decades younger than himself – he'd sort of hurl in on this person and just feed into them.

So, you felt that's what he did to you?

Very consciously. And then a year or two later when I came up to Jo'burg I made contact with him again. I directed "National Madness", which was James Whyle's play about conscription. Barney came to see it. I also had a kind of secondary role in it. There was one scene where James got fucked up by a vicious corporal in the army. I just had to stand aside and watch this happening. And Barney said for a moment he realised that I was an actor, you know, a real actor, when he watched me watching this assault, and there was a kind of relish. I always used to say to him that was probably me as a director, because I was watching with anxious involvement, trying to make sure that this was happening in the way that it should. And he said, 'No, no, no... I can see your understanding of the ambiguity of that moment, the way that when you see violence, it is not revulsion pure and simple – there is actually this part of you that really enjoys it.' So then he asked me to get involved in this process that became "Black Dog".

Tell us about that?

"Black Dog" started as poor old Brendan Butler's play. Brendan was at varsity with me, and he was the sort of leading light of the English faculty at UCT. But what was always curious about him was that he'd been a parabat in the army, and he wasn't terribly ashamed of that fact. In the early '70s at varsity, you had to be ashamed of the fact, you had to kind of run it down and talk about the trauma. Brendan refused to do any of this. You had to also be a Marxist, and he became a Marxist, or he pretended to be a Marxist. But he would always say what an incredible experience it had been. He'd been into Angola. But he was a well brought up boy. He'd been to a good private school, and he was very sharp. He was an incredibly good academic. And then he wrote this play about being a parabat that, I think, won an Amstel Award, or it certainly got some kind of recognition. And Barney had read the play and met with Brendan and said he'd like to do something with the play. Brendan being a little naive in his understanding of what Barney was about, sort of thought that this meant that Barney was going to do his play. But actually, what Barney would always say – after the whole thing had been shot down in flames and Brendan had a nervous breakdown – was that he was never really interested in Brendan's play, he was only interested in Brendan, because Brendan was a fascinating sort of ambiguous character. So he'd had long talks with Brendan. But the play didn't last longer than about three days in rehearsal.

He actually rehearsed it?

I remember reading through Brendan's play, but we never got much further than that. And we were all a bit perplexed because by then we all kind of knew what Barney's work was about, and this wasn't really a Barney type of play.

Why did he choose the cast?

I think he chose them because they were interesting people. And I think he pretty much knew from the start that this is what he was going to do, to use the play as some sort of springboard. But he wasn't quite sure how much of the play he was going to use, or how important Brendan was going to be to the process. Maybe Brendan would write alongside him. But as soon as Barney started, Brendan became aware of the scale of the kind of renovation that Barney was proposing for his play. He became increasingly furious. Barney would hold his ground and say, 'You don't understand, this is the process, and I feel that something really good will come out of it'. And Brendan sort of said, 'Fuck that' and left after the first week. He felt betrayed and discredited, foolish. And all that remained of Brendan's play was the character that I ended up playing in "Black Dog", which became Raymond.

I think Barney found the germ of the play was the ambiguity of a sensitive boy going into the army and having to do terrible things. And the effect that it has on his personality and the way that he accommodates those contradictions. And the effect, the kind of ruin that he can create in other people's lives without even being vaguely aware of it. Having to block it out, but not being fully aware of it. If you were fully aware of it you'd go mad. So the necessity of screening the horror, the true horror. And then there was a seminal time when John Ledwaba spoke about his experiences in 1976, and mentioned this character that had led the school, the kids, at the forefront of their march, the initial march. It was very compelling. He got very emotional recording this, the whole incident. That was the turning point for Barney. He realised that there was a lot more that was happening here, and these things were too valuable to just be ignored. We had to incorporate that. It was enormously important as a kind of counterweight to the white story. That then became the core of the play, the opening speech of the play, that story, what happened to that guy, the leader, "Black Dog", who started out swinging his chain above the marching school kids of June 16th. That was John's story.

SONG: "Inj'emnyama! The Black Dog"

During '76, we children also had our own helicopter. Inj'emnyama! The black dog. We had many leaders and he was one of them. The song "Inj'emnyama" was his song and we sang it with him. He was our leader.

He was there when the police came with their guns and hippos. He was there when Hector Peterson was shot dead. He was there when we screamed and cried. He taught us to have courage. He taught us to find our own weapons, dustbin lids, stones and bottles.

I remember when he came to our school. It was on June 16, 1976. We were all sitting in our classrooms waiting. We knew something was going to happen but we didn't know exactly what. And then we heard the voices of mnany children singing outside. The voices came nearer and nearer.

SONG: "Sizobadubula Ngombayimbayi"

We all ran to the windows and teachers tried to chase us back to our desks, but we ignored them and shouted 'Bayesa! Bayesa! They're coming! Bayesa! Soon their head was Madoda Dhlamini, Inj'emnyama. He swung the chain over his head and everybody had to duck. He shouted 'Amandla! Awethu!' He said: 'Fellow students, we would like to apologise for being so late. Things have already started. The protest is on. As you all know there's been a boycott of classes. Do you know why? Crowd? Yes! Because we want to have a say in what we learn... Do you want to learn maths in Afrikaans? No! Do you want to learn Science in Afrikaans? No! So this is what is happening today. The Soweto Students Council have organised a protest march to Orlando Stadium where we will meet. Please! Please! Try to be strong. There's been some trouble on our way. And in Orlando West some people have been killed. So when you see the police come don't throw stones, don't do anything. Just sing, and if they charge at us, we will all sit down and shout peace. Do you understand? Crowd? Yes!'

Soon we were in the streets.

'Kubi Kubi yoo!'

'Siyaya!'

People ran out of their homes. Women left their polishing and washing and joined the march. Private cars, police and soldiers moved with us in helicopters, motorbikes, hippos and vans. Hai man!

John's character always sort of straddled an easy divide between being the commentator on that story, and being that man who ultimately was harassed by the police and then went into exile, and was killed in Lesotho during the raid. I can't remember whether we discovered that that was actually what happened to him, or whether we constructed that as his history. But that then became the kind of core structure, the story of the white crack army boy, and the story of this black guy. The white boy bursts into his room and kills him in Lesotho, and the effect that that has on black life, and the effect that that has on white life. And the tragedy of the destruction in both areas. It became a very, very delicate story. It was, in a sense a lot more narrative than "Born in the RSA" was, because there was that central thread and the other characters sort of clung onto one or other of those stories. We decided that Brendan's play had really nothing to do with the process. Barney would work individually with each actor. And to varying degrees dictate pretty much what their story would become. It was a curious process because there would be a lot of empty space, certainly for an actor.

Where did you start?
In the first week Barney was saying, 'Does everybody remember where they were on June 16th 1976?' and we all from our personal perspective would say where we were.

Where were you?
I was in Rome. And I couldn't speak a word of Italian. I just remember seeing the newspaper and getting such a shock, because I could see that these were South African policemen on the front page of a Roman newspaper, and I couldn't understand that. It was only quite a few days later that I heard what had happened. I remember at the improvisation thinking, 'Ag you know, '76 is a little bit passé, it's '84 now.' '76 created enormous ripples and it was already part of a national culture of resistance. But at the time to me it didn't feel very contemporary.

I thought it was amazing that there was this cast of people from such different backgrounds. That felt incredibly exciting and very important at the time. Doing what we were doing, and getting on in some fashion. I remember one night taking Gcina back to a women's hostel in Alex where she was staying. And that being such a rebel action for me. I'd never gone into Alex before. Such a confrontation with the real difference between us. We all go on as artists, but if you saw how she lived in this four storey, incredibly overcrowded, grubby building in Alexandra township... That was a shock.

Then Barney got us all to write. It was another seminal moment between us. We'd have our one meeting with Barney, and then he'd ask us to go off and create. I would go off and write, just long, long speeches, developing intricate versions of one's background and past lives and things. After a couple of days Barney said to me, 'I think you're writing too much, I think you're pushing ahead too fast. You have to pull back.' I shouldn't try to write finished productions, speeches that I could do. Some I wrote did last and stayed within the piece.

What was the relationship between your character and the play?
It evolved. The focus was not on me, it was on my character. I think the same could

be said for everybody. Barney would come in and say, 'I've decided that so-and-so is actually John's sister.' And you'd go, 'Oh okay, all right.' But it felt like, 'Ag well, you know, that's John – why are you talking about that? I want to talk about me.' He'd slowly make little connections. It was quite far on into the process that he decided Marie and I were going to become lovers. I thought it would be five stories of people witnessing the same events as we'd started out with. I didn't understand for a while the way that Barney had conceived of the stories all tying in together, and creating one story. When we did "Born in the RSA" I was much clearer about where we were headed.

When you opened in Johannesburg with "Black Dog", how was it received?
It was surprisingly well received. I hadn't anticipated the kind of response that we got. We used to get standing ovations, which in Jo'burg was amazing. And there was a real sense of to what degree this information was surprising to people. It came as a surprise to me that so many people who came to see the show found this shocking and new, that they didn't understand the black reality, or the black experience, or the kind of emotional story behind '76, its ramifications. Likewise for a black audience, the thought of the white oppressor also having a painful history was an incredible eye opener.

There was this whole subliminal message that "Black Dog" and "Born in the RSA" projected, merely by the fact that all these actors were sitting on stage together. There was a kind of Brechtian device, I suppose. We'd all join together and play a little part in whatever group scenes there were. And we'd all sing the songs. The song at the end of "Black Dog" was this song of mourning. But everybody joined in, and the mourning became as much about the fact that my character was on a fence, completely raging out of his mind, as the fact that the "Black Dog" character had been killed. There were always these currents of meaning that crisscrossed each other. I never felt that there was a danger of me being victimised or alienating the audience. It was a challenge and, in those kind of confessional monologues that that piece consisted of, one had to speak to the audience as if you knew they would understand, they were confidants. And I think that that was also the liberating aspect of the pieces, that audiences were asked to make this imaginative jump every time a different character spoke to them. They were being rocketed, sort of dumped into a different world, because the character just assumed that they were there with him.

Barney was always very aware of the danger of one standing in judgement of the characters. And I think it particularly applied to whether you were playing the white character, though it wasn't exclusively a white problem. There was a temptation to make it clear to an audience that, 'This isn't me, this is a terrible person.' But that was the kind of risk that one had to take. That was how the piece functioned. It actually became quite comforting not to have to make any comment on it, but just to be in it. I think I was responding initially from a politically correct view, that if we were going to create something really novel, it should be about now. I started to understand the real emotional impact of the piece, that it was really profound. A lot of that impact was due to the fact that '76 had entered the collective South African psyche as a defining moment, there was a sense of things never being the same again. So it became important and right what we'd chosen.

On tour how did Barney keep it alive and together?

Barney never stopped working. And it would sometimes be infuriating. You'd get to another venue and he'd want to have another rehearsal, talk about changing that inflection. I remember sometimes really having to contain my irritation. I thought, 'Is this really going to make a real difference to the piece?' But he would never back off, and he would never entirely trust a good performance without himself being there regularly.

Tell us about your relationship with him as a writer?

My writing is not very similar to Barney's. It wasn't, certainly, in those days. I was preoccupied with satire and kind of larger-than-life characters. He was able to plug into that world, bring in his own sense of humour to my pieces. It always had to do with finding the quirky detail that would bring something to life. For a lot of people the process was too invasive, the way that Barney would intervene in other people's work. It just became too... obliterating because there is a certain kind of hubris in writing anyway. It became his work and not theirs. And there was, there certainly was, a temptation, in the early days when we first started working on my plays together, to feel that. But I think, through the "Black Dog" process, that I did understand that there was always something incredibly special at work with him. And that even though it might feel like a compromise at the time, when one looked back afterwards, it wasn't a compromise, it was just an augmenting of a vision. And it was an incredible learning experience for me. I feel now, in my writing, that Barney's legacy has come home.

Tell us about "Born in the RSA".

"Born in the RSA". You know, the process was certainly hugely influenced by what we'd done with "Black Dog". With "Born in the RSA", when we started out he asked us what kind of characters we found interesting. There was a certain amount of that trudging around the streets of Johannesburg, looking at people and coming back and reporting on who you found intriguing. And then for myself I remember saying, either a campus informer, or there was a neighbour who lived opposite me. I was intrigued by either somebody who was involved, from that angle, or somebody who was totally uninvolved. I remember talking about a man I'd watched mowing the lawn in the house opposite mine. Just fantasising about what his life was about, and the degree to which the world around him didn't seem to impact on his life at all. He also found that interesting, but I was kind of seized with a horror of going back into that world. So I went with the campus outjie. I went to the police, to John Vorster Square, and applied for a job there. It was a little terrifying. In fact I never got as far as applying for a job, because all I did was sit in the waiting room and talk to the other people who were applying for jobs. And there was this chap, he was a policeman from '76, and he'd left the police force because he thought they were getting too soft, and had become a traffic policeman. Now, he'd thought, he was going to come back into the police. I had to consciously roughen up my accent, because I thought everyone would see through me as this softly spoken boy from Cape Town.

Opposite – Neil McCarthy in "Born in the RSA", September 1985.
Photograph by Ruphin Coudyzer.

'I suppose my fascination was, how do you live in the kind of double world where you're pretending, your entire life is around something that you are not'
Neil McCarthy

A TEEK

Why did the police spy fascinate you?

I suppose my fascination was, how do you live in the kind of double world where you're pretending, your entire life is around something that you are not? That the real centre of who you are is expressed in a few moments outside of this whole fictitious world that you've created, and how is it possible to do that? I suppose the discovery for me was how much it was about vanity, and about the thrill, the incredible excitement of fooling people, being an actor in your life, convincing people that you were something that you weren't... and the lack of imagination that had to go along with it. The fact that one had to be a sort of thick person. So that was the breakthrough for me. It was a rather horrible discovery that there were parts of myself that were capable of that.

It used to astonish me that people had such a profound reaction to it. They found me so unlikeable. I was totally inside the role and it often used to come to me as a shock when people afterwards would say, 'How could you? How can you play that kind of character?' Years later I remember going with Barney to visit Joe Slovo at his house in Observatory. We'd been sitting there for a while when Barney said, 'But you remember Neil because he played the police informer in "Born in the RSA".' Joe just looked at me and said, 'I was trying to work out why I hated you so much.'

I spoke to a few lawyers at the time, people like Fink Haysom, and Charles Nupen, because they'd all been involved in student politics at the time of those big spies like Craig Williamson. And Craig Williamson's story was uppermost in my mind when I was creating the character. In fact I was convinced that Craig was in the audience at our first preview.

The second State of Emergency was declared while we were rehearsing. So that became quite crucial. I remember talking a lot about how bleak things appeared then. How sort of uncrushable the apartheid state seemed to be, and how much violence and oppression there was around. And when the book of the plays came out, reading the plays again was such a reminder of the mood of the time, which is, I think, quite easily forgotten. You know, what we all want to forget probably, is just how obscene the level of oppression was, and how much despondency there was about this ever being resolved without rivers of blood, which I think was what Timmy Kwebulana's character became about. Barney put us in touch with this sort of 'amazingness' of the concept that all this had happened to black people yet they didn't rebel. Ja, they didn't crush skulls in the street. And that's really what was behind Timmy's character.

Can you remember a moment as a performer?

It was the moment when Vanessa had to explore the inside of her mouth with my finger. Maybe I was exploring the inside of her mouth with my finger, I can't remember. But we would always, both of us would say, 'Oh no...' Barney would go, 'Oh no, no, no! You've got to take longer, because it's the way that the finger approaches the mouth, it's the quality of the way that you receive that exploration.' We'd get to New York and you'd think you'd done the finger moment by now, but he'd say, 'I'd just like to look at that finger moment again.' And Vanessa and I would just go, 'Aargh!' because we'd been pulling back from the finger moment, and now we needed to be brave with it again.

Opposite – 11 June 1986, Police patrol outside Khotso House, where the UDF (United Democratic Front) held a public meeting. The following day the ruling apartheid government declared a National State of Emergency. Photograph by Anna Zieminski / iAfrika Photos.

How did the processes of "Black Dog" and "Born in the RSA" compare?

I think in "Black Dog" Barney had to do a lot more work himself. There were characters that he pretty much constructed entirely from the ground up. In "RSA", I seem to remember the process being a lot more communal. There wasn't so much of that separating off and then putting people together. It was a lot of verbal improvisation. I suppose what we would call brainstorming now.

Barney would arrive in the morning after some sort of brainstorm that he'd had in the night, and say, 'I've got a great idea – she smokes dagga.' Often it sounded like tiny little things, but it became very important because it was all about textures and the language of the nation. The reason we'd had this set plastered with newspapers and headlines was because he was very preoccupied with what was going on. There were these shadowy explosions and violence in various places, and a sense of half-reported things. I think to a large measure, the success of "RSA", certainly in Jo'burg, was due to the fact that everyone felt that there were things happening that they weren't aware of. The society and the community was being defined by forces that they had no access to. And so the theatre really became a way of understanding what was happening to the whole Johannesburg society. And there was a sense of a kind of liberation, of catharsis, in our Jo'burg audiences. A sense of relief that there was a little bit of truth being told. That became a very important component of the whole production.

When we were overseas it became a very different thing. It sometimes became quite disturbing. At home it was very heart-warming to feel that one was part of a process that people did find important. Whereas overseas it became a kind of nostalgic thing. ANC exiles would come to the show often and get drunk in the bar afterwards and want to talk to you in Afrikaans and that kind of stuff. It was quite strange. So that was a big eye opener. I wasn't aware of the culture that had been created overseas. And I thought exiles just went and lived as part of English society. But there was this whole exile community that existed on fantasies, on dreams of what South Africa was, or could be. They had, I suppose, to sustain themselves. We became a kind of rallying point for that community. And sometimes I found that a bit disturbing. I suppose it was just the enormous difference between living inside the country and living outside it, as a South African.

Why was it disturbing?

When we were in Washington DC we were invited to a party. It was a huge party. It was all black. They were all wearing mock African garments. And they were singing, chanting: 'Africa must unite, Africa must unite.' And at one point a woman leaped forward. They said, 'Stop the music, now Jubie is going to give us a tribal dance!' And this woman did this sort of shimmy dance in the middle of the place in improvised tribal outfit, and Gcina was just totally appalled and said, 'This is rubbish, this is not African, this is kak, she just made it up.'

We felt like complete aliens in this place, because I don't think anyone had seen the play, they'd just heard that there was this South African group and we were very political, and they'd invited us to this party. I don't think they even realised there were white people in the play. It wasn't about the work, it was about what you symbolised – some sort of liberation spirit. It was clearly very uncomfortable that there were whites in the play as well. They wanted it to be an all-black thing. When we were in New York, there was an Africa festival organised by Duma Ndlovu, who is back here now, a very PAC-inspired event. On the final night, everyone joined on stage to sing Nkosi Sikelele, but we were told that we weren't welcome on stage. I was a little relieved because I wouldn't have been able to sing Nkosi Sikelele in front of a PAC audience. I don't remember Barney's response. He must have been there, because it was a gala occasion, a huge fund raiser. Harry Belafonte and Joanne Woodward were there and they spoke. I think they just wanted to create this sense of a unified black struggle.

Our final performance in America was at Amherst University in Massachusetts. Huge hall, completely packed with students I presume. Horrible conditions, just terrible. It wasn't a theatre. They just banged up a few lights. You just got on the stage. It felt like an appalling performance, just really bad. But we'd never got a response like this. I mean these people could not have known what they were watching. They just knew that it was from South Africa. We hadn't even got to the final line and they just went ROAR! Rose as one person, they just screamed and threw things, and it felt quite disturbing because it couldn't have been about the work.

How did you feel when you did the classic "Hedda Gabler" with Barney and he began tampering with the text?

I understood because I knew that that's what Barney did, but I found it intriguing that he did it with Ibsen. You know, that it wasn't only Brendan Butler that had his play tampered with. I think Barney benefited from the isolation of South Africa because one could evolve a different way of working with texts. Whereas the rest of the world was going on about the sanctity of the writer. You had to respect the writer's vision and it was the role of the director and the cast to implement that vision. Barney was completely opposed to that view. When he came to Ibsen, ja, he didn't have any qualms about fiddling with the text. He didn't fiddle with it to any large degree.

How important was Barney's Jewishness?

I think Barney's Jewishness was very important. Jewishness is not about going to Shul. It's a sense of a history and a sense of a culture and a kind of bitter laugh. The laugh that comes out of pain. But it was about celebration. The sanctity of objects was a very important part of it. That each object has a soul, and you know that it's not just about people, it's about things. It was about the God in everything. It wasn't about God being some remote force, but about it being reflected in every aspect of your life, every aspect of one's world containing an element of sanctity. Barney's work was about expressing that sanctity, that nothing was without its sacred aspect, even liars and complete con artists, like the Dugmore Boetie guy that he latched up with at one point. I suppose that's why I chose to play that role in "RSA". A con artist is somebody who creates his own life. I think Barney was also fascinated by the workings of a storyteller, somebody who creates fictional lives within life.

Images from old scratched contact sheets of rehearsals for "Black Dog Inj'emnyama".
These prints were found amongst Barney Simon's desk items after his death.
Photographs by Ruphin Coudyzer.

The cast of "Black Dog Inj'emnyama", James Mthoba, John Ledwaba, Marie Human, Neil McCarthy, Kurt Egelhof, Gcina Mhlope. April 1984.

Gcina Mhlope

'Knowing and working with Barney was like being with a man with huge breasts'

I was going through this delayed reaction. I don't know what to call it, but it was a very ugly thing going on inside me. Vanessa Cooke phoned me up and told me they would like me to come and say a few words about Barney. They were having a commemoration. 'Of course I would come'. So I went – to walk in there and see people like Dawid Minnaar and his brother and all the people who really cared for Barney. It was really great for me to be there. For the first time I was able to cry about it and grieve for him. I felt really privileged to be in that family of people, he made family for himself. And after that I somehow slowly began to heal inside. Now I remember him with lots of affection.

I remember Barney with laughter sometimes, about all kinds of things. I can think of times when he used to say, 'I am not coming to see the show. You can be free today.' And we would go on stage and we would be in the middle of a show and we might make a mistake and you think, 'It doesn't matter. Barney is not there.' Then you hear him coughing somewhere on the stage, hiding, coughing and he can't stop himself because he is so upset about the mistake we made.

And sometimes I am doing something and I wish I could just share ideas with him. Phone him up and say, 'Barney I'm working on this thing' and he would ask questions: 'What is it about? What do you want to say? You shouldn't be stuck.' I miss those lovely times when you were able to talk to Barney. But I think, maybe a better way of missing him is to share whatever skills I have with other people. That's a better way of missing Barney because he was about sharing, not about boasting 'I know so much, I'm so clever, so wise.' He had so much wisdom but he was very accepting as well. That is one of the things that put him in my heart.

When I was in theatre I felt very much an outsider – criticised for not drinking and then for not smoking, and people wanting to know whom you are sleeping with. I felt like I was alone. I did well. I was successful, but I never belonged. I was never one of them. I used to say to Barney, 'I am flying with crooked wings. I don't belong here. I don't fly the way everyone else flies.' And Barney says, 'But you are doing your work well. Go on.' Another director would have been pissed off with me. He never shooed you off. I would have difficulties with other actors, tensions on tour. When we went to New York, I would cry so much and Barney would be tired. What was he supposed to be now, a social worker or director?

You never doubted his sense of commitment to what we were doing. His greatest wish for us was to grow and grow. Every time we worked with Barney it was a revelation of what you are capable of doing. Doing "Written by Hand" and working in Boston was like a confirmation that maybe I could attempt directing, because I was assistant director to him and I had never directed before. An accepting man like that. It was an experience. There were times when the students we were rehearsing with were worked up with what was happening with their shrinks, and they would cry and cry

Opposite – Portrait of Gcina Mhlope.
Photograph by Ruphin Coudyzer.

because the work was digging inside as well, looking for things inside, and they would cry and make us promise that we wouldn't tell other students. To watch Barney handle situations like that was a privilege for me. I have been lucky with Barney.

What is the process of creating a character in a workshop?
He would ask what you wanted to be, off the top of your head. Dentist – and he would never argue. Now all of this sits on your shoulders: make the dentist credible. Is she female, black, where does she live? Where was she educated? You have to find a biography for this person.

Tell us how you approached one real woman from Alexandra that you based your character on.
I asked if I could interview her. I told her, 'I am doing a play and I would like to use your story for the play.' I had a tape recorder because I used to work as a journalist.

Did you meet her by chance?
I went to see Daphne, a friend of mine at the detainees' support committee. I am one of the founder members. I came across this woman who told her story. It just shook me so much. So I asked if I could come in the evening and interview her and she said yes. I did not go back to rehearsal. I went home, took my recorder down to 20th Avenue and met this woman and she told me the whole thing. I saw her also after Fanie [a child detainee] was released from jail. We spoke. The boy was shaking. He was forgetful. It was a horrible thing to see.

Did she ever see the play?
She came. I invited her. She cried. She was glad that her story could be seen by other people. For me Barney did not particularly stand out as a white person. I'm not the kind of Africanist who would be selecting people according to their colour. He was a very skilled and giving person. That was what mattered. Barney embraced my different types of expression and I am grateful. I am flying with straight wings and I am where I belong. Knowing and working with Barney was like being with a man with huge breasts. He has breastfed so many of us in the theatre business. The best part of it was that his breasts were so nourishing and they never ran dry. He was such a blessing of a man. Now it is up to us to take his example and to nourish others.

'Barney embraced my different types of expression and I am grateful'
Gcina Mhlope

Vanessa Cooke

'Is it chicken or is it Kentucky Chicken, or is it Nando's chicken? There's a huge difference'

Before Barney went to America, he got the group together and said, 'When I come back we will work on something.' He knew exactly who he wanted. But he went to America for quite a long time, and during that time there were all the arrests. Kids were arrested. When he came back things had changed, they had got much worse. So he didn't know what was going on as much as we did. So whatever ideas he'd had before, which he'd never told us, he couldn't work, and had to start right from the beginning. He knew that he had to talk about what was going on. So I think perhaps there would have been a very different play if he hadn't gone away to America.

The whole world had changed. He had to deal with that. He was freaked out at what was going on. So he kind of imposed a little bit on us in "Born in the RSA". Politically. The kind of research we had to go and do was political. It was going to see victims, going to detainees, and their parents. It was very, very different from "Cincinatti". Extremely different. For "Brecht on Brecht" we tried doing a workshop, and it didn't work. "Cincinatti" was done with members of The Company. We'd done "People". We'd done "Storytime". We'd done "People Too". And then the whole Market thing happened. The Company started to, not break up yet, but I think that was the last play.

We started talking about what was going on. The New York City, a huge club in Fordsburg, which was where we all used to club, had just closed. It was a multi-racial club which completely freaked the government out. It lasted for quite a long time. We used to go there after shows, one place where we could all meet. In those days you didn't mix that much. We talked about what was going on with the country. Also we were thinking about what kind of character we could relate to, who could feasibly be in that club. Either you'd come up with your character or Barney would.

I based mine on a girl I saw there often, who just danced all the time. Nobody knew where she came from, why she was there. She just danced, and then she'd go. She was only about seventeen, eighteen. I'd never spoken to her. It was just a visual kind of thing. She never came with anyone, or left with anyone. She wasn't a prostitute. I imagined where she came from, where she was living. You know, those three things that Barney always said: 'What does the character know? What does the character want? Where is the character from?' When I was seventeen, what would I have wanted if I was a person who went to clubs? What are her dreams? What are they going to end up as? What was her knowledge of politics, what was her knowledge of what was going on here?

I'd done a lot of that work with Barney before. There had also been the thing with Arthur Molepo and Danny Keogh. When they were building The Market, Barney got us to come every day. Danny and I were building the Upstairs Theatre. So we'd fetch Arthur, who worked at World Furnishers, and then we'd meet Barney and work from five until it got dark, which was like two hours at the most. There was no electricity there, so when we left we'd always have to find out the time. Barney came up with this idea that the world had ended and that each one of us thought we were the only person left. So we didn't see each other for the first while. It went on for a long time, this improvisation. Like months. We each made our own little place. It was like playing. And then it got really scary, because the strongest would start to steal from the others. So Danny ended up with this mansion. Arthur and I collected corrugated iron and we were living in like a squatter camp. Arthur and I had nothing. We had one little piece. We had to move in together. It was terrible. I remember crying. I said, 'Barney you can't do this'. We got very into it after a while. Barney would waltz off home and we'd have to take Arthur to Diepkloof. Then Barney went away to America again. I've been through quite weird experiences with Barney in terms of improvisation.

It was just an exercise. It could have made a fantastic play. I was constantly with Barney because he constantly wanted to do workshops. All the time he was trying to carry on with this South African story somehow, and in the meantime, we had to do plays to keep The Market going. Barney would talk about "Cincinatti" being softer in comparison to "Born in the RSA" as a play, because people could talk to each other actually. That club had given people hope that it was possible to communicate with each other. Whereas by 1985-1986 it was not possible anymore, and "Born in the RSA" was about being isolated from each other in this country because of the political situation. "Born in the RSA" was definitely a political play. As was "Black Dog". "Cincinatti" was not primarily so. With "Born in the RSA" it had got to a point where it was no longer possible, really, to talk about someone's life without being political. One could not ignore that situation anymore.

So you say he came back and saw things were very bad here. What was the premise when you did get together?

When Barney got back he wanted us to tell him what was going on. He was away for six months or something. I think he'd heard things there. But he wanted to know. He felt very out of place. Then we went onto the streets and began to research. While we were together, the second State of Emergency was declared.

We had done "Four Paces by Two" in The Laager. It was not Barney's play. It was for the Detainees' Parents Support Group, while everyone was in detention. Barney had been asked to do a play for this group but he had to go to America. So he left it to me and Lisa Dyzenhaus to continue it. We'd started research on it already, going around to all the parents, and whoever, because everyone was in detention. It was a very different process, in terms of going to interview someone to use the story in the play, compared to going out on the street and observing somebody, and observing the ordinary un-dramatic things. Neil Aggett died while Barney was away. Then the detainees started coming out of detention – Barbara Hogan and Maxine Hart.

I didn't have a terribly hard time with "Born in the RSA" because I had interviewed Maxine, and I had also interviewed parents for "Four Paces by Two". It wasn't easy performing these live people in terrible situations. For me "Born in the RSA" was a much more serious play than any of Barney's other plays. I felt it was a responsibility. Even more so than "Black Dog". For me "Black Dog" was emotional. But this wasn't. It was really bleak, as the situation was. And really uncompromising, because it could not explain anything, justify, or try and reason why. It just was that, as it was. Barney called it 'newspaper theatre'. Because the newspapers weren't telling the stories.

That must have been awesome, that feeling that you were the only people in South Africa telling that particular story. The papers were trying to, but they weren't allowed to. For some reason you got away with it in the theatre.

In "Born in the RSA", you have to imagine yourself in that situation. You've got all that information, but then you bring it down to finding your own... person. That was the magic of Barney. We could have just played Maxine [Hart]. But for Barney that was not 'being interesting'. He had to make it into drama. He had all his own images as well. And he would impose them on you. And sometimes you wouldn't agree about what that person would do. In a normal play, you would have to bow down to that because he was the director. And that's the point where actors tended to fight with Barney. Especially in workshop stuff. All this stuff, it's yours, and there is this guy saying, 'Go off and do it again,' and you just have to.

He would never say you must, but he would go on and on and on and on trying it a different way until you had to just accept it. He's the audience at that point. You must never assume that people know what you're talking about. You have to be fair to them, and give it to them, even though you may think that that's being too obvious. I mean, is it chicken, or is it Kentucky Chicken, or is it Nando's Chicken? There's a huge difference. And if you just say chicken, somebody is going to not know what you're talking about, really. If you say roast chicken, or steamed chicken, or chicken that's off, they're going to know what you're talking about. But if you just say chicken, then they're not. They may not get the full picture. So you've got to, you've got to explain yourself, as a character or as a writer. That was Barney, that was his genius.

Barney was also criticised because of those things. On the one hand people were saying Barney was not bashing the government enough. The other side was protesting and saying we don't want to know. Barney's whole white consciousness thing was important – conscientising white people as to what was going on. He believed quite rightly that if they didn't learn what was going on here, the consequences would be terrible. He really was serious about that responsibility. I was shocked by the way all of us in the cast treated each other on tours. Barney couldn't understand that once we got out of South Africa the black actors were without any fear, and were able to say, 'We hate white people.' We were the white people who were there. It was terribly sad. Barney didn't cope very well. It was very, very hard. And you couldn't say, 'How dare you!' It was understandable.

Thoko Ntshinga

'Then, I had no voice as a black person. But on stage, I had a voice'

It was about 1975, 1976. We were a group of young and restless people who wanted to do theatre and we worked with Rob Amato at the Space Theatre. "The Sacrifice of Kreli" was my very first professional production. It was written by Fatima Dike and directed by Julius Mtsaka. We knew nothing. There was this energy from the township, this bursting energy that said, 'I want to be on stage.' It was the only place for black people at the time. We were flocking to the Space Theatre. We came to Johannesburg on tour with "The Sacrifice of Kreli". Barney rehearsed us when we got to The Market Theatre in November 1976. This was the first time we met Barney.

Do you remember what you thought of him then?

He was a forward old man. Barney would scratch his beard and say whatever he wanted to say, and I actually felt, 'This is not your play, who do you think you are! You are here to advise and not to take over.' He did not talk much. He just sat there and watched and listened. Then you would hear this voice shouting to the stage this and that. Barney used to make me furious. I used to think, 'Do I really want to be here? What is it that this man wants from me?' You must understand we were young and used to township theatre. The discipline of this kind of theatre was new to us.

What was township theatre?

Township theatre was: look at me, rather than this the message I have for you at the moment. When you are first starting out you just want to be seen, and the impact of what you are doing is not the same. Also the battle of coming on stage and finding yourself with a predominantly white audience means: 'Gee, I must push myself even more to prove that I can do it... Do these people understand me? Do they know what I am talking about or are they just sitting here because they have paid? Or do they hear my story?' That was my first experience.

What made you come up to Johannesburg?

Cape Town was so limited. The Space Theatre was the only place that had black people on stage. You know that CAPAB painted actors to be black. There was no chance of growing in Cape Town. I went to CAPAB once. I wanted them to say to my face that they cannot use me. There were going to be auditions that were advertised for PACT. I called to see if they were going to give me an interview or not and they said I must come in. I think it was Francois Swart who spoke to me then. He said, 'Do you know that the place does mainly Afrikaans work?' And I said, 'I believe so.' He asked if I could speak Afrikaans and I said I can understand and I am an actress and, being an actress, I could learn to do anything. Then he said they did not know what the cast would be like, and I said, 'But you advertised the play with a black face in it. How are you going to do it?' He scratched his head and said, 'Well, let me give you an Afrikaans script to read.' I said, 'Is that your way of pushing me out?' I felt it was not worth it,

Opposite – Thoko Ntshinga.
Photograph courtesy of The Market Theatre.

and I said, 'No sir, I will come back next time when I have learnt thirty pages of Afrikaans to recite.' And I left. That made me go into theatre even more, because I felt nothing is impossible when you are on stage. People learn if they get time to learn.

So I came to Johannesburg and the only place I knew was The Market Theatre. I met Barney and I told him I was looking for work. And he said there was nothing happening yet but he might soon be rehearsing a play. He had not cast it yet, but I must keep checking. I did not have a telephone at the time, so I kept coming to The Market Theatre and auditioning for this and that. He gave me a date and we began rehearsals on that date. Workshop at the time was a foreign word to me. I was here to learn. If they say I must workshop, then I'll workshop. But I was living in Berea and I did not have money to come to the theatre. Barney said he would lend me the money to move between Berea and work.

We had to collect material for "Cincinatti". We used to sing and chat about apartheid and its effects on people and how we felt. Barney used to find the anger and push you to a point, like a psychiatrist wanting to really find out what makes you tick. The one thing that comes to mind was him pushing me to go and sit in Hillbrow and watch how prostitutes worked. During the ins and outs of moving to Johannesburg I had lived with a prostitute. I had worked with this woman in a musical here. We were shipped form Cape Town to Johannesburg and back. This woman took me in.

During the workshop we were trying to choose characters. Once he made us lie on our backs: 'Close your eyes and imagine a light bulb being switched on. Then imagine it switched off. When the light bulb is off – it does not go dark.' The light would fade and during the fading of the light he would say, 'Tell me what you are thinking at this point, what comes to mind?' And in my mind I saw this woman. Another time he made us lie on our backs, take off our shoes and look at our toes. 'Don't think of anything. What do you see?' Again this woman came to mind in a different situation. Then he said, 'Maybe there is something fascinating about this woman. Something you never understood about this woman. Let's find her and maybe you can play that woman.' So I ended up playing a prostitute.

Did he do these exercises with you alone?
No, this is how we chose the characters.

Had you been having a discussion before he told you to lie down?
We would just sit around and talk about situations. What interests you? What fascinates you? What makes you angry? Then you got to a point when you felt okay. These are the kind of exercises he would do. When you would battle to find a character to play, those are the exercises he used to eliminate everything else from your mind and see what remains.

So it was through those exercises that he wanted you to go to Hillbrow?
I didn't want to go to Hillbrow. He made me go to Hillbrow.

Why didn't you want to go to Hillbrow?
It was scary. What would you do standing at a street corner, evening or day,

depending on when Barney would send you? He would send you at a time when he thinks you will find what you are looking for. One afternoon he sent us all out. I remember him saying to Sam Williams, 'Go to the corner of Bree and West and just sit.' 'What do I do?' he asks. Barney says, 'Just go and sit on the pavement. And you, go to Park Station. I will pick you up at 8 o'clock. Go at 5. Watch people come and go.'

The next day you would come back and talk about everything you saw. It was amazing what came out. You would be sitting there watching people and you'd think nothing of it. Then Barney would try and find out what else you saw. 'I saw a woman in a red dress.' 'What woman? What did she do? What did you think about this woman? How many other people had red dresses?' He used to dig. He never left anything as A, B, C, he wanted to go to Z. So you would sit. I sat at Park Station for three hours that day. I remember getting angry, getting calm and then laughing. You see people going. You see people fighting. You see people pushing. All sorts of things. One day I saw a man biting an apple. It was like: 'I want this finished in one second.' Barney made you do those kind of things to create a character. Those were the little things we wrote down.

He was very pushy. Maybe I say that because Thoko as a person is bright, but in fact I hardly talk about myself as such. I always block out. I am the kind of person who will give you this happy face all the time. If there is something else, it is mine. Barney used to try and get in there, and this is what made us fight. I didn't know what he wanted besides what I was giving him. Actually what he wanted was genuine material. He didn't want you to assume. If you were going to the shop he did not want you to assume that you would buy cigarettes. Why? Why?

So you got all this research, and what would happen then?
Then he would write the characters. He did the writing.

What happened in Hillbrow? Tell us more about that.
In Hillbrow, first of all you became a suspicious thing. Men want to pick you up. And you are like a prostitute eventually, because why would you just pace up and down the pavement unless you are trying to pick up a man? You would fight with people because they want to chat you up and you do not want any of this. In those days it was not as open as it is now to be a prostitute. People were sneaky. I discovered prostitutes used to walk around in maid's uniforms because it was freer. You were somebody's maid and these people were making passes, and talking with their eyes. I would not have known that if I hadn't stood on the street. Those times you could not be black on a Hillbrow pavement at night, trying to chat up a white man. When you were black you were not allowed to be in public or across the colour-line. It was dirtier then. Now people are more open. Then people would even klap you, because you were a dirty woman. The dirty white men who were into prostitutes were maybe fascinated by the uniforms. I don't know. Black people were not allowed to live in the flats then. The only way they could move in and out was in maids' uniforms, because they were 'cleaning flats'. In the meantime there were thousands living in the flats with white names. So if you looked at the resident cards downstairs, nothing looked unusual.

'The only way they could move in and out, was in maids' uniforms, because they were "cleaning flats"' Thoko Ntshinga

Some white people rented flats for their black lady friends. It was tough, and people had to work hard at getting their money – when they did it was cash. This I picked up as I paced the pavement for three hours. You begin to recognise faces and pick up that this is how it is done. Barney got you to go out there and find things. Because no matter how much material you brought you would still be questioned as to what else. What more, surely there is more? I'd met that friend who was a prostitute when we did "African Odyssey" with Clarence Wilson and she was part of the cast. She was very open. She never hid that she was a prostitute. She introduced the whole cast to Cincinatti [the club]. She used to take us there. We were scared. We were from Cape Town and lived in a hotel. We did not know where to go.

When you talk about prostitutes in maids' uniforms, was she like that?
Yes, during business time she was in a maid's uniform, and at the club she was one of the smartest girls. At one stage she said to me to come to her flat and she would show me what happens. She lived at the corner of Klein and Van Der Merwe streets in a block of flats there. She was in a maid's uniform. She said, 'When you walk in the building a dog will bark. It is the caretaker's dog. Don't get in the lift on the ground floor otherwise it will catch you.' The caretaker didn't know that she lived there. So what she used to do was push the button on the ground floor while the dog barked and then run to the first floor. It was that kind of life. You could not be seen coming out of the flats in smart or private clothes.

When you say maids' uniforms, were they smart?
No, a blue overall, blue apron, a blue doek and takkies. You would find the women in short skirts under the uniform, because they were in business.

So did this fascinate Barney?
It fascinated me and helped me create a character. After collecting material we would come back and sit in a circle and read out what we had seen. Barney would cross out things and tick things. The cast would help develop what you got. We would criticise and help each other. People would be reacting – like, I wouldn't want to see that on stage, or, it's too much, it's not believable. You would write all the ticked pieces in, and Barney helped create the character. He re-wrote all the pieces and gave it back to you to read before it got into dialogue.

How did it get into dialogue?
Let's say I would bring this woman. I would go to someone and get them to question me about those things. Like: 'I cannot go into the flat today because the madam is so-and-so and I have a client.' You question – 'Client for what, where?' Dialogue comes into place. But in the end Barney wrote the script. He took all the material and put it together step by step. The next day he would come back and say this is how far I have written, if you are uncomfortable with this, this is not all there is. There is still more to come.

Opposite – Domestic worker in Yeoville, Johannesburg, 1981.
Photograph by Paul Weinberg / South Photos.

It must have been hard for you to have someone else write the script when you had done all the work?
It was hard. Because he would come back with a different idea. You would say, 'I gave you this. In actual fact this is what happened,' but for theatre purposes some things needed to change and be able to flow.

What was in your mind while all this was going on?
It was an exciting process. I was doing it intensely for the first time, and so for me this was a training process.

When he spoke earlier about workshopping a piece did you know what it was? Had you seen it?
No, for me it wasn't a workshop, because I did not know what a workshop was. I was still waiting to go into a workshop. I would ask, 'When do we start the workshop stage?' And Barney would say, 'You are halfway through the workshop stage.'

How many weeks would this take?
He got angry with me because I said we were fucking around the first two weeks – putting things together, taking paper and pen and saying, 'You are a prostitute, let's talk about it.' It was different to asking someone to experience it. I am an impatient person. When something takes too long I want to push it. He never forgave me for that. Barney did not work like that. He waited for a certain stage before he said, 'Okay, we are ready for rehearsals.' It would take two weeks to collect material. And we would only start rehearsal on the third week and then rehearse for 4 weeks. It was 6 – 8 weeks, I would say. We had decided what play we wanted to do before we went and researched. Because we were a mixed cast, we had to come to a level where everyone was placed in a black and white "Cincinatti" kind of scenario. I remember Barney sending us to the club one evening to dance and come back with material. We had a fight. Lesley [Nott] was not much of a talker, and Vanessa [Cooke] came back with being in a club trying to talk to Lesley. Lesley had said she could not hear her. What came out was a scene where people are talking about dancing at the club: 'You don't go to a club to talk. That is why the music is loud. So don't talk to me.'

At the club Sam Williams was fascinated by the security guard. He was sitting by a little fire. He had lit his pipe as if nothing was happening. But he had stories to tell, because he would sit there and watch people come and go. The Immorality Act was still in place then. It was strange. From this night at the club, characters became secure.

What was the rehearsal like? How was Barney different from other directors?
He rehearsed individually. Suddenly you find yourself face to face with this man who is going to push you to the limit. I screamed. I was so frustrated. I would cry because he had taken everything that I thought I could give him. And he said, 'Not enough.' Somehow he did find something. You would learn your lines to a certain point and think, okay now I am ready for whatever. And he would say,

---

Opposite – Affluence and poverty live side by side in Hillbrow, 1987.
Photograph by David Sandison / The Star.

FAST FOODS
FAST FOODS
& PRINTING

'You are not giving me enough. Why are you holding back? Find more!' and you'd say, 'From what?' He'd say, 'From the script' – 'But I gave you material, you wrote the script, we discussed the script, and this was the end. Where must I get more from?' So, okay, maybe he wants me to scream this line. So you do it again. 'Hold it right there. I didn't say you must scream. I meant you must find the character.' 'Yes, I have found the character, remember we found it together.' And he would say, 'But now the character must be found by you. Remember, Barney Simon is not going to be on stage. YOU have to be on stage and convince me.' 'How can I convince you? You know the script.' 'Pretend I do not know about this.' – So you constantly try to find little things in the character. You would walk differently. I would go back home and think about things like the way you pick up a cup, and you think, your character would not do it like this. Your character was with you all the time. You ended up enjoying it, so much that you wanted to come back and share something new that you had found. He made you comfortable in character. One week you'd rehearse by yourself, and then you would do the portions you had rehearsed together with the rest of the cast. For two weeks he would work with the groups, but you still had your own hour, kind of thing.

When did you realise there is actually something in this?
I think when we started doing those individual rehearsals, when we actually wanted to know more about our character and it started to be fun. You actually loved this character. Barney's rehearsal never ended. The last day of performance Barney still gave notes. I bowed for the last time and still got notes. It was never over.

After all this, had you changed?
Yes, a lot. I began to realise that theatre is not only entertainment but a vehicle whereby people can learn and messages can be put across, where you can influence people. Then, I had no voice as a black person. But on stage I had a voice. On that stage I commanded and demanded respect. I made people listen to me. Not by force, but by talking and sharing a part of my life. People came out of the theatre understanding something of a black person.

So even when you worked in township theatre it wasn't the same?
Like I said earlier, it was a different discipline. Township theatre was more raw material. Township theatre didn't spare any punches. It went full out. So I learnt the two disciplines. "Cincinatti" was very successful. We took it on tour to Cape Town. It played for 10 months – historic for South African theatre. After that it was "Born in the RSA". It was quite some time after, although we kept in close contact. I was one of the lucky people who never stopped.

What was it like going to another director after Barney?
Other directors were easier and others didn't workshop. I did another play with Barney before "Born in the RSA", called "Call Me Woman, Colour Me Black". Again for this play we had to go out and do research. Myself, Saira Essa, Barrie Shah, Nomse Nene, Pat Maboe. It was the same process all over again but this time I knew what to expect. Barney's work was a painful process but rewarding in the end. "Born in the RSA" was

another painful process. We were talking about how the State of Emergency affected people. Again a mixed cast. I chose to find out about detention. I was married to an activist who had a banning order and could not leave Johannesburg or be in a room with more than two other people at a time. So I wanted to find out what happened to women in detention. I went to political meetings and found out who had been in detention, and ended up with some names. I asked permission to interview them. They had learnt by then that theatre is a form of communication, and it meant for them that their stories would be told. That's how I sold the idea. So I would go out with my tape recorder and interview people. There was one woman whose story wouldn't leave my mind. She was so strong that she told her story with a by-the-by attitude. And these stories became the monologues of the play from beginning to end. But still you came back with material and Barney edited it and put the storyline together.

This woman was in detention. She was six weeks pregnant when she was picked up by Special Branch. She was made to stand for 24 hours for three days. She miscarried while standing on that table. Policemen and policewomen would come and have sex with each other while she watched, drowsy and standing on the table. The way she told her story was like 'So what!' That for me was so painful, because she accepted her situation as being normal. And Barney, 'the grey man', would send you back for more. And you would go back and ask more questions. And it came out that the only relief she had was by asking to go to the loo where she could steal five minutes to doze before she went back to the table. Barney made you find those moments in yourself as an actress, and made you go back for more.

What happens to you and your psyche while this goes on?

It breaks you into twenty different pieces. One, you do not want to believe that this could happen to a human being, and yet if this person is telling this story she couldn't be lying. So you end up with two conflicting things in your mind and you have to fight to discover which is true. It is so unbelievable and painful that you doubt it ever happened. It was a trying time and it was only then that I understood what my husband was going through.

What is it like to play the character of such a story?

Painful, to tell the same story every night, and what makes it painful is the different reactions. The pain of the audience comes through. We did this all over the world. "Born in the RSA" never became automatic, it couldn't, it was too emotional, too painful. It was an invitation to know what South Africa was really like.

How did you make this story your character?

It was different in the sense that with the prostitute story you couldn't understand unless you had gone through it. The prostitute would never have said to me, 'I've got a sexy nightie under this uniform.' It was something you discovered. This detention story was being told on a one-to-one basis. The woman was going through the process of telling me how it happened. She came on opening night and she cried. She said, 'It's been such a long time but I can actually see those policemen.'

How long ago had she experienced this?

Around 1979, '80, and she told me like it was yesterday. She was an activist when I interviewed her. I interviewed a school child in Daveyton who was in detention. Her head was put in a rubber thing with water so she couldn't breathe.

When you toured around the world, what was it like?

Doing a story here, you were talking to people who had a taste of what South Africa was like, and some who refused to know what was happening in South Africa. When we went overseas, it was more fascinating because people tended to think they knew more about us than we did in South Africa. We were packing houses. I remember playing at the Edinburgh Festival. People were responding to things in South Africa, and yes, they knew things were happening, but not to this extent. It felt like it was being well understood and well received. What hit me at first was that the overseas audience was too quiet. I could not relate to that. The English don't move in their chairs, and at first you do not know if you are making any sense. It was only in the end when they went crazy and applauded that you knew they were actually listening.

Did Barney go with you?

Yes, of course, he wrote us notes while sitting in the audience. It was rehearsal all the time. I don't know how, but you would see him. He would make gestures in the wings and you would turn and see Barney Simon trying to tell you something. You try and figure it out without the audience noticing. He gave notes all the time. Even after the show. Vanessa told us that once Barney was trying to say something to her through the floorboards of the stage. He was fun once you got to know him. He could work wonders.

So when you look at your life what do you think he gave you?

He gave me a life in theatre and understanding of the theatre. He gave me tools. I work in television now, which is different to theatre, but not the tools. He always said, 'split the difference'. When you go on stage you can be big and when you go on television, you can be nothing – so you split the difference. To work with that man for so long taught me a lot in theatre. I can find myself in a situation, even out of theatre, and try to understand it before I react to it. Patience – that's a very good thing he taught me. When you choose a character you have to find what makes it tick. In "Call Me Woman", we spoke of childhood and womanhood. We all came from different backgrounds although we were all shades of black. We had to use that sexuality, individuality and humanity. You had one white man and seven black women talking about womanhood. I remember a journalist once asked how we felt about being black women working with a white man. I said to him, 'Darling, if you can't take white and mix it with black to make coffee or chocolate, then there is no point in us being here.' He never felt differently. I remember us discussing him saying, do you think he is gay? Why would he want to do an all-woman play? He was just fascinated by people.

Opposite – Thoko Ntshinga in "Born in the RSA", September 1985.
Photograph by Ruphin Coudyzer.

PW SNUBS
THE CITIZEN
GERMAN 'NO'
TO SANCTIONS

"Born in the RSA" being such a painful play, was there ever any conflict with white people in the cast?

Because it was a working relationship, we never had conflict. We had Neil McCarthy playing the spy, and that could make you angry because here was a woman who lost a child in detention. And here was a man who infiltrated an organisation to get someone into detention. But we were over that step. Terry Norton played a dumb housewife, one of those people you wanted to punch for not knowing what is happening in South Africa. We had our fights as people reasonably contained, and were careful with each other. I believe that if I want to tell you something then I need you to listen. If you shout, people do not listen. If you force them to listen, they will not listen. So I want audiences to listen and I would like them to go back home and laugh and cry at the same time because it had so much impact. I know that the impact comes from the soft person in me. Through that I learnt that if the punch is soft, it stays longer with the person.

Fiona Ramsay

'No blonde ever gets sympathy'

When we did "Born in the RSA" I was tired of people exploring stories in South Africa that were about victims and the underdog. I believed there was a huge community of South Africans who were articulate professionals who also needed a voice. So with a wry smile, when we were discussing what I could play, he said, 'How about a lawyer, is that articulate enough for you?' I played the human rights lawyer, Mia Steinman, and I wanted her to be as close to my background as possible. Barney thought a White Anglo-Saxon Protestant from Forest Town, Johannesburg was just not a warm character, and instead suggested I play an Afrikaans Jewess. We argued and struggled to get the character, and I'd look on as he worked with others with such seeming ease. I got Mia's essence about ten days before we opened in England! One of the insights about Mia he gave me – which proved pivotal – was his remark: 'Remember Fiona, Mia is a great cook!' He too was very fond of delicacies and delicious foods, and many a rehearsal would be spent over tea and some creamy delight. Because I actually played a character a lot older than myself I used to wear a lot of make-up and 'did' my hair. Now Barney seemed to dislike 'blonde' hair – whenever I worked with him he would suggest I dye my hair darker – or 'warmer' as he used to say. He would come to me at the half-hour call and say, with a curled finger beckoning me and a smile, 'Come I need to work with you!' He also thought I spoke too fast – and spent hours getting me to give weight and value to words. 'Come, say that bit again, when the child has been arrested and your colleague does not offer to help you' – which was: 'And your fucken telex-machine breaks down.' I would say, 'Andyourfuckentelexmachinebreaksdown!' 'NO! Slower! Chew the words' – he would say. Meanwhile my time for preparation with make-up and hair was rapidly running out. I'd say, 'Hey Barn, it is now five minutes to eight!' At about two minutes to eight, he would agree I could go back to the dressing room. He'd be sitting in the audience and couldn't believe when the show began, that the person he'd left only two minutes before had transformed so on stage. He would mutter with disbelief, 'How did you manage to get all that make-up and hair right in two minutes?' I realised all he was doing was working with me before each performance in the hope that I would not have time to titivate. He thought make-up was a mask – and always wanted to see the whole character without filters.

Why?

He felt my make-up was a mask that I did not need, and we always argued about it. In retrospect I wish I had been able to say, 'Okay, I will do it tonight without any make-up and see how it works.' Barney always wanted to uncover some unexplored part of you as an actor – and to nurture you through dealing with that exposure. At the time, I think I felt I didn't need nurturing in that way – the toughness and arrogance of youth!

How did you develop your character with him? What was your journey?

He just said, 'No' a lot, until you dug further and further down for more information or insight that would interest him.

What do you mean 'No'? To what?

Well, we were writing our own histories for our characters, and as a human rights lawyer I remember going to sit with Kathy Satchwell, Priscilla Jana and a whole lot of other lawyers. I used to sit in the waiting room and just watch the clients and interaction. I would also sit with the lawyers during consultations. I would come back to Barney with what I thought was fascinating stuff, which he thought was all too factual. He just looked at me – still with a twinkle in the eye – and said, 'No, go back and find out more about the person!' I was also supposed to know Ruth First (a friend of Barney's) and talk passionately about her and Joe Slovo. I was too young to have first-hand experience of some events around that time – so I had a cerebral understanding – but had to imagine more than I really knew.

Did you enjoy working with him in this way?

He could be unbelievably frustrating to work with – because he never made you aware of just how much you had achieved in creating and portraying a character. Which is probably a very good thing. The moment you are aware of certain achievement, there is, or can be, a tendency to just relax and not continue working. Barney always gave you a challenge, or 'obstacle', before going on stage – even up to the last night. I think that is what people now miss in directors, as not many of them work in this way. I wish I had had more opportunities of working with Barney.

So what do you think of him as a director?

There always comes a time when you think – when working with any director – that you have to take a chance and go along with his/her vision and ideas – respect that. Or the whole ship will go down. There is always some part of one that does question, and may be sceptical – but it is all part of the process. I think working with Barney – although often frustrating – was usually exciting and fun. He was interested in you as an individual rather than your persona. Many directors are more interested in the persona, and as the individual creeps in or emerges in the work, they go 'uuughh uughhh' and patch over so that they do not have to deal with the individual.

What other plays did you do with Barney?

I was in "Oedipus", where we were all in hessian robes with our own masks, strapped by an elaborate contraption to our heads, which moved as we did. In "Still Life", I had just returned from time spent in London, and was excited at the prospect of working with Barney, and Aletta [Bezuidenhout] and Wilson [Dunster]. Barney wanted me to chain-smoke through the play. One evening, after a dress rehearsal I had felt was particularly good – or I'd enjoyed myself on stage (one never quite knows the difference) – I remarked to Barney, 'Wasn't the new way I did that amazing.' He answered naughtily, 'I didn't notice. You did not have the right cigarette. I could not hear anything.' During this run-through, he had decided my cigarettes should be filterless. He wanted to see me pick the tobacco from my tongue. He was always into detail, specifics. That was one of Barney's ways of working – giving you an obstacle. My obstacle was I ended up smoking Gitanes plain. As I said earlier – I used to think he never wanted me to be me on stage. In retrospect, that is all he wanted me to be. I had felt that my clothes, make-up, hair, etc. were all just me – whereas he wanted me to be comfortable with just me and none of those accessories. I also think that Barney's enjoyment of working with actors was his relationships with them – to find out how much we knew about each other. The process of 'sussing' one another out fascinated him. I thought he had a stereotyped vision of me, he probably thought I was defensive. Apart from not wanting some of the physical manifestations of portraying character I have mentioned, he also never wanted me to speak with my natural voice or accent, saying it was too 'posh'. I remember arguing with him, saying, 'I am South African, for God's sake!' And he said, 'I want warmth in your voice, and you must dye your hair darker. No blonde ever gets sympathy. Just look at Marilyn Monroe.'

"Born in the RSA" was filmed for BBC TV – and now many years later when watching it I understand what Barney was saying. So he taught me an invaluable lesson about acting, although it has taken time to be learnt. Barney loved beauty and saw beauty in many different places. He loved beautiful things in people and he was always trying to extract it from every actor he worked with, and to show it to them. He seemed to strive for actors to understand and explore their full individual potential. After having worked with Barney on "Oedipus" at the Baxter Theatre, Cape Town, then "Still Life" at The Market Theatre, and again in "Born in the RSA", which toured South Africa, the UK and America, I have a lasting and recurring image of Barney saying to me, 'Fly, Fiona, Fly!' – which seemed to be an acknowledgement that I had arrived at the character. I would think, 'Fly? Where can I go – I'm not allowed to wear make-up, I cannot fly without make-up? Happily now I could say to Barney, 'Yes, I can.'

Fiona Ramsay in "Born in the RSA", September 1985.
Photograph by Ruphin Coudyzer.

'So the end product was… elegance.
And elegance means maximum effect'

Terry Norton

Terry Norton

'So the end product was… elegant is a good word'

I thought there was something wrong with me because Barney had never asked me to work with him. But then he approached me to do "Born in the RSA". I came into the rehearsal room a little in awe. I'd never really been politically aligned – looking in from the outside, never really being involved myself. I felt it to be an issue maybe for the rest of the cast, but certainly not for Barney. He wanted me to play a hooker. I was quite bold in saying, 'Well look, I'd like to play somebody that's totally middle-class, and uninvolved.'

I found him to be incredibly open, and non-judgemental. He allowed me to pursue that avenue, which was quite in the opposite direction of what he was suggesting really. And so Nicky evolved, and she was this wife of Neil who was the police spy. I drew a lot on myself really, in terms of research. And the metaphor he used of betrayal was something that was very personally mine. We spent a lot of those early days compiling the character and how she would see the world. It was a completely new experience for me, because I'd always been given a script and told what to do. Suddenly I was in a position where I had to take over the reins and really drive and search and create. Barney taught me how to create. After that he would gather all that information, and slowly a story started emerging from the situation of the characters. The process was actually very fast. We did it all in about six weeks.

I didn't really know what I was letting myself in for, just knew in my gut that I wanted to work with this person. The State of Emergency had just descended. He opened my eyes to a lot of stuff that was not published in the newspaper and never spoken about. And I started to become aware of what a protected life I'd led, and how cut off I was from the majority of people that lived in Johannesburg or South Africa.

I was typically white, playing out the white female middle-class world of being a victim, being submissive. You know, waiting, as opposed to creating, or taking responsibility. And you know the atrocities that were going on at that time; we all just turned, or part of the country, just turned a blind eye. That was very clearly played out for me. It was terribly shocking to realise that grandmothers were being shot down and their grandchildren watched this happen. It was quite a humbling experience, and opened my eyes, opened my ears. I certainly began to see the world very differently. It was an enormous gift to have that thrust in my face. Barney introduced a passion and a sense of urgency to take responsibility for who I was as an actor. He made me conscious that I had a responsibility to educate and to heal myself, and maybe anybody who watched that play.

He certainly made one aware that one had those unique qualities to create with, and to have an impact. Taking responsibility for who you are, and what you have to do, and what you chose to do. The choice was very open. I never found him to be dogmatic. He would guide, certainly, and he would question, but he gave you a choice.

Opposite – Terry Norton and Ramolao Makhene in "Death and the Maiden", June 1992.
Photograph by Ruphin Coudyzer.

I think the only time he didn't give me a choice was when Neil and I were outvoted because everyone else wanted to come home. I think we were in Boston performing on tour. We were upset that we couldn't go on travelling with the play. Ja, he gave you a choice, and he certainly got those brain cells working. And more than that, he got your heart feeling.

The motivation for the play was a feeling that things were getting completely out of hand, violent politically, and, as far as I remember, we were going to workshop something in reaction to, or coming out of that, situation. What I learned about myself during the process was that I'd always been told what to do. You were told what colour you were. You were told what sex you were. You were told where to live, or how late you were allowed to stay out, and all those kind of things. And I feel very much so still, that we as South Africans are still trying to find our voices. We're trying to take our places, because for so long in whatever way, in some subversive way, we were told what to do. And we listened like little sheep. Most of us. So all of a sudden it was like one was given freedom, absolute freedom of choice, freedom to play, freedom to do whatever you chose to do.

Barney was guiding and, being who he was, you felt in a safe place. He was just so courageous. He was doing stuff that nobody else would touch with a barge pole. He allowed me to discover that I had a choice, which I didn't really understand before that. And that to perform work that you've workshopped has a very different quality to working from a written script, somebody else's work. One really understands where everything is coming from, and there's no question, it just is. So there's an enormous commitment and caring for the work. I suppose it's like having a baby.

Certainly he gave value to things. One was always wanting to do this hot play, that hot play or part. He made me value where I was coming from in the whole South African context. Before that I kind of looked to England. Suddenly I was acutely aware of the value of where I was coming from. And the value of where I was living, and the dignity, the sense of, 'God, this is all so amazing.' That dignity came from being truthful. You knew nothing was glossed over. So the end product was... elegant is a good word. And elegance means maximum effect.

Compared with other directors I've worked with, Barney didn't let you get away with a thing. He would not let you do something that was not truthful. It was as simple as that. He didn't dictate. He'd let you discover and claim stuff for yourself. It was an incredible kind of gentleness. Ja, most directors, you know, if it looks okay you kind of get away with it. But it's not based on fact. I think that's what made a difference, that something's alive, it's living. It's alive each time you do it. I've also worked with terrible people who tell you, you have to move then, you have to say it this way, and you have to wear this dress, and that's that. Aahh, but I'd give anything to work with Barney again.

Opposite – Police clash with Alexandra Township residents, Johannesburg, 1992.
Photograph by Graeme Williams / South Photos.

STOP

Chapter 7. Woza Albert!

"Woza Albert!" created by Barney Simon and actors Percy Mtwa and Mbongeni Ngema became an international and national hit. The workshopped play was inspired by the hypothesis that the second Coming of Jesus Christ would include a spell in South Africa. Christ is put in jail by the South African government, and then escapes and raises the country's black heroes from the dead. Of it Barney said:

'The form is sophisticated but the ingredients are simple. It reflects South Africa as people. We're making real people in the streets. It is important for me to give an identity to what surrounds us. To the shadows. I think it uplifts people in despair and informs people who are ignorant.'

Quote from The Star, Adrienne Sichel, February 8, 1984.

Mbongeni Ngema, Percy Mtwa and stage manager Dixon Malele describe how "Woza Albert!" originated, what Barney gave to the process, and how they made "Woza Albert!" the success it became.

'Woke up this morning feeling happy and full of hope. What is this? My mornings are gloomy. The headlines are grim. What happened? "Woza Albert!" happened. That's what. And if I had a rooftop handy, I would climb up on it and shout this review.'

Quote from the critic of the San Francisco Examiner.

Opposite – Percy Mtwa in "Woza Albert!"
Photograph by Ruphin Coudyzer.

Gibson Kente with the cast of "Now is the Time".
Photograph courtesy of City Press, Media24.

Mbongeni Ngema

'Working with Barney was a revelation that became consistent with my work up till this day!'

It's always a pleasure for me to talk about Barney.

Why?

Because Barney came at a time when I needed a pillar to hold on to. When I needed guidance. When my creative energies were very, very high. But I needed a mentor. I went to Barney. I remember his first work that I ever saw was "Call Me Woman", in 1979, at The Market Theatre and I didn't like it. I didn't like it because it didn't have the theatrical magic that I always look for in a production. It was ten African women and it was a beautiful, smooth little piece. It didn't have the energy, the vibrancy of African people, but it had very clever writing. So I felt like, well this man is very creative but this particular work is weak. It could be so much better.

Anyway, I wasn't intending working with him at the time. I was still working with Gibson Kente. And I had always told myself that I want to work with Gibson because he had what I did not have at that time. He knows how to orchestrate these beautiful harmonies. He's a genius musically, but also he has the vibrant energy of the African people. And he co-ordinated so well that I wanted to know how he did it. So I went to him purely as a student. Even though he didn't know it. He employed me as one of his artists. But for me it was not an employment, it was a training course.

In 1977, I had told myself that I wanted to work with a person like Gibson, and with Athol Fugard. I had seen "Sizwe Banzi is Dead". It didn't have the energy or magic of Gibson Kente's work. But it had something strong, so powerful. The writing was so clever and the timing was perfect. I decided I wanted the best of both worlds. I wanted to work with Gibson and I wanted to work with Athol, because I could then combine the two techniques and come up with something that no one has ever come up with. We had been workshopping many pieces, and one of them eventually became "Woza Albert!". For two years I had been researching, reading the Bible, talking about 'What if Christ would come back to South Africa?', which is a subject that came about by accident in a bus when people were arguing.

And did you hear them saying that?

Yes. Finally, we started rehearsing, Percy Mtwa and myself. After nine months of rehearsals, after being detained and all those other things in the Transkei, our passports were taken away. We came back to Johannesburg – we worked and worked for months and months and we kept on coming to see works at The Market Theatre. Work by Benji Francis, and different people who we thought, honestly, had not worked hard enough, researched enough. They brought work onto the stage that was half-baked. They didn't spend enough time with it. We felt that we had to spend as much time as we wanted to. And people were laughing at us. They kept on saying, 'You guys are still in rehearsal?' After nine months we had a run-through. A lot of people came to see it. And a lot of people came wanting to work with us, wanting to direct us.

James Mthoba is one of them. Peter Sepuma... We were these young dynamic two guys with an incredible theatrical piece that needed guidance. Mannie Manim was one of the forty people that came to that first run-through. Mannie said, 'You have a piece of diamond which is uncut. You can take it out as it is, and it may be worth ten rand, or you can find a diamond cutter and cut it properly, and it could be worth a million rand.'

'Somewhere, he is a guiding angel for me as a director'
Mbongeni Ngema

We said, 'Okay, we do need a diamond cutter. We've worked for so long, we're not in a hurry to open this play.' I told Mannie that we really wanted to work with Athol. But he said, 'You know, I think I have someone else who will understand your work better than Athol.' And we said, 'Who is it?' 'Barney Simon.'

Now when he said Barney Simon, I wasn't that enthusiastic. Both Percy and myself had seen "Call Me Woman", and this was a different kettle of fish. But we said, fine let's have a meeting with Barney. We had a meeting. We had a run-through with Barney. He was very tired. He was the only one watching that day. When we started he was half asleep. He was really tired. But halfway through the piece, when we did that Coronation Brickyard scene and I played Zulu Boy, he became alive up till the end of the play. We met with him the next day. He expressed the greatness of the idea and the endeavour, but also expressed that it needed much more work to turn it into a great theatrical piece. But he was afraid to work with us because during that time the Black Consciousness movement was very strong. A lot of writers were against working with white people. He felt that he would be seen as a white opportunist who has come to snatch this black effort. The more we talked to him, the more we understood. I particularly understood that this was the right man to work with. We had several meetings and in all those meetings he gave us notes, but he didn't want to work with us. Not because his love wasn't there. He was afraid to work with us. And then finally he gave in. He said, 'Okay, let's try.' He and Mannie organised. We worked for six weeks. And that six weeks of our work was one of the best times in my life.

Why?

Because he understood what we were trying to achieve. And he came right at the centre of it, of our beings and he kept on challenging us more. And sometimes it was annoying. But I had a vision. And I would listen and listen and say, 'Okay, let me try what you are saying.' For instance, he sent us to the streets to go and watch people, to see people and bring those people to the theatre, to the rehearsal room. Through those people we could express the things that we were only expressing in words. And for me that is the greatest achievement in theatre. In his words, 'Don't tell me, show me.'

I then began to see the difference between him and Athol. Athol was too involved in the text, in the words. Each paragraph has to be so perfectly written, and he'll spend months and months or years doing that. Barney's work was not about the words. It was about people's emotions. And I then understood that actually Barney was closer to Africans in his technique than Athol was, because African theatre or drama is not really about words. We say so few words and we do so much in action and emotion. I must also say that I have never worked with Athol Fugard, so I stand to be corrected.

I have based what I have said about Athol on what I have seen rather than experienced. Perhaps if we'd had a chance to work together, history would have been different. Working with Barney was a revelation for me that became consistent in my work up till this very day. So then after six weeks "Woza Albert!" was born and became a phenomenon in South African theatre. We toured all over the world for five years and collected whatever awards were available. Barney was not a great innovator but he was a great diamond cutter, as Mannie had said. So I understood why "Call Me Woman" was so weak in comparison to "Woza", because they didn't give him enough to work with. He had to work with the material that was available. That is why other works that he did were never in the same league as "Woza". Percy and I had worked so hard in compiling material. We had spent two years in research and spent nine months in rehearsal. Barney knew exactly what to do. So if you were to ask Barney to invent something from the beginning, that was not his skill. He could have a great idea but he needed someone to actually move that vehicle and then he would come and say 'Okay, this is how this is supposed to look.' He would give it the spirit that it needed. And no one, to my knowledge, is as good as he is, to this day, in this country. No one could touch him.

So can you remember, in those six weeks, a scene or something specific that you worked on?

There were so many things. I can remember the old man that I played. Barney said, 'Tell me a story about the old people that you know.' I told him about my grand-father. And he said, 'What did he look like? Show,' he said, 'show me how he looked. Wear something. What did he like to wear?' I found a coat somewhere and I wore the coat, and I started mimicking him. And he said, 'What do you think this old man would say about Christ? Think like him. Don't put politics in his mouth.' And that's how part of that character came about. And part of the story. One day Barney had flu and couldn't come to rehearsal. After two days he came back, and said while he was lying in bed he read the New Testament, and the play should be exactly like the New Testament.

Talking about the old man – then were you playing your grandfather?

Yes. And talking about apartheid. He asked me how my grandfather would relate to Christ. Of course my grandfather was never a Christian. He died over a hundred years old. He would say, 'What would happen if Christ came to South Africa? They would do to Christ exactly what happened with Piet Retief. This is South Africa. Christ would be crushed the same way that Piet Retief was crushed by King Dingane at uMgungundlovu Palace. "Come inside, Mr Retief, leave your guns outside." PW Botha will say, "Come inside, Morena [Lord] – leave the angels of your father outside." What will happen to Christ is what happened to Piet Retief. His bones were found at Kwa Matiwane long after he died.' But there were many, many changes that Barney brought about. For instance the very title "Woza Albert!". He said, 'Okay, who would Christ want to resurrect if he came back?' And we thought of a lot of different people, and then finally it was Albert Luthuli and all these people. Hence the title. Barney would look at what you've got and dissect it to the core. You may have something wonderful but don't know how to get to the centre of it. He had that skill.

When you rehearsed, before working with Barney, were you using people that you knew?

Yes, we were using people that we knew in some scenes. But we didn't know what technique we were using. What Barney helped us do is to understand that it's actually a technique that we needed to develop. So when he sent us to the streets it opened our eyes to a new technique.

'And that six weeks of our work was one of the best times of my life'

Mbongeni Ngema

You've said what he gave you as a theatre director. As an actor, what has he given you for life, for your career?

Sometimes you create something that you think is so special, and it is always difficult for you to censor your own work, or to cut something out, or to write a beautiful song and then decide it's a great song but it doesn't belong to the show. He had a skill of coming to you and saying, 'You actually don't need that, it disturbs the plot. It's great but maybe it doesn't belong to this show.' When I have tried to tell other people, 'No, you don't need that,' they become very defensive. He taught me not to become defensive and to be more objective.

And how did he do that? How did he teach you that?

Just talking about it all the time. Making you understand that sometimes you love your child but maybe you have to separate from your child. From Barney I also learnt simplicity. For a director to make an actor as comfortable as he can, and not demand a lot of words. Sometimes actors struggle with words, and they can't come across because, especially we African people are communicating in a foreign language most of the time. So Barney would say, 'Say it in your language until you feel that you understand it, and then let's translate your words from Zulu. Let's translate word by word into English. It doesn't have to be correct grammar as long as we can understand it.' And that's a great technique. As long as I live Barney is very close to my soul. He's one of those great artists who didn't reap what they had planted to the fullest. He was very selfless. But while he was alive he was never given the respect that he deserved, that Peter Brook gets for instance – actually surrounded by the community, the French community. He is given a theatre and money, where he can do whatever he wants to do. But Barney lived in this society which is so crazy, during a wrong government. And even if he lived during this new government, I think he would be in the same position.

Do you think so?

Yes. Because nothing has changed, in terms of supporting artists and arts, that has made a difference. This government is like a church, it wants to be good to everybody. Giving to everybody all the time.

Opposite – Mbongeni Ngema and Percy Mtwa in "Woza Albert!", October 1981.
Photograph by Ruphin Coudyzer.

How did you feel about the white/black issue? Because those were heavy times.
I just said, if someone is good, they're good, that's it. If we are fighting racism we can't be fighting ourselves along the colour lines. I defended Barney to the last because I believed in him. We were criticised a lot. People would come and say, 'Barney Simon has diluted "Woza Albert!". He's put in a white element.' But "Woza Albert!" was the most successful theatre piece of the time. So how did he dilute it? And those pieces that they were claiming were not diluted were not successful. The white/black thing was never an issue for me. In fact we always wanted to get back together again and work, but it didn't happen. It didn't happen for many reasons. One was that Percy at that time wasn't too keen for us to embark on another work for whatever reasons. And then we started going different ways. My career then took off in another direction. But Barney was always there. He spent endless hours in the rehearsal room helping me to shape "Asinamali!" and "Sarafina!". Because we didn't write another piece together after "Woza", it didn't mean that we didn't continue to collaborate. Even when I direct I sometimes will hear his voice. It's like somewhere he's around with me. Somewhere he's a guiding angel for me as a director.

Mbongeni Ngema and Percy Mtwa with Barney Simon and Mannie Manim.
Photograph courtesy of NELM.

Percy Mtwa

'Ja, we were like with Morena himself on that stage with Barney'

Percy, you say the positive outweighs the negative, and you feel that is how a lot of South Africans survived apartheid. How did this influence your work?
As it was with "Woza Albert!", with "Bopha!" and now with "The Patriot", I celebrate the triumph of the human spirit over adversity. I believe that the positive outweighs the negative. Barney, I remember, once said something about a hooligan running around with a knife, seeking to stab anyone he meets. But at that moment should his mother show up and call him by his name, he answers and says, 'Mum.' There is a soft spot in all of us which always puts us in a position where we are ready to forgive and forget the past. It is in that spirit that I write my work. I have dedicated my latest play "The Patriot", which I wrote and directed, to Barney.

How did you know Mbongeni?
In 1979 I was staying in Soweto and working for Gibson Kente in "Mama and the Load", and I met Mbogeni through Gibson and we immediately became friends. There was a lot of affinity between us, and we were talking about creating our piece. Then I met Andy Mabizela (may peace be upon him – he passed away recently) who was an actor who then became a stage manager. He had with him a book entitled "Towards a Poor Theatre" by Jerzy Grotowski. I borrowed that book and studied it with Mbongeni. This book taught us how theatre can be simple. How it can exist without technological aids and huge sets. Grotowski was talking about the preparation of an actor, the training of an actor and exercises for actors. He also has exercises that are designed to remove psychological barriers, to remove obstacles, so that the soul, the spirit, is free to play. It is that book, in fact, that inspired the inception, the conception, of "Woza Albert!". We worked on it and visited The Market Theatre quite often to see plays. We were quite fascinated by Barney's work. Later when we were in Cape Town Barney was also there with a play, I think it was "Call Me Woman". He was at the Baxter Theatre and we were also there, performing Gibson Kente's play. He approached us and asked what were we doing.

Mbongeni said he didn't like "Call Me Woman".
What I liked about Barney's work was the experimental nature of it. He knew how to make an actor discover himself, take him through the experiences that could possibly have been locked in the subconscious of the actor. Barney had this ability to dig this out till the actors could finally be free to express themselves. Well, "Call Me Woman"... I do understand what Mbongeni said. Of course, it was not such a great piece. It was polished, and Barney had a special tenderness in the way he handled his work. And that did come across quite effectively. He knew Jerzy Grotowski, but I do not think that he was using all the techniques Grotowski was providing. During the nine months we were rehearsing at FUBA, we did showcases of "Woza Albert!" for Barney Simon. Now when Barney came to see us he said that he had always wanted to work with artists like us, actors like us, very inspiring [Laughs]. I assume it was because of our style of

It's like a journey of self discovery to find out – to bring your soul even closer to the person you are about to portray' Percy Mtwa

presentation. Never mind the standards. I mean we were groping at that time but we were highly inspired, highly enthusiastic. It was because of the preparation we went through inspired by the Grotowski book. We kept pursuing Barney. At some stage he complained about Black Consciousness – that artists would feel that the show should be directed by a black person etc. I was very stubborn when it came to that. I kept on insisting that Barney is the person who could lift us up and place us where we can find a way to go on our own.

I think to a certain extent Barney was not aware of the amount of preparation that went into the type of work we presented to him. I was saying to a friend recently that I believe that there are other actors somewhere out there who can do "Woza Albert!" as well as we did, provided they go through the type of preparation we went through. It is possible. Many people have performed "Woza Albert!" throughout the world, but there is a mark which they have not hit with it. Why? Because of the preparation. There is a lot of subtext, quite a lot of hidden emotional content that needs to be brought out. It is quite a physical piece, so you get on that stage and exhibit a lot of energy if you've got it. "Woza Albert!" is also about the finesse of acting.

How did you discover the finesse of acting with Barney?

He had patience. He was able to let you try things out. It is like a journey of self-discovery to find out – to bring your soul even closer to the person you are about to portray. At that point your soul can give way and the soul of that person takes over and plays. That's what you deliver to the audience. Barney used to do it quite well.

So he did that through patience and... what else?

And of course there was also Jerzy Grotowski whom we were studying. I tell you, we studied that book until it was in tatters [Laughs]. Grotowski also taught actors in the conventional fraternity that they cannot move from one production to another with a bag of tricks. Grotowski taught actors to transcend that and be able to look at acting as a trance... an actor must be in a kind of trance. You must lose yourself. So that what we see is a projection of the person you are portraying. And I found that it could work wonderfully once you are in a kind of a trance – focused. Those exercises, designed to remove psychological barriers, put an actor in touch with his emotions. So that at one second you can be in tears, and as your tears are falling, you can burst into hilarious stuff. And "Woza Albert!", being as physical and highly paced as it was, I needed to get that kind of focus, alertness.

So you got the idea from Grotowski and Barney...?

Barney helped us realise it. As an experienced director you get exposed to a lot of varieties of emotions of people. The problem with most directors is how to get that out of a person. I think Barney technically and artistically was well-equipped to do that. For instance, me playing the part of the young boy swatting flies in "Woza Albert!": I have watched some actors playing that part and, because it is quite small, they take it easy. I think because they managed to sit there and hold that paper and swat the flies

---

Opposite – Mbongeni Ngema and Percy Mtwa in "Woza Albert!," October 1981.
Photograph by Ruphin Coudyzer.

away, they do the scene and think that they've got it. I have often said to actors – and I quote Grotowski's words: 'You can surmount completely the audience's own capabilities in order to arouse a sense of magic.' It is that magic that "Woza Albert!" was about. Every little thing we were doing... Barney at some stage, as he was directing me, said something very important that let me come to grips with that scene. When the boy starts talking to the interviewer and says, 'Yes, Baba I want people to come and buy all this meat,' then moves on to say '... and I want him to take me to school,' there is a lot that comes into this boy's mind.

Those lines are telling us so much about why this boy is here, why he is selling this meat. It is because he has been telling his mother over and over again that he wants to go to school, and the mother says go and sell this meat so that we can make money to go to school. And all that is encompassed in those few lines. Barney would say to me, 'Can you imagine how much emotion is involved in those words? How much power is involved in those words? Imagine this boy always crying. Every day he sees his friends going to school and he has to go somewhere else and sell meat.' This is the kind of journey Barney used to take you through. So much so, that whilst he is speaking you can even feel yourself getting the emotion of it. Even before he has finished speaking you want to go on stage and do it, because you really understand. That is how he worked. And we learnt a lot from that. And that is how I approach my work.

That is how you direct?

That is how I direct. Of course there is also something that is uniquely me. But we draw influences from a lot of people. In this case Barney Simon was one of the greatest inspirations. Barney said he wanted to work with actors like us. It was because deep down inside Barney had always wanted to do work like Jerzy Grotowski, but it was a question of finding actors who will be just as prepared and able to execute that kind of work. Not really anyone can do it unless you go through this kind of preparation. When Grotowski spoke of exercises designed to remove psychological barriers, Mbongeni and I were doing meditation. Now meditation is also a technique designed to remove psychological barriers. So that is what we used, because some of Grotowski's exercises were quite weird. Grotowski considered theatre as a modern version of ritual. Now every director, as he goes through preparation for production, takes actors through some rituals. We Africans are quite ritualistic. We even surprised Barney Simon in "Woza Albert!". One night, at the end, we were running around raising Morena in some ritualistic stuff. We did not know he was in the house, and I tell you, after the show Barney was the first in the dressing room [Laughing].

What did he do?

There was some guy who used to help us. He used to finance us before Barney joined us. He owned some kind of a church, and sometimes we would watch the worshippers running around. There was this spirit that these people were running around with. So we intended to include that, but it was particularly that night, and Barney, unfortunately or fortunately, was there. He was the first person in the dressing room: 'Guys, what are

---

Opposite above and below – Traditional ritual prayers are offered in the sacred mountain caves of the Free State.
Photograph by TJ Lemon / South Photos.

you doing? What was this thing, katcha, katcha? No, no, no, let's keep it simple.' That's another thing, sometimes he used to protect what an actor can do well. Some directors have a problem with helping an actor to protect a beautiful thing he is doing in rehearsal so that he can give it to the audience on the night. Barney was good at that.

'He had that kind of heart, that of tenderness within, which I believe we need as artists'
Percy Mtwa

How?
Let's say, for instance, you have done something wonderful in rehearsal and you were not aware of it. To make sure that you understand and to help you remember it, Barney would ask you to try that once again to make sure it is embedded in your mind. He used to be so concerned about performance opening nights. Sometimes he would stand at the back. Rehearsal is beautiful, but opening nights are like death – they come. It is something I have adopted too. Opening nights I stand at the back. So if something goes wrong, you sneak out. It is only when you realise, 'Ah, everything is going smoothly,' you start looking for a seat. I have done that several times, even overseas. You never stop being anxious about your work's coming across to the audience, how it is going to be received.

If Thandi in the Free State who is 15 is reading this, she is still saying, 'Ja, but how did he protect you? How did he make you understand? Is he still saying remember you did this and this and this?'
Here we have to find an incident.

Okay. What did he tell you about the flies and the newspaper?
The customer asks me, 'What have you brought today?' and I say, 'I have mutton, chicken and nice sausages,' and then I smash a fly. Barney says, 'That was wonderful, it was spot on. But now understand why you did it like that.' It is because I want this person to buy something because I am thinking about the money I have to make to go to school. So when I smash this fly, it's like this little fly becomes the biggest enemy to me, because this man may change his mind from buying because he has seen that fly. So it is like a dialogue, saying, 'Get the hell out of here, you are spoiling my business.' And since then it stayed with me, and it has helped me protect that which came spontaneously in the beginning. And of course like mime itself. I believe anybody can go on stage and hold a piece of paper and wave flies. But what makes it aesthetic is when we give it meaning.

I think you must be a great director.
I am flattered.

How did Barney protect you overseas?
Barney at some stage was telling us about our articulation, that we had to be careful: 'You must work on that, guys, because over there you will find people do not hear a word you say.' And one time we were at a garage somewhere when a guy talked to our American stage manager. When we drove off, one of us asked what he had said. Barney said, 'That is exactly what I am trying to say: as much as you did not hear what he was saying, that is exactly the way you may sound to him on that stage.' So that is when we started working on adapting our speech to the American audience as well, and even

changing little things. He understood the tapestry of a piece of work – that if something is missing, it may cause the whole piece to be cut into two. He knew how to keep a piece together.

So how did he?
Oh Irene, you keep digging and digging. Even in performance he knew how to keep things together – how to balance up a performance.

How do you balance it up?
Besides the tapestry of the text itself, also the performances of the guys – how they keep the audiences on the edge of their chairs. Barney was wonderful about that. At some stage an actor may go on stage and perform a piece five days in succession without being aware that each performance, and each audience, takes something away from him. He diffuses this energy which quite often has to be refilled, recharged to meet the standard of performance that is required each night. So Barney knew how to do that. He would say, 'Remember, your life may not be just your own, it belongs to this production.' As a result he would start preparing us from the minute we woke up – what we'd eat, what time we'd wake up. And during the day, where we'd go, who we'd speak to. We would even decline some interviews, because that night is very important and we'd need to rest. The energy that is going to be required that night to sustain our purposes is very important, and we cannot squander ourselves by maybe going to a party somewhere, or taking a walk, even in the zoo, or sitting and speaking to Irene [laughter], because it takes a lot of energy as well. Which is something I always emphasise. So Barney knew how to protect a performance, even like that. These are a lot of things that he has left me with. When I heard that he had passed away, I was in Cape Town. I cried like I had lost my father. I only discovered three months after he had been buried that he had passed away.

It seems like, on every level, articulation was such a practical and technical thing, yet the trance was the opposite. It is almost like you could embrace...
... All of them at the same time. Ja, we were like with Morena himself on that stage with Barney. We were taking upon ourselves the souls and spirits, the thoughts, of the people that we were portraying. Barney would never let you get away with anything. He would just stop you and ask why did you do that. If you cannot answer, then he is going to tell you it is because you did not do this and this. Try this and that and that. Then when you get back to performance... it was wonderful working with that man.

And then of course he was a wonderful human being. He had that kind of a heart, that kind of a tenderness within, which I believe we need as artists. I am a Christian-humanist, Barney was a mystic-humanist, which was just a point of departure. We have to understand, as artists, not to allow ourselves to be trapped or imprisoned by our philosophical and religious, even political, ideologies. We need to be quite flexible. Because as a director I learnt that I may be requested to direct a piece whose message I totally disagree with. Sometimes it does happen. But then as a director you have to try and solve the problems inherent in that play in order to make it work – and to protect the intentions of the author and be as faithful to him and the audience as possible. Amen.

Words

baas, basie – subservient words for boss

baba – father, a term of respect

bra – brother

hostel – all male housing compound serving the mines and industrial areas

kaffir – nigger

Morena – Sir, or Lord, term of respect

Passbook – Every black man and woman over the age of sixteen is forced by law to carry at all times, a passbook, also known as a dompass. It contains information about birth, family, background, employment taxation etc. If at any time the police discover a person without a passbook, immediate arrest follows. The passbook is a major symbol of oppression in South Africa.

rand – South African unit of currency, one dollar

woza – rise up

Places

Albert Street – This Johannesburg street is the location of the Pass Office that controls the influx of black workers to and from the city. Workers often line up for days awaiting permits to seek work. A black born outside the city becomes an illegal immigrant if he loses his job and can be 'endorsed' out of the city back to a homeland. Black men, legal or otherwise, wait in Albert Street for whites driving by who are looking for labourers.

Homelands – Also known as 'Bantustans' and 'Reserves', the homelands are the tribal areas set aside for blacks. They are run by governments set up by the South African regime. Rather than being 'homes', they are areas of great devastation and poverty that offer few opportunities for employment. Because young men are recruited away by white industries and mines, homelands such as Kwazulu, the Transkei and Bophutatswana are populated largely by women, children and old people. Blacks employed in white areas may not bring their families with them. Consequently they often live in all-male hostels, and are able to see their families for only a few weeks at Christmas. Through the apartheid policy of homelands, only 13% of all South African territory is ceded to more than 20 million blacks. The rest of the land, which includes the richest agricultural and mineral areas, is reserved for five million whites.

Robben Island – Surrounded by the icy Atlantic Ocean off Cape Town, Robben Island is the high security prison where black political prisoners are confined.

Soweto – This huge black ghetto outside Johannesburg was the scene of the Childrens' Uprising in 1976, which began as a protest against poor education, became a protest against all government policies and ended in riots and the massacre of at least 467 people.

Sun City – A huge pleasure resort and gambling casino in the heart of Bophutatswana. Here top entertainers like Frank Sinatra, Liza Minelli, Olivia Newton-John, Ann-Margaret perform for enormous fees. Here gambling, bare-breasted dancers, miscegenation – all illegal in South Africa – are permitted to South Africans. Sun City offers employment, but it is surrounded by terrible poverty.

People

Albert Luthuli – Born in 1898, Albert Luthuli was a Zulu chief instrumental in organizing the 1952 Defiance Campaign – a civil rights crusade in which thousands of blacks demonstrated against apartheid. The same year, Luthuli became president-general of the African National Congress. Arrested in 1956, he was released after a year, but in 1959 was banished to his small farm under the Suppression of Communism Act, which prohibited him from attending meetings, from writing for publication, and from being quoted. He was awarded the Nobel Peace Prize in 1960, published abroad his autobiography, *Let My People Go*, in 1962, and died in 1967.

Robert Sobukwe – Born in 1924, Robert Sobukwe was a militant college leader and one of the founders of the Pan Africanist Congress. He was elected its president in 1959. One of the leaders of the 1960 anti-pass laws protests, he was arrested and charged with inciting the destruction of pass books. After being sentenced to three years imprisonment, Sobukwe was released in 1963 but promptly detained through an act of parliament for an additional six years on Robben Island. This so-called "Sobukwe clause" permits indefinite detention of political prisoners after their sentences have been served. Finally released in 1969, Sobukwe was restricted by bans and confined to the Kimberley district until his death in 1978.

Bram Fischer – Born into a prominent Afrikaner family in 1908, Bram Fischer was the son of a Judge President of the Orange Free State and grandson of a Prime Minister of the Orange River Colony. He became radicalized as a law student at Oxford. After becoming a lawyer, he led the defence in a number of political trials, including the Treason Trial of 1956-1960 and the Rivonia Trial of 1963-1964. In September 1964, he was arrested and charged under the Suppression of Communism Act, but fled underground to continue his political activism. Re-arrested within a year, he was sentenced to life imprisonment, and died in 1975.

Lilian Ngoyi – Within one year of joining the Women's League of the African National Congress in 1952, Lilian Ngoyi became its president. Her eloquence as a public speaker and energy as an organizer made her a target of the government. In 1956 she was arrested and became one of those prosecuted in the massive Treason Trial that did not end until 1960. Restricted for many years by various bans and forms of house arrest that confined her to her home and prohibited her from having visitors and from holding a job, she died in 1980.

Steve Biko – Born in 1946, Steve Biko became the first president of the All-Black South African Students' Organization in 1968. It and the Black Peoples' Convention, which Biko also helped form, were at the forefront of articulating the emerging philosophy of black consciousness. He was served with a five-year banning order in 1973. In 1975 he was arrested and held for 137 days without charge or trial. Following the Soweto riots of 1976, he was arrested and held in solitary confinement for 101 days. In 1977 he was again arrested and twenty-seven days later became the twentieth person to die in police custody over an eighteen month period. Despite numerous arrests, Biko was never convicted of a single crime.

Ruth First – Author and teacher.
Born into a politically radical family in Johannesburg, she studied social science. From the mid-forties she worked with African mine strikers, and with Nelson Mandela and others of the African National Congress. She was Johannesburg editor of radical journals which were successively banned, and acting secretary of the Communist Party. Among the 156 accused and later acquitted in the Treason Trial in 1956, she was then banned and house arrested. In 1963 she was held in solitary confinement for 117 days. A leading member of the A.N.C., while running a university department in Mozambique she was killed by a letter bomb on August 17 1982.

The stage is lit by the house-lights. The set consists of two up-ended tea-chests side by side about centre stage. Further upstage an old wooden plank, about ten feet long, is suspended horizontally on old ropes. From nails in the plank hang the ragged clothes that the actors will use for their transformations. The actors wear grey track-suit bottoms and running shoes. They are bare-chested. Around each actor's neck is a piece of elastic, tied to which is half a squash ball painted pink – a clown's nose, to be placed over his own nose when he plays a white man.

WOZA ALBERT!

Woza Albert! was created in collaboration by Percy Mtwa, Mbongeni Ngema and Barney Simon.

It was directed by Barney Simon and performed by Percy Mtwa and Mbongeni Ngema.

It was first performed at the Market Theatre, Johannesburg, in 1981.

It was subsequently performed at the Mark Taper Forum, Los Angeles (1982), the Berkeley Rep., Berkeley (1982), the Traverse Theatre, Edinburgh (August-September 1982), Riverside Studios, London (September-October 1982), the ACT Theatre, Seattle (1983) and the Annenberg Centre, Philadelphia (1983).

Was it overseas that there was this issue about black and white?

These are the politics. Of course we have had such problems. We came from an apartheid situation here. Overseas we were viewed as people whom the government had allowed to go, and therefore for that reason we may not be as important or as effective as we claimed to be. That is particularly how Black Consciousness politics tended to view us. "Woza Albert!" was against the system as it were. Not against the people – which are two different things.

Percy, wasn't there criticism about working with that white man?

Well, we came from an apartheid situation. When we came to work with him, Barney had already worked with lots of other black people. On the basis that there is nothing wrong as long as we know that our values are protected as much as his right to protect his values, we came together to create that which we feel we need to give to the people. It is a question of making sure we treat each other with dignity and work on that. Politicians always want to drag each other to one side. As artists we cannot afford to be imprisoned by narrow-minded ideologies. We need to be transcendental because we are regarded as the conscience of the society. Politicians tend to play dirty and we artists are always trying to clean up society, basically, and throw in some light so that they can see where they are treading.

I think also Barney wanted people's stories...

Ja, people's stories, because there is a lot of mystery in those stories. Remember, I said he was a mystic-humanist? He was fascinated by these mysterious things, but his objective, basically, was to try and unravel these mysteries for an audience. Which I believe theatre is all about. Peter Brook said: 'Theatre: the objective of theatre is to make visible the invisible.' Where things might seem accidental on that stage as we tell that story, people can begin to see that 'Oh, it is not much of an accident after all. It is because A became B and C became D.' Barney has helped us to investigate our very own lives, to find these mysteries which we will seek to unravel for an audience on stage. Barney had this spirit of a child in him, which I believe constitutes an artist. I have often said theatre is such a vivid experience for many people because it recaptures the unspoilt awareness of children. There is always that readiness to play. You always found that in Barney. Inside him, and in his mind, there were these people playing on that stage. He was able to get it from the actors – to play just like that.

And that is why he wanted an actor to play with?

Ja, that is what made him a great director. For a director to be able to integrate all those elements, there is one instrument that is paramount – the actor and his spirit. You need to revive the child in him. Sometimes that child dies. When he is dead – the child hurt, broken, stifled at some stage – then we die. And if we are dead inside, how are we going to play? We need to revive that child. When we revive that child, it is done with the innocence that characterises the child – the innocence that is able to embrace the souls of the people we want to portray. It is very important. So far, it is that innocence that keeps me going, that unspoilt awareness of children and artists. I hope I am not sounding like a saint.

Opposite – Glossary from "Woza Albert!" published by Metheun Drama.

Dixon Malele

'He was sort of a mother, you know'

The first time I met Barney Simon I was still a young boy. They were doing "Phiri" with Sophie Mgcina, Cyril Magubane and Felicia Mabuza in Diepkloof. There was this old white man with a white beard in Diepkloof, where I lived. He wore this heavy jersey. You know the one the Wits students used to wear.

A polo neck?

Ja, those cheap ones, ja. Hey, it was amazing to see a white man in a township and all that, and then in a black shebeen. I said, 'Hey, broer, man, I want to see the show.' I saw "Phiri". Then the next time I met Barney was when I was working with Mbongeni Ngema and Percy Mtwa doing Gibson Kente's "Mama and the Load". They hinted to me that they will be leaving the production to go and do something on their own. They went to Transkei and they got arrested as they were working on their material to do "Woza Albert!". They wrote me a letter to say, 'Dixon, we are working on a very good thing and we want you to be in it.'

I went to Mannie Manim: 'Mannie, this is what is happening: there are two young men and they have got this thing they want to do and they would like to show it to you.' We had hassles – we didn't have any money when we were trying to put the whole thing together, then Vusi Magudulela gave us R35. We just knew him as a rich person. He was not educated, he just loved the concept of "Woza Albert!" because it was talking about the sufferings of the people, specifically about jail. He said, 'What you two young men are doing – this is very good, I love this, you are talking about me.' After we got the whole thing together we said we were ready for the people at The Market. Mannie Manim went through his appointment book. He pointed to a day and said, 'Fine.' The guys said, 'That's all we want.' And then we didn't sleep, we were just thinking about the day. "Woza Albert!" was auditioned by Mannie Manim and Barney Simon. Oh man, it was very rough. We did our thing, and at the end Mannie Manim said, 'I want this show.' Barney said, 'No, I am not going to do it, no, no, no. I don't want people from the Black Consciousness movement saying, "How can a white man direct this thing."' At that time you know Black Consciousness was very, very heavy. We said, 'Barney, we don't care who sees you, but this is us, we are also black. We want you to direct this show because you are the only person who can understand what we are talking about.' Mannie put a lot of pressure on Barney, but we also put a lot of pressure on him. It took a while for Barney to accept the job, and then on condition that he will help and not really actually direct. He gave the guys a lot of homework. Then when they came in the morning he let them go through their physical exercises. Then he would ask them what they think about what he asked them to do, and to look into it when they were at home.

And do you remember what the homework was and what he asked you to do?

It was basically about the characters in their script. Like when Mbongeni would talk about his grandfather, you know, and then Barney would ask about a lot of details.

'How was your grandfather, how did he walk, how did he talk?' These are the exercises that he would give the guys to go through in their minds when they were at home. And in the morning he asked, 'Can I see what you have been thinking, what you are seeing in your mind?' Then the guys would stand up and give Barney what they had been working on. Then there would be a lot of laughter from all of them. 'See it works if you go through this exercising of your mind, visualising, thinking about, or preparing yourself for, what you are going to do tomorrow.' And the guys became very warm and it kept getting stronger. Barney felt he had got beautiful boys to work with – they gave him a lot of enthusiasm. I think Barney started neglecting some of his work that he was supposed to do at The Market – he was mostly with these guys. He became like a possessive, caring father. Mbongeni was always late, and Barney would really freak out and say, 'Man, you know, I need a fuck as much as you do... be prepared to come and work.' All Mbongeni could do was smile and roll up his eyes. Barney really cared for those guys. He said to me, 'Please make sure they go and shit in the morning, and wash, and eat breakfast, and then they are here at the rehearsals in time.' They were very, very naughty. He was sort of a mother, you know. Barney was obsessed with the ANC. He had his favourites – like Ruth First. When he heard of her death, he dedicated the show of "Woza Albert!" to her that night. We were on tour in Australia. Chief Albert Luthuli was also loved by him so that's why his name is in the title.

Was this when you travelled?

"Woza Albert!" started at The Market Theatre and then it carried on to Los Angeles, and to London at the Criterion Theatre, Piccadilly Circus. Barney was very, very worried about his actors. He wanted to make sure that he protected them – even from the critics. When working he would always ask: 'Are you comfortable with what I have given you?' If not, then he would suggest another way of getting the actor to be comfortable, so as to do what they are supposed to do on stage. Again he would ask, 'Are you comfortable?' And the guys said, 'Yes we are comfortable.' And still Barney would check again. He didn't want to impose on an actor but work with him. Barney unearthed feelings from the inside. 'Tell me tomorrow what you think. What you have seen.' And then when the guys come to work the following day they'd say, 'Man, you know, when I looked at this character, this is what I discovered.' Then everything becomes like a ball of fire.

Do you remember any examples?

Ja, there is a lot in the old man that Mbongeni was playing. There is Albert Street where the guys were begging for work from the passing cars: 'My baasie, asseblief, man.' Barney would send them out to Albert Street to research. He'd ask, 'What do you think if Jesus comes back to life and chooses South Africa as his second home. Where do you think he would go to? Do you think Sun City?' Then the politics would erupt from that. Barney would say, 'Hey, come on guys, let's not get too excited – there is too much politics here. Let's just be specific on the play... Sun City, why Sun City? The people there are swimming and the people nextdoor don't have water. Would Jesus be pleased to see this kind of affair?' I remember one lady, Evelyn Leveson, writing for the Sunday Express, being very critical of Barney Simon for allowing black boys to show their behinds in public. But this was what was really true about what was happening at Number 4, that jail in Hillbrow.

What was true about that?

If you are arrested for anything, they book you in and then before they lock you up you have to go through an inspection. Maybe you have a stompie of a cigarette hidden in your ass to smoke later, or whatever. It was called tauza. Barney was excited by this and said, 'No, we are going to keep this. It's going to be in the play. You have to tell the truth.' Barney really wanted to expose the horrors of the grand regime at that time. Theatre was like a platform for him to do that. He didn't pull his punches. He went beyond, and we were scared. Man the police! The guys came out with a lot of stories they wanted to tell. Barney dealt with this information artistically.

When you work with Barney you don't see what he is telling you immediately. It takes time. Most times we didn't really understand what this Jewish old man was trying to say, why is he always nagging. We find out later that it is just that he cares. If you are late, he cries a lot. If you didn't do his homework, he cries a lot. He loved honesty and he would always get honesty from you. When he is working with a black man and a black man tells him a story about the township, Barney doesn't live in the township, but something tells him that, no, we are not telling the truth. Aah, he has got his own way of getting the truth out of you. He says, 'Okay, if what you are telling me is the truth, look at me in my eyes. If you blink you are not telling the truth. If you don't blink then I am going to accept your story.' We start laughing and say there in no going away from this old man, let me just tell him the truth. There were just so many exciting things with Barney. Everybody wanted Barney to direct them. If they were not directed by Barney Simon, then they were not pure as actors – he was a springboard. Barney would bring you a book to read and discuss that book. He would always want to open the door for me. With the costumes as well as the props, he made sure that everything is right. Like using that ping pong ball as a nose to depict a white person.

Tell me more about tours – I remember, you were quite instrumental in looking after people, because tours are difficult.

He always wanted the guys to see the theatre that they would be playing in. He loved giving the guys information about the kind of audiences that they were playing to. He was very helpful in a lot of things. What to eat. Always saying, 'Taste this, it is very good. This water, Evian water, is very good.' I remember him telling us that to be an actor you have to keep an athletic fitness. If you are a stage manager, you have to keep athletic fitness because you will need that energy in theatre. He loved his guys to go to gym, because there were only two of them and they had so much work to do for ninety minutes. They have to eat properly, they have to rest. And then he had a problem with the guys and their girlfriends. Because at that time they were very famous. It would be a problem with the women. Barney was a perfectionist. You know, once the show has opened it was not a closed book with him. He would go back and give notes. His notes are the ones that you yourself as an actor long for.

Opposite – Dixon Malele and friend.
Photograph courtesy of Dixon Malele.
Overleaf – Mbongemi Ngema and Percy Mtwa in "Woza Albert!", October 1981.
Photograph by Ruphin Coudyzer.

Chapter 8. Research

Barney's inspiration often came from stories originated by others, and this approach sometimes gave rise to questions around authorship and rights. Nicky Rebelo had researched and written a play about homeless people, which became the play "Outers". He talks of the complexities of his relationship with Barney. Actors Gys de Villiers and James Whyle tell how their field research in preparation for the play empowered them.

Matthew Krouse wrote a poem about 'rent boys' which was the inspiration for "Score Me the Ages". In this chapter Krouse describes the journey from poem to play. Robert Colman and Lionel Newton relate how important the research process was to the creation of a Barney Simon play.

Opposite – Barney Simon.
Photograph courtesy of The Star.

Nicky Rebelo

'I got up to leave after a while… he said, "Are you going to go like that… two guns swinging?"'

I had seen Barney's work as a student. "Cincinatti" just blew my mind.

Can you remember why?

When you are a student you are keen and interested in seeing vibrant theatre and dynamic theatre. And that it was. It was about what was happening in Jo'burg in the late '70s. At varsity Fugard was the only South African playwright that we studied. Then we were introduced to Barney. He came and saw one or two of our productions. Then we saw "Cincinatti". As a drama student you dreamt of going to work at The Market.

In my fourth year at drama school I did a creative writing course under Mike Kirkwood. He was running Ravan Press at the time. We all had to find some kind of project, to interview people and from that make a play or make a TV programme. I decided to go to Joubert Park and sit with the hobos. I had a tape recorder. I did not want to have an interview situation where I am asking questions. I actually allowed them to pick me as it were, pull me over and sit down. I befriended them. I would go and visit them every day, buy them food and take them stuff. I had this tape recorder running all the time. From that I wrote a play, and Mike Kirkwood was blown away by it. He introduced Barney to the material after I had graduated… that was in about 1984.

Barney called me over and said, 'I want to do a play.' Then he says, 'I want to do it in the main theatre. I'm thinking of Marius Weyers and Marcel van Heerden.' I can't believe this. You've just come out from drama school and you see your name in lights – you think this is it, you're made. It was a weird experience. The text that I wrote wasn't a complete play. There was still something missing, and the main problem was my character. I did not want to have a play where this drama student comes along and sits with the actors. I needed to find something there. Barney liked that idea. I wanted to be in the play as well, obviously. He wanted me to be in it and I didn't want to play myself. I wanted to play one of the hobos. He agreed to that and he wanted me to do some more work on the text.

Before we started rehearsals Barney was directing "Antigone" in Israel. The Haifa Theatre agreed to fly me over to be with Barney and work with him for two weeks in Haifa. While he was rehearsing I would be sitting in this cold flat writing. I wanted to talk about the work with Barney after his rehearsals, but he would be more interested to know if I was enjoying myself. What have I eaten? And making me chicken soup. Meanwhile I am just this young drama student who got this opportunity to do this play and just wants to like write and work, get it together, so I can say 'That's it… it's done.' After we got back from Israel I went over to his house hoping to get feedback from him on my newly completed text… but he wanted to talk about other things… about what his friend Charlie had done… a new patio with railway sleepers. I got up to leave after a while… and he said 'Are you going to go like that… two guns swinging?' I explained that I had hoped we would talk about the play and felt upset that he did not seem to want to.

When we started rehearsals the actors were given the text... but Barney still wanted to workshop. He was in the workshop mode. So we all went out into the streets. At first to the labour department to look for work. We were all dressed as hobos and we all had different stories. We would come back each day with stories. We would sit around the table and speak about what happened. I would go home and work in some of the things that we'd got. My feeling was that in a workshop production a cast would arrive at a rehearsal and start afresh to create and find a character and write the text. But here we had characters and a text. It was difficult for the other actors to rewrite their parts because they had the original playwright sitting in the group and they'd confessed to me that they really liked what I'd written. Out of respect they left the re-writes to me. Barney was happy with this process. When it came to the character based on myself, Barney worked with James Whyle to find a different character based on James's experience, and Barney wrote new scenes.

I was very hurt when I walked into the foyer a week before we were to open and saw some pre-publicity about the play. It said, 'A workshop play by Barney Simon'. So I went to Barney and said why did you put that there. You know it is a play that was written. Seventy per cent of it is the original material. So he said: 'Well how do you think it should be?' I said it should be something like: 'Workshop play based on the original text by Nicky Rebelo'. So he said, 'Okay. Fine.' He took his pen and crossed it out and wrote, and said, 'Are you happy?' It stayed like that, written in pen. It looked so tacky. It just hurt me so much, and our relationship from then onwards was not easy. We did not communicate very well after that. Other people heard about it. People who were in the play knew the text and spoke about it. So that is how this whole thing evolved, which was unfortunate because I still respected Barney and he still respected my work after that. It was just unnecessary.

And do you know why he did that?
I think it's the way he worked. I used to go to his house in the early days before we went to Israel. Instead of sitting in the lounge, he would make me sit on his bed with the text and read it there and talk about it. It was very strange.

So when did you get a warning signal in your mind? Was it right at the beginning, when Barney said we are going to go and do more research and workshop the play?
No, I didn't mind that. That was important work. It was important that people went and spent time as an acting exercise with Barney. People told me about spending nights in the bush and that kind of thing. I was ready for that and happy to do that. So that was fine. I was the only one writing and wrote some things. He did do that and I acknowledge that. But 70% of the writing was mine, and with Barney we added 30%. With The Market play I got 30% and everybody else in the cast got a percentage of writers' royalty. Meantime they did not write anything.

How do you recover from something like that?
Other work came and you just carry on to the next play. It was an eye opener because it was naive to think that I'd had a play at The Market with a cast like that and that

work was just going to flood in. In fact it didn't. I think the big reason why the play didn't get the kind of praise that we would like was... if we look at theatre, at what was happening in the mid eighties... it was the time of protest theatre – Mbongeni Ngema's "Asinamali!", plays like "Bopha!" – a play about a group of white hobos doesn't fit into that genre. It will be forgotten when we talk about the history of SA theatre at The Market in the eighties. In fact when we did do "Outers" a lot of people said to Barney, 'Ag, what are you doing with a play about white hobos?' Barney wanted me to try and work a black character into it and I tried. That was false, because it was a real play, about real people. That was the whole point. To suddenly attach another character on just because you want to have a black face there was false, and I said it was. I followed a black hobo around for an entire day trying to get to know him and get to communicate, but there was just nothing there. He was not interested in talking to me. That's the way I worked. I didn't want to say: 'Excuse me...' It had to be natural. It had to be him talking to me.

It sounds like what you did in the beginning by yourself was in a way what we have come to understand as the Barney principle. When you interview someone you don't do it with a formal code of questions. You just go and be with the person?
That's what I did and Barney recognised that in me. He knew I was very good at that, because after we went out into the streets my stories were always better.

If, as you say, the writing was 70/30, you must feel you did the basic development of the play?
No, we did fill in certain gaps and try to develop some characters. Give them a bit more material.

But your play gave the defined characters?
The defined characters were still the central thing. The character of Derrick (Hennie in the text) and the fact that he had this special friend who came and brought him stuff... that was the whole core of the play. This community was only held together as long as this relationship of the benefactor and the receiver existed. Derrick was king of the circle because he had a special chommie. As soon as that was broken the whole thing fell apart. And Derrick died... he died in real life. All the characters were based on real people and we just found a few other little bits that we added to develop them more.

What do you think you gained from that experience as a director and then as an actor?
Sitting in on the rehearsals was a very tense period for me. Seeing a thing being put together. I would watch everything. Backstage every day I would be sitting and listening to every single line and how it worked. I had done things before, other cabaret stuff, so I knew my writing worked. But to have a full-length play with good actors doing it, was an experience. It gave me the tools which I now have, to direct with confidence. Barney always looked for a quality in something and he always tried to push and push and get the actors to understand this quality. This worked for some

'I decided to go to Joubert Park and sit with the hobos…' Nicky Rebelo

actors while others struggled. I felt he could have found more direct ways to get across what he wanted, rather than his vague alluding to something. It was like dagga speech, a lot of it. He would say something and you weren't quite sure what it was, but you got the texture of what it meant and you kind of went on that.

Why do you think he did that?

He always communicated like that, whether it was directing or just a normal conversation. You always felt you had to concentrate 100% and be on your toes when you were speaking to Barney, to really try to grasp what he was talking about.

What you said is very precise about the ownership of the writing and accreditation. But you don't hold a grudge?

No, not at all. It's just what happened. A lot of it is other people picking up pieces from something they heard. Then you start hearing from people how Barney started it. "Woza Albert!" and "Black Dog". That is the kind of thing he was wanting to go for. He found it difficult to work with ready material. I think he would have preferred it if there wasn't any material. But there was this material, which he had acknowledged was great. That was the problem too.

Did he say this?

He said it was brilliant. At a party one night Barney actually said to me, 'This material is better than Fugard.' That's not something you want to hear as a young playwright. You want that aknowledgement only after you've proved yourself over a period of time. It soured our relationship. In fact we never worked together again. I could have learnt a lot from him and we could have worked well together. Because when we did speak about things we were interested in the same subject matter. We were Jo'burg boykies from the same side of the railway tracks. When he saw "Apparently or so I Heard", four monologues I wrote and directed for Jennifer Steyn, he particularly liked the one about a schizophrenic girl. He had a sister who was a bit mentally retarded who used to sit on the stoep all day. He just related to that character. I think that there are certain people that work in the industry who you can relate to and say, 'That's my kind of actor. That's my kind of material.' I recognised Barney's "Cincinatti" was based on the first multi-racial club that opened. I used to hang around the end of town in those days and watch that stuff because I found it fascinating. I still go into Hillbrow and find it fascinating. That's why I still live in Yeoville. Barney lived in Yeoville a lot of his life too. What is important to me is in Jo'burg. There are people like us also running around the streets at night looking for stories there. The main thing is about creating new South African work.

When you worked at The Market again, would Barney come and watch?
He was fine, yes. Absolutely. I just think that there was always going to be a tussle between us if we had to work again with me as a writer/actor. I am not the kind of actor that a director takes complete control of. I am too strong about my own ideas. When I read something I bring a lot to it, and some directors are happy with that. Other directors feel intimidated. It is not that I don't want to take direction.

You just want to be heard?
Not so much want to be heard. I trust my instincts. I don't come there completely blank. I think he preferred that kind of actor. To me theatre is just an empty stage. An actor walks onto the stage and the audience sit there not knowing what to expect and being held spellbound by the word and by the performance. I concentrate on the word, the text and the performance, and that's what exciting for me. I have worked with some really lousy directors here who sit there staring. To me that just doesn't work. I think a really good director is somebody who lets the actor know he is listening to every single thing. Really listening and really caring. To have a director that listens to every single word and cares about everything you do. You feel safe in that environment and you feel you can experiment and trust him. Barney was that kind of director. And he was also caring about what you had eaten. Making the chicken soup. Nurturing. It's like your granny sitting there taking care of you.

It's the nurturing of the word as well? What was it like then being in Israel, seeing Barney work?
He couldn't speak the language either. So he was directing a play in a language he couldn't understand. I have just directed in French, but I can speak a bit of French. Not perfectly but I can still direct an actor in it. You can still feel rhythms. You can still hear the truth, hear the music of it.

Previous page – Barney Simon and the cast of "Outers" in Joubert Park.
Photograph courtesy of The Market Theatre.
Opposite – Boy having his head shaved in Johannesburg. Photograph found on Barney's desk.
Photographer unknown.

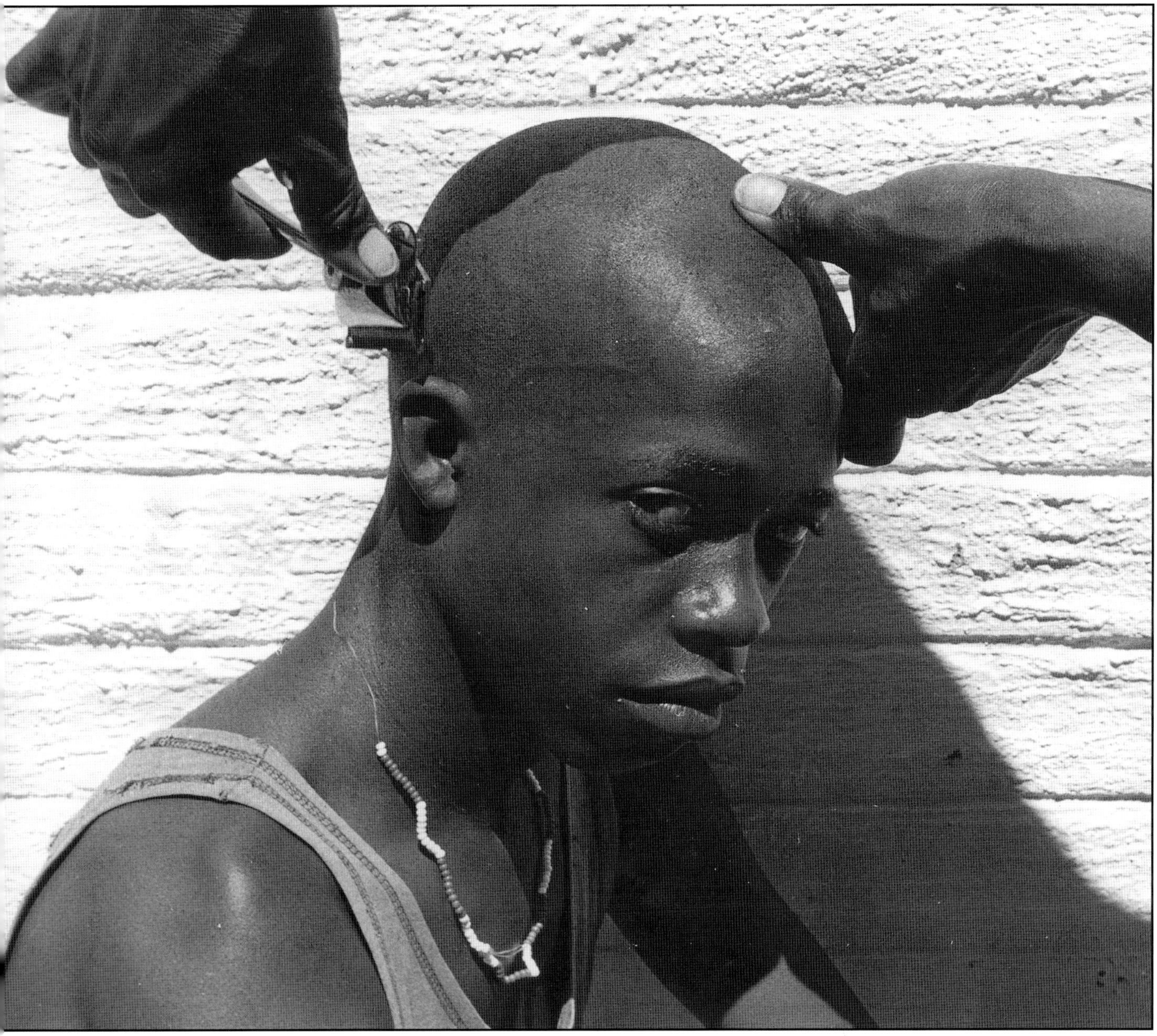

Gys de Villiers in "Outers", 1986.
Photograph by Ruphin Coudyzer.

Gys de Villiers

'Your eyes just fucken' go wide'

I went to sit at home with him and got goofed and thought, 'Yissus, this ou's head is fucked, ek se.' Then we started working on "Outers". We had a standing script that Nicky wrote. Let me just say, Barney made you look three hundred and sixty degrees at life. The three hundred and sixty degrees become relevant to the project that you're working with. And then after you've worked with him you can never not look three hundred and sixty degrees to find inspiration and things relevant to your piece. That was the main thing that he taught me. Your eyes just fucking go wide.

And how did he teach you to do that?

He sent us into the field, into the streets for two weeks to come back with scripts, with stories that we could filter into the standing script. Even things that people say, or the way they do things, the way they roll a cigarette. Just things to enrich your project. The way he'd make you look three hundred and sixty degrees was, you'll tell him a story. I saw a woman, she was wearing a red dress, and she bought one apple and a banana, and she sat down and ate it. Then he'd say, 'Tell me again, you didn't tell me the story.' I'd say, 'What do you mean, I didn't tell you the story?' He'd say, 'No, you didn't tell me the story. You must start fantasising. See the person's life behind the little image that you've seen. You know, the tip of the iceberg that you see there. So much more under the water.' So you'd have to go, 'Okay, I saw a woman. She was probably about forty-two. She's definitely overweight. It looks like she's got two kids. I don't think she's married anymore. Her husband probably beat her up. I think she comes from Rustenburg. She doesn't have a car. That's why she takes the bus. She only bought an apple and a pear because she's on diet somewhere in her mind.' So you have to start fantasising, and explore. That way he opened your eyes to not just see the outside but to really go and look for things. Then you'd have to write it, rewrite it and rewrite it again.

And did he give you the leads why you should rewrite?

I once read a piece that Barney wrote and I thought, 'But why doesn't he work like that?' Because when he wrote it down, it was just so clear and straightforward, what he wanted from actors. He was saying thing like, 'You can not show the actor where you're leading him to.' He knew what he wanted from you. He worked in a cloud. A cloud is not clear-cut. It's not a clear shape like a building. It's changing constantly. Reforming. He never gave you a straight-line answer.

Yet, in writing he could be straightforward and say, 'You make the actor always vulnerable, so that he is never settled and sure where he is at, otherwise it becomes a tame, just rehearsed, flat performance. Whereas if he's never sure, he's always reaching towards it.' And for me it's like dancing. Once you've reached your final position it's already too late. You should, on your way to reaching it, already be moving towards the next moment, so that it never becomes a stale flat thing. I think for him it was always about reaching and letting the actor explore every night. Not working towards final moments, not to ever make you feel settled.

Do you think it was worth it?

In retrospect it was worth it. The second time he used me in David Lans's "Flight", he used me exactly like the first time. He used only my energy. I said to him, 'But Barney, don't use me like this again.' And he said, 'Ja, but you mustn't be angry with me. That's not how I want you to use your energy. You must be like a karate man.' If you asked him a question, he would not give you a straight answer. He would tell you a story out of his life, or something that he read, or he'd show you pictures to give you kind of obscure leads. With "Flight", I was pissed off. I felt I'm not moving. I thought, 'Ag, fuck you, you lazy director, why don't you challenge me and put me on a completely different angle. Take me somewhere else. Please, for fuck's sake, there is more to us than that, you know. We're busy with a craft.' It was the first time I was really fed up with acting. I'd say, 'I'm not fucking English.' So I was just saying, 'Barney, this is it. I don't want to see this fucking business ever again.' And he just turned to me and said, 'Gys, you've got the responsibility.'

In retrospect there was a lot one learned from Barney. But while you were working for him it was always in a cloud, and kind of frustrating, because you never felt like you'd reached a point where he was satisfied. I understand it now. But it was frustrating.

What do you think you learnt?

I learnt from him about observation. That everything is relevant in the end. Everything that happens in the streets around you, society, your family, whatever, is all relevant to a project. And the thing he said about responsibility. In later years, I worked out for myself that as a performer one carries a responsibility for the character one plays. He also said, 'There, but for the grace of God, go I.' So, even in a killer there is some good, or even you or I could become a killer if we were in those circumstances. That made me look at every part that I played for the truth of that character. The responsibility of carrying that person's story to the audience so they can see also, 'You can't just write off a character and say, yes, he's just that, he is only a psychopath.' The whole history is very important, where the person come from, the circumstances in which he grew up, is all very important to where you find him at a particular time in the story. I've taken that through with me to the part I play. This has made me choose very carefully.

How do you choose?

When I choose, I read the script. If I trust the director, then it doesn't really matter. Barney made a massive impression on a lot of people. I mean Charlie, the guy he kind of took under his wing, was a kind of street kid that he gave a life. And after Barney died he was shattered.

Why was Barney attracted to you?

Raw energy. I did one year at UCT. I didn't finish a course. So I wasn't over-trained.

What do you mean over-trained?

It is that thing about people feeling too safe. They start singing scripts. They make nice noises because they have so much voice training that they think they can gargle. And that's why he went for Marie as well. Marie was also raw energy. And I think also because I was Afrikaans. I had a different angle. I wasn't only working with a lot of head, like a lot of other nationalities, like many English people. Raw energy was something that he could use.

I don't think I did my best work for him, but what I learnt I could put in other plays. I didn't want to think too much, and talk too much. I wanted to get down and do the fucking thing. But obviously that was the lesson I had to learn from him, to really explore. If the head understands where you're going then the body follows. So you have to kind of tweak the brain firstly to let the rest come. But at that stage, I just lived. I was young, and energetic, and mad. I was exploring this business that I just found fascinating and wonderful to be in. I saw "Black Dog", because Marie was my mentor in a way. I was looking out for her and what kind of work she was doing. I saw in her there was definitely a verdieping, more depth in character, in Marie. And in John Ledwaba I could see raw energies and what Barney did with that.

As an actor you'll find your safe little pocket and sit in it and not push yourself. And that's what he always broke. He didn't want you to be safe. Ja, as an actor you also have a responsibility to take an audience to precipices of immense fucking dungeons and not fall. You can hang out on a precipice and show them the danger of those precipices. But, ja, you cannot let the audience be safe, otherwise they are just going to sit back and go to sleep. It is a live performance. You throw the ball to each other, or to the audience. A great thing that he taught me is you must earn a pause. In the storyline where you can take a pause is again like music. You learn the score from the character, the breath spot where you can breathe, and take your next passage.

He also taught me another thing. Every sentence has got a heartbeat, so it's about meaning again, which I later discovered with other directors. It's about meaning. And you've got to find the heartbeat of that sentence, where you put the exclamation to make that heartbeat for that sentence work, so that you can follow on to the next sentence. In "Outers", people were talking quite a lot across each other. If you watch a play, and there are three people on stage, each one has got his own rhythm, his own beat, and his own direction that he's going in. That makes interesting theatre, where it's at cross-purposes, cooking all the time. Otherwise the audiences are lulled into complacency. Jesus, but I'm clever.

'Let me just say, Barney made you look 360 degrees at life'

Gys de Villiers

James Whyle

'Barney's glimpse of God'

I got to know Barney Simon in Yeoville, Johannesburg in the 1980s. I was in my twenties. I had recently lost my last parent and inherited enough money to live on. I had also just aided and abetted my expulsion from the army on the grounds of insanity. Yeoville, bless it, was full of artists, activists, students, musicians, actors and other misfits loosely unified by their hatred of the great white lie. Thus ensconced, and with encouragement of Clare Stopford and Lynne Marie, I wrote a play about my military adventures. It was called "National Madness". It was the vanguard of a small column of army plays that followed it into the decade, each one at war with the lying idiocy of the media and the state. Nicky Rebelo, also still horrified by his army experiences, saw "National Madness". Nicky was going into production, and, as I understand it, a very difficult relationship with Barney, on a piece he had written called "Outers". "Outers" came out of research that Nicky had done among the white tramps in Joubert Park. The writing was, is, remarkable, unequalled in its ear for the lyricism of the gutter. But there was a clash between writer and director/writer. The result was that while "Outers" is unequivocally Nicky's play, Barney was writing the part of Richard, which I played, well into the rehearsal process.

I got what I was always asking my agent for: to be challenged as an actor. And Barney, I think, got challenged as a director. While sometimes effective, I was a limited actor. So Barney and I did a lot of one-on-one work over weekends. We'd break to get a boerewors roll from the Steers take-away round the corner from his house next to the park. These, he said, were subtly spiced. When we were eating he would say: 'Do it now.' I'd have to work the speech we were busy with around the boerewors roll. He was persistent like that. And sometimes frightening. Three quarters of an hour before we opened he was still rehearsing me. 'Don't worry about the moves,' he said. He just wanted to believe in what he was seeing. And now, when I am directing, I have exactly the same feeling. It either works or it doesn't. It's true or it isn't.

"Outers" was well received by the public and the profession but not by the critics. The piece frightened them. But years afterwards I found myself at a table at the Troyeville Hotel with Lara Foot Newton, one of South Africa's most accomplished directors. Somehow the subject of Barney came up and I told her about three young schoolgirls who had watched the show. Their wide-eyed awe and excitement as they experienced the production from the front row had lived with me ever since. 'That was me! That was me!' said Lara. She told me the production inspired her to study theatre.

It was certainly extraordinary to rehearse. Barney sent us, temporarily stripped of privilege, out into the streets of Johannesburg. Because we went dirty and worn, doors opened into new worlds. I got a lesson – the street is richer than you think. It has levels that you cannot experience if you walk through it in a suit.

Opposite top and middle – Marius Weyers and James Whyle in "Outers", 1986.
Photographs by Ruphin Coudyzer.
Opposite bottom – Marius Weyers, Gys de Villiers and James Whyle in "Outers", 1986.
Photograph by Ruphin Coudyzer.

James Whyle

Looking for something in the character of Richard which I was not prepared to explore for him, Barney sent me three times to the public toilet in Joubert Park. He was sniffing around the gay world that he would navigate later in plays like "Score Me the Ages". I met a man whose injured arm oozed through a bandage. He told me that he really should go to the Jo'burg General, but he was scared that they would hurt him. The gay thing never happened and Richard became, as I had been briefly in real life, a deserter from the army. Barney never used me as an actor again, but the experience had made us friends. I'd have breakfast at his house and we would share the occasional joint. And once or twice we walked dogs together. We laughed a lot. When my second play, "Hellhound", appeared at The Market Theatre it opened under his sheltering wing.

I didn't go to Barney's funeral but I write with a piece of sculpture from his house close by my head. I believe that he comes to visit me occasionally when I do certain kinds of work. Barney's roots were in downmarket Jo'burg suburbs. He had a profound moral insight, a delightful sense of humour, a love of Durban's finest hemp, an ability to alchemise high art out of authentic South African experience. He died around the time apartheid did. Barney knew when a thing was true – a performance, a play, the delivery of a line. He saw it, and he knew. He had a glimpse of God, Barney. He ruled nothing out. He didn't judge. He knew that the good, like the evil, is in the detail. His eye stripped off all status and made us equal. He had a glimpse of God, and he stayed true to it, and it made him great.

Opposite – Afrikaner Weerstands Begeweging, rightwing recruits practise shooting in Mpumalanga Province, June 1992.
Photograph by Paul Weinberg / South Photos.

Matthew Krouse

'I wanted the play to show how amazing and exotic and incredible the gay community was'

I took all my friends for my birthday to see "Cincinatti". At that stage it had already moved to the Brooke Theatre. It must have been about 1977. I think it was the first time they had ever put a strobe light on stage in Jo'burg. We all went to see the strobe. Anyway, we were late. We missed the strobe and I was outraged. That was the first time I saw Barney – in the foyer of the Brooke Theatre. In "Cincinatti" there was a gay scene where Marcel van Heerden is cruised by, I think, Ron Smerczak. That was very electrifying. The Market Theatre crowd in the first generation was very sexy to people. One was in awe of them. And Barney was the head of it all. Barney decided The Market Theatre was not enough, that there needed to be additional experimental space. We sat down and Barney said, 'Hi, everyone. I want to initiate a new idea.' We had been running the Weekend Theatre which Barney came to. That is why we were invited to that meeting. His perception was that there was need for new space. John Nankin, who had come from Cape Town from the Space Theatre, said, 'Tell me one thing, is this Rehearsal Room going to be Barney's Rehearsal Room or is it going to be The Market Theatre's Rehearsal Room?' Barney was outraged. I think that must have plagued Barney a lot – whether The Market Theatre was his venue where he was making decisions or if The Market Theatre was an autonomous venue that ran on its own steam. And that is when I thought, 'God, cultural politics is not a simple terrain.' There were encampments functioning in opposition to The Market Theatre which was essentially set up to work in opposition to the Performing Arts Council.

After a couple of months the Rehearsal Room put on some interesting things and, not least of all, became a place of progress. It became the home of Possession Arts run by John Nankin and Ivor Powell. They did outrageous things there. Not least of all, if I remember correctly, circulating a syringe. Everybody took the blood in their arms and put it in a coke bottle. They didn't change the needle. They filled up a coke bottle with blood and they smashed it against the walls.

How did you get to "Score Me the Ages"?

I mentioned to Barney, in passing, that I was living in Braamfontein right on the renting strip. I was suddenly noticing in my loneliness that there was all this male prostitution going on. I said to Barney, 'Wow, that is really going on around me.' I was watching the most outrageous things happening in the trees outside my flat. And I said, 'Now, that is an interesting subject for a play.' And he said, 'Well, why don't you write the play? That is an incredible idea.' I went away and wrote the play. I called it "Forgotten, Forbidden" and it was just abysmal. It was terrible. It was a poem.

Did you think it was terrible then?

No, I thought it was absolutely brilliant. Lionel Newton went away and learnt it off by heart because he was convinced that that would be the play. Barney looked at him and

Opposite – Matthew Krouse.
Photograph courtesy of M. Krouse.

said, 'This is absolute shit. I won't do this.' Barney just kicked it out. Barney was very single-minded about his standards. An ongoing conflict started between me and him over that particular play. Barney said, 'You have to soften the subject matter in order to accommodate the audience member who does not know about life.' He also said, 'What do you want to be in the play?' I said, 'I want to play a queen who likes to wear woman's underwear and likes being burnt with cigarettes.' Eventually he said to me, 'Hey listen, this is not going to work like this. We are going to show the world that everybody is a lunatic, sick, depraved, unfortunate. You are going to show very unhappy people.' And he swung the whole thing around. I was terribly immature. The play was being taken away from me because of Barney's method of appropriation.

Which was?

As he did with Nicky Rebelo on "Outers". He worked himself into the project and made it his own, which is quite unacceptable in retrospect. He got involved in the subject matter. He eventually landed up directing my play and I landed up transcribing by hand, if you don't mind, every fucken improvisation. I had no role in the end. I refused to be in it after I couldn't play the queen in the negligee getting burnt by cigarettes. I had no role. So I had to be assistant director for R2000, which was hardly a desirable role as initiator of the project. Laurens Cilliers was brought in for the role that I was going to play. So I worked myself into a corner and had no role and function other than hanging around. Eventually when I had my big fight with Barney he said, 'You should be paying me as opposed to them paying me.' Because I was learning so much. I was in my own way learning a lot but I was grumbling through it. Mannie Manim at some stage voiced disquiet around the way things were going and said to me, 'We don't want to get this play banned.'

On the opening night, believe it or not, Peter Brook arrived. And before the dinner Barney said to me, 'Why don't you come out for supper with me, Athol and Peter.' So we watched the play and afterwards I went for dinner. Me, Barney, Peter and Athol sitting in Gramadoelas eating supper. I was angry because I thought the play was a complete success. The mayor of Johannesburg had arrived – he was an old geyser – and said to Barney after the play, 'Can you believe these things are happening in our Johannesburg? Isn't it amazing how the play shows us that even though these incredible things are going on, these people are just human beings like you and me?' Barney was happy as a lark because that is exactly what he had wanted to show – the humanness in everyone. But Edwin Cameron, the gay rights activist, had come to see it and had nearly walked out before the play had even started, because he had read in the programme note, 'the desire and the shame', and he wanted to murder Barney. He still says to this day, if we ever have these conversations, that completely misfired – to say 'the desire and the shame'.

Why?

I can only imagine that it stereotypes gay men. That gay men are sort of overwhelmed by desire and because of their desire they are afraid of the shame. That is not good for gay liberation politics, to say that you have got this shame horny thing. According to Edwin, Barney showed himself to be a fool by that programme note. After dinner Athol said, 'This play shows that everyone is the same. It doesn't matter whether you do A, B, C, or D.' I said in front of Barney and Peter Brook, 'Athol, what makes you think that we are all the same? Do you go renting at the station at night? Ever had it up your bum?' And I started to bait Athol. Barney was terribly unhappy with me because I put a damper on his dinner with his influential friends. They were three of a kind those three.

What did Athol say?

I don't think he could say anything because I was just being petulant like a school kid. I wanted the play to assert a kind of difference. That is why I was outraged. I wanted the play to show how amazing and exotic and incredible the gay community was. Just saying this – 'We are exotic people who dress up, so accept us for that,' – you know. Barney was very closeted and completely grey in a sense. He wasn't an out gay man. He would prefer to live a life of upfront ambiguity. Nobody was really sure whether Barney was gay or straight. That is fine. I still won't even say in an interview whether I thought he was gay or straight, because he was what he was. He was that generation of man who had his own identity. They did have an identity, that generation of men of fifty or sixty plus. It made me also understand that The Market was Barney's baby. He definitely worked a thread through the work that happened. He used his incredible strength to assert a kind of morality – not that it was negative morality. It was Barney's world.

My play was a celebration of our gay colourful selves. And he didn't want that. And you can see how that goes with his personality, because he wasn't one of those people. He did send people out on field excursions standing on street corners or going to bars. I tried going with them. They did not want to go with me at that stage, because they realised that I was coming from this place of resentment and bitterness and depravity, and I wasn't going to help them. I was too angry, too gay and exotic to go into theatre experimentation invisibly. With those kind of field excursions there was Marie Human walking through Joubert Park as a hooker or Lionel walking through Jo'burg station as a rent boy – it's the invisibility that counts. Not walking with Matthew Krouse who is obviously a Jewish fag from around the corner.

A couple of months before Barney died the Wits students did a student production of "Score Me the Ages", the workshopped play that grew out of "Forgotten, Forbidden". Barney and I went along to see it ten years after the fact. He phoned me and said, 'I want you to come and see this.' The audience gave it a standing ovation. They did not know that Barney and I were in the room. It was quite a relevant play, although it was too white, because we could not really find a black perspective for it. There weren't many black rent boys around in those times.

Before Barney died I did an interview with him because of the Yiddish heritage in this country. The South African Jewish community had just been surveyed by the World Jewish Centre and they found some very interesting things. How close knit it was and how they laagered. It is one of the last of its kind of Jewish communities on earth. Jewish orthodoxy is dying. It won't exist at a certain stage. Likewise, Yiddish is a

language that is nearly dead, because they killed off a generation of Yiddish speakers. Barney's observation was that he wasn't Jewish, he was Yiddish, which is very pivotal in the Jewish community. The working class Yiddish community theatre developed at the same time as communist community theatre developed in Europe at the time of the revolution. And you have to understand that the left wing instincts that Barney carried with him, as well as people like Joe Slovo, come out of that mindset. You cannot divorce Barney from the development of left wing theatre that happened from the 19th century. You cannot because that was the legacy of his theatre. That is how you get plays like "Black Dog Inj'emnyama" – any of his political plays. That is how it works. That is Yiddish theatre. That is what it brought to the world.

'It is one of the last of its kind of Jewish communities on Earth' Matthew Krouse

Opposite – The Bishop Suffragan of Johannesburg East, the Rt Rev. Simeon Nkoane, prays for peace in Temple Shalom, alongside Rabbi Ady Assabi.
Photograph courtesy of The Star.

Robert Colman

'He would give you an image of water running over rocks instead of running down a river'

I had been working a lot with Matthew Krouse.

What work had you done with Matthew?

Matthew, Irene Stephanou and I had done satirical, political cabaret. Barney had seen that and the one show that Matthew and I had done – "Famous Dead Man". Matthew had this obsession about rent-boys and that led to "Score Me the Ages".

What was the fascination with "Famous Dead Man"?

It is a style – queer theatre. The kind of humour, the gender changing. And I think it was mainly because it was something he hadn't done himself. It hadn't been explored or done very much here at all, except a lot of camp cabaret, I suppose, with people like Adam Leslie. So I think Barney appreciated the humour of it. He appreciated, I'd imagine, the political sentiments of it.

Which were?

Which were the then apartheid government. And drawn very much from Matthew's and my experiences of having been in the army. The incredible anger about that. At the time it was very much sort of attacking Afrikaners, which was the government, in a very vicious way. Which was certainly cathartic for us and cathartic for the audiences who saw it and enjoyed it. And even cathartic for Betsie Verwoerd who ended up having it banned. It was about her late husband. She brought the whole case to the censor. All that stuff must have attracted Barney. "Famous Dead Man" ran at The Black Sun, which Barney had a lot of respect for.

Why?

Because it was the only fringe venue at the time. It has never really been replaced. A lot of important work was being done there. It was very accessible to work in. You did not need budgets. You hardly made any money. You changed in the kitchen. But it was very popular and it gave a voice to a lot of young writers, actors and singers.

And specifically sort of anti-government or anti-establishment?

Ja, really kind of political cabaret. "Famous Dead Man" did very well. It played once a week and we were packed for about eight weeks. It was a story about Hendrik Verwoerd and Dimitri Tsafendas, the man who assassinated him. Through Verwoerd's history, we traced the history of apartheid and a lot of the apartheid laws that Verwoerd was responsible for. It was a two-hander, myself and Matthew. A journalist came to see it and she thought she was doing us a favour by giving us this huge back page of The Sunday Times which sensationalised things that were sensational in it. Like Verwoerd's mother giving his father a blow-job on the train. Another scene was two Afrikaner society women masturbating to their rousing climax of Afrikaner Power. There was a

lot of really shocking stuff, chosen really to make the point that we were trying to make. When we went to the Censor Board, one of the people who defended us, in fact he paid for our trial, was Pieter-Dirk Uys. He was astounded at the chutzpah that we had and how far we went in debunking and dealing with these things. The next thing we knew, Stoffel Botha, who was the Minister of something or other, phoned the Censor Board personally without having seen the show himself, and the show was stopped. This was at the instigation of the Verwoerd family who had read about it in The Sunday Times. We had to do a performance for the Censor Board, because they are not allowed to ban a show without seeing it. They all shuffled in in the daytime. All the lawyers and Edwin Cameron. It was terrifying at the time. We completely over-reacted. We were going into hiding and terrified of being attacked on stage – which in retrospect is real.

Robert Colman in publicity photograph for "Score Me the Ages", 1989.
Photograph by Ruphin Coudyzer.

score me
the ages
BarneySimon

How did you become involved in "Score Me the Ages"?

I had heard about Barney's method of working and I wanted to work at The Market Theatre. We started meeting once or twice a week and just talking extensively around and about the theme, which was male prostitution. To get back to your original question about who I was when I met Barney. As an actor, I had lost my confidence and for me in retrospect it was ideal to be working with Barney. I worked completely without vanity. I really wanted whatever it was that he had to give and I was completely open to it. As an actor I have never worked as hard, as dedicatedly. I suppose in a way I idolised him. I just really wanted what he had to give. I loved the whole process.

Tell us about the working process.

The working process was sitting and talking around the theme and then going out and finding characters. Barney could be quite vicious – intentionally and unintentionally. He would actually pick one person out of the cast and say this one is so good at character research and the rest of you are shit. 'This isn't how you research a character. Look how well so and so has done.' It is a human failing. Directors tend to fall in love with someone in the cast. So some of those things were very hard at the time. But I was just so open to what he had to give, so those negative things I only thought about later. It was hard at the time to see that Barney did have favourites when he worked. My whole perspective on that changed since I have started workshopping and directing. It is very difficult to avoid. It is ultimately quite destructive to the person it happens to, who gets given a false sense of something. So then it was going out and researching characters. I came with a few ideas. One of the first things Barney said to me was, 'Wouldn't you like to play a working-class character?' I went out to the hospital to do research about being a hospital porter.

What did you do?

I went dressed obviously to look like the sort of person that might look to get a job as a porter. I spent the day at the hospital with these porters and heard their sort of hospital jokes.

How did they relate to you?

I just kept very quiet. I did not speak very much, just followed them around and helped push trolleys. I did not do any hands on. They showed me around. Then we had lunch in the canteen. I was getting a bit desperate that I could not find a character. The people working that day were not the right kind of people. Then I saw this man at lunch that I did not even speak to. That became the character. It was quite amazing, an incredible process for me, something that has served me as an actor since then.

Just that impression of somebody and that instinctive response to him. You can capture a whole living character. I think that, in the best way of working with Barney,

Opposite – Barney Simon photographed in the foyer of The Market Theatre, 1989.
Photograph courtesy of The Market Theatre.

is what one achieved. The actors met with Barney one-on-one and created biographies. Part of the process was writing your own biography. And then incorporating events from your life into the final biography of the character.

If you want to delve you have to be someone who likes to listen don't you?
That is what I mean – patience. It was something that went as deep as possible without becoming therapy.

How did it not become therapy?
Because at the end of the day, the production, the production was the important thing. I think what broke the group-therapy thing was the next stage of the process – the improvisation, which at the time I was quite terrified of. I'd done improvisation at drama school, but I came into it as an actor who had very little confidence, so I was scared about not being able to improvise. Again there, Barney was quite cruel, picking up one person in the cast and saying, 'What a fantastic improviser you are! You guys don't know what you are doing.' The end result, when he picked out and kind of fell in love with someone, was not a very good performance from that person whose ego he pandered to. I think he himself had his own fears and his own needs from the people he worked with. He had a side that was blinded when he encountered someone who was dynamic, extrovert and confident... If you played the right game you got Barney's full attention. You got to places. If you were not prepared to play the game you were just another of the ten million actors wanting to play with Barney. I tend to idolise people. I put people on a bit of a pedestal, which I did with Barney. Then they must be perfect. You cannot expect that from somebody. An institution that is about a personality goes through a very difficult time when the personality is gone. Because there isn't actually an infrastructure. The infrastructure was that person's energy and dedication, drive and passion. And vision. There are people left behind who share Barney's vision and who worked with him over a long period of time. It is very good that they are there.

Tell us about 'Score Me the Ages'.
I ended up with Barney developing this character for me called Alan who was a hospital porter who fell in love with one of these rent-boys. The amazing thing about it was the level of reality every night. I realised since that it was very rare and very valuable experience. While we were doing the show Peter Brook came to town. Everyone was in a complete state as you can imagine. I imagined turning Peter Brook into somebody in the story that night. So for the character there was some important dignitary coming to the hospital.

Did you meet afterwards?
Ja, I did. He said something that I really held onto. He said it was an incredibly important work. It was fantastic. The performance was really the level of reality. I was probably very irritating to some of the actors in the cast because I took Barney's principles very seriously.

Can you think what some of the principles were?

Well, preparation. A good five-minute silence before you perform. Being involved in every single moment of the story, having read and thoroughly worked out relationships to everyone on the stage. Holding details sacred. I found some rehearsal notes, like: 'Every reply is a response to something you have learnt, received, experienced.' 'Don't anticipate, everything that happens is the first time for the audience.' 'Monologues are dialogues with yourself.' 'Each thought leads to the next thought.' 'Care what matters to Alan and his life and his story in the play.' 'You are not listening at all. You are denying James a presence.' They were technical notes but many of them were not technical: 'Deal with the audience.' 'You cannot always tell the story as we did last night – they set the rhythms, we do the dancing.' 'Don't ham – you're overdoing it.' 'Alan's becoming a type, you're losing the person.' 'Be careful of riding the laughter.' The notes I really liked were when he gave you an image in trying to explain what he wanted – say an image of water running over rocks instead of running down a river, which was wonderful. He loved telling stories which I always enjoyed. It was probably about the rhythm of the whole play. 'The river flows over rocks, past them, around the corner and out to the sea.' Then something about the story: 'Understand the range and the story. We are co-storytellers, with the lighting, with the stage-manager, with everyone.' It was important to listen to the story and the actors in the scene. 'Rehearsal is the work. Performance the release.' There is also a fabulous one. 'You're being eavesdropped on from the back of the theatre.' 'Be bold tonight.' 'This space is mine. This man is mine. This moment is mine.'

Ja, the notes, just the detail of the work was incredible. In three months of working with him I learnt more than I learnt in drama school. It has taken me a long time to just be an actor. It made it difficult for me to work with people who did not work like that. It did not suddenly catapult me into fame and constant work, but I suppose it really laid the seed for me to build up my confidence again as an actor. As it turned out I was rarely in shows like that. He has given me a method to workshop and devise plays, which is very much drawn from the way he worked. Another amazing thing about Barney which I sense was that in "Score Me the Ages" every character had an aspect of Barney. The women and the men. One was like Barney's vanity, or Barney's humility, or Barney's closeted-ness, sexually speaking. When he demonstrated, when he gave notes, he was brilliant. He just knew the character, the intonation and the emotion.

Would he demonstrate by doing the lines?

A line or a word, or physicalise it for you. That is part of Barney the writer. That he also fed – he was not just sitting there looking. It was a real journey. A real person and real humanity.

'You are telling this story about rent boys' Lionel Newton

Lionel Newton

'Beware what the camera can see. Just bring back the photographs'

We were at The Market Theatre doing "Thina Bantu" (a University of Cape Town production in 1988). I saw Megan Kruskal in the bar and she said, 'Come, you must meet this beautiful friend of mine, Barney Simon.' I knew nothing of him, never heard of him. I'd missed all the plays in Cape Town because they never toured there. I was quite cocky, about 22 or 23 in a leather jacket. My image at the time was brash and bokkish. He was this old man and he had a white beard and white hair. 'I thought Megan was going to introduce me to this Italian model. I was also confused by the fact there's the guy on the radio who is Barney Saayman (on Radio 5).

I'd done workshop process with Mavis Taylor but never to the extent Barney used it. Although Mavis probably spent the last 15 to 20 years of her life doing workshops at UCT, I found something in Barney that I'd never seen before. The closest way of describing it is that he would really tune you like an instrument. He wouldn't just like take your information. He would really get to know you as a person, or he would try and open every possible avenue getting to know you, quite personally. I think he got turned on by people, by getting to know people.

When I was younger, just coming out of drama school, I was very straight. When I went into drama school I was obsessed with knowing what people's sexuality was. Barney – I could never tell his sexuality. I was dying to ask him. If I knew I was dealing with a guy who was gay I would show a certain side of myself that was I suppose gay friendly. But with Barney I couldn't 'cos I didn't know. I asked him have you ever been married? Ja, I think he was engaged once. And then we talked about living with someone: 'Do you miss that?' He said, 'I am a bit in love with all my friends.' He would always ask me about myself and it was never about theatre. He'd ask, 'How did your father come to South Africa?' and I'd tell him. He loved the story about my parents. My mom was 14 when she rode on the back of a bike from Krugersdorp to Pretoria to watch my father racing in front of 50 000 people. My father was an international dirt-track motorcycling champion. My mother would sit there and pose. He'd carry on about that story. He wanted more details, more details about it.

So Barney was just after stories?

Ja, he was just into my world. My stories in childhood, because I was always the Engelsman in an Afrikaans family. By the time we started working, we'd started forming a character. I remember he wanted to work with people who would turn him on. So he would choose people. We knew he wanted to work on rent boys. We were obviously isolating the characters. He'd say, 'Come back in a week's time and tell me what you've seen.' I'd go and spend whole days in Jules Street walking up and down, I used to come with lists of stuff. Then we got closer and closer to this character.

Opposite – Gideon de Wet and Lionel Newton in "Score Me the Ages", 1989.
Photograph by Ruphin Coudyzer.

How?

I'd give him five characters and he would say, 'Why did you speak to this character?' And I would say, 'Because I found him interesting.' And he would say, 'Why?' I'd say, 'Well his hairstyle, he had such a cheesy hairstyle.' 'What kind of hairstyle?' 'Well, combed backed up and he had this one eye that just tics and tics.' Barney loved that kind of detail. We would have about 5 or 10 characters. We must go and find a rent boy, because you are playing a rent boy. So I say, 'Cool.' He says, 'Do you have any ideas?' I say, 'I know they hang out at rent boy corner'. 'What's rent boy corner?' 'It's that block there in Braamfontein, because Matthew, every time we go past, is always checking the rent boys out.' He says, 'Didn't even know there was a rent boy corner.' I don't know if he was feigning innocence, I am sure he was. We went there. I showed him where it was. He was fascinated, and we carried on driving.

'Take care, take care of that skill'
Lionel quoting Barney Simon

I remember him giving me really tit advice. 'Don't ask the guys questions, just sit there. You don't have to talk to anybody.' And I said, 'Why?' He said, 'Well, they might not like you and they might not want you around.' I sat there for three and a half months, for three nights a week. For the first two, three months I would have okes winking at me. I had stone-wash jeans, quite kak takkies and quite a tight T-shirt. I had quite a body then, had my hair up, would not shave for a bit. I sat there for a long time. After a while I started seeing the situation from the moffie's point of view. What times so-and-so took place. And none of them actually talked to me. Then, one day, I hit an angel. I'd just been sitting there for about three months. He just told me everything. It was about 11 o'clock on a Saturday night. He came up to me he says, 'How's it? What's your name? Where are you from?' I told him, 'I'm from Kimberley.' 'Ah – Kimberley.' You see I had a history of Kimberley. So I bullshitted half of my life story, and half of what I knew. So he started, 'This is Tjokkie – don't worry about him, he will take you around the block, and show you his cock if you give him 15 bucks but don't let him touch you.'

He started giving me all this information. 'You see the okes will pull in here and wait until lights are red so they can view you. They won't just stop. They will slow down till they hit red and that's when you have to show your wares. That's Willie, he likes you to piss on his headlights. He'll take you into this alley and give you 10 bucks to piss on his lights. That's so-and-so, he likes to suck your dick through his car window. That's old Frikkie, if you fiddle with your dick...' He just went right through. He knew them all. Of course when I went to Barney we just wrote this stuff. Barney said, 'This is the play, this is the stuff.'

Just in terms of the process, you wrote it down?

I went home. It was about three in the morning and I wrote it down. It must have been about 15 foolscap pages of detailed notes. I was getting the environment and textures. We weren't even looking yet at the play and how people interact. The second time Barney said, 'That's cool, but try and get a bit more personal and get more information. But be careful, don't get into their personal life, don't break down.' He kept on saying take care of yourself. 'Take care of what you find out. Beware what the camera can see. Just bring back the photographs.' The second time I met this oke I could start getting more personal. I was saying to him, 'Why are you doing this? It's horrible. It's a kak job.' Then what his life is about and how does he handle things. Then I was forced into a situation there. I had to do something. All these okes were stopping for him. I went for all the easy options. Pissing on window screens, jolling with the okes' dicks. I would not let anyone blow me and I would not blow. I couldn't. I did a lot of wanking okes off or talking rude to an oke.

How did you do that?
I went into complete character. I'd get into the oke's car and say, 'I want my five bucks – if you touch me, I'll cut you in pieces.' I always had a bottle with me. I became pretty astute. Now people just shoot each other. Then they didn't. I was quite a rough boy then. I had a lot of aggression and a lot of madness. I fucken felt scared. Always nervous in terms that something could happen. We used to play pool together. He lived in this garage. He would look after cars at night and people trusted him because he was white. Instead of a black oke from town.

The second part of the process an extraordinary thing happened. One of the great lines from the play, and it's a fantastic play, is, 'Just close your eyes and think of chicks.' This is what this oke said to me. I said to this guy, 'How do you actually do it? How do you get it up.' 'Just close your eyes and think of chicks.' That was the great line. Barney just wept, when I told him. He was devastated.

But when I went through the second week of being close to this guy, I just flipped and said cheers buddy. I got on to my bike parked far away and went to Barney's house, banged on the door just sobbing and crying. It was also about three in the morning. By the time he got to the door I was just so exhausted from banging and crying. I said to him, 'I just feel like such a leech.' Barney says, 'Why?' – 'You know, it is such a rough world out there. These people are fucking for money and for drugs and are being treated like scum. I go in there with all my knowledge and my skill and I meet this guy who has basically taught me how to live. How to look after myself in that world, and all I am doing is fucken stealing it and sticking it in a fucken play. What a complete fucken jerk. It just feels wrong!' So we carried on talking until about eight o'clock the next morning. I was really freaked out. I said, 'I don't think it is fair, I don't think it is right.'

What did he say?
He said, 'You are not telling his personal story. You are telling this story about rent boys. What we are trying to do in this play is not to glorify rent boys or the business of buying and selling sex. We are basically telling a story in which the world happens to be that and in which humans are touched by each other in that environment. We can only do that if we observe that environment with complete articulateness. If we did not take care then we would be creating a disservice to this guy. The best way we can serve what's happened is to play that character as honestly and truthfully and with all the knowledge that you have.' By the end of the conversation I was convinced.

One lesson he taught me. I will never forget that opening night of "Hello and Goodbye". I was really nervous. It was a period piece. It was written the month that I

was born – 1965. Fugard was there, it was all that pressure. It is not an easy part to play, that Johnnie. You start with a ten-minute panic attack. I walk in, I say, 'Howzit Barney?' He says, 'How are you doing?' 'Shit, man I am really nervous', and he laughs and laughs at me. So he does this to me (goes out of the room and comes back in holding a bunch of keys). He says, 'Now look into my eyes.' I start laughing. He says, 'Stop laughing. Just look in my eye.' I say, 'I am looking.' (He jingles the keys.) 'Don't go anywhere else just look in my eye.' 'I am.' 'Without looking,' he says, 'tell me what this is?' 'They are keys.' 'You are not looking, you are looking in my eyes.' I say, 'Ja.' He says, 'There is the audience, there is the press, there are the other actors, there is the opening night – those are all the keys. You must ignore the keys and just play the character.'

Internal monologues. He often used to do that. Speak what you are thinking, what you feel. It was an amazing technique. He would alter it while you are speaking. It was quite interesting, because he used to walk amongst us. Even if you were doing improv on your own. He would look at you and walk around the back of you. He would generate productivity and get the ball rolling.

The way he structured his rehearsals was episodic. Say it starts off with a bar scene. Create characters in isolation. Step A – See what characters are available. Step B – Choose a character. Give the character an environment. Start finding possibilities of how characters could react. If they do not react find possibilities with others. Then from there the play just kind of grows and starts forming its own life. He used to love skinnering. The way he would mix direct questions with psychological questions was just pure gut feeling. The way he would skinner to you about a character or a person. He had amazing photographs. It all started with that famous Italian photograph, I think a 50s photograph, of that beautiful woman walking along the road, and all the men looking at her, and all their different responses to her. I started understanding what he was saying. He had books and books of portraits.

Do you remember what he was saying about that photograph?

Well, it was one shot but it was how each guy was acting with a different sense of lust. I mean you could just read exactly how they felt about their own sexuality. Barney put me through a lot of time with old, old, old portraits. I would say to him, 'Barney, what fascinates you with all these photos?' He would say, 'People are coming with all that dignity of who and what they are. So simply. They are sitting, looking at something, and it's magic. They don't know what is coming but they have seen the results of it. It is because they want to be remembered, and that being so, is that how they want to be remembered? If you look at the way they are posing, they are posing with their absolute self.' Then I began understanding. It would help with everything. In the streets... I used to hate airports, now I love them. He used to make me feel like I was the best actor in the world.

Opposite – Postcards from Barney Simon's desk. Clockwise from top left –

1. Berliner Ensemble – Helene Weigel ais Natella Abaschwili in "Der Kaukasische Kreidekreis" von Bertolt Brecht 7 Oct. 1954. Foto – Vera Tenschert (All Berliner Ensemble copyright issues direct to Hersteller: PGH Rotophot Bestebsee).

2. Berliner Ensemble – Helene Weigel in der Szene "Die Judische Frau" von Bertold Brecht, 15 Feb. 1957. Foto – Percy Paukschta.

3. Josephine Baker, Paris, 1937. Photograph by Lucien Aigner, Musee de l'Elysee, Lausanne © Aigner from ANA, Paris, News Productions, CH-1446 Baulmes 55516

4. Berliner Ensemble – Helene Weigel als Volumnia in "Coriolan van Shakespeare/Brecht", 25 Sept. 1964. Foto – Vera Tenschert.

What do you think he left you with?

He left me with a sense that I still consider myself special in whatever it is that I have. There is a lot of theatre happening in the country and it's all going in other directions. Often I get discouraged. I say just go and learn building, plumbing, painting, and learn some basic skills. Then Barney revisits me and tells me, 'Take care, take care of that skill. Take care of that talent because it is really worth it.' So that's it. Barney's belief in me still lives in me at times when I really need it. Also a benchmark of quality. Of commitment. He allowed me to perceive things in a different way. Allowed me to be less critical and more open, to let the information come in. Which is a great gift.

You told me once about that evening and the stars?

It was here in my back garden. We were stoned and we were sitting on two stools and there were stars. I was quoting Shakespeare. We were rapping and it was a full moon. Barney and me and Lara [Foot Newton]. We used to talk in our Newtown/Jeppe language. I say to him [in accent], 'Hey Barney, where do you go when you die?' I think it was partially related to the rent boy. 'Where do you go when you die?' He says, 'Hey, check the moon, see the hole in the sky there. That's the hole that God breathes through. In the beginning there was the tide. It was blue.' It was poetry, poetry from Jeppe. It was beautiful. That ended up being the last line of the play.

Opposite – Lionel Newton and Gideon de Wet in publicity shot for "Score Me the Ages", 1989.
Photograph by Giulio Biccari.

POOL
POOL
8
7

Part 4.
New Times

PATRONS OF THE MARKET THEATRE
COLLINS BROS.
JOHANNESBURG
PATRONS OF THE MARKET THEATRE
RETURN SEASON
THIS IS FOR KEEPS

Mr Binger, we thank you and Jujamcyn for the honour of recognition that you have given to us for our role, you say, in proving that art can change society. When I was fourteen years old I had a girlfriend of fifteen who was always telling me never to contradict a compliment, because I always did. I hope that I'm not offending her now, wherever she is. But may I submit, rather, that we at The Market Theatre are part of a changing society and that we have attempted, consistently, to nuture it. Of this I am proud and I hope that we can keep your award. Again, perhaps inappropriately, because I'm standing in Freud's study, may I quote Jung? He wrote that artists often serve their cultures and epochs in ways that are veiled and not immediately understood. That art is constantly at work educating the spirit of the age, conjuring up the forms in which the age is most lacking and compensating for the one-sidedness of the present. I think that that is part of what we are trying to do too. I believe that we live in a place of miracles. I haven't seen a burning bush, except in a veld fire or two. I've never followed a travelling star or even fantasised a flying saucer. But that's not a complaint. The miracles that interest me are not wonderful or delightful or much to do with the divine. The ones that I like best are those that give evidence of the grace that is in all things. They're the hardest to come by in a world as tormented as ours. There might be miracles in heaven, but I suspect that they're not nearly as rewarding as miracles in hell. Every adult South African sitting in this auditorium was born into an insane world. Insane because it denied and confused mankind's greatest gift, the equality of our humanity. We were forced to behave as if cultural differences between human beings were stigmas, separations; chat, curiosity and passion could be crimes; and we were denied the dignity of even comprehending the lives being lived beside us. Johannesburg was not founded beside a river or a bay, as sensible and decent cities should be. It was built on a barren stretch of land because gold was found beneath it. And because of that gold, the greediest and most dangerous men in the world gathered. And here's a miracle: despite our beginnings, our landscape, our grace is our people. Multiple, vivid, absurd, treacherous, generous, adventurous, divinely pragmatic and always capable of our sound of survival - laughter. We who began the Market Theatre did it out of love for this landscape and committed outselves to it. Freedom through legislation has come suddenly and swiftly, and that is cause for great celebration. But freedom of the heart and mind is lagging far behind. It is that freedom that has always been our concern, and remains it. We know that for a time we will continue to live in contradiction and confusion, we have watched like celebrations wither, rooted as they were in devastation. Our new South Africa is very, very young. We struggle every day to realise the difference between what was and what is. To render justice finally imaginable, if not yet real, in a world so long abused. You honour us for what we have been. I hope that it is also for what we are. We undertook a task in the terrible year of 1976, that many called, according to their prejudices, absurd, criminal, or superhuman - which is my preference. It's not a vanity. Camus said that tasks are called superhuman when men take a long time to complete them. We're very far from completion. Our journey is as various and difficult and extraordinary as any that strive for dignity and clarity in our time. Thank you for helping us continue.

Transcript of the speech Barney gave on receiving the Jujamycin Award, 1995.

Chapter 9. Permit yourself what you know

Whatever sort of play Barney was directing, he gave the same importance to storytelling, and allowed stories arising from the life of the rehearsal room to inform his workshopped material. Dawid Minnaar tells how Barney used the treatment he was receiving for flu (inhaling eucalyptus) to help describe the moment in "The Dybbuk" when the spirit enters Leah's body. John Kani recalls how in creating "The Lion and the Lamb", the focus was on telling a good story. He also recalls how Barney encouraged him to use his own knowledge as an African warrior when playing Othello, and not concentrate on matters like 'iambic pentameters'.

In his Jujamcyn speech at The Market Theatre in 1995 Barney Simon declared:
'Every adult South African sitting in this auditorium was born into an insane world. Insane because it denied and confused mankind's greatest gift, the equality of our humanity... But here's a miracle. Despite our beginnings, there's our people. Multiple, vivid, absurd, treacherous, generous, adventurous, divinely pragmatic, and always capable of our sound of survival - laughter. We who began The Market, did it out of love for this...'

The Jujamycin award is an award given in America to theatres with a human rights affiliation.
This prestigious award is usually given to American theatres, but in 1995 it was given to The Market Theatre.

Previous page overleaf – The Box Office at The Market Theatre.
Photograph courtesy of The Market Theatre.

Dawid Minnaar
'It was like drowning'

'A dybbuk is a wandering soul which has attached itself to the body of a living person and has assumed control of that person's thoughts and actions.'

"Background to the Long Search" by Ninian Smart

In "The Dybbuk" he wanted the two characters to be physically together after his spirit enters her body. It had never been done like that before. We – Megan Kruskal and I – improvised a lot. Well, it made sense. Because normally you would have the girl wandering around the stage talking in a deep voice. But they're really one. The two spirits are one, and he wanted to show that physically. Through the whole second half we were physically together. She was always in front of me. She would mouth exactly what I was saying. We thought it was completely melodramatic, but people got such a shock. Eventually a circle is drawn around her, and I think he does help her step through it. She dies and they are eventually together. It has to do with destiny and meddling with it.

We found this thing for when he enters into her body. We couldn't hit on anything that really worked for Barney. I had a cold during rehearsals and I said to him, 'Look, you know I am not well.' He asked what I was taking for the cold. I told him that I would take boiling water with eucalyptus oil and put something over my head and inhale. So he says, 'Show me how you do it...' I demonstrated, feeling a bit stupid. Cloth over my head, I am sick and I have to go through all this and inhale. So he says, 'Make it bigger.' So I made the whole thing bigger, and then the character just started becoming something different that eventually entered her body. That was so amazing about Barney. It was like he had hundreds of tentacles and he could take anything out of the air and use it for work. To tell the story. He could have given me off for the day, but we would not have found the moment. It was one of those magical things that sommer happen. The first time we did the whole thing where his soul enters her body, Bess Finney reacted and stepped back off the stage and broke her ankles.

I'd never worked with Barney before "The Dybbuk". I wasn't as relaxed as I was by the time we started working on David Lan's "Flight". I had obviously learnt to trust him implicitly by the end of "The Dybbuk". He made me feel that he understood me as an actor. He knew what my needs were and how to work with me. Barney could see so clearly through one. He was acutely aware of ego. I had the feeling that he could see what you were, like relying on things that you know already. Maybe that's not completely to do with ego. But in "Flight" I found myself in love with someone. I could not sit in the evenings and work for hours on my script. I would sit in the garden and just dream. I got worried. I said, 'Barney, this is the situation. I am a bit worried...' He said, 'Just let go.' Both times I went through a process where I felt like I was drowning, I didn't know where I was. One always goes through it anyway, but with Barney it had an extra thing to it: he stripped me. Not in a negative way, not in an attacking way. I've heard of directors who can strip actors and it's a personal thing or a power trip. Where they first have to destroy the person and then start rebuilding them in their image. Barney did not do that. He just wanted you to shed all the excess baggage so that you could empty the barrel and be receptive to the work.

Do you know how he did that?
Continual probing and prodding. Barney had a thing about innocence. What was that quote he always gave? It was in Mary Benson's book I think, that a man spends his life looking, searching for the first few images that touch him. That life is a process, a journey where you can continue to search for those moments – the rediscovery of innocence. A very tricky thing. I think that if one can achieve that as an actor... it's always something that one always tries to do. You know it is fucken difficult to reach that point. It's a kind of Zen thing.

Why do you think that innocence was so important to Barney?
It's not so much innocence in the sense of not having experience. It is more an openness and wonderment. To see something for the first time. That tricky thing in acting, to make it fresh every night. To be able to see it again for the first time. That kind of innocence and readiness to step into the moment.

And do you think you achieved that?
It has got to do with simplicity. It must have been, at the end of the day, a very simple thing to achieve. For example, the opening night of "Flight" was the most relaxed opening I have ever gone through. What he did was, he just took us outside at the five-minute call. I think it was raining a little bit, and he had little sparklers that he gave us. We lit our sparklers and we stood there. That just did something amazing. The opening scene was tricky because I had to shuffle a pack of cards in the air. And so I went like this [he gestures cards dropping to the floor]. It did not faze me in the least. I collected the cards. The story got told, and it was just wonderful. It had to do with that moment with the sparklers. So what do you do before you go on stage? You get yourself into such a state, and that released us. There was a sense of wonderment and the childlike experience. It gave us maybe a little bit of innocence for the evening, you know. That is how it was so wonderful. Never since. "Flight" was about people who came from Lithuania, a lot of the Jewish population. These people fled for political reasons and they were very politically active, a lot of them. Most of them belonged to the Communist Party. "Flight" was about that. It starts off in Rhodesia and then independence happens and they flee to South Africa. My character was the old patriarch.

Did the production close earlier because the Jewish community objected to it?
I wasn't aware of that. Oh yes, things like Megan lighting a cigarette at a Shabbat candle caused controversy.

Was there ever an issue that you were not Jewish yet you played an orthodox Jewish character?

There never was. Another important thing I learnt from him was I never asked, 'Am I doing the right thing?' If he didn't say anything, then you were on the right road.

So how did he work with you on "The Dybbuk"? The first day you sat down and did a read-through?

Oh, we watched an old black-and-white film called "The Dybbuk". Old. Melodramatic, like old Yiddish theatre. Some people felt he was too vague. That is one of the most misleading things about Barney. This vagueness. He created that impression with a lot of people. That airy, vague, drifting... I never had that with Barney. As far as the work was concerned he was never vague for me. I always felt that he knew exactly what he wanted. And he was allowing you to go through these insecurities, if that was what you needed as an actor. You need to feel insecure, but you are not insecure. I knew he had a plan. There was always a specific.

I often wonder, what would have happened if Barney had had the resources like Peter Brook. There seem to be similarities between the two men and their way of working and approaching actors. But Brook always has three months or longer. Once they worked for a year on something. That was always Barney's problem, too little time, because he used

Barney Simon directing Joe Stewardson in "The Dybbuk", with Charles Comyn and Michael Maxwell in the background, February 1986.
Photograph by Ruphin Coudyzer.

'Truth – it is very complicated to get there, but the truth itself is simple'
Dawid Minnaar

to work so carefully, he used to be so careful with people. You have to deal with where we are now and the textures around us and where we come from. The history with which you come into the room, into the scene. So that the result of being specific is that then there are no empty moments. Because you are stitching one little thing to another, ending with one tightly woven fabric. Intimate stuff so that nothing is obvious and nothing is generalised. Through being specific the picture becomes filled and full.

Dawid, what do you think working with Barney did for your career?
I always felt with Barney that, ideally as an actor, one would have to work with him once every two years, just for him to get you back on the right road in case you had strayed in the meantime. The thing is to get to the heart. He always made one aware of how much is still to come. He could change things like five minutes before curtain rise on opening night.

Truth – it is very complicated to get there, but the truth itself is simple. You do not want to have to get there on your own as actor. It is a terrible thing because I feel incompetent. I need to work with a director. So I opened myself. It's like drowning. He knew he could take me and stretch me as far as I could go at that stage of my development. I may resist but I would give in eventually. And you don't want to do it on your own.

Dawid Minnaar in "The Dybbuk", February 1986.
Photograph by Ruphin Coudyzer.

John Kani

'... number two on my list of white friends'

Barney was special, vulnerable. He impacted on my life and I on his. I met Barney in 1969. He came to visit Athol in PE (Port Elizabeth) when I was with the Serpent Players. Immediately we just clicked. At that stage to know one white person was enough for me. I didn't want to know more. It took a long time to get to know Athol. We were both interested in workshop experimentation. I was confronting why I am in the arts and how my work contributes to the struggle as a black man in this country. Barney was talking about what life is, really. How can you celebrate life? How can you enjoy the arts?

There was something similar between the two of us. He spoke of the new work emerging, the work that articulates the new voice of South Africa. Of the struggle for a decent South Africa. That is where we clicked. While people were excited that "Sizwe Banzi is Dead" was about pass laws and doing away with apartheid, Barney saw the deeper meaning. The truth of the lives of these people. He gave Winston and I a deeper reverence for these lives. It made me feel honoured to tell the story of these people's lives, and grateful for the gift I have, the ability, as an artist, to make those lives meaningful and true in an artistic way, and thus feed the meanings of those lives into a broader community. And that is when I really liked him and could list him as number two on my list of white friends.

Ian Bernhardt and everybody were milling around us trying to take us on. We were exposed to this stinking affluence and arrogance of rich white people and the way they treated us, like curios, like some strange phenomena that emanated from that dust of the township. We were surprised that they said what a great classic quality we had. So those were the compliments that were heaped on us. I couldn't believe it.

When I told Barney he just laughed and said I was paying for being greedy to have a meal there. Following this we were invited to a dinner. I never saw such heavy sterling cutlery and china cups – you felt by lifting them you might break the handle and be made to pay a fortune. Barney again laughed and said I paid for my greediness. I could have gone to his place and had lovely fish. We could have had everything; we could have made it together, and eaten with our hands. I think at that stage Barney was mischievous and knew I did not like being teased. Barney was aware that I was very serious about life and the struggle at the time. But what Barney was trying to do was to sprinkle within that intensity a bit of humour. Nothing is very serious at that level. By 1972 I realised this is a guy I would like to be good friends with.

After that we went to London and the world became a big stage for us. We went on to win a Tony Award and got recognition. We travelled in England, Australia, North Africa and Kenya. The Serpent Players were a very creative and hardworking group that used Athol and his experience to interact with him, show him and take the work forward. After the overseas tours I came back and met with Barney and Mannie and we started talking about this space. This space was a mess with dust all over. Mannie was talking about the theatre that was going to happen and Barney was talking about the work that was going to happen in this place. Barney was filling us with the history of this place, the dust, the pillars, this space where people would work, how brilliant it was going to be, how many plays were going to happen. We were on our way to Australia and I thought, 'These bloody dreamers, you know!' We came back from Australia and Barney met me at the airport to show me the Upstairs Theatre. So there was this mass of rocks. Barney was walking and showing me that this is where this was going to be, 'Can you feel the space?' Barney was calling me aside, luring me and trying to get me. But I wasn't interested in Johannesburg at all.

However in 1977 we came to do "Sizwe Banzi is Dead". Barney talked us into doing "The Death of Bessie Smith" just as a late-night show in the main theatre. So we agreed to do this incredible play, with Vanessa, Danny Keogh and Janet Suzman who was in town. We started the rehearsals with Barney. It was unusual, because when you work with Athol rehearsal is a process and there is an order. This follows that and the script is the text and that is what we are working on and we understand. The research into characters is a normal rehearsal. I know what a rehearsal is.

Barney was present and we waited for rehearsals to start. The stories began to flow, story after story about his experiences when he was in New York. I could see that Janet Suzman was starting to freak out, because we spent the whole day without coming to grips with why we were doing the play. Everybody was being a little tense telling their stupid story, and I thought, 'Ooh Lord, maybe he'd be a nice friend, but only as a friend, not as a working director. I don't think this guy knows what the hell is going on. I think this guy is a bit looney!' And there was Winston, who is a method actor, and Danny, who hadn't studied anything, Vanessa, who was just a flippant young girl, who seemed to like everything around the room. There was also this guy, who was to play Janet's father, a Pieter Toerien type who was also really pissed off with the process. I thought, 'What is going on here?' So in the first week we really had absolutely nothing, and we only had three weeks of rehearsals. It was crazy.

You never mentioned the play?

Nooo. We had the scripts. We were reading them and learning them. It was only in the second week that we did a read-through. We got a sense of understanding what the work process was about. He would research inwardly within your soul, the meaning of the play and the character. So the stories you were asked to tell were bringing you closer to the stories of the character you were going to do. So you would do a character analysis in a very broad sense before getting into the normal way of doing it, first reading the play and then doing a discussion about the characters. We did that in a more casual way, which was an initial breaking down of inhibitions. There was Janet Suzman, the best Shakespeare actress from England, and two black men from the Eastern Cape who had taken the world by storm, Tony Award winners, and Danny Keogh. He was very uncomfortable with the attention around and was defining his space as an actor.

Then I became quite excited about the way he worked. You had to know who Barney was. It was about lives of people. Lives tell their own story, and your life coming into the part tells another story. I am a great storyteller. My grandfather had three wives

so my grandmothers used to tell stories day after day. So if theatre was not storytelling it was not good theatre. Up until today I am a sucker for 'once upon a time'. If you say 'Once upon a time there was this little girl...' I will sit the whole night and watch it. When I miss that in a play I am disappointed. It could have a brilliant set, lights, design and acting, but I just miss the little story, 'Once upon a time...' That's what I found in Barney.

Janet Suzman and I were working together – I just came in to say that Bessie Smith had been in a major accident and she was bleeding to death. Janet had to tell me that I had to go to another hospital. Janet was trying to say it, and Barney said, 'Again!' 'Again!'. Janet said, 'What's wrong with the way I said it? Why do you keep saying again, again?' and Barney said, 'I want you to... [smacking his lips and licking them]... that is what is missing.' And Janet said, 'What?' He said, 'You are not savouring the words. The story is delectably interesting, the nooks and crannies of it. If you are not enjoying it and if you are not excited by the opportunity to tell the story, if you are not finding it, then you are just telling it.' Why wasn't Janet understanding it? I was enjoying the frustration and Barney knew I was having fun. Finally, he said, 'Tell it like you have just swallowed the world.' When you look back it becomes an incredible landmark, how we did that play. The way we worked with Barney was something for my career that I was always grateful for. To tell the story is exciting and dangerous.

And did it move the rest of the cast? Did it gel with their methods?

No, I still believe the other actors enjoyed the success of the play but they queried how Barney worked. I could balance it because I learnt to tease him about being the Jew. Then we could laugh at each other. Barney would tell me of new ideas and new things. What I found with Barney was there was no connection between the creative process and the production process. If it ended up there, it was okay, but he was more interested in the experience around the creative process. The exciting investigation. The journey of people and things happening. If you told him what happened in the newspaper, he would spend the whole bloody morning discussing what that is about more than just reading the article. We would talk about South African theatre, not necessarily working on a project, but rather working together in trying to form an identity, some character of what our work was about. To look at things that were happening. I would spend the day discussing the world with Barney. I would learn a lot from him just questioning what I saw. He would push it so much that the truth would come out when you find the word to express it without the bullshit of being general. Very specific and in detail.

So tell us, politically those were heavy times?

In the riots of 1985 my brother was shot and I was looking for my brother in the mortuary and the police were visiting me and I spoke out because I got angry. Back in Port Elizabeth, my father had just died. I buried my brother and I was nearly shot by a soldier because I talked back. So I decided I was leaving South Africa. Barney knew I was leaving. I had already spoken to Janet and made contact at Royal Court Theatre. People were trying to find work for me. I knew my family would follow soon.

Opposite – John Kani in "The Lion and the Lamb", 1992.
Photograph by Ruphin Coudyzer.

Marcel van Heerden, Barney Simon and John Kani pose for a media portrait during rehearsals for "The Blood Knot", December 1987.
Photograph by Ruphin Coudyzer.

Barney asked if I could postpone it for three or six months and work with him at The Market as assistant director. Just to work with him, see the work that is done, maybe direct and be involved in some of the things. Mannie also called me aside and said that he needed an assistant in running the place – 'This place can no longer be run by two white people. It needs an experienced black person who commands respect in his community and can be in a senior management position.' That began another tussle, tug-of-war between Mannie trying to teach me administration and Barney saying, 'No, you have got nothing to do with that, you have got everything to do with this side.' So I had to not tell Barney that I met Mannie and not tell Mannie that I met Barney. Mannie would show me the balance sheet and the budgets and he would want my input in places. Barney started to use me on stage as a director. He kept asking me questions about directing, until it became obvious to many that I would be on the artistic side more than the administrative side. So then I became the associate artistic director. I still had the responsibility of management, but mostly, at the time, I was responsible to Barney, concerned about artistic development. We discussed talent that was unmanaged and untrained. We had to find a place where we could train people. Then in 1990 I was trying to raise money for The Market Theatre. When I spoke about The Market everybody was very concerned and passionate about it. People were signing cheques for R5 000, pledges for R10 000 and R15 000... Janet Suzman, Athol Fugard and Joseph Papp spoke.

In conversation with Suzette Sata [of the Rockefeller Foundation] I mentioned young people and their dreams and the way we as The Market could serve their dreams. She said to me, 'I am not going to give you money from the Rockefeller Foundation, I am not interested in your deficits and capital and administrative expenses. Could you tell me more tomorrow at breakfast about the dreams of these young people.' It had no shape in my mind. Mannie had overheard this and decided to go to this breakfast with me. I began to understand that what Barney and I were talking about was the Lab [The Market Laboratory]... It was a place for training, a place that could give opportunity, a space for artists to experiment, explore. I managed to articulate this, and I walked away with 150 000 dollars from the Rockefeller Foundation. That's how the Lab began.

So we found this place, we rented this space. I have seen a man's eyes twinkle at a dusty rubbish place under a freeway, in Goch Street, number 63. It was almost like that flame that keeps us artists burning, that we must nurture and guard. It is a candle wick which can be blown out even by a movement of a hand. This lit both of us up and we knew that here something special was going to happen. Barney said, 'You are the architect, you will always know that you are responsible for this.' I said, 'You too Barney.' He said, 'Both of us.' And that little flame went up at that moment when we stood in that space. We brought in Mark Fleishman as the administrator. He bought into our mad dream.

And you and plays and acting?

We decided, one of those crazy decisions, what I and Barney should do was a play based on the Bible. Barney said to me, 'You are going to create something now...'

So we discussed this and Rose watched us. She asked, 'Are you making up a new church, Barney?' [Laughter]. I wasn't aware that Barney as a Jew didn't know about Jesus Christ. We worked in Barney's office, every piece of the Bible was on the floor. We did not know what part was Luke, what part was Matthew and what part was Mark, and we finally put together a story. Christ from the Annunciation to the Resurrection. I was going to sit and tell the story, reading it. I have a special gift of not having to learn my lines, I read something and it stays with me. In the second week I knew these passages like 70%. Barney was aware of this and would ask, 'What does Luke say?' And I would tell him what Luke said about the passage. Barney was trying to make me learn the lines without reading it. Explaining what Matthew says, or Luke or John, I was trapped by him: '... and which one do you think is best?' At the end of three days Barney says, 'I want you to learn it.' I said, 'Barney, no man.'

Mannie mentioned there was someone who might be able to help us. We agreed that while I am telling the story Merle Thompson would play the harp. Then Sophie Mgcina said she wanted to be in it. When Sibongile Khumalo heard that Sophie was in it she wanted to do it too. Then we put in Lydia Hannibal who didn't have any work because of her strange American accent, but we thought she would be different. In no time we had created "The Lion and The Lamb".

In 1987 when I was doing "Othello" I had a problem with Janet Suzman who was directing. She was constantly telling me about the performance. People explained why she was using a black man for the first time, rather than a big actor playing the part. They were explaining the political viewpoint of using a black actor. One felt the problem of not having the proper accent or gestures. I was struggling, trying not to be an idiot. I was trying to understand it for myself when Barney says, 'We need to talk. I can see you need help. Come I'll help you.' And he did. We went to the Bailey's home for a smart tea and we walked around. We looked at these paintings, one of them was a black man on his knees, crawling. It was Nebuchadnezzar. Barney finally said to me, 'Can you walk? Look you have been dropping your shoulders for years. How can you be taller than Richard Haines [Iago] if you are dropping your shoulders?' I said, 'Barney, we have to talk about the play.' He said, 'What about it?' 'You were going to help me.' He says, 'I did.' I said, 'But Barney we have not discussed it?' He said, 'I have to leave now.' I thought, you swine. He left it to me to make the choice. So I walked in like an African warrior and did what I had to do, to hell with the blank verse and iambic pentameter. If it would make sense to me as an African, I changed the accent and forgot about the gestures and all the blood flowing thing. How would an African do it? Janet came and said, 'It is different, but I will go with your way if you want.' I said, 'This is the way I want to do it, or I am out!' John Whiteley said, 'Why didn't you do this the first time while everyone was thinking it wouldn't work?'

Now I am often too busy with the big picture of fundraising and negotiating with government, getting the money to get this place to work, getting the marketing right. When that happens and I lose the little people with their little stories, I hear Barney slowly saying, 'It is your job to listen to those stories.'

Opposite – John Kani, Barney Simon and Marcel van Heerden in December 1987, during rehearsals for "The Blood Knot".
Photograph by Ruphin Coudyzer.

Chapter 10. Style

"Starbrites", "Silent Movie" and "The Suit" all express innocence and childlike qualities. Nelson Mandela had been released and a spirit of renewal pervaded the country. Basil Jones, Adrian Kohler, Fats Dibeco and Arthur Molepo describe their collaboration with Barney in the world of puppets. From "Silent Movie" Seputla Sebogodi, Tony Bentel and Leila Henriques talk about the use of visual images in Barney's unique theatre language.

Barney Simon reflects on his motivation for "Silent Movie":

'Well I was sitting here, I think it was with Jennifer Ferguson, at the kitchen table, and somebody else was watching CNN on TV. It was about Yugoslavia. And there was a heavy sound of gunfire and then the person swapped channels and managed to hit some sort of Rambo thing on M-Net, and all these sounds of violence were coming through. You know, effects and bodies splattering and all the belongings of pop art. I thought about it, we were living with that as if it were here, as if it was the sounds of birds and children in the park. We've become so accustomed to the sounds of violence that I wanted to return to a kind of beginning - what people feel about each other.'

Charl Blignaut, Vrye Weekblad. May 14, 1993.

Sello Maake Ka Ncube describes how he was empowered by Barney's strong and delicate direction in "The Suit". "The Suit" was a short story by Can Themba who had been one of Barney Simon's contributors when he edited The Classic magazine. "The Suit" toured internationally to critical acclaim and was playing in London when Barney died.

Opposite – Women enjoying music concert at Jabulani Stadium, Soweto in 1981.
Photograph by Rodney Barnett / South Photos.

Basil Jones & Adrian Kohler

'It was intoxicating working with him, like a love affair'

Basil: Mandela had just been released and the idea of "Starbrites" was to make a play about renewed hope. It was centred on an old down-and-out. That was the basic idea and Barney wanted the puppets to play all the characters apart from the old man and his nephew – the main characters. It was a completely fabulous period for me. Barney of course was impossible in that he would have an idea and not really help you make it practical. You would be sitting round the coffee table in his house chatting, most nights actually in a type of crisis. But of course he was so enthusiastic that it was infectious. I had to come up with a way of doing it. But we hadn't discussed where or what or how these puppets were going to fit on the stage. He was just sort of throwing elements in.

It was intoxicating working with him, like a love affair. Because he was phoning, or you were there, or he was here, and you were working through ideas. But once the play was up and running and people were coming to see it and it was doing well, suddenly you were out of the picture because he was working on something else. It was the end of the love affair, you sort of wondered where it had gone. It was the intensity of the working period and the sense of loss at the end of it which characterised that time for me. You thought you were more important to him than just to be dropped, but he had gone on to other people. He was working with a new idea. That separation was a bit sore. The show ran in the Upstairs (which is now the Barney Simon Theatre) for nine weeks I think. It was extended, it was packed, and people loved it. Albie Sachs and Joe Slovo and Helen Suzman came. So did Harry Belafonte.

So you both came up with ideas and you would make the puppets to fit?

Basil: Ja, I developed the 'dancing petticoats' because the main character was a lingerie salesman. It was meant to be a dream of sexy petticoats dancing in the air. And the actors thought: how the hell are they going to do that? Barney wanted them on a washing line originally, but then the washing just hangs. We thought we could blow it with a fan. But then how does it really come alive properly? Barney was experimenting with things that come alive around this man who was dead spiritually. He's told to get off his backside by the ghost of his grandmother who spends the whole time sweeping the yard. So that was something that had come alive in his face. Eventually I hid wire inside three petticoats. It was a bit like a wire body, which had some hip movement and chest movement in it, and the wire held the petticoat straps up. They were controlled on quite long rods, side-lit in lilac, with the puppeteers in the dark. And the petticoats floated into the space, in the air. So that became the solution to the washing-line idea, but only after much talking, smoking, joints, sitting round the table.

And was this before the actual rehearsal?

Adrian: Yes, because we had to have all the puppets made by then. After the Lab workshop Barney went away and I went away to work on the figures.

Opposite – 'Dancing Petticoats' from "Starbrites", 1990.
Source unknown.

Basil: And a lot of the Lab period was also about Arthur Molepo and Fats Dibeco, because it was largely based on Fats's life and Fats's experience. He had sold lingerie in the townships.

Adrian: Basically it was about Fats's life, and sometimes Arthur also contributed. It was a little tricky because Fats had had a very difficult life and Barney didn't really want Fats to think it was about him. But it was. Slowly Fats was coaxed into telling a very painful story about himself.

Basil: Because Fats wanted his real story to be better than it really was, it was a matter of Barney coaxing his true life out of him. The bed came in quite by chance. The bed on stage had a mattress, and during performances Fats often used to go to sleep on it.

Adrian: Fats really asleep on the bed, with the ghost of the granny sweeping outside and complaining. Basil was doing the granny, and when the time came for Fats to respond, there was complete silence. They say there's no more delicious sleep than the sleep you sleep on stage. Basil had to prod him rather roughly with the broom to get him to wake up.

Basil: Fats is a very eccentric guy. He loves English. He loves languages. He loves the profession. He used to talk lovingly about London. His nickname was the professor, but he wasn't really that able to look after himself. It's a classic story.

Adrian: A classic story of art imitating life imitating art. Because Barney wanted to do a play about regeneration and he chose an actor who he knew needed to be regenerated. So Fats could give a tremendous amount to the role automatically because he was the person who fitted the part. He was the person.

So could you remember how Barney did the probing?

Basil: I think the clue was when he heard that Fats had sold lingerie door-to-door. That was a nice sort of comedy element and Fats would have had experiences of who bought it and probably would want to tell those stories. I think that that was an important lead.

Adrian: This was one of Barney's really strong theatre instincts. Once he discovered a deeply personal detail like that, he would allow it to create its own resonance throughout the piece. So, to some extent, the play became a trip through the townships with Fats selling his lingerie. And the petticoats came out of that and the women to whom he sold his wares became puppet characters in the piece. In London we got a lot of flack. An old friend said, 'How dare you bring a play like this to London!'

Basil: It was six months after Mandela's release. The 'Third Force' was rampant and everything was upside down in the country. So the play seemed like complete nonsense to anyone outside of South Africa. It didn't represent anything that was happening in the country. It seemed misplaced. Whereas here it had done very well because of the mood of optimism at the time. But ja, during the rehearsals of "Starbrites" Fats couldn't go home. He spent a lot of nights with us. The townships were in a hell of a state then.

Adrian: The elements of the piece were the two human characters, and then there were Doreen Mazibuko, Basil, Busi Zokufa and me. We were the four puppeteers. And we did the people in the street, neighbours in windows (shadow puppets), ladies in the shebeen. And there were other elements, like fighting cats, because Fats's character used to eat chicken and throw the bones out the window and the cats used to fight over the bones. They were made out of wire springs. They fought pretty well. There were dancing shoes. There was an imbatata scene of sandals dancing.
Basil: Barney wanted Florsheim shoes, which were worn by the band in the good old days.

Did Fats also speak about the shoes?
Adrian: Yes, he spoke about Florsheim like they were million-dollar shoes. That's what set Barney off. They were dream shoes. So you can dream shoes.
Basil: I suspect "Starbrites" was the first play that was written specifically for puppets by a South African writer of real stature. However, the two main characters were human people. And of course behind the puppet was an actor. It is two sides of the same coin to us really, about whether a puppet can hold the audience's attention. Barney still had his reservations about that. That was his risk. He was more accustomed to making 'poor' theatre.
Adrian: Nothing on stage except the people.

It was the actor's process?
Adrian: Yes, so the difference between that kind of theatre and puppet theatre is: lots of objects. It is not Grotowski. It is about using objects and things that move like people to suggest people and aspects of people. Auntie Betty, the woman singer in "Starbrites", had had a car accident and had been crippled. We made a fabulous puppet for that. Because she was walking on crutches, it meant that we didn't have to work her legs. They just kind of swung and therefore you only needed two operators. Busi and me worked her. She had a very pathetic presence, because of the crutches and the swinging legs. That was definitely a puppet idea that worked strongly for the character. The sense of illusion and the frailty of the figure. Despite all his other talents, William Kentridge is primarily a visual artist. He can propel you very powerfully in a visual direction. Whereas Barney's plays grew from the centre out. So of course you are never sure where you are until you get there.
Basil: Ja, you were never sure about that because he had new ideas during the production process and you had to be ready to respond. Whereas actors can change an aspect of the thing that they have rehearsed quite quickly, a puppet requires a lot of hours in the workshop to become something else. That was the difficult side of it, because opening night is coming and you have a lot more to make. And when you are working with these things up front you don't have the broad picture, aesthetically it may not hang together so beautifully. Whereas with William the visual aesthetic is central to the project from the start. Barney's 'centre out' approach was primarily what was so strong about working with him. By the time you are halfway through the rehearsals you really do believe in the people that are in the play.

So what do you think you have learnt or taken from Barney?

Basil: Well, respect for the character is for me very central, that respect for the person, and allowing characters to develop out of their personal histories. That deeply felt respect for someone's intimate, secret history is something that other directors don't necessarily value. We often return to the memory of this way of working when we are doing new work. Sometimes I feel that there can be almost too much respect. I think that it can sometimes become slightly sentimental, particularly with "Starbrites". I felt that we were teetering sometimes on the brink of a sweetness that became cloying to my sensibility. In a way, I wanted the director to take a slightly, not less respectful, but more directorial attitude towards a character. But his delicacy and respect for the back history of the character, that I think is very much what I learnt from him. And also the fact that you can direct a play successfully and not be nasty to the actors... The other astonishing thing was the phenomenon of Barney's skin. His skin was a map of his emotional state of being and his productions were a kind of extension of this skin. All the delicacy and rawness and vulnerability that was in his skin was alchemically transferred into the characters he created.

Adrian: Why did he have so much magic over people? It had something to do with what Basil is saying: he was living his life through the performances he got out of people or the truth of the story they were telling.

Basil: It was a form of lovemaking. We never knew what his love life was but his main love life seemed to focus on the interaction between himself and his actors.

Adrian: During the process of "Starbrites" we kept on thinking time is running out: 'We don't have a script yet Barney, you know. We don't have a story.' And he said, 'I can go and sit down tonight and write the thing. I can do that. No problem. But it is much more interesting to draw it out of the people who are involved here.' Not just going for the obvious or the overly constructed is what is important about his work. Because he would rather hang on and wait than...

A quick fix?

Adrian: Ja. With a project like "Starbrites", he had assembled a group of people who he believed could do a job. But rather than rush in with a formula, he was waiting for the moment when people would be completely familiar with the parameters of the play. It's then that the subterranean ideas emerged.

Basil: Don't be afraid of the process. What was that movie we saw recently which you talked about?

Adrian: "Reservoir Dogs".

Basil: "Reservoir Dogs" has a guy lying on the floor bleeding. And rather than be afraid of that and going into another visual and another visual, Quentin Tarantino stays with it and just allows it to develop and take its course. That's the kind of thing Barney knew really how to do. Not be afraid of the situation, and not be afraid of the process. Not feel that he has to impose a structure onto the process. Allow the process to develop on its own structure. This is always more surprising, more interesting.

Adrian: I have two other things that I remember Barney for. After "Starbrites" we embarked on a TV project "Spider's Place" where I was going to direct the puppet side

of things. I felt insecure, had a lot of doubts, but Barney said, 'Go for it, on one condition, that you protect your work like a tiger protects her cubs.' This always comes to mind when things get tough on a new show and people look to you for strength. The other thing was the opening night of "Woyzeck" in Grahamstown. Barney knew the play very well of course and wasn't happy that we were working on it with William, because he wanted to do his own version with Solomzi Bisholo. In fact he had come to see a run-through a week before we opened and had very little to say other than to comment on the face I'd made for "Woyzeck". He said, 'That's the face of how he looks at the end of the play. But you are stuck with it right from the beginning.' However, he was there in Grahamstown when the show opened. All of us from the production dispersed afterwards. Like we weren't able to see that we'd made something good and that the audience had, in fact, been completely with us. So it was with Barney that I celebrated that night. I was with him when I heard from people how moved they had been by what we had made. It turned into a magical night. We drank a lot and the world felt wonderful and he said something, which was very touching and revealing about his own hunger for the theatre. He said, 'When a show works doesn't it make you feel sexy?'

Adrian Kohler, Barney Simon and Basil Jones pose with a puppet from "Starbrites", April 1992.
Photograph by Ruphin Coudyzer.

Fats Dibeco

'He was an actor who didn't physically act'

That's when Madiba came out. Barney says, 'Now we are free.' I said, 'We are not free...' I said, 'That's the end of the road. Now we are going up the mountain. Now we are at the mountain, there is still a long way to go, this is the harder part now.' But we enjoy the freedom. Because freedom is within the limits of order, is that not so? We performed and then we went overseas.

How did you work on "Starbrites"? Because it wasn't scripted.
It was scripted afterwards by Barney. But we were trying things. I was playing a salesman. I had failed in the music – from booze, or from being taken by the studios. Now I had a bit of money, and I invested in selling lingerie.

How did you decide on selling lingerie?
I know some of the guys who are selling that. They make more money than anybody, because when it's stockings and this and that, ladies just buy. I know the whole of Eloff Street there are more ladies' shops than men's. I said this will be the alternative, since I am not getting a job. My "Starbrites" job just fell on the wayside, but Barney kept on pushing: 'No man you can do it, you can do it.' I think somewhere along the line I was feeling heavy again, with him. I wanted him to be an activist, but those are the kind of things that didn't happen. I don't know how it was side-tracked.

Did Barney side-track it?
I think he did, because he was always not wanting to be direct. Hey no, he always did things subtly... 'Barney, no man, this thing, let it be direct man.' 'No, it must be subtle.' I say, 'You must tread on toes sometimes.' He says, 'No, no, no, you don't have to do it that way.' Every day he was there doing things. There was a time when I went to Park Station to look at the salesmen.

So you researched in Park Station?
Park Station and all the others, but I couldn't get it... because these guys were too ordinary, there was nothing like being sort of flamboyant. I expected such talk, like 10, 20 minutes... guys who were fun, wouldn't leave you just to pass by. But these guys were sitting there and they had a cigarette and started smoking. Now you can't put that on the stage. When I was growing up they were over the top, the way they laughed, you know, with the Fisherman McGregor shirts, Stetsons, Crockett and Jones suedes. Do you know the Crockett and Jones suedes? Ja, in Sophiatown teachers used to love it. Crockett and Jones suede! They were beautiful, beautiful shoes. On stage I had a checked trouser, I made it purple. I thought, no, we must have a checked trouser and shoes. What I didn't do was to bone them, I should have boned them, you know so they shine. But the fact is I was down and out because I was boozing myself almost half to death. I was just going

---

Opposite – Fats Dibeco in "Starbrites", August 1990.
Photograph by Ruphin Coudyzer.

about and doing this lingerie. I said, 'No Barney, I must call it like they call it, I must say lingerie (pronounced linger-ee).' He says, 'No, because people won't know what you are talking about.' I said, 'No, what is this high falutin' thing of 'lahngeray'? They will think it's laundry'. We work, work and then stop and then we started again, following year. We got it together. We worked at that guy Adrian's place, that's where we rehearsed. The fact is I was rehearsing on my back, I burned myself. I don't know what happened. It was in winter when we started, I burned myself with water, all over me. I still have the marks.

So you rehearsed on your back?

Ja, because I had to sleep through the whole thing. I was reading a script. Mostly I am sleeping and dreaming, you see. I am dreaming my grandmother wants a tombstone. She says, 'I am lying cold.' This getting burned was timing because I couldn't react properly, in the sense that I couldn't stand. After a month or so, I said, 'Bugger this. I don't want to be lying here.' I couldn't, you know. I am not used to lying on the ground. I knew the script already. I stood up. Barney said, 'No, no, no.' I said, 'No, forget it, I have to walk.' I started dancing, and I stopped smoking. I decided I didn't want to go overseas smoking and drinking. I left off. I came back and I started smoking and drinking again.

What do you think set Barney apart as a director?

That is something difficult. He didn't want to be set apart. He was an actor who didn't physically act. He was a person who was an actor who becomes a director, knows exactly what actors are like, their heart, their temperament, their likes and dislikes, what to do with them in giving them words. Because some people write and they are not thinking that you have to use those words, and they are like weapons, you know, sometimes they slip off. But work! Heh heh heh... Hey, Barney used to work for a very long time.

What made him laugh?

I would say anything: 'Police...' He would say, 'But when are you going to be serious?' I say, 'But what's the use of being serious. It doesn't bring any money into anyone's life being serious.' I say, 'You must laugh! I've saved myself from becoming crazy by laughing and joking when things are bad.'

Fats Dibeco in "Starbrites", August 1990.
Photograph by Ruphin Coudyzer.

Arthur Molepo

'For me, Barney was like Bob Marley'

When fishes flew and forests walked, sometime when the moon was blood and donkeys smiled, I met Barney. I was still with Workshop '71 then. Workshop '71 was a theatrical group operating from Wits with Robert McLaren, who is now in Zimbabwe. Barney Simon was also involved in the workshops here and there, and whenever there was anything happening at Dorkay House. Barney was a rabbi in theatre, he was teaching theatre. That was his gospel.

What gospel was that?

Every little thing you see anywhere, do not undermine it. It is there for a purpose, use it, find something to do with it, that's what Barney used to say to me. You can't just be in a corner and wait for somebody else to deliver a line. Don't just wait for your cue – that was Barney. You are not upstaging. If you are busy washing dishes, I am not going to sit and wait for you to finish your dishes – no, I also have my life. I have to carry on with whatever I am doing. Barney had his own vision, he wanted to improve this place. Where The Market stage is today there was a grader, with water gushing out of a burst pipe. Barney gave us an improvisation there and then. We had to start building shacks as our houses, because a twister came and blew everything away. We started building shacks.

And why did Barney make you do that?

Barney's a person who likes to explore things. You cannot just do a thing or come with a script and say this is it. That is not Barney. You have to explore every line. Go through it carefully. Explore whatever you are doing. When I did "Starbrites" with him I did not know what we were doing in the workshop with Fats. I suffered in that workshop for Fats.

For me, Barney was like Bob Marley. This guy has written so many wonderful songs, so much meaning, if he were alive today I wonder what song of his I would be singing. With Barney I am wondering what I would be saying, because he was wealth like gold is to South Africa, not even gold, like platinum, worth more than gold or diamonds. It is a great loss.

I was given a task as part of the workshop to fetch Fats in the morning. He was still drinking then. He was bloody brilliant on stage. Maybe that is one thing about being a genius, you actually become useless but you know your business. When I got to Fats's place, from the door as you entered it was like the foot of a mountain. Fats was lying in his bed next to the door. The whole room smelt of paraffin. He showed me a wound, he had burnt himself overnight. He was drunk or something, he didn't know what had happened and he wanted to go to the clinic or the hospital. So I went home, phoned Barney – that was the days before cellphones – and he said, 'All right, you can take him to the clinic.'

What do you think Barney left you with?

Awareness. It is like being on the road driving. You don't only drive your car. You watch who is coming to smack you, who is coming to break your window. Be aware. Be alert all the time. Don't be on stage and start relaxing. You know, Barney was just white in colour. He was black inside. When I tell you about black life you do not understand, you do not know what it is like. You are only telling me about jacaranda trees. There are bombs in Soweto and you are telling me about flowers. Barney used to understand the bombs though he was from a flowery life. He knew about the problem but he was more into the battle. That is what made me trust him. He was black.

How did you find that out?

By working with Barney and the tasks he put us through I realised that he understood the black man's problems. He never put us in situations where everything is like The Bold and the Beautiful. Every time we had to scrape for things. You want to eat? There is nothing to eat. You want to drink? There is water and it is full of rust. What do you do with it?

What do you do with it?

Either you strain or you boil it. You do not know whether it is right to drink or not. He used to know what suffering means. He used to know what pain is, especially from the ghetto. He lived a lot. Every time he told stories about the ghetto it was never about living with roses but he loved his dog as well.

Opposite – Arthur Molepo and Fats Dibeco in "Starbrites", August 1990.
Photograph by Ruphin Coudyzer.

Seputla Sebogodi

'I felt like God took him early'

Barney gave me a wake-up call. I had a small role in "The Meeting". Barney saw the first run-through. To be honest with you I was just going through my motions. I was in the first scene and the last scene. And he said to me, 'Hey wait a minute, do you know how important your part is?' I said, 'Aaag, no, this old man. What is he talking about?' He said to me, 'You can leave an impression with the people.' He said, 'You know there are small actors not small roles.' And he actually did it. I couldn't believe it. It was like I had one of the leads or something. All credit should go to Barney because he worked with me and it was a painful experience but it paid off in the end.

And what was the play and why was it painful?

Here I was thinking I've got two scenes. Here's this man who says to me, 'Do you know what this line means? Do you know what you can do with this line? Can you tell me in your language what you want to say with this line?' And he says, 'That's the key to the play.' He made me say that line over a hundred times. I nearly cried.

Barney had this thing about body language. He said, 'You're a big man. You can push it even further.' I started discovering all of those sorts of things. He didn't want caricatures. He would tell you, 'Look, I don't believe you. You are lying to me, listen to your heart. Are you really telling me the truth?' And you would be honest with yourself. He says, 'Okay, now I want you to find it.'

He said to me one day, when we were doing "Silent Movie", I must go to my ward-robe and watch what was in it. When I was home I thought, aagghh let me cheat. I didn't watch it. And so the next day, I thought he had forgotten. Puffing his cigarette he says, 'Seputla, I want you to tell me what you saw in your clothes... You didn't look, go and look again.' When I went, I looked and saw different clothes. And he said to me, 'Okay, I want you to tell me, what did you see in your wardrobe?' I explained about my white T-shirt, red-what-what. He asked, 'When you take out the white T-shirt what do you say you are going to do with it?' And I said, 'I am going to wear it.' 'But where are you going? Are you going to a disco? Are you going to a soccer game? Why would you choose that white shirt? Why don't you like to wear the red T-shirt? Now this is what I want to know. The way you move, it's all like those clothes. This move is meant for this and that move is meant for that. This is how I want you to move. I want you to move like a person who hasn't had food for three days.' And that really made sense. He would say I must go to Park Station and look for a character. I mustn't just get a character from nowhere. It must be something that I see.

Okay. Seputla, you did say you felt you could work in comedy after "Silent Movie"?

When Barney wanted to do "Silent Movie", I was thinking, Aah! I am going to do another "Woza", another hit, you know, only to find that he's doing something completely different. I said to Barney, 'Look, I don't see myself funny.' He says, 'Okay,

Opposite – The cast of "Silent Movie" with Barney Simon – from left, Seputla Sebogodi, Leila Henriques and Richard Carter.
Photograph by Ruphin Coudyzer.

let's wait and see.' The way we went about it, the way we rehearsed the play, I thought that was great. And all of a sudden I enjoyed comedy. Since then comedy is my breakfast now.

Is there any secret to comedy?

You have to be truthful to every moment. That's something that I have. He also said, 'If you believe in what you say and really mean it, nothing is impossible. But if you try and make it funny, forget it, it won't be.' He says, one day he was driving – I don't know whether he was telling a story or, you know, the truth. He said, one day he was driving in his Beetle somewhere in Somerset West, or whatever. He had a bag of oranges in his back seat. And as he was passing he saw these kids clinging to the fence with like sad faces. When he saw those faces he stopped and went back. Because they couldn't speak English he just took some oranges and gave them to the kids. The kids didn't say anything. He just saw a smile. And that's what it's like, when you do comedy. The people have paid their money and they had problems during the day, some of their marriages are not doing well, and some of them are experiencing a bad time. So the only thing that you can do to them is make them laugh. You know, that's how simple it is. I did a play, Paul Slabolepszy's "Once a Pirate". We performed in Grahamstown. Later Lara Foot Newton took over and we took the play to an African festival in New York. A lot of South African plays at the festival were slashed by the critics. All the shows were getting not-so-good reviews. I got a fright. I wished there was somebody that I could talk to before the show. Lionel Newton was in New York as well. During the day I said to him, 'Baba, do you mind giving me a class?' He says, 'No, sure. No problem.' So he gave me a class and something happened. We started talking about Barney. The last words that he left me with were, 'Remember the old man, what he would say – it's how you tell a story that's important.' I was far away but I felt like he was closer. To me it felt like he was listening to our conversation. I don't know what I did with the play that day. It was like I'm gliding on the clouds. The feeling was different. I was honest and I gave it my best shot. And we got bloody good reviews. And that's why, even now, I feel cheated. I feel like God took him early.

What was the inspiration for "Silent Movie"?

Well, Barney saw Megan Kruskal's wedding. At her wedding he saw her veil flying, with the wind... It was the first time he saw Megan smiling from ear to ear. From that inspiration he just thought of a runaway bride. I've done plays but that one is very close to my heart.

Why?

I mean, we had no script. We had nothing else. It's the first comedy play that I've ever done. Since I worked with Barney I was never the same.

In what way?

What do you do with the role? I just imagine if Barney was still alive he would say, 'Okay look, Macbeth, let's do it like...' It would be possible with Barney. That's why I said he changed my life, because what I am doing now with industrial theatre, it's all his teachings. It's what I saw and what I heard. Some of the things he taught me.

Tony Bentel

'It had to be a "magic waltz" – those were Barney's words'

The story that transpired in "Silent Movie" was a love story. About love found, love shared and love lost. It was very much in the vein of the old Chaplin movies. We started working on the music. It was a difficult process because a lot of the movement had to do with the music and the music had to reflect the movement. It was a symbiosis between music and movement and story. The music had to strike chords with the audience. It had to relate directly to what was happening in the story so that people would say, 'Ah, I know that song, that's "Moonlight Sonata" or "Clair de Lune". I know now that is a night time scene.'

On top of that there was the whole personality of the pianist, who was very much part of the silent movie. He used to sit in front and was absolutely an essential part. It was a whole stylistic approach. The music would create tension, or romance, or whatever the feeling was. Each and every piece of music we used for the piece was discussed at length between Barney and me. One of the most challenging parts was to find a signature waltz for love. It had to be a 'magic waltz' – those were Barney's words. We must have worked our way through 250 waltzes before we came up with a Strauss piece which had the right effect.

There was a scene where Seputla Sebogodi was teaching Richard Carter how to kick a can that keeps running away. The music was "La Cucaracha" which was very apt. We tried it with the action to see how it worked from Barney's point of view, from his vision. I remember the scene when the three derelicts – now led by the beautiful Leila Henriques who has come into the lives of these two clowns – are sitting on the side of the highway eating breakfast, and these cars zoom past. I remember that Bongani (the stage manager) was holding up a placard saying what kind of car it was: BMW, Mercedes, Toyota, Mini. They would watch the car go past with great longing and yearning. Especially the big cars. The music we chose was Janis Joplin's "Oh Lord won't you buy me a Mercedes Benz".

So there wasn't one piece of music that didn't have something to add to the action. It was really an amazing process. There was a song called "Come all ye fair tender maidens" that was a favourite of Barney's. He lent me the record and we made a piano piece out of it which was Leila's signature tune, so that you would know something was going to happen with that character at that time. But we couldn't just choose a song that had the right words and the right title if the music wasn't conducive to the scene. I found it very easy to work with him because we were always thinking in the same direction. It was the first time I had ever done a workshop piece.

I didn't tell Barney, but I decided to do my final performance in drag, and Barney was there. Not just any drag. I was this old lady who sits at the piano and plays for these kinds of things – some of whom I know. It was a complete surprise for him. I thought he would be quite upset.

Afterwards he said to me (he was absolutely serious, there wasn't a hint of irony in his voice), 'Tony, that was very nice, but you really should have looked at the character further, because she would have had a little brown packet in her purse, you know, with some booze in it. And really, when Leila leaves in the dead of night, your character should have wept.' And I thought, well of course, here I was trying to make a superficial statement, and he just said, 'Whatever you do, it doesn't matter if what you do serves the story. If it hasn't been thought through deeply enough, it is not going to serve the story as well as it could.'

We did "Silent Movie" at the time that Chris Hani was shot – something that I think Barney communicated to most of the cast. We felt guilty that we were doing what to all outward appearances was this light-hearted, frothy fairytale. We should have been doing strong political theatre. It was a very difficult time in the history of the country. I remember driving to The Market with the kids in the car and saying to them, 'When I say duck, it means get below the seats. Don't look out the window and say "Where daddy?" because people are shooting at cars.' It was really a dangerous time. I remember talking to Barney about it and him saying, 'But it is a very strong political piece. It is not a whimsical fairytale. You do not have to look at something that has strong politics – it doesn't have to be a literal protest theatre. What we are doing is an appeal for a return to a simple dignity and integrity, which is really a political issue. It is what we are going through at the moment.'

It was this fantastic learning curve. It is not being literal about the big issues like politics, or religion. You can be a great politician but you will still, in essence, have to get up in the morning, brush your teeth, go to the toilet and lead the life of a human being. He looked behind those great things at very simple issues that have their own dignity and integrity. The characters were all united in love for each other, which went through its ups and downs, because they both fell for the same woman and she fell in love with both of them. Eventually she realised that she loved both of them too much to be able to stay there, because it was going to create enormous conflict. So she did the only thing that she could do which was to leave. She left the two clowns to the devices of a drunken pianist.

Barney was always trying to understand conflict and why it happened and how it could be resolved. In "Silent Movie", it was resolved by somebody turning around and walking away. What appealed to me was the power of music, which in this case was used deliberately without words. If you make a new word you are actually making a sound and a sound is music. You are trying to convey an idea. All we have is words and music. I used to get tears in my eyes every night when Leila left and I was playing "Somewhere Over the Rainbow". That was to Barney a song about yearning. I wept at his funeral. I found that he meant far more to me emotionally than I had ever realised. I thought, I never wept like this when my father died and I realised that I had actually spent a lot more time with Barney at that stage of my life than I did with my father. I would say that what he gave me emotionally was the courage to carry on – believing in the simple dignity that simple people have.

Opposite – Tony Bentel in "Silent Movie", 1993.
Photograph by Ruphin Coudyzer.

I wish
there was a
mossy bank

Leila Henriques

'You didn't have to pretend anything because he didn't need that. You could be small, pure, uncluttered'

I never had a conversation with Barney. I never knew what to say. We didn't talk. You didn't have to talk to him. I think Barney took a person on what they were at that moment. Every now and again he was fascinated in little areas of your life. Every tea break I put on a lot of red lipstick. He found that funny. He would see what you were at that particular moment without judgement... The actor, and the journey and the truth of that journey. I suppose I was already aware of this from watching Barney's plays. I didn't know they were Barney's plays at the time. I saw "Born in the RSA" when I was at school. I remember thinking, 'Well, this is interesting, this is something that's something, and that's what I want to do.' I am sure he has done that to thousands of people, just touched them through his visions.

Tell me about rehearsals.

By the end of his rehearsals I was so dead that by the time opening night came, nothing could be as bad as rehearsals. I came to the project all fit and organised. I came thinking I was quite good. Then by about the third day I realised I knew nothing. I felt like the most useless person on the planet. And then his interesting stuff started. I don't know how.

Why didn't you leave if you felt so useless?

I don't know. In "Silent Movie" I spent every fourth day in the toilet crying. It was absolutely terrible what Barney did. But you couldn't leave. The other thing about Barney, he was always inviting a lot of people to come and watch us in rehearsal.

You are joking?

It was actually a good thing, because I'd died so many times that I really just had to find my own little story and my own little thing and be safe in my own little thing, so that I didn't have to worry about all the rest. As a result, by the time the run came, I had something that was special because it was honestly part of me, because I had gone through hell to get it. I suppose he was a very brave man to believe so strongly. So the feelings of the actors, their egos, don't matter, the pressure of opening night doesn't matter. Yet it did matter to him, because he would always get that eczema. But when it came to the work, there was no compromise. He just wouldn't lie.

You would never know what Barney wanted or what he was after. In "Silent Movie" I thought, 'He is busking,' but he wasn't. He just gave you that feeling. Sometimes he was harsh. 'You didn't learn anything in your training,' I heard him say. He could be very impatient. If he felt strongly about something he would make it known. He wasn't scared of terrifying actors. He donnered for what he believed in. If he saw falseness he really, really didn't like that. But he wasn't writing you off. He would disarm you. He was going with his instincts; your feelings didn't come into it. There was a far greater

Opposite – Leila Henriques in "Silent Movie", 1993.
Photograph by Ruphin Coudyzer.

thing happening. He would never tell you if anything was going well. A lot of the time things were going well but, because he carried on pushing and pushing and pushing, you never realised it. He worked on people, and he saw through any affectation. He wanted the truth. 'Why do you think that's good, do you know why?' Slowly you found a better way. He would never say, 'Do it cheekily,' or 'Be more cheeky.' He was always asking questions, never giving answers. Oh it was terrifying and exhausting, all the questions he asked. It's not like when you work with a dictator director – you know: Da! Da! Da! Sit! Stand! Cry! In the performance you could grow. It was literally like a journey. You became attuned to what was real and what wasn't in a way that I haven't discovered with anyone else. He removed that ego part of you. The work is so detailed and so full you don't have time to think about the other stuff. There was just so much to achieve, just in one glance. Masses to do in one look.

But still, on opening night I felt it was the worst thing in the world! I thought, 'I can throw myself down the stairs, break my leg, pray for appendicitis. I can try to have a car crash.' But because there was nothing more to lose – rehearsals were so debilitating, and the piece was already so dreadful – I thought, 'I might as well just do it and be damned.'

Barney took risks: the fact that he even employed me for "Silent Movie" was a risk. He thought I was a dancer, I don't know why he thought I was a dancer. I can remember during rehearsal one day, a really terrible day when I had to try and march but I couldn't, I just couldn't. I marched with my same leg and my same arm, I couldn't do it, you know in that dyslexic way? He turned to Phillipa de Villiers, the choreographer, and said, 'I thought she was a dancer?' He took a massive risk, but at the same time he didn't mind that I wasn't a dancer. He was just amused by what was happening... I think.

How did he cast you?

He came to see "Six Degrees of Separation", in which I played a tiny little part, and then he phoned. I was completely terrified. He said all he had in his mind was a burnt out Volksie on the side of the road. He said he would like to do it in a Chaplin style, and that was it. There was a Chaplin festival on at the Mall. I went to some of them and saw Barney there. I was with Bruce Laing and I was so... terrified I sort of hid, grovelled along... pathetic. I just didn't want to get into a discussion about anything.

Eventually rehearsals began and he thought I could be a runaway bride. I have a history of runaway brides in my family and he found that out somehow and thought that would be a nice idea. Chaplin normally uses part of your own name for the character, and I think Barney did this as well. My second name is Fleur so it was Fleur, the Runaway Bride who ran into a squatter camp where there were these two clowns, Seputla Sebogodi and Richard Carter. We spent ages learning to juggle things. By the end of the first week we had an outline. I don't know exactly how that happened, we just suddenly had an outline. She lives in the Volksie. They all get on well. They teach her how to do clowning tricks and she cooks them pap and washes the clothes. They both fall in love with her and they start fighting. And then she has to leave. Barney's things were so simple that you doubted them. I'd think, 'Where is it?' They were so simple but so full. During the run I began to realise it was profound. And because it was so much a part of me, I could start to play. I was creating the character through his eyes. The task was to make it more like me rather than to try and pretend to be someone else. He seemed to give me so much space yet none at all at the same time. It was like a whole new world. He was constantly telling stories and I listened and my mind started thinking of its own stories. He was beautiful. He would create images and it was like walking in an incredible poem. He took me off guard. I was actually writing, creating. I wasn't just trying to be something else. It was a big shift in my mind about theatre and about myself. You don't have to shout, you don't have to do anything, yet what you are doing is valid. It was such a relief.

He had such a sense of time, he was never afraid of time. When Fleur was leaving he kept saying, 'Slower, slower...' I felt I was doing it in slow motion, and he kept saying it was still was too fast. Gestures meant so much. He created close-ups on stage. Did you notice he did that with a lot of things, like in "The Suit" for instance? That kind of stillness that those actors had, it was Barney zooming in.

Once I had a rehearsal with him on the telephone for about two hours, during another play. He had seen the play and had come back that night and phoned me at about 11pm. He said, 'Okay, just say that line? Ja. Just say it again.'

He phoned up on the day that "Silent Movie" was to open, and said, 'How are you feeling?' I said, 'I'm feeling terrible.' He said, 'No, no don't worry. You know what Fleur is like, she is like a dog, she is like Sally my dog.' And he was dead right, that is exactly what she was like.

It's very difficult to define actually what he did, which is so bizarre because he was so full of specifics, but I suppose I was so caught up in it that I just can't remember. He was so extremely delicate, very gentle. He gave me the feeling that anything could have happened. I could go anywhere, and not in a big grand massive way. I didn't have to pretend anything because he didn't need that, you could be small, pure, uncluttered. I trusted him. The actress part didn't trust him at all, but that calm bit trusted him implicitly, completely. There was an enormous amount of pressure. But when I was in the right groove, or whatever it was, everything else seemed to become still. Then I could do anything. That wouldn't last all the time. That would go, and then I wanted to jump out of the window.

Sello Maake Ka Ncube

'I think that was the beginning of my liberation'

It is like I haven't mourned his death. On Sunday I was chatting to my girlfriend and somehow we got talking about Barney and she said something and I broke down and cried like a child. The first time I worked with Barney was in 1986. We were doing "Woza" there with Dixon Malele. When Barney came in we had been rehearsing for about six months with Dixon.

Six months?

Ja. I remember I quit my job in November 1985.

What was your job?

I was working as a clerk for Hoechst Pharmaceuticals, it is a German company that deals with chemical products. Dixon had called me to come and do "Woza" with him.

Were you good?

I guess so. It was like someone had told him about me. And he came one Saturday. I was springcleaning the house. And Dixon came and said to me, 'Come, please, I want you to read to me.' It was about eleven o'clock and I asked what time and he said to come at about 2 o'clock at The Market. I came and I read for him and he said, 'Okay, but I want to start rehearsing now. You are working, so what are we going to do now?' I said, 'When do you want to start working?' And he said, 'Monday.' And I said, 'Okay, Monday I am here [laughter]. That was it. Instead of going to work on Monday I came to rehearsal.

When did you first meet Barney?

When I first met Barney I remember I dithered like nobody's business. We started working in November with Dixon. And I think also the reason why we rehearsed for six months was that there wasn't any slot open. Just two weeks before we started previewing, Barney came in to watch a rough run. It was h-a-a-a-r-d, you know, Dixon was h-a-a-a-r-d. I remember many a time there were afternoons that I walked out of the rehearsal room blowing my top. The first remark that Barney made was, 'Dixon, the guys have got the play but only mechanically.' I also remember he said, 'Guys you have got the play, but what we need to do is work on the line.' And then Barney started, and those two weeks made those six months we had spent seem like we were playing. Barney in two weeks just eliminated the hardness... Rehearsing "Woza" with Barney became meaningful, individually.

And how did he do that?

It was amazing. Aah, it was amazing! I remember thinking, 'Gosh, this white man understands black people.' Sometimes he would actually show you something. I remember in particular when he was trying to show me the threading of the needle. I had seen Mbongeni do it. It was like I saw Mbongeni in him. And then he would do something and say, 'Okay Sello, tell me what would you do in this situation?' and you explain yourself and he would say, 'Okay. Alright with that in mind let's try it.' And you would do it. And as I was doing it I saw how clever. And he would say, 'Okay, stop there. Why don't you, when you get there, maybe say... What was that Zulu word that you said?' And you would tell him and he would say, 'Aha it's there, use that word.' And you would do it and use that Zulu word there and he would say, 'Okay, how do you feel?' And naturally, because somehow you did something that sort of sprung out of you, you would say, 'I feel nice, Barney.' 'Does it make sense to you?' 'Ja, ja, ja, Barney.' 'Well if it does, then keep it.'

I think what I observed was that as an actor what you explain and end up doing are two different things. Barney would find a way of connecting what you were explaining and make you interpret it in your character. He just listens to you, and he is understanding what you are saying. That is the impression that he has left on me, and the sensitivity and the pride that he made me have. Barney came at a time when I wanted to express myself. Having lived in a time where, if you lived in South Africa as a black person, you didn't have the platform to express yourself. Barney was the only person that trusted that I had it.

How did you get that feeling that he was trusting you?
He said at one stage, 'Everyone has a story to tell but in their own way'. Also working with him in "Woza" was not making us duplicate what Mbongeni and Percy had done. What Barney did was make us discover what we want to do or what we can do. That's how he gave me that sense of pride that you have got what it takes. You just need to have it unblocked.

There is one thing that actually captures that brilliantly for me. It is in the programme of "The Suit". I have never really understood the whole thing about biographies and programmes. Instead of writing, 'I did this production here and here,' I decided to write a dedication. It was just realising how a lot of people have contributed to my life, and I really haven't thanked them. For instance, my mother. Sometimes you think about this when they're dead. When I was attempting to do plays, in my teen years, my mother said, 'Go and do it, my child.' That was the first sign of somebody having confidence in me and encouraging me, and mothers are like that, I think, most of the time. Anyway, I thank my mother and also a lot of people who contributed to my life, but specifically Barney. I remember thanking him for opening the door, which is beginning to let light come through, because where there was darkness now there is light.

Then we did "Flight", David Lan's play about the Jews. "Flight" was a little turning point. Talk about the respect that you can get as a performer! Barney was going to direct this play somewhere in September, and by January Mannie comes to me and says, 'Sello, Barney wants you in the play.' That just warmed my heart. It was a small part. I don't have really very specific memories about that, but I can just remember the delight, just the fact of working. Barney was working with Dawid Minnaar, helping with a whole movement thing. And Barney saying, 'Ooh Dawid, there is too much energy now, break it down'. He was an amazing man, he really was. I don't think I would have been what I am today if it wasn't for Barney. I think it takes a very special

person to give so much. There were moments when I would just be understanding my environment and I think I had a little confusion as well. I would speak to Barney and many a time he gave me the courage to go on. I was waiting through a phase, especially in the early '80s, for something I wanted to do as an actor. The roles never really delved into life experience. The people that I worked with forced me, or locked me, into a corner. I mean, South Africa has been horrible in many ways. I remember working with directors that made me feel that I was not complete.

Not complete?

Ja. Basically, that we are not intelligent enough. That is why I say if it wasn't for Barney in my life... He gave me courage to just go on. In '89 I was even actually thinking of quitting. Giving up acting, because I was just losing faith. I was doing Paul Slabolepszy's "Smallholding". Maybe it was that part also just made me want to give up. It was a silent character. He got his throat torn off by a dog when he was like three years old, so the character couldn't speak. I was constantly on stage, so watching people who were speaking. That play also added to the inner frustration. When we were in Grahamstown I just felt like giving up this bullshit, you know, because there was no food for me to grow on. The thing that changed my life was going into a bookshop and getting "The World of Can Themba". I read that book and I realised, 'Yes, but here are our stories.' I got a collection of Can Themba's work and showcased one at the Lab on Goch Street. Barney saw that, and we were talking about Can Themba until Mothobi Mutloatse came and said he wanted to do "The Suit", and it was like yes! Then we started working on this with Barney. Wow! I think that was the beginning of my liberation. If ever there is a liberation to be attained, I attained it when I was doing "The Suit". In the rehearsal room I was just sitting and pouring out my life, my feelings, my emotions just pouring out to the director. Sometimes I would do something and he would say, 'Sello, that was nice, but it's dangerous on the bad night. We have got to find something to protect you'.

Why was it dangerous?

I never used to ask him why. I did something vulnerable, and he would say, 'Ja, it is good that you are doing it now, but now let's just find something to protect that.' I looked forward to rehearsals. It was one of the most splendid times of my life.

How closely did you work with the script? What made it more exciting?

Mothobi Mutloatse had given us a script and we read it and it was just not going to work. We ended up taking the short story itself and we started reading that. And then from there, Barney said, 'Okay, what would happen here at the bus stop?' Then we would start workshopping that. And he would say, 'Go off and write those lines in Sotho or Zulu.' Then after that he would say, 'Okay, what does that mean?' That's how basic it was. It was a moment of having to prove to myself whether can I act. I had heard many times that black actresses cannot play character roles, black actors can't play cerebral parts. But for me it was – well, let's see if it is true.

Opposite – Sello Maake Ka Ncube in "The Suit", September 1993.
Photograph by Ruphin Coudyzer.

How would you describe that role in "The Suit"?

It was as though I was battling, or questioning, my manhood as well. In questioning it I realised I was very unconventional in my addressing it to myself. There were a lot of black ouens I have known that I began opposing personally. How to treat your woman and all those things. Barney said to me, 'Sello, one thing that makes you the actor you are is that you are constantly questioning things, questioning yourself.' That is something that I constantly did throughout my life.

So when I was dealing with "The Suit" it was like wanting to show, or deal with, the rough edges and psychological rough edges that we as men have. This whole thing of being socialised not to express our pain. The character in "The Suit" had a very strange way of dealing with his pain, and the way of dealing with it was like shutting it in and not expressing it. It was an elating feeling for me to do that character.

Barney said, 'Okay, walk this way. What happens when you feel this way and someone looks at you?' You can almost feel that that person is seeing through your pain. Just playing with those kinds of shades. Playing with shades of pain and of joy. Basically like showing what is inside and living it and working on telling the story. It was brilliant working with that man. He was remarkable.

In what way?

I remember one time we were at a party. I think Sean Taylor was attacking him. What was amazing was to see the vulnerability that Barney had. He was like a little boy and he would say, 'Sello, why is he attacking me? All I want to do is just work, that is all I want to do.' I was trying to sort of comfort him. I remember acting in Greg Doran's "Titus Adronicus" in 1994. He didn't like the production at all. We were still doing it and Barney went into a tirade of condemning the piece.

Was it the first time you experienced a white criticising a lauded fellow artist?

Ja, for a white person to become so sincere about what they didn't like and really make no bones about it. And it was like, 'Oh Sello, you are in the play.' I would say, 'No, Barney I understand.' For me it was like he shared the most intimate feeling he had at that moment with me. Just before we went to London (I think he was going to go for the operation the following day) we had tea at The Periwinkle, and he was kind of questioning me: 'What needs to be done? Has there got to be a new way of telling stories?' I can't find the words [Sello is crying]. Ja, for me it is just like a last memory. That man has given me so much.

And now that you are directing?

Even now I am working with a group in Alexandra and I keep saying, 'Barney once said this to me.' He constantly comes into the picture. Experience is totally shaped around his approach and his delicate way in wanting to get to things. He said, 'You can understand something, but until you have your own vocabulary to try to explain it, then you don't understand it.' With "The Suit", which I directed at the North West Drama Company, I was beginning just to find my own vocabulary to deal with actors. It was a hard experience. Just discovering that way of communicating with actors.

And for me with black actors it was like this going back to the basics. Having to ask ourselves why we are doing certain things.

How black actors perform bothers me a lot, because I have realised that we are not dealing with our life's experiences. Most of the time we are hiding things that are unacceptable to people. Our people have a certain understanding about our behaviour, which we constantly shut out of the rehearsal because we are relating some kinds of behaviour that we don't understand. So, for me, it was like discovering the vocabulary to get to explain things amongst my peers, my colleagues. Discovering my own vocabulary. Most of the time I have worked with new actors, mostly black actors.

Barney just had that way of making you feel that you are whole, this package in this life. In many little ways... having time to listen to you. In many instances when I would be trying to explain something to whatever director, I see in their eyes that they are not listening to me, don't hear me. Barney would hear you and be there for you.

Chapter 11. Relentlessness

Barney's approach did not soften with the years, despite an unsuspected heart condition. He continued to challenge actors to search for the life of the piece, applying what he had learnt from Joan Littlewood in the 1950s.

Actor Robert Whitehead wrestles with Barney's 'short emotional leash' in "Death and the Maiden", and Dorothy Ann Gould reflects on Barney's often bewildering exercises and processes. In 1995 Barney directed one of his favourite plays, Berkoff's "East", of which he said: 'It is his most personal and passionate statement.'

In 1979 his production of this play was staged late at night to avoid its being banned because of its explicit nature. In 1995 it was expected to draw audiences and boost box office sales. It was to be his last production.

Jamie Bartlett and Joss Levine are exposed to the challenge of Barney's gruelling direction, and Gilda Blacher brings testimony of Barney's relentlessness in vivisecting his actors to attain the depth of intimacy he demanded.

Opposite – Barney Simon in an American hotel room during a tour of "Born in the RSA".
Photograph courtesy of Wesley France.

Robert Whitehead

'What does it smell like to pick up a cup?'

I don't think I was necessarily Barney's can of worms as an artiste.

What was Barney's can of worms?

Well, he wanted somebody sort of malleable and enthralled, who could be tortured into something. Obviously, with my association at The Market, we knew each other and we had loads of laughs and loads of chats about everything. But we had actually never worked together. We talked about the work but we never really, for a long time, were interested in talking to each other about working together. I started getting cross around the time of "Born in the RSA", because I could do that stuff. In retrospect I realise that while I was busy acting in and directing other kinds of work at The Market, which Barney paid close attention to, he was keeping that going by not pulling me into his projects during that time. When I did work with him, Barney's glorious kind of intellectual and emotional wandering seemed an enormously broad space that you were entering. In a way it was, but however much he let the actors wander around and encouraged them to feel that there were actually no bounds to the stage at all, they were all, in fact, on a very short emotional leash. In a way it seemed enormously free and experimental, but the actors didn't necessarily know that they were being tightly monitored. But the sheer raging insecurity that was happening on stage triggered an energy that gave his work that extraordinary quality. I mean, that's the whole school – Peter Brook and Barney – that sort of beat generation behaviour.

What school would you say you came from?

Post-beat. I was trained at the Drama Studio, which was kind of international and very contemporary European but essentially British training. Barney started working in theatre with people who weren't actors. I think as he grew and matured, that was germane to his work. He had to deal with the 'actor' and his rehearsal process was much concerned with de-constructing the trained actor. Like going to art school and trying to find out how to draw like a child again. So, that, of course, is very valid. The production I worked on with Barney was Ariel Dorfman's "Death and the Maiden". This was '90/'91. It was in the Upstairs Theatre, designed by Nadya Cohen and lit by Wesley France. Barney had the play set across the middle of the space, a wooden deck overhanging the water of a beach house. The audience was seated to the left and right. It was very beautiful. Also, it was very difficult to achieve.

So what happened when you started with Barney?

I screamed and shouted.

Did you have a read-through on the first day?

Yes. Lots of lovely investigative read-throughs for days.

Opposite – Robert Whitehead in "Death and the Maiden", 1992.
Photograph by Ruphin Coudyzer.

We've heard that the read-through was like reading a telephone directory?

Oh yes, you weren't allowed to do anything at all, which was so nice for the first week of rehearsals. That process is not unique. Of course in "Death and the Maiden" it was ambiguous. "Death and the Maiden" was so unresolved at the end. It was a sort of a moral and human victory on one level. I was playing Dr Miranda who may have been a torturer, this unspeakable doctor to the Argentine military regime, who went down to the basement every so often and had a whole pile of fun, not least with the woman in question. From the beginning what was absolutely vitally important to me as an actor was that I shouldn't know whether he did or didn't do it. The character Dr Miranda's absolute ambiguity was vital to the story. Barney kept pushing me to make up my mind, but I knew, if I make the guilty/not guilty decision it was going to colour it. Once you've put that knowledge into yourself then everything you do is going to be the business of masking that knowledge.

So you'd say to Barney, 'Why? Why should we do that when the essence of the character is utterly ambiguous; when it is very important for the character, if he is guilty, to have psychologically blocked his past, so that he can believe himself utterly? How much unblocking do you have to do to yourself psychologically and emotionally? How much distancing? Heaven knows how much of that has been going on here in South Africa through the Truth and Reconciliation Commission. I wasn't precluding making a decision about Miranda's guilt, at some point. Barney of course wanted a decision before we finished coffee on the first morning. So that was a huge fight. I was aghast. That was such an un-Barney sort of demand of me. But I think maybe he made it because it was me. We changed positions, which might have been, probably was, a devilish Barneyish ploy. I mean, for him with all his assumptions and knowledge of the type of actor I was. And me, with all my assumptions and knowledge of what sort of director he was. I like to imagine that, while trancing out one evening he might have thought, 'That is how I am going to nail this Whitehead fucker. I'll change shoes with him right at the beginning!'

Was this an ongoing fight then?

Ja, it was ongoing for a long time. He would just say, 'He's guilty, he's guilty.' I was lumbered with it. I must say, jokes apart, I am very happy to have done that particular thing with Barney. It was very interesting working with him on Dorfman's text.

What was happening exactly at the time?

Mandela had been released. The Kempton Park negotiations had begun. They were in the early stages of formulating a negotiated settlement. As you know, we the people did not know from one day to the next whether the whole place was just going to explode into civil war. There we were at The Market basically doing a Truth and Reconciliation play three years before the elections. There was a tremendous amount of violence in the country. There was terrible tension in the city. The play was very harrowing, so it was quite hard and frightening. I often wonder what difference it would have made, how different the production would have felt in the theatre at the height of the Truth and Reconciliation Commission investigations. As opposed to the desperately uncertain, brink-of-civil-war situation that we were in. Would it have been healing?

Or would people just have been unable to endure it because of what they had to endure watching television or reading when it all came spewing out? That certainly would have been true of the white audience anyway. I honestly don't think Barney was trying to manoeuvre the play to suit what was going on politically. I think very much to the contrary. That if we had tried to inject it with the 'here and now' when we were doing it we would have skewed the whole thing. So we had to keep it intensely personal. The work was very personal and very private, which did give it the beauty and delicacy that it had. It was dreadfully prophetic. Saying, this is what is in store for us – if we are still around to face it. The way Barney worked was actually what the heart of the moment was about. Barney would want to put the ingredients in and then take some out with a spoon, or dip your finger in, get burnt and then take that piece. The whole kitchen, every pot, everything. All one's equipment was all over the place. And the mess.

What did he do?

Quibble with the moment. Not let you explore the beginning, the middle and the end of any moment. Like me going to pick up a cup. Picking it up is the middle of the moment. He would fuck with that. Picking up the cup that way. Barney would be busy with the end of the moment before I wanted to deal with it. Then, one would have to work out between all of us, why that should be. Largely, a lot of the time, because it amused him, I felt. He was concocting something or thought it was fascinating to watch. He could talk brilliantly for hours on end about nothing, which cumulatively became a remarkable sharing of everything.

About nothing?

About nothing, about everything, about something or about picking up a cup. It was different when he was telling a personal story, anecdote, about his bobba and his nanny, when he was growing up. That was an entirely different story. Clear, clean, simple and beautiful. But when you all got into the rehearsal room to try and tell a story. Oy-oy-oy! Going around and under and about. What does it smell like to pick up a cup? I picked up a cup because it smelt nice. Why? What was the smell? Why do you think the smell was like that? Was it nice like my bobba's chicken soup? And then you'd have a nice ten-minute break while he told you a story.

Did the story help?

Not immediately but perhaps it cumulatively did.

Over and above that, were you glad that you worked with Barney? Did you gain anything as an actor?

Yes, Barney had seen everything I had ever done at The Market. Ten, twelve years of work, so he knew my tricks, my shortcuts, my safety zones. What was valuable was he was not going to allow me to get away with anything. In principle his whole premise was of not actressing yourself all over the stage. Be true, and be busy, with your terrifying uncertainty and insecurity, which is what he engendered so brilliantly in one... How dismal it is to realise one's arrogance. How cavalier I was in the past. Of course, now in the theatre, I should like to work with Barney again more than anything.

Dorothy Ann Gould

'He was Lee Strasberg, Jerry Grotowski, Peter Brook, rolled into one'

I always felt with Barney that I wasn't his kind of actress, which is why it took him so long to want to work with me. I just always wanted to please people. So I am the kind of actress who says to the director, just tell me what you want and I will do it. I think that Barney found me facile in the most positive sense. I could technically do things easily, but I did not live or work in the now. The first time I auditioned for him I was twenty-one. He was auditioning for "The Crucible" at his house in Loch Avenue and I went to audition for Abigail or Mary Warren. I obviously launched into my little sort of RADA piece on the verandah; with the traffic going past. I'd no sooner said two or three sentences than he said, 'No, okay, no, this is wrong.' And he took me through to the kitchen and gave me a bowl of strawberries. I didn't know what was going on. Finally he took me to the bedroom, but not for soliciting – he was just trying to disorientate me so that I could stop my learnt thing. I suppose he wanted to see me enjoy strawberries with some sensuality. He obviously didn't cast me. Years later I said to him, 'Why won't you work with me?' And he said, 'Because you are not strong enough yet.'

So what do you think he was trying to teach you?

I wish he could have been more articulate about it. I just needed some pointers. I think he was trying to teach me to be in the moment, to forget about my skills, to forget about my neutral accent, to forget about trying to be perfect, to let the rough edges show. And yet it is ironic. If that is what he was trying to teach me with something like "Hedda", I ended up so smooth. There was no wildness. I always thought that Barney had insight into my personality, into the fear. He actually never said be wild. He would probably tell me a story and I would miss the point because I would switch off.

When I came back from England the first thing that Barney asked me was to co-ordinate a storytelling festival at The Market. I had only been back like three weeks and I was full of energy. I was spending a lot of time working from Barney's office co-ordinating the thirty-seven storytellers. The man was respected. When one thinks of the tributes that came in after he died, those tributes came in because of the man. They did not come in because he was a director in this country at a very important time, socially and politically for the people. It wasn't just that. It was that he gave them as much as Brook or Grotowski when he had little interactions with them. Barney had wonderful stories about these people and they had ones of him.

I spoke to directors in London who did the National Theatre Workshop. He was one of the directors chosen from all over the world to lead workshops there. They just said it was fantastic. Take someone like Sean Mathias who is this huge international director now. He tried desperately to get into that workshop and he couldn't because it was full.

Barney asked him to come and direct at The Market and then he died, so it couldn't happen. Barney had never seen his work, he hadn't done Barney's workshops. But Barney felt or saw something in people. And I don't think he was wrong because if you have that belief in people you can make them believe that about themselves. He took some actors in the early days who were virtually off the street. They were hardly actors but they gave us such astonishing performances. So he was right. You don't necessarily need four years of drama school.

Dorothy Ann Gould in "Hedda Gabler", written by Henrik Ibsen, 1994.
Photograph by Ruphin Coudyzer.

Ramolao Makhene

'Barney was waiting'

In 1992, PAWE (Performing Arts Workers' Equity) and members of the artistic community groups and other artists went to The State Theatre to support the handing over of the memorandum demanding the transformation of PACT – one of the infamous state-funded arts councils. The memorandum was to be handed over by Wally Serote and Carol Steinberg. But hardly had we been there for five minutes when we were surrounded by the police force of Pretoria.

Lots of exiles had come back and the Alex Arts Centre had also sent a lot of people, so there were many of us, and they couldn't find a big enough prison. We were driven around for ages to different prisons and we ended up in Pretoria Prison.

No one had eaten anything from 9 in the morning. I said I had to be in a show – Ariel Dorfman's "Death and the Maiden" at The Market Theatre – I said that I had a show – but they just delayed. Alan Joseph organised my release after discussions with the police. I came here and found the audience were just leaving. Barney was waiting.

Ramolao Makhene in "Death and the Maiden", 1992.
Photograph by Ruphin Coudyzer.

Jamie Bartlett

'He was a voyeur of sex'

I was amazed to work on "Hedda". For me it was a process of totally stripping down everything. Strip, strip, strip to the point where you wanted to burst into tears. At times, I did burst into tears. He'd phone you at night and sense your incredible frustration. But then he was unabated. The next day he would be at the strip, strip again. The minute you tried to shape a gesture, he'd say, 'Why?' He'd strip you down to absolutely nothing. I totally started to doubt everything, my talent, and the fact that I'd done any work before.

Barney suffered. He was incredibly overworked. I felt very bad at the time because I don't think any of the people around him, including myself, and at The Market, really realised the pressure he was under. He was taking strain. He wasn't admitting it. His close friends had not seen that this guy was going down – big time. He became vague. He was unable to concentrate. "East" kind of got there, but it was far from being successful as a piece with a vision. Being inside the work, it really lacked muscle.

One thing that I do remember, and that I will treasure for the rest of my life – he said, 'Jamie, why won't you show me your pain, show me the shit, show me how embarrassed you are, show me that you are not a warrior anymore.' He said, 'Go and look at John Kani and Winston Ntshona, go and look at Winston's scarred stomach, go and look at that belly hanging over that belt as a prisoner and see what nakedness is.' When I went there I was very touched by that. I saw Winston with his big stomach, this man of fifty years old with children, and his pain, and his life as a man and as a political activist. This actor with all this hanging out. And Barney had wanted me to do more of this in "East" and I didn't have the guts to. I was hiding behind little bits that I knew how to do and that produce something technically proficient. It's only now as a man, as an actor, I can roll around the floor with belly exposed. I've become a bigger man. Maybe Barney wanted me bigger, or I wasn't big enough for him. I am bigger now to do those kinds of things like roll around naked and maybe masturbate, or take off my shirt, and kind of vomit and cruise around the floor without any thought for how it might look. I wasn't ready for what he was asking me to do in "East".

A lot of his stories were tied to sex. Barney was fascinated by sex and the power of sex. He was a voyeur of sex. Male and female were intriguing to him sexually. It was quite a powerful tool to dig into various people. He used to try and touch you. He liked to try and find a key to your brain. I never found that key. But one of the greatest gifts was he had a gift as a leader. I know he had a relationship that was actually beautiful and true with each individual. We never quite connected on that level. Although we used to laugh. I did feel that one of the prerequisites was you had to actually surrender, in a sense. There was a status that was required there and I wasn't part of the status thing. Barney was an old man. If you didn't buy into a little bit of that as well, then the relationship could become tenuous. It was a prerequisite.

So you say he was like an acting teacher?

Ja. 'If you want to be great, Jamie – you have too much vanity. You are overly caught up with muscular speech, with the incredibly powerful use of the consonants and vowels.' My father was terribly disappointed in "Hedda Gabler". My parents flew from Cape Town for the play. They came to the first preview. So it was our first audience. My father said, 'I have never ever been so bitterly disappointed in any play I've seen in my life.' Needless to say the National Theatre were there at the time, Ian McKellen, Sean Mathias, Anthony Sher and Greg Doran. I think everybody was quite flabbergasted. They all sat there and shuffled and whispered and squeezed each other's bottoms. I can remember just feeling such a failure. Like the biggest idiot. What amazed me was that Barney knew it was so dreadful and so embarrassing. He knew. But he came back and said, 'You've done what I wanted you to do.'

Barney touched me as the person Jamie more than as the actor Jamie. I have never known anyone of that age that can talk to you like you are talking to a mate. His incredible knowledge. He was prepared to say, 'Hey Jamie, I really think you are a bad lover, I'll tell you why.' I said, 'Fuck, why am I a bad lover?' 'I can see you're a kak fuck.' 'Why Barney?' 'Because you are afraid to show your stomach. If you are not prepared to show your stomach how can you be a fucken sexual athlete? You're a fucken coward!' He had powerful insights. He challenged you on many levels. But I can never forgive him, as a man, for some of the things he said to me, God's truth.

Gilda Blacher

'Doing tricks for Barney'

I got an inkling of what Barney was like when he told me the reason he was auditioning me was he'd seen me dance Swan Lake drunkenly at a party one night. Somehow he equated what he saw to Sylv in Berkoff's "East".

You'd be in the middle of a monologue, or in a middle of a scene, and he'd stop you. And you don't know why he's stopping you. He's not unhappy, or happy, or anything, but he'll just stop you to tell you a story, and he'll go, 'So do you know what I mean?' You're desperate to understand because you think that everyone is so much cleverer than you. Everyone understands what he's telling you this for, except you. Or, he'd say things to me like, 'Won't you just walk across the stage like a mixture of Bette Midler and Katharine Hepburn.' And you go, 'This is beyond my capability, I cannot walk across the stage like a mixture of Bette Midler and Katharine Hepburn. I don't understand that note.' 'That's not a note.' And you want to hit him.

He found out that I had been at Habonim Camp when I was little. Barney had also been. So we'd hear stories about his experiences at camp, about his first girlfriend at Habonim. They took roast chickens on the train with them. And he was so nervous because suddenly he was alone in the carriage with his first girlfriend that he really liked, and he didn't know what to do. He was suddenly at a loss as to what to do, and he gave her a quick kiss, and then he was depressed. 'I don't know what to do with this note. Barney, help me – I'm being raped onstage in Berkoff and you're telling me about Habonim.'

He found out that I could tap a bit, which he thought would be interesting. 'Show me.' And you'd go and show him. You feel like a child at a birthday. You have to do tricks to impress Barney, you were terrified Barney wouldn't be impressed with you. So suddenly you were tap-dancing on stage for Barney. You know, whatever tricks you could do he'd want to see.

The brutality that he found in the male characters, and the way he expressed the brutality, I found so extraordinary. Because no matter that it was set in the East End of London in the '70s, for me as a woman, it was still real and so frightening, but he wasn't scared. He would take it to absolute extremes, the notion of brutality. At one point she gets raped. And he says, 'Imagine a huge, big penis being thrust into you, when you're dry, repeatedly, until you are so sore that you're splitting up and you're bleeding inside.' And he'd use these kinds of images, until you actually are broken. You're finished. You feel like you're being raped. You had to go as far as somebody who hadn't experienced violence could go, into the imagery of it, and he would emphasise penis and cock the whole time, and thrusting. And it was hard. It was very, very hard. He didn't treat you in a gentle way, because he took you as far as he thought you had to go to be able to tell the story of somebody who is brutalised. And I thought that that was incredible.

Suddenly I was working with somebody who wasn't letting me play at being an actor. Who was actually saying, 'Just throw away all that shit, get rid of it... You're

Opposite – Gilda Blacher in a one-woman show.
Photograph by Ruphin Coudyzer.

lying, you're scared. That's not who you are. Find who you are, find the core of yourself before you can use it to create a character.' So he got rid of stuff, and I had to create from nothing, rather than packing on with what I already had.

He tore away everything I imagined Gilda to be, and made me recreate myself as Sylv, which was very scary. It was kind of everything I had wanted to avoid. He'd say, 'Do you think you're sexy?' or 'Do you think that men find you sexy? If a man walks into a room what do you think he thinks of when he looks at you?' And you go, 'No, you're not allowed to ask me these questions. You're not! I'm not paying you two hundred an hour for this. We're here to rehearse. No Barney, I don't want to discuss.' 'No, we must, we must,' he'd say, 'Are you sexy?' And you'd go, 'I don't want to deal with this now.' And he'd go, 'What do you think of sex? Do you climax? Do you enjoy penetration?' You know, questions like that. And you'd think, 'Oh my God, I can't!'

That is stuff I avoided thinking about for 25 years, and you're suddenly asking me to tell you about it. And you know, he asked in such a matter-of-fact way. It's like, 'Did you go to Checkers today? You bought that? Oh that's nice! And are you sexy?' And it's too huge, but somehow you find yourself thinking about it as well, and you go, 'No I'm not, I'm a big, fat, ugly, Jewish girl from the North, and I'm not sexy! I can't be sexy!' 'No, you can. Just feel sexy. Go against that wall and move sexy.' I eventually did.

Do you know the part that sometimes made me angry is that you did sometimes get the feeling that he had no right. I wasn't sure of his right to be phrasing things in that way. Although, maybe what we are saying is that if you want to be an actor that's where you have to go. But I sometimes felt Barney was a bit voyeuristic. 'Do you feel you have the right to know so much about me, or to take me to places that maybe I'm not entirely ready to go?' But you were always scared, you always had this fear at the back of your mind, he's going to think you are not talented enough, or you're not ready to be an actor if you can't go there. So you'd push yourself maybe to places you weren't actually ready to deal with. In that way I sometimes did have a problem, and I did disagree, and I did doubt his motive sometimes. Because he also always remained that little bit distant, that little bit aloof, like somebody watching a laboratory experiment, seeing how far he could push the rats. What tricks he could make them do. Or how they could perform. And I used to get cross about that. I never had the courage to say, 'Barney, I want to ask you, do you think you're sexy?' You were so taken aback by this enormity of the questions and where he was taking you, it was only afterwards often that you got angry.

Do you know what I think Barney loved, and what I loved? Berkoff writes stories about tiny people. People who aren't noticed. He knows that there's a story whether it's in Vrededorp, or in New Brighton, in the East End of London, or wherever. What is happening to tiny people who the world doesn't know, or notice, is what makes true and beautiful people. Maybe that is the correlation between Barney and Berkoff. Their acknowledgement and their recognition that what is tiny and what appears insignificant is what is the greatest in humanity, what really counts, and what makes the world unfold. It's not the huge historical events.

Opposite – Interior of dressing room at The Market Theatre.
Photograph courtesy of The Market Theatre.

Joss Levine

'And that is how it happened'

Barney wanted you to win. He kept working with text, kept carrying on. He needled me one day because it wasn't coming right. Then I got into a bad mood, and he said, 'Now take that, put it in.' So I took that feeling and put it in. And that was the grip. Then I could layer emotions concurrently running into a sentence. If you're saying something and you're using different emotions I think you're on top of what you are doing. To get that takes a very skilled person to find.

There was a joy that we had. I kind of felt that he was treated very badly by us during "East". He didn't take as much care of the production as he usually did. He was rushing from meeting to meeting trying to organise funding. He had about forty things on his plate all at the same time. And he was dealing with the play. Barney explained a lot of things to me when it came to the character in "East". For one hour I lay on stage with him. I lay on the floor and he said, 'Make yourself comfortable.' My legs were dangling over the bar or something. He said, 'Just say your lines.' And so I started to say my lines. And he said, 'No, just lie there and dangle your legs a bit longer.' And I said, okay, I am ready. He said, 'No dangle your legs.' I think for about fifteen minutes I just dangled my legs. I was starting to fall asleep. And then he said, 'Now just start talking.' And that is how it happened. That was in one rehearsal. Then we went to another rehearsal room a couple of weeks later and when I got into a very bad mood he said, 'Put that feeling inside.' From dangling my legs to being in a bad mood – I had to put those feelings together. You start working with two states.

If you say the same monologue twenty times and you are not getting anywhere, what do you do? You start thinking, 'Why aren't I getting it?' You cannot understand in your head why you are not getting it. The emphasis is always being changed on certain things, which then changes things in the monologue, but you are not adding anything to it. And then you get upset with yourself, thinking, 'What am I doing wrong?' Then he got you in and took that feeling of not being able to get it right. He went further and further. He'd say, 'Take what you have and put it in the monologue. and then go back to where you were lying on stage.' I kept saying to the stage manager, 'Well, I think we better carry on.' And the stage manager kept saying, 'No, Barney wants you to relax.' So there I was lying with my legs up. But I am busy thinking, 'Why am I doing this? Why am I doing this?'

Well I find that fascinating, because you say that he was going to all these meetings. The play wasn't being blocked, the actors were upset, yet he had the time to spend twenty minutes with you, with your legs dangling.

Well, you know those moments when people say things and you feel embarrassed and you just want to bury yourself in the sand? He knew how to make that so alive. He just knew how to extend those moments. He knew how to take moments.

Opposite – Joss Levine.
Photograph by Ruphin Coudyzer.

Part 5. Legacy

Why Theatre?

'There are those who believe that God created man because He liked to listen to stories. They also believe that we are created in His image. So listening to stories, if we believe as they do, is fundamental to us all... But telling stories is a circle of respect. If the storyteller (even of jokes) is without the focus of vision, his story will die. If the listener is indifferent, the story will die. If the listener is careful and caring, the storyteller will be inspired to dig deep into his treasure house of memories and talent for the colours and textures that will honour the attention he has received.

'Theatre is communal storytelling. The actor, approaching his character, will journey through the gardens and deserts of himself to discover his kinship to the man that he will play, to understand that there but for the grace of God goes he. And when he does, he will move his audience into equal empathy. With his director he will spend hundreds of hours exploring and discovering the gestures, the reflections, the silences and the images that best express their vision of the text that they have chosen to tell. The set and lighting designers collaborate, with their own sense of space and shadow and light. And when their work is least remarked upon, in a story that is understood, it is usually at its most successful.

'Each night the story is different because the audience that receives and feeds from the darkness outside is never the same. Sometimes the communion is total, and when it is, it is a miracle. It is for these times that theatre exists and is necessary to the souls of man.

'Theatre in South Africa is among the most vital and thriving in the world and the world recognises this. Theatre happens everywhere. Not only in the centres of culture, but where people gather to learn about history and literature, the roots of violence, health and nutrition, sanitation and the growing of successful crops. Trade Unions teach through theatre. Poetry is read at political rallies. New groups are springing up all over the country – from Nelspruit to Oogies to the suburb of Berea.

'Because we choose to reflect our country, to tell its stories about itself, The Market Theatre is a meeting place, a training place, a sharing place for people of all cultures and intentions. We remain committed in this new and complex time to join our community in its quest for a world of peace, justice and greater understanding. In order to continue we need your strong support.'

Previous page overleaf – The revamped Market Theatre Laboratory.
Photograph by Ruphin Coudyzer.
Opposite – Barney Simon.
Photograph courtesy of NELM.

Chapter 12. Writing

Barney Simon is quoted as saying:
'I only do dangerous things - there is so little time.'

Barney's love of writing had begun when he was at school. His story "Elizabeth's Baby" was published in the literary magazine Trek, edited by Bernard Sachs, while he was studying for his matric. As we heard from Lionel Abrahams, when he was in his twenties, Barney and his friends self-published a collection of twenty stories called "Twenty", which they 'printed' by means of a Roneo duplicator. He took over the editorship of The Classic, South Africa's first literary magazine specifically hospitable to black writers when Nat Nakasa, the founding editor, went into exile in New York where he died. Later Barney sponsored and helped Dugmore Boetie to record his autobiography, "Familiarity is the Kingdom of the Lost".

In the epilogue of Dugmore Boetie's autobiography, "Familiarity is the Kingdom of the Lost", Barney speaks of where he got his sense of 'no time'...

'Another factor which propelled me towards commitment is one which I am a bit reluctant to mention. But it is the most personal, the most important. It is a sense of urgency, of "no time". A terrible sense of the mortality of so many African talents I've come to know and love. I am afraid that I mean the man, not just his work. It's as if, through surviving as a whole man, not unbitter but capable of functioning free from his bitterness, he has to pay the price of his life. True, people die every day from suicide, alcoholism, gangsters' bullets, jaundice and cancer. But it has been with a kind of superstitious horror that I have watched some of the most tender and rare of our men and talents go. Nat Nakasa, Can Themba, Julian Motau, Todd Matshikiza, Duggie. Some in exile, some here. It is with the same kind of horror that I sense mortality in faces around me now.'

From the Epilogue of "Familiarity Is The Kingdom of the Lost", written by Dugmore Boetie and edited by Barney Simon.

While in America Barney became an associate editor of the New American Review. And in 1974 "Joburg, Sis!", a collection of his stories and monologues, was published by Patrick Cullinan's Bateleur Press. Barney wrote screenplays from short stories by Doris Lessing and Nadine Gordimer. Writing and encouraging actors to write was integral to his process.

He describes how he wrote with actors:
'I am a writer. I've written short stories. I've written film scripts. I've also worked as an editor. But, to me, what's exciting is composing with the actors, because every human being has a biography as individual as his fingerprint. Everybody contains enormous surprises if you can release them to explore themselves. And that's part of the process I go through... So what excites me is to "turn on" my actors, get them to find the stories in their lives. When they've found the character to be played I help them build the character's biography. Next, I take that biography and place it beside another, then put them in a situation, and then we improvise. The story develops that way, and then I begin to give it a form and we edit it into a play.'

In the following chapter Nadine Gordimer describes Barney Simon's adaptations of her short stories for screen. He wrote lyrics with many composers: Mackay Davashe, Victor Ntoni, John Oakley-Smith, Sophie Mgcina, Jennifer Ferguson and Cyril Magubane. Jennifer Ferguson describes this process. Playwright Paul Slabolepszy and writer Sipho Sepamla tell of the influence Barney had on their work. Mtutuzeli Matshoba speaks of Barney's New Directions play-writing workshops for TV channel M-Net, which he was busy with in his last years.

Nadine Gordimer

'We both saw it as an immense jigsaw of the consciousness of our time'

There were films of two stories of mine, "Country Lovers" and "City Lovers", and Barney scripted "City Lovers". Barney was going to adapt my story and so of course we talked a lot about it. Six stories were adapted for television. I wrote some and he did several. In "City Lovers" Joe Stewardson played a surveyor for some big overseas company who was a stranger here and had a love affair with a coloured girl he picked up. Barney chose Joe Stewardson. He interpreted the role wonderfully. Barney's casting was usually very, very good. And the girl was somebody from Cape Town. She was also excellent. I remember one wonderful line, a mixture between the actual text of my book and direct speech – obviously, when you adapt a short story, unless it is completely in dialogue, you have to transform narrative into direct speech. This is always the problem with people who attempt to adapt my work, especially foreigners. They think they know the way white South Africans speak, they think they know the way black South Africans speak English. But of course with Barney it was different. He had a perfect ear for differences. And for the ironies of the way poor people see rich. In his script, the girl is now living with the man in this rather nice Killarney flat. Looking out of the window she sees some Northern Suburb youngsters. It was just at the time when you had to cut off your jeans and have them unravelling on the end. He says to her, 'What are you gazing at?' She says, 'Mmmm look at them – I think you have to be very rich to dress like that.' And it was a typical wonderfully perceptive Barney line.

How did he work with you and your story "City Lovers" for television? Did he take the story and just adapt and write it by himself, or did he write it with you?

First he read the story twenty times, and I think he must have made many notes. We discussed them, particularly the enlargement of the dialogue between Stewardson and the young girl. Then he obviously went away and wrote a script. I am sure he probably brought it back to me and we discussed it again. But it was very good. That is the only good experience that I ever had with scriptwriters. But Barney – he just understood that story as I had conceived it.

So Barney and I had a working relationship for this period. He introduced me to Dugmore Boetie, a coloured writer who wrote a remarkable story about working in OK Bazaars. Barney and I were very enthusiastic about his talent. He was very, very good but a bit of a con man. But Barney was, as you have probably discovered, the guy for every con man that walked. That was part of his sweetness. His trusting nature.

So Dugmore Boetie was sort of our mutual charge. I was encouraging Barney to bring out a book of Boetie's writings. It was published as "Familiarity is the Kingdom of the Lost". There were inevitably terrible problems for about ten years after Boetie's death. His relatives were absolutely sure that Barney had made a fortune out of this

Opposite – Nadine Gordimer on a Johannesburg mine dump, 1987.
Photograph by David Goldblatt / South Photos.

book. So we were pestered, I was particularly, because Barney was more slippery to get hold of, by these relatives. They must have their share of the money they believed Barney had made. Of course, it was quite the other way round because Barney had to do everything for Dugmore Boetie, endless expenditure of money and time. Barney was a great one for giving you advice about everything. He wasn't a father or a mother but he really behaved like an old mom sometimes. Always telling you how you ought to run your life while not always being so expert in running his own. But that was his way. On the other hand he was unbelievably supportive and more than helpful if there was any problem, any crisis. So one can only say he was a really wonderful, wonderful friend.

We have asked most people, and I would like to ask you, who were you and where were you when you met Barney?
I think we must have met through Lionel Abrahams.

What happened, did you just sort of click or talk about writing?
The chemistry was right from the beginning. Then we became genuinely very interested in each other's work, not scratching each other's backs, but we recognised and saw qualities in each other that were genuine. And so that was an ongoing dialogue so to speak. Barney's stories were good, very good. "Men should Cry More Often". Splendid story. But then I think, of course, the theatre was really his great talent. If he had lived on, he might have done much to bring real quality to television drama.
Barney had intense but different relationships with many people. With Athol for instance. They were always quarrelling and then getting together again. I remember one occasion – Athol will probably be furious with me but that doesn't matter. I forget what part it was, it might even have been Boesman – Barney wanted Athol to take his teeth out for the authenticity of the character. It seemed that Athol was born with false teeth... There was an argument, either Barney wanted Athol to put them in and he didn't want to or it was the other way around [laughter]. So this sort of thing was always very, very serious indeed.

Sometimes Barney used to phone me and say, 'I have found a real talent, and I want you to meet me.' Once it was, 'I want you to come and listen to these two chaps improvising.' And do you know who they were? Mbongeni Ngema and Percy Mtwa. He had been talking to them about their experiences and said, 'Now you go back to where you live and talk to people. The woman who is selling mielies on the street. The people who are queuing up to get on the train. Talk to them about what they think would happen if Jesus came back, if Luthuli came back.' And that's how "Woza" was developed. This day was the first time that they had returned to talk about their experiences. I sat there transfixed. The two of them were absolutely brilliant. The dialogue began to be set in the graveyard, or at Luthuli's grave. I am happy to have been present at the genesis of that marvellous play. One of Barney's greatest collaborations with black artists.

This was part of the curious dichotomy within Barney over his political allegiance. I would say he was politically engaged in a very general, high-level way. He was totally against all racism and all injustice but he would never have been able to subscribe to any particular allegiance. He always said, 'It's the work that counts, you don't have to take up a stance on anything.' That was his main way of dealing with the injustice in our society. Indeed, what he did so wonderfully was to foster incredible talents. Few people know that he quietly also took political risks, hiding people on the run from Special Branch persecution.

Without Barney and Athol I don't know how black theatre would have emerged, how black playwrights would have emerged. I know it is not a popular way to suggest that's how it began, but it did, with Athol's Serpent Players and with Barney. And somehow with Barney, in the end, much more selflessly, because Athol became famous. Athol's plays were his plays in which other people acted. But Barney did the kind of collaboration he had with Mbongeni and Percy all the time. Think of some of the talented women that he not only nurtured, but, if they fell by the way in the hard times of apartheid, brought them back into theatre.

Politically he was, as I have said, privately incredibly committed. He kept a deep friendship with Ruth First and Joe Slovo. Ruth was such a very doctrinaire person when she was young. So quite how Barney fitted into the friendship I don't know. But his whole life was bold, courageous theatre, wasn't it? I don't know whether you have been able to talk to Rose the maid?

She died.

Oh that was a saga, especially since eventually she moved the whole family into Barney's house and he had to leave [laughter]. Do you know that? Well, he had this nice house in Yeoville, a nice outhouse at the back, which he then converted into a study. Well, the next thing, poor Rosie brought along her family, so he moved out of his study and they occupied that. But then slowly more and more family members needed shelter and eventually they were in the house and there was no more room for Barney. He had to move somewhere else.

I didn't know that's how it happened.

I remember long before that, he lived, oh donkeys' years ago, near Joubert Park in an old flat building. It was always a dubious area, even then, with lots of prostitutes hanging around. One night he came home and there was a woman sobbing, beaten up, outside the door. So, being Barney, he took her in and made cocoa for her and gave her a Kosher bun. And to cut a long story short, she spent the night, he made a bed for her. But she stayed on and on. She was frightened that she would be beaten again by her pimp. Barney didn't know what to do with her. Then there was, what was his name, that young man?

Charlie.

Charlie, is he still alive?

I think he is around but we can't find him.

Charlie, and the gun that he kept under his bed with him. It was all very mysterious, but that was Barney. A man with a boundlessly good heart. No wonder it wore out too soon, too young. Barney also wrote advertising copy when he was young. I remember this changing his appearance, because when you are in the advertising world you have a certain kind of chic. You don't wear three-piece suits but you wear designer jeans and so on. Then that changed. I would always say, 'Barney, you look like a garage attendant with those overalls.'

Barney was such a generous person. He was always bringing me things he thought I ought to have. Gadgets, or books that I was to read. But he also brought the most terrible cakes. I think that's what killed him in the end, eating that rich muck he used to buy from the Kosher Bakery in Rockey Street. He never could understand that nobody else liked these things. When you went to his house to discuss something, he would have gone and bought cakes. You were expected to eat them.

Another thing we were involved in together was "Marat/Sade". The Cultural Boycott was in force. Anybody that had any principles, overseas, wouldn't allow their work to be done here. Now I knew Peter Weiss. Barney came to me and said, 'Can't you get him to let us have it, so we can have it for the opening of The Market Theatre?' Nothing could have been more appropriate, more defiant of apartheid's onslaught against the freedom struggle. Our people were in the streets saying, as the actors in the play did, we want our revolution now. So this was really a very daring play to put on. I wrote to Peter Weiss and phoned and talked to him and persuaded him. Although I was the last person to tell somebody to break a boycott I felt that this instance was justified. This was going right into the battle lines. He finally gave permission, and, as you know, it was a triumph. I will never forget it. Peter Weiss always wanted to meet Barney but it didn't work out.

It is incredible — so far sixty-three people we have interviewed have all said that they were his best friend and that they had lived with him.

Well, he was a best friend, I think, to many. Toward the end, the last years of his life, he and I weren't as close as we had been, not seeing as much of each other as we had. We both became so preoccupied, so caught up in other things. But when we met there was that old intimacy. He was always so terribly, lovingly interested in everybody else's children. I last spoke to him after his heart-bypass operation at the home of Hilary Hamburger, and said, 'How are you?' and he said, 'Much better.' So I said, 'In the next couple of days I will come and see you.' The following night he had this terrible attack and he was dead.

Some people said that he didn't look after himself properly as he should have.

No, he didn't. After the operation everybody looked after him. I mean nobody could have taken more care of him than the Hamburgers, but I am told by doctors that if you have this operation your chances of recovery depend pretty much on the lifestyle you led before. And you know he didn't exercise. He lived on junk food. He somehow fell victim to this, though he never struck me as someone who really suffered that much with stress. He had an inner calm, don't you think? Everybody would be raging around him and he would just say, yet again, 'It's the work that counts.' That is my rubric for him.

You were obviously very good friends for a very long time, but is there any way you can say he contributed or gave to you as a writer?

I would not say as a writer. Maybe some writers come greatly under the influence of others but if any writers have influenced me it has been in their books that I read when I was very, very young. Once you find your own voice and your own preoccupations, it's always a discovery and pleasure to find someone else who's perhaps moving along the same dark channels. There Barney's vision and mine met. I would say that was the basis of our relationship but I was not influenced by him. Perhaps if I had written for the theatre...

His love life was always absolutely mysterious. I think he was a kind of cupboard gay. Why, I don't know, because none of us would have cared a tuppenny damn. Even though he spoke about other emotional things, especially my own emotional entanglements that happened a long time ago, we never talked about his, when I come to think of it. It was something that he kept to himself, so I couldn't give him any advice. I have the feeling that he is listening somewhere and saying: 'No, no, no... It's the work that counts.' I still can't believe that he's gone... When I go to The Market and I see the Barney Simon Theatre and that terrible bust that looks like anybody but Barney...

'The chemistry was right there from the beginning. Then we became genuinely very interested in each other's work' Nadine Gordimer

Jennifer Ferguson

'You had to enter the accuracy of the biography and at the same time unveil the shadows, and then bless them'

I met Barney in Muller Street at his house. Christo Leach and I were working on a double bill "I, Ulrike, Cry" by Dario Fo, and Franca Rama's "Women's Play", which I did with Katie Tindle. The original work "Women's Play", had taken so much time that the Dario Fo monologue had been left to the end. Halfway through the monologue I just couldn't do it, and it was two days to opening. Christo was totally overwhelmed. So we called Barney in for a run-through. Barney came right into this crisis. It is a very harsh monologue. Ulrike is in prison. It could be pre-suicidal. She is a terrorist. She is the voice in some of us, the potential bomber. At the end of the monologue, which I had done with a fair amount of wrath, Barney said to me, 'Now I want you to say it like a love poem.' That ricocheted in me. When you receive that sense of directional insight as a performer you get lightheaded. It was an awakening. The whole experience was totally transformed. I had to bless my character. I had to forgive myself and the world.

Barney in his pursuit of truth was almost always totally free of judgment. He demanded of you your nakedness. Barney's power as a director was to scrape through all the sediment of your defences. He saw the divinity in all of us and as a director managed to touch it. Because then you become a vessel for the mystery of a performer, the mystery of the writer. Which is why he was often so difficult to work with, he never would take the obvious choices. And he would always push you as a performer to look under, to look beneath, to look round again – to throw out. His directing was stripping. It wasn't putting on. It was surrendering to a state of nakedness – where you had to go.

After that, Megan Kruskal and I were working on "Kentucky Fried Chickies". It was a crazy time. Now, in retrospect, you can see how easy it is when a lot of your own personal shit and unresolved anger can so easily find a home in the political struggle. Through our art we tried to harness that explosive energy without hurting ourselves too much.

Many of the people that Barney was working with were incredibly damaged given the history of our world. Barney provided a very important refuge for a generation, two generations in fact, who were working with changing their relationship to this world. If we are creating our worlds then surely we have to understand ourselves firstly? Barney was working on a deeply personal level in relationship to us and that made him wonderful. It was like honey, nectar, in this time of drought. Ja, just to come and suck a sweetness that was insightful, and also all the time holding a mirror back onto yourself. That's probably why I think everybody who worked with him felt that they had a deep, personal relationship with him.

The process with Megan was hectic. We were working with a bottle of brandy on the kitchen table every night that we would finish, the two of us, while we improvised. "Kentucky Fried Chickies" was bulimic theatre of extremes.

Opposite – Rehearsing "Inyanga" in 1989, from left Rashid Lani, Gcina Mhlope, Jennifer Ferguson, Thembi Mtshali, Barney Simon and Sophie Mgcina.
Photograph by Ruphin Coudyzer.

You sliced your theatre under your skin. It was a theatre of cruelty to change the world, but in the process you were also incinerating yourself. I remember while we were writing the script it being a time of blind, inner turmoil. I remember Barney coming around to my house in Regent Street. I was very upset. But I remember him sitting there. We were sharing a joint and he sat on the chair opposite me and said, 'Well, I am going to teach you something very important that was taught to me when I was in great trouble.' He spoke about this interview that he had to attend in New York for which he was totally unprepared. On the way in the subways he meditated. By the time he had left the subway he was entirely at peace. 'I want to teach you how to meditate.' It was such a gift. He gave me the first lesson in going inside, quietly, to listen from exactly where you are.

Toward the end, before he left his body, we were talking about the possibility of doing "The Passion" in Grahamstown. He was asking many questions about Jesus the man. He had a fascination with the mystical – but he abhorred dogma. He was wary of conclusion. He was in life-process all the time. His constant questioning amplified itself at the end of his life. I read a similar account about one of the Buddhist masters who was in great pain at the end of his life – after all the years of training and preparation for facing the passage of death and dying. At the end this master had to let go of his own mind. The pain confused him. At that point the child returns. The state of absolute bewilderment that comes because the world is not what it seemed. So it was a privilege for me to spend time with Barney at that juncture. The emergency bypass and surgical procedure was a total shock to him. The shock of the invasion of the heart. It was such a massive, uninvited and anonymous entry into the most intimate space of yourself. He was so very bewildered by that. He was desperately trying to understand what had happened.

Ah, the deliciousness of his friendship, his Jewishness. There was always something to celebrate. His love of sweetness, of deliciousness, of trees. There was so much sensuality in his relationships though there was also a voyeurism. And his skin. He lived with his skin. He lived in daily charting of the state of his skin. On an esoteric level psoriasis seems to be the soul of a bird that battles to be at home in the confines of the body. There was a deep desire to transcend – and at the same time go deeper into the world, into the sediment of "Joburg, Sis!" for example. Without judgment – without morality.

Aah, the music. That was incredible. His relationship to music was very special. We did "Inyanga – Woman of Africa", "Eden and Other Places" and "The Lion and the Lamb". You know, he couldn't really sing. He couldn't keep a tune. But he had a totally instinctual, innate sense of music that was impeccable. Collaborating with him, he would have a sure idea about what he wanted. Sometimes we had to battle. He would introduce a different sort of rhythmic change, or an energy that could be absolutely appropriate.

We were writing a Hillbrow song, so we went riding through Hillbrow. I was working Pretoria Street at Club 58. I adopted this incredibly old elephant mother woman who was a homeless angel with a shopping trolley. She had these huge, very swollen legs and her trolley was full. She was too big for the city. Once when I walked past I looked over and saw she was reading a book by Camus on her trolley. So she was an incredible song. Riding through the streets all those landmarks that aren't there anymore. Café Wien, Café Paris. There's a woman with her hair on fire moving through the streets. Setting Hillbrow alight, God. And at the end the Black Madonna rises – to beautify / to sanctify my childhood. Thank you Barney.

With Barney there was an imperative for accuracy, and at the same time you had to unveil the shadows, and then bless them. I think that is why I battled to end things. When is it complete? Even the workshop stuff was never complete. It was relentless. There was just no resting in it. Because the biography is continuing. The mystery is constantly amazing.

He was working with people that had big holes in their hearts. He could not understand the self-damage. Self-depreciation. Wanting to hurt yourself. It would be interesting to see who he reincarnates as. I wonder if he's black. Where would he be? My greatest collaborator and dearest mentor/friend. I miss him so much.

'Dear God, Qamata, Mveliqangi – you are the one who came first.
You are the creator of the universe.
You created the moon. You created the sun.
I am not sure in what order.
Did you create the moon first with all the gentleness and care.
With the soft light and mysteries that it seems to carry.
Did you get bored with the way it is, then you created the sun,
so hot, so confident, that overpowered the moon.
So hot that it could scorch the earth and all that's in it.
I am not sure whether the moon and the sun are supposed to be
male.
Whatever the order is.
I know sunsets can put people in a very romantic mood,
but isn't the full moon wild!'

Opening praise song to "Inyanga".

Paul Slabolepszy

'He had given me my legs to walk and then I had to run away'

Barney was the first person to encourage me as a writer. He was doing a lot of workshop plays at the time. I would take a monologue to Barney and he would say, 'Explore it further.' I would have all these ideas but no one would take them seriously. Barney would say, 'Ja, that's great. More. Tell me more.' More than anyone else he actually made me believe that my characters had a voice in the world. All a fledgling writer needs to hear!

In August 1981 I saw an article in the Rand Daily Mail about a bizarre attack at a roadhouse. Two youths ride up to the roadhouse and throw a smoke canister in the window. A black waiter comes out, they beat him up and they ride away. That's all it said in the paper. That kind of gave me my skeleton for "Saturday Night at the Palace". I wrote it in two weeks drawing from my experiences as a youth in roadhouses across the East Rand. I always had the sense that Barney felt that I should have taken it to him and we should have workshopped it. But I was very precious about the story because I knew exactly where I wanted to go with this play. I was anxious because of my experience of working with Barney. It was an ego thing on my part because I was scared that Barney would take it in another direction. No question it would have been a powerful play but it wouldn't have been my play. He had given me my legs to walk and then I had run away. I wanted to follow my own instincts. Looking back to 1981 when it was written, I wanted it to be as real as if you were sitting at the roadhouse in your car watching it all unfold before you. Which is exactly as it turned out.

I remember Barney coming in a week before we opened and saying, 'Hell, you know, you must throw the play out the window now and take risks.' I remember Bill Flynn being completely thrown. I said, 'No, no, no, I know what Barney is saying, I know exactly what he is saying: It's that we have gone so far and actually we could go a lot further.' It might take another six weeks or three months or six months, but we couldn't do that because we were opening next week. It wasn't a kind of like parting of the ways but in a sense that's where I lost the umbilical cord. Up until then I'd been one of the guys from Barney's school.

Going on a trip with Barney was something completely unique. It actually made you thrilled to be an actor. It took our acting into a dimension where we could do the same as what they were doing in that American school of guys like Pacino, Meryl Streep, all those people. Barney could do that, he actually made your acting brilliant because you could explore endless possibilities. Barney's method did that. So when Barney and I took a split after Palace in '82 I felt that afterwards he couldn't ask me to do the things he had before. It was kind of an unspoken thing that Barney was going to workshop "Saturday Night At The Palace". It's hard. If I could speak to Barney today he might say, 'No, it's not like that at all.' But that's what I sensed.

Barney's method, the workshop, was completely different from the conventional play. Barney gave me the taste of writing plays and I couldn't go back to the workshopping option. He told me not to be precious about my stuff, and that's why I let my actors have quite a lot of free reign in rehearsals. So although I write a play with a beginning, a middle and an end, I let it travel if it needs to travel, but only a certain distance. Whereas Barney's experience would be that you all come with your own idea and it could travel until wherever it stopped. It is interesting now looking back at a lot of Barney's things like "Score Me the Ages" and "Cincinatti" – they are almost like a chronicle of the times. So that's what Barney was bringing to his work. If you went to see a Barney Simon production it would be what is happening now. When we did "Fortune and Men's Eyes" it was already an established Canadian award-winning play. What's fascinating is that Barney – funny, I loved what he did there but I would hate it if someone did it to my work – what he did was he chucked the ending completely out of the window. He said, 'I have seen "Fortune and Men's Eyes" in America and in Cape Town, and it's pathetic. It's so sentimental.' Barney took what was a potentially strong play and made it more powerful. I have never had a greater experience on a play than working on that one. Mannie had the rights for certain plays that we weren't allowed to change. Some playwrights were saying, 'You will not change this play.' Barney was quite subversive because he didn't change the play just until we got to the end.

I think of delightful things, like when we did "Show Me Yours", where he made us play five-year-old-kids – me, Davey Eppel, Sue Kiel and Vanessa. It was a very hard thing to do. We were in nursery school. It was incredibly insightful, ahead of its time. In fact years later Steve Martin made a thing like this. I remember there was a big play on Broadway. But Barney was experimenting with these things long before. There was an article, I think it was in Newsweek, about South Africa's best-kept secret. It was about Barney. Wherever he went to work in America or even in England people picked up very quickly that he was a very special theatre practitioner. But Barney's whole life was 'the work'. Barney never ever turned an actor away, ja, that was his genius as well. Danny Keogh is today one of the greatest South African actors. I'm in awe of Danny's talent. Danny was a stage manager who was never going to do anything but knock nails into walls and tell people when to go on and off. But he was hungry to act. Barney held his hand and gave him courage and the opportunities and led him to where he is now. Barney had this amazing nurturing ability. If some people had ever gone along to audition for PACT in those early days they would have said, 'Voetsek man! Don't waste our time.' In drama school I had Mavis Taylor to thank for keeping me at UCT. Others look at the 'obvious' things like, hey, he can't speak properly. Barney saw right through all that. He was looking for the essence of what acting is all about. Something coming right from deep inside.

Barney hated Peter Shaffer's "Amadeus". He'd say this guy has just got involved in his own pyrotechnics. He hasn't brought us the characters. They are very cardboard, one-dimensional. That was the most fantastic thing about Barney: when you were in a Barney production you were never one dimensional – no matter how big or how small your part was. You created something special. It is sad that more of his work didn't reach a wider audience. It was so wonderful that "Woza Albert!" was able to travel the world. If that was his only contribution to world theatre, which it's not, then it would have been huge anyway.

Paul, how was Barney politically involved, if at all?

Throughout the '70s and '80s there was a side of Barney that always remained hidden from his actors. Periods when – at the drop of a hat – he would either suddenly up and leave a rehearsal, or simply disappear for a couple of days at a time. We were all aware of his absolute abhorrence of the government and its apartheid policies. In fact most of the stories Barney worked on reflected the pain and suffering this systematic enforced racial separation caused. He would often return to work disturbed, distraught, preoccupied. If anyone asked him if he was okay, he'd shrug and say he's just heard some bad news or a friend had been in some kind of trouble. He'd never say what it was.

But there were times after rehearsals or around his kitchen table, late at night, when he was weary – he'd express his fears for the future of the country – the absolute horrors that were going on around us – all the time. 'You have no idea of the wickedness, the depths to which these people sink.' He'd go into a decline, like his brain, his whole being, had gone walk-about. And yet, to my knowledge, he'd never share his pain with the group of young actors that were forever around him.

It was only recently – when I laid my hands on the Mary Benson books, "A Far Cry" and "Athol Fugard and Barney Simon – Bare Stage, A Few Props, Great Theatre" – that part of Barney's 'secret life' suddenly emerged for me. In these books she described her great friendship with Barney – going back many years, of how he drove her around in South Africa when she was under house arrest, or not even supposed to be in the country. Of how he himself could have been imprisoned, not once, but many times.

In one of the pictures in "Athol and Barney Simon" there is a wonderful fun-filled shot of Joe Slovo, Ruth First, Barney and Athol taken in London in 1966. Mary Benson talks in her book of how Ruth First's death at the hands of the apartheid assassins in 1982 affected Barney. He was in London at the time with "Woza Albert!". He was shattered, absolutely torn to shreds, and yet had to return to South Africa to continue working. I get the feeling, in hindsight, that deep down, Barney was torn between the work he felt he had to do to tend the wounds that the apartheid regime was inflicting on his fellow South Africans and a genuine desire to do something more drastic, more concrete in the struggle.

But Barney was essentially a storyteller, a lover of humanity, and in the '60s, '70s and '80s South Africans needed him to be just that. And he was. And we are richer for it. As he said in a BBC interview immediately after Ruth First's state-sanctioned murder, 'There is so much drama in South Africa. As somebody once said, you touch a person, and a story flows like blood from a wound.' Barney Simon gave those stories a chance to be heard.

Opposite – Paul Slabolepszy in "Cold Stone Jug".
Pphotograph by Ruphin Coudyzer.

'Who needs a degree? If you are a writer that is your degree, so do not spend sleepless nights reading notes for exams, because your abilities are your certificates. What you are able to produce from writing will earn you respect whatever you are hoping to achieve'

Barney Simon's advice to Sipho Sepamla regarding his studies through UNISA.

Sipho Sepamla

'You must not always be reading other people's work, you must write your own books'

Yes, I would consider Barney a friend, someone that I trusted and therefore would discuss some of my creative work with. Barney used to meet with Dugmore Boetie. He wrote the last part of Boetie's book. They worked on the book practically every day for weeks on end – I got to know what they were doing. I admired the way they worked on this thing. These were partners rather than master and student, it was more like equals meeting. So later on after Boetie had died and the book came out, for me it held a certain fascination. I had seen it grow. I think Boetie was not a writer at all and Barney was helping out.

Why would you trust him? He was white.

Well yes, it was a bad time. There were definitely suspicions between blacks and whites. But you see, I was working at Dorkay House at the time and I got to know that Barney was a knowledgeable guy, I kept discussing things with him because I liked the way he gave advice. If you gave him a poem or a short story, as I did, and then later a play, Barney did not give you advice that gave the impression that he wanted you to rewrite the script. To me, I suppose because of my age, he tended to make suggestions. He was very tentative about it, allowed me a lot of room. If he gave an opinion or an idea, it remained an idea and it was up to me to decide whether to incorporate that idea or not. That is why I enjoyed working with him, because other people that I had advice from had a different attitude. That is why later on I did my play with him.

I have always been unsure and tentative about my creative work. I gave my play to Barney and he was really thrilled. I asked him to direct it, but unfortunately at the time he was busy with some other work. He couldn't handle it and later, when he wanted to do it, I was not available. I was into other things. When I made the announcement that I was going to start a magazine, Lionel Abrahams suggested that I speak to Barney because at the time he was looking for someone to take over the editorship of Classic Magazine. So I approached Barney and he was quite happy to let me try my hand at editing it. I think I did three or four issues. The first edition was paid for by the remainder of a grant, which Barney had received for the production of the magazine. So I was really dealing with someone who had faith in my capabilities.

In the relationship he encouraged you?

Yes, he was big in encouraging. He always wanted people to make attempts at whatever they could lay their hands on. He gave me some very interesting advice. One time he said, 'You must not always be reading other people's work. You must write your own books.' I respected Barney a great deal. I remember seeing one of his rehearsals when I was working at Dorkay House. I saw a presentation of "The Death of Bessie Smith". It was memorable. The way Barney presented it was wonderful. I had read that Bessie Smith had been a leading singer in that period, but to see how she was treated at the hospital after the accident... Memories like that one keep Barney alive to me all the time.

Opposite – Sipho Sepamla.
Photograph by Ruphin Coudyzer.

Mtutuzeli Matshoba

'I remember him making an example about locking your ego in the wardrobe before you could go out and do any sensible work'

I had this dream to write something that would be directed by Barney Simon. Each time we met we kept promising each other these things. I was impressed by his work and by his standing in the community at large and in the arts community.

In 1994 Barney was involved as a co-ordinator of M-Net's New Directions short screenplay workshops. I'd always wanted to be a screenplay writer. I entered a short story, "Chikin Biznis". It was included amongst the six texts chosen for the course. My assumption was that they'd bought the script, they'd paid and why should I bother. On the first day of the workshops I did not attend. I was at home. A lady called Sheila, who was like an art director in movies, was also involved in the workshops. Sheila phoned me and said I must come over, I was delaying people. The thing started at nine and she called me at ten. I hadn't even taken a bath and she says, 'Barney says this thing is not starting until you are here.' I walked in there, embarrassed, around lunchtime. And there was Barney in his own humble way. Nobody was upset. He had insisted that I be there because he liked that particular story. So I went in and that was my first direct interaction with him. I was impressed by the man for the way in which he respected people's creative integrity. You'd expect that a person who is editing your work would be brutal like movie people are. But he was so patient with us and actually assisted us to understand that writing anything like plays, or screenplays, is about rewriting. I remember him making an example about locking your ego in the wardrobe before you could go out and do any sensible work.

Barney was absolutely anti-violence. You could see when a violent script was placed in front of him, or when we were doing scripts that had violence, he worked hard to tone it down, or make it subtle. I remember him saying that things happen, rape, violence happens, but for him it was the aftermath that had the impact. While it was happening it may even entertain a sadist to see a man raping a woman. You understand what I mean? It's either you prevent it, or if you look at it in terms of movies and how to express it, it's the result that you need to deal with. You need to deal with how people cope. I had written protest literature almost all my life. I just felt so relieved after 1995. We had forgotten how to laugh in South Africa. Barney said it's ordinary people that have to be built into characters that work in literature. The character that is already there, cut and dried, is too big. It is very difficult to cut them down to the size of life. So he encouraged us to write about these things. I remember him saying the little man on the street is like epic. His story becomes epic. It may be a little story to you. So that is what "Chikin Biznis" was about.

I get to the workshop and I realise that we will have to read all six final scripts, and mine has got to be read. You can imagine how one feels: 'Now these people are going to sit here and tear it to pieces.' So they actually sit there and they criticise your work and you think they are doing it because they are in competition with you. Barney is guiding these things. With a lot of patience he is sitting there smiling sometimes. You think he is not listening and then he throws in a word. At the end of the day he demystified the whole thing. He said that the moment you had entered the competition the work was no longer yours. It belonged to all of us and, finally, it is going to belong to audiences. We were sitting really roasting each other. He did not stand up there like a teacher. He became one of us. He would ask soft questions. I remember him asking one guy, 'Why?' about ten times. This guy would say he is talking about a character. And Barney would say, 'Why?' This guy starts wondering if he's being pressured by Barney. Then Barney says, 'Take your pen and each time you give me an answer write that answer down. Once you look at the answers and the questions and the why, why, why, you are going to arrive at a conclusion that is going to satisfy me as a person who is reading your writing.' So it built your confidence to be able to stand there and present your work amongst strangers. Right now when I'm actually pitching a script it comes exactly from that. Barney defined that when he broke down the fears that we have, and our wanting to hold onto the work. And it actually made me believe that when I'm writing something I'm writing for people out there. So that is the essence of what I learnt from him – to pitch. He would put a pile of scripts there and everybody would take a script. When the time comes he asks you, 'Why do you think that story should be made into a movie?' What a question! 'What's in the story that you think people would invest money in?' That was the constant question. It was about learning to write a story for the future. He insisted that writers should be involved with the scripts from the beginning right up to the end of the process, to post-production. People should understand the whole before they can specialise. If you understand all phases of making a movie, when you write you consider the practicalities and impracticalities of what you are writing about. From their input he would judge where people's strength lay in movies. If you were lazy, Barney would have looked at you as if you were a disappointing child. He wouldn't scold. He wouldn't criticise. He would say it through his eyes. He would have a sort of surprised look about him.

Mtutuzeli Matshoba, 1979.
Photograph courtesy of The Star.

Chapter 13. Directing

Barney Simon mentored many artists. His incessant notes on other directors' productions inspired and infuriated them. Lara Foot Newton and Robyn Orlin relate how Barney shaped their work. Clare Stopford points out that Barney, rather than trying to control directors' work, wanted them to ignite and maintain their own creativity. Actress Grethe Fox describes the impact Barney had on the filmmaker Manie van Rensburg.

In the second part of this chapter Richard E. Grant, Jana Cilliers, Michele Maxwell, Peter Piccolo, Wesley France, Michael Maxwell, Bruce Koch, Janet Suzman, Busi Zokufa, Motshabi Tyelele, Gina Benjamin, Sheila Fugard, Megan Kruskal, Kate Edwards and Christo Leach all pay tribute to Barney Simon.

Opposite – Barney Simon during rehearsals for "Silent Movie", 1993.
Photograph by Ruphin Coudyzer.

Lara Foot Newton

'Before the scrambled eggs are ready you take them off, because you've got to respect the heat of the egg'

I had just finished at Wits and I asked if I could watch some of his rehearsals. He said he would phone me if he needed an assistant. He phoned me six months later. I had watched his plays "Outers" and "Born in the RSA", so it was like getting a phone call from Steven Spielberg. He said he needed an assistant for "Starbrites", and could I come today? He used to pay me from his own pocket. The petrol money, that was my pay. I was broke, paying back a student loan and doing all sorts of jobs. He would put his hand in his pocket, give me twenty rand. I would feel awkward because I was taking his money. Then Mannie came and said he had this little bursary at The Market for exactly what I was doing. He gave me six hundred rand for my work. I thought I was so rich.

We had a constant thing of eggs, me and Barney. There are so many memories of how we used to make eggs, scrambled eggs. Me wanting to talk about a play and him teaching me how to make scrambled eggs. Of course everyone knows how to make scrambled eggs, but he had his own method. He used to say, respect the heat of the egg [laughing]. He was telling me something else but by the time we had finished making the eggs the problem of the play was no more a problem, you had isolated the one thing that you needed to go forward.

He was different things for different people. So he was what you needed. He was like water, flowing into little cracks in you and making you better, making you visible. When I first started, I tried to remember: What did he say about directing? What did he do? How can I engrave that in my memory? Those things have become less and less important now as the years go past. He used the saying 'Work makes you visible to yourself.' Things like that, and you use them and quote them. You actually don't understand them totally, but the years go by and you understand them more and more. That is because you live in him. He used to show me movies and I never realised what he was showing me, but as the years go by I start to understand more and more. And in ten years time I will know more. Talk about immortality.

How did he direct?

He was fascinated by how people affect each other, how people perceive each other. That is how he directed. That was for me everything he ever told me about directing: what dialogues people have, what people do to one another, how people affect one another... You just work from that. I don't even think he ever thought of anything else, like lighting, vision. No, it was just that, just that. Watching me directing one time, he said to me, 'You are not working properly.'

And what did he mean?

He meant that I wasn't seeing a moment. Seeing how it is affecting that person, and where it leads to. Going in and giving life to that moment. And that has a natural consequence. I was working blandly, in other words. I know what it is like to be told in front of actors that you are not working properly as a director. It is hard. But Barney could tell one. I felt mortified. I never argued with him. I just had respect. If he was right, he was right. What could I do? You can direct by rejecting certain things, or you can direct by being fascinated about what you are looking at. And that was Barney. Sometimes maybe I lacked something. I was directing to get from point A to point Z. But if you are at A and you stay at A, you get somewhere in the end. It is much scarier because you won't necessarily get a good product but you will get a truthful one.

Do you just stay on things that interest you?

A thing that has life. That can live and live and live. If I can't get it right, hey, that is what I challenge myself with. I try to do that. The tendency is get to Z and polish it. But if you follow the truth of what you see, then you have to stay there and keep allowing the truth to tell you where to go next. That is very hard to do because you have the pressure of people who have paid you and actors who are worried about what is going to happen, how it is going to end. If you trust that you can stay there, you will get there. Barney once discussed a director that he said just wanted to see the product before she had seen the life. He had asked her what she thought of what he was doing and she had said, 'It needs rhythm, it needs pace, it needs polish.' He was appalled. You never heard Barney say, 'Let's polish this' or 'It needs pace.' He would rather be going, 'What is she doing there? Why is she looking at him like that? Is the floor cold there that he is walking on?' I spoke to Yoshi Oida who worked for Peter Brook. 'You have been working with the same director for years, surely you get bored?' He said, 'No, because he is so curious. It is never the same.' I think that was very true of Barney, just curious about life. So that is what kept him so young as well. If you are fascinated by something, really explore it.

Lara Foot Newton.
Photograph by Ruphin Coudyzer.

Could you describe what happened to Fats Dibeco in "Starbrites"?

The process was ridiculously hindered because the actor just didn't want to work. He was old. Barney dealt with that. It was nothing to do with, 'This is going to fuck up my play', which is how most directors would behave. How I would behave. It was more like, 'Why is this man there? How do you encourage a man in this state?' That was the last time that actor was on stage, and that epitomised the process of "Starbrites". It wasn't about how to get puppets to interact with human beings. In a professional world most people would say, get rid of Fats. Casts come and go. Ultimately your cast is not your family. But this man's life... Barney said he was like an old walrus lying on a rock and just couldn't budge. In the end he did budge and he did a jolly nice performance. So that was my first experience with Barney. He just moved in with the story and whatever was obsessing him at the time: how there is not enough light in the actor's eyes, or life. How do you teach that?

On the opening night the lights failed. I was sitting next to Barney in the lighting box of the Upstairs Theatre and the lights tripped. They had all these little intricate puppets and you were only supposed to have tiny little lights on the puppets, not see the puppeteers. I tried to sort things out. Then ten minutes later the lights came on again, and the stage manager put on the house lights, so the actors were standing in the house lights. I said to him, 'What are you doing, what were you thinking?' I wanted to shoot The Market Theatre for having bad lighting. I wanted to murder that stage manager. Not Barney. Barney was like, 'I was watching what the actors were doing'. He was in love with actors! It is what he made important, made him a director, a beautiful director. To Barney the most important thing is the actor. Right, I can say it. I can learn it. I can intellectualise it. I can to a certain extent believe it, but I don't feel it like Barney felt it. As the years go by I begin to understand what he meant.

I feel like I can still talk to him. I know that perhaps he wouldn't have given me an answer, but he certainly would have tried to make me think differently. He'd say, 'Stop sort of nagging about all of this, just make scrambled eggs, get rid of all the flack and just think about where is the truth.'

But how did he make scrambled eggs?

Okay, he mixes eggs with a little bit of milk and quite a bit of herbs. If you have got garlic and salmon, then that is fantastic. Put garlic and little bits of salmon. And if you have got some red onion, eat it with the eggs afterwards.

Raw?

Yes, on the side. You heat the pan and you put the eggs in and stir constantly. Before they are ready you take them off, because you have got to respect the heat of the egg. Then by the time you serve it, it is perfect. You see. That is exactly what he told me. Don't eat the egg yet, don't lay the table. Just be there for the egg. Until I totally and utterly have that understanding of what actors are going through, I am never going to respect them, or love them, in the way that Barney did. When I understand more about myself and life, then only will I be able to embrace actors in the way that Barney did. I asked him if he ever considered marriage and he said he'd had every intention to get married and have children. I said, 'And then what happened?' He said, 'Then your Market happened.' So in a way I suppose it was his family. [Silence – Lara cries]

Clare Stopford

'Space is an adventure'

Barney became the voice in my head. It was devastating to work with Barney because he didn't know how to lie. You're sitting there, you're writing, and you just hear Barney's voice: [whispering] 'Oh, we must just look at this again.' Barney would be the angel on your shoulder – trying to make everything real and very honest. He was trying to protect against potential lies, conceits, and mere effect. One of the biggest things that Barney taught me is to do it with taste. As a director you're reflecting taste and honesty in every decision you make. Barney's taste was sort of old, leftie, hippie, scrubbed floors, white walls – that pure organic thing. You could see it in his house, and his love of organic and recycled things. He loved glamour in the shape of Marilyn Monroe and Greta Garbo, Bette Davis – real glamour, real depth and dimension. Velvet opposed to tinsel. Barney adored glamour, but it had to have a very special dimension. He hated tinsel and cheap. Ultimately, because of his own sensibility and his constant challenging, he helped me realise something of my own taste, and that is to avoid affectation – effect for effect's sake. Barney would never ever go for effect, and that is why some people would take him to task for maybe being dull, or maybe too naive. He would want to go from one pure moment to the next without any tricks connecting them. He was like this truth monitor, this lie detector in one's work. 'But why is that there? It's got nothing to do with the story, take it out.' He gave me the courage to start sticking by my own ideas and concepts. So I can't be Stoppard. Who am I? What can I be? And I think he gave anybody else who wanted to listen, the courage to access their own sensibility. Particularly black actors, and women. 'What is your story? Your story is valuable to me.'

He taught me that every single piece of matter on the stage had a life. How somebody picked up a cushion could reflect the whole world. Barney's way of telling a story was through texture. I remember him telling me he spent hours working with Megan Willson on the texture of being pregnant. About the feeling of lying in a bath, and feeling the largeness of her breasts, the new weight of her belly. How would she walk if she had to answer the door bell, having just got out? That thing of trying not to slip as you're getting to the door, because you're dripping wet.

He would spend an enormous amount of time on texture. When that worked it's what made his work extraordinary. Barney's visual pleasure was provided mainly by the use of actors in space. The suspension of a body in space, a point of light hitting the side of the face at just that and that angle, the arch of the back expressing a world of emotion, an arm lifted – flesh-tone merging into soft light. In "The Dybbuk" for example the creation of the creature was a simple joining of two bodies – a more frightening moment I've never seen on stage. He was a master of the use of space. Perhaps at times he was trapped by hasty design decisions made because of conditions at The Market. For example, he often used platforms with different levels, which in a sense limited his exploration of space. I think he wanted the limitations – in keeping with the economy of activity he was practising in every part of his life towards the end.

But as a teacher of the use of space he was unsurpassable. 'Space is an adventure.' I've absorbed this as a key of my own aesthetic. To me it was liberating. The telling of an emotional story through the arrangement of bodies, the distance between them, the planes on the stage that are endlessly there to be explored to tell the story. What attracted Barney to people had to do with some life, or light, or story, or a connection to something he could see. It was like he would want to be part of igniting it. But, so often, what happened was that people couldn't then fly. He wanted to know whether we would still be doing it if he wasn't there. We were energies, or lights he could ignite. Was there life in us that would happen whether he was there or not? That was what he really wished for.

I think people misunderstood often. They felt that he wanted the power. Because maybe of the obscurity, the puzzling way that he spoke sometimes. He seemed so inaccessible, his approval was so slow in coming. People felt often at his mercy because of that, but really what he wanted was for people to empower themselves through the contact with him. That's what he really wanted, which is why, if people initiated something anyway, whether it was politically correct or not, he would be there. He was attracted to energy that could ignite on its own. He wanted to be part of it. He would go anywhere. He would go across the townships. We used to go everywhere to see work.

It takes massive energy and courage to ferociously attend to standards in the theatre, as Barney did. He was responsible for unleashing numerous unformed energies into the world, people who carry his lessons today, who are informed by his impeccable taste and rigorous notions of a truthful moment. When I was getting divorced, two months after Neil left, it didn't faze him at all that I was like this piece of straw, this shoelace. I said, 'Barney, I can hardly stand up, my marriage has collapsed and you're asking me to direct one of the most complicated things?' He said, 'Just get a comfortable chair, and just work from another place.' And I did.

Opposite – Barney Simon and Clare Stopford, December 1987.
Photograph by Ruphin Coudyzer.

EXCLUSIVE TO THIS THEATRE
CRY FREEMANDELA
– THE MOVIE!
PIETER-DIRK UYS
CHRIS GALLOWAY
AS

Robyn Orlin

'One cannot rehash another Robert Wilson, another Barney Simon'

There was a neurosis in Barney that I really understood and loved. A lot of people were very frustrated with the way he would distract us and start talking about other things, but I loved that. I found that interesting. You'd get frustrated with him but you'd know that he was doing it for a reason, because he was trying to work through something else. Only afterwards did you realise why he was asking all those questions.

Barney used to make out like he was a nutty old man and he really was not. I mean, he was sharp. He kept on saying to me, 'Why are you so scared of breaking through? Why are you so stuck on this whole dance thing?' He respected it but I think he saw other stuff. My experience of the dance world is that there is little encouragement to form one's own thoughts. Everything is very beautiful, very physical, but actually ugly. Barney exposed me to a literary background that was not available from mentors I had in the dance world.

I believe in actually exposing everything. So I understand completely where Barney went with his work. Barney really understood the pain of why things are, that was really what I learnt most from him. Even his niggling questions. You knew that he understood something about pain and suffering and how deeply things mean to someone. We live in a society that is extreme, that is really in pain. It was during the time of apartheid, and still is. Barney really had a sense of that.

He created a South African theatre, a very important theatre. The work was idiosyncratic in a very true way. I'm only discovering now what Barney was saying to me a long time ago. It's only making sense to me now, and I am not really in theatre. I'm still somewhere bordering on the edge of art, theatre and performance. I think that it is sad that we actually do not have anyone to carry on where Barney left off. That's the real tragedy. People learnt from him and worked from him, so where's the follow through?

The Market Theatre Lab was his baby and Barney's spirit is being sustained there. But I worry about the future of the students. Survival for actors today is only in the commercial world, there's little opportunity to explore, the way we used to with Barney.

Barney had a way with actors, he knew how to push an actor and he made actors work out why they were acting. He was idiosyncratic. The same can be said of Robert Wilson, Peter Brook and Tadeusz Kantor. One cannot rehash another Robert Wilson, another Barney Simon. It's like when the Polish director Tandeusz Kantor died, his company just fell apart because he was the company.

Opposite – Robyn Orlin in "Dark Continents", August 1987.
Photograph by Ruphin Coudyzer.

Grethe Fox

'Manie would come to Barney with a story and Barney would turn the whole thing upside down'

Barney became very important to my husband Manie van Rensburg, who was a legendary filmmaker in South Africa for his time. He tried to examine the Afrikaner in a very special way in TV films like "The Fourth Reich" and "Verspeeld'enter". Politically Manie moved further and further away from his background and ended up on the left, going to Dakar to meet the ANC in 1987. That was the anguished kind of part of him. That's not, I think, the reason why he committed suicide, or why he was shredded into a million pieces.

I introduced Barney to Manie who I had worked with in "Oedipus". And like everybody, Manie needed some kind of guide or mentor. He used to bounce his scripts off Barney a lot. I remember, he would say that it was quite disconcerting when he would come to Barney with a story and Barney would turn the whole thing upside-down. Manie would get completely frustrated because he would have to go back and rethink the whole thing because Barney would always be totally revolutionary in everything he told you. A lot of people found that disturbing. But in the end it was incredibly valuable.

The version of the one script that they were very close on was the film "The Native who Caused all the Trouble" written by Danny Keogh, Vanessa Cooke and Fink Haysom. Barney was a lot of help to him on that. The idea was to film as many South African productions as possible. Sadly, the money ran out and we didn't get very far. (Though "The Native who Caused all the Trouble" at The Market was made quite successfully.) The second one they wanted to do was Mbongeni Ngema's "Sarafina!" Manie set up the whole film and was trying to get it under way, but then "Sarafina!" hit the stage overseas. It became a huge hit, and then it had to become an international film. It eventually was done by Darryl Roodt ten years later with Whoopi Goldberg. So that was a lost opportunity. When my brother came back to this country in 1994 he got involved with New Directions, and Barney was his mentor and adviser on one of his scripts. He described the same frustration with Barney. So there's always this like mixed thing: 'Oohh he's driving me crazy!' But in the end you just love him so much and how much he did for you.

What was important in those very dark days is that he was a very important political guide and mentor for people. I think his example was crucial. People were really lost. The whole theatre community was led in a certain direction which would not have been possible without him. He was definitely very powerful, not only as a theatre practitioner but also as a moral guide. His principles were very important to everybody. Barney was a person of impeccable integrity. He was a pure soul. Somebody whose whole existence was bound up with doing things for other people, helping people to get their plays on. He was always helping and guiding other people, non-stop. I mean, his whole life was devoted to that. It's this enormous legacy. People forget where this form of theatre came from, that we have. Actors get up and they research their story, and they tell their story. In a way we are almost stuck to that kind of thing. We've got to move on from there. That's the phase where we are now – trying to move out of this huge shadow of Barney Simon with his personal testimonies. Yet theatre that comes out of protest theatre and human testimony will be with us forever, because in South Africa these stories will continue to have to be told.

Opposite – Grethe Fox in "A Doll's House", April 1990.
Photograph by Ruphin Coudyzer.

Richard E. Grant

'His guru-elder-statesman-rabbinical-confessional style was very seductive'

I was a teenager in Swaziland in the early seventies when The Company brought a modern dress production of "Twelfth Night", directed by Janice Honeyman, to the Mbabane Theatre Club. I'd never seen professionals before in Swaziland, nor Shakespeare. It was so inventive, genuinely funny and sexy, that I went to all their performances. I didn't meet Barney Simon then, but I memorised every actor's name and his, for the future.

Fast forward to 1978, mid-way through UCT drama training, and I directed Berkoff's "East" for the first Grahamstown Festival. Barney saw it and made contact, softly, guru-like in his whole persona. As though he had spent his whole life in slippers at an ashram. Already bald and with a habit of telling you something phrased like a question, with a trademark codicil – 'you know?' at the end. Which had the effect of making you feel that he was forever trading in the currency of ideas and curiosity. Never satisfied with an easy answer or pat response. Always accompanied by hand gestures, as if he was subbing together ideas and possibilities before your eyes.

Stories, personal histories, acute biographies were his focus, addressing what it was like to be a South African in the here and now, rather than the rarefied land of Ayckbourn, Aeschylus and other luminaries. So the effect was as immediate and recognisable as catching an unexpected glimpse of yourself and everyone else in a shop window. Monologues and a penchant for detailing the lives of the white underclass characterised his devised plays, giving a 'voice' to people usually dismissed as ignorant and inarticulate.

His guru-elder-statesman-rabbinical-confessional style was very seductive, making you feel that your own stories were as significant as those of many more celebrated human beings. At a time when the very fact of being a white South African was riddled with guilt, he unashamedly held a mirror to everyone, examining with compassion, curiosity and humour, in lieu of harsh judgment.

At a time when I was particularly frustrated within the confines of drama school, he encouraged and advised me to pursue the dream of co-founding a theatre company beyond university. Treating me like a professional adult, rather than a student with 'ideas above your station, young man'. To be 'gifted' by his endorsement at this critical stage was of inestimable value and gave me courage to follow through. Which we did in forming the Troupe Theatre Company, with a group that included Fiona Ramsay, Lamie Shoba, Sean Taylor, Joko Scott, Ian Roberts, Fred Abrahamse, Brumilda van Rensburg and Hillary Jones. Making it clear that The Market Theatre was going to be our 'home from home'.

I only once worked with him as a director, when he did "Oedipus" at the Baxter Theatre in 1980 – an experimental effort involving wax masks of each actor's face and a hessian costumed puppet body that each actor manipulated. It did not really succeed but the restless pursuit of a new way to express an ancient story was worth the journey. Whereas most directors have a clear-cut pre-conceived idea of the end result, I felt that

Barney was forever questioning. However, simply extracting every detail of a character or actor's biography, were his greatest strengths. His days as an Ad-man in a previous incarnation made him an easy target if ever one felt manipulated by him, which sometimes happened on a particularly difficult rehearsal day. But this never lasted. He was too clever, and compassionate, to ever let anyone get away with that.

Witnessing Yvonne Bryceland performing his "Miss South Africa (6)" monologue at the People's Space Theatre was to experience theatre at its most visceral and potent. In 1981, struggling to get started as an actor in London. I performed his "Joburg, Sis!" monologues at a theatre-pub, which led directly to getting my first agent. So again I am indebted to him for getting me started as it were, although he was not physically present. His work focused attention on the power and importance of the individual, no matter how insignificant one's life seemed to be. Ironically, the last time I saw Barney, he was directing "East" in the Laager Theatre, and he asked when I was going to direct something again. His encouragement is something I have never forgotten.

Actor Richard E. Grant holds a British Academy of Film and Television Award (BAFTA) at the British Academy of Film headquarters in central London, January 28, 2002.
Photograph by Ferran Paredes / Reuters.

Wesley France

'He was always up for a jol'

When I met Barney I was the production manager of The Market Theatre and a lighting designer. In terms of the technical side of the production he was usually very vague and couldn't really visualise anything unless you physically showed it to him. I am sure he could, but that was just the way he operated. So we spent a lot of time showing him stuff, which was in itself quite exciting.

Why was that exciting?

Because one would go down a long road and explore a lot of routes. He was obviously discovering at the same time what he wanted out of a piece. I got frustrated and angry with him a couple of times, because it is frustrating, expensive and time-consuming if you are changing things. On the one side you know how he operated was beneficial for the work, but then on the other side, does the guy really know what he wants? More often than not it was a workshop process. It just becomes problematic from a logistical point of view, that's all, not frustrating because he as a person was frustrating. He was a great person.

Did you feel like you were a friend of his?

Ja, ja, you could drop off at his house any time, day or night, and have a discussion about anything. Travelling around with him on tour was quite fun.

Why?

Because he was very forgetful. He liked to travel with a lot of books, so his baggage was very heavy. Once in America he decided to buy a set of wheels. I was behind Barney as we went up the escalator. In the distance looking up there was just blue sky and a few fleecy white clouds, and the silhouette of Barney going up in front of me with his bags on his wheels. And the thing got caught, or broke, and all his bags just came tumbling down. Oh God, stuff like that could only happen to him. But it was fun though. He was always up for a jol, that was good about Barney, he liked partying. I think it is a great loss to the theatre. Not many directors that I work with today have the same capability of working. The one thing that I will always remember about Barney is, it doesn't matter where you are in the production, all you have to do is just keep on fixing what is wrong. And that applied right up until the very last performance. The times that I remember were good.

What do you think Barney left you with?

For me, a big hole.

Peter Piccolo

'Art should imitate life, rather than a smooth formula'

Theatre demands from its workers a mental focus, a technical awareness, the ability to stretch one's imagination and a willingness to share. Even an uninspiring play, put together by an inspired director, can be a lot of fun and a challenge. Those of us who worked with Barney enjoyed the dual blessing of his very carefully selected material and his radiant insight into human nature.

Barney was never impressed by elaborate caricature, but demanded that we dig deep and reveal rather than imitate. Somehow he taught us that pretense and truthfulness are not mutually exclusive. How often we watched him coaxing the umpteenth articulation of a single word from a perplexed actor, watching for honesty, not mere effectiveness. There was no clear distinction between real life and the stage, and Barney's alchemy certainly made me re-examine and refine my everyday performance.

On more than one occasion he corrected my swing, drawing my attention to something phoney in my arsenal of cool. It was not a judgmental thing, but simply a perceptive director troubled by a performance that was not honest. After a brief sulk I conceded the point and we had a good laugh about it. That soft safe-like laugh of his came from a deep place.

Those were the days of mayhem and The Market was a calm but exciting haven. We enjoyed a strong sense of belonging, inspired by Mannie's vision and Barney's meticulous translation of that vision into creative, flawless and demanding theatre. Barney's reputation was built not only on his long relationship with our very best writers and actors, nor his collaboration at Dorkay House, but also on his limitless ability to give, to inspire and to guide.

During the unusually long run of "Cincinatti", complacency and a sense of false security were setting in. Barney suggested that we re-establish contact with the play as originally conceived. We had slid away from the delicate centre, but he reminded us that art should imitate life, rather than a smooth formula.

In my relatively short career in theatre I worked with some exceptional people. My life was enriched by them. Barney stands out as a friend, a teacher and a visionary whose influence remains with me in the world I now inhabit, far from the stage.

Michele Maxwell

'I have a vague recollection of chicken blood being present. Did we drink it?'

My memories of Barney begin in 1975, when I came up to Jo'burg from Cape Town. He was living in Loch Avenue then, and I stayed in his cottage for a few months. He sort of took me under his wing. He was very kind and encouraging to me, when there was always so much going on around him. An endless stream of actors, artists, musicians – rehearsing on the front porch, in the kitchen. Mannie had left PACT and they'd formed The Company on a wing and a prayer and faith and hope.

And faith in what?

That money would come, that they'd find a 'home' for The Company. And faith in the quality of the work. That was the thing. Going for the internal, rather than just the external. The internal – that's, I think, what made everyone want to work with him. The possibility of 'magic', and finding the truth, and simplicity – which of course we all knew we had somewhere, but Barney would bring it out.

You were in "The Crucible" at the Alexander Theatre. What springs to mind?

Barney's casting of Annelisa Weiland as Abigail. He wanted the image of an innocent, vulnerable little girl to bring the powerful, big John Proctor (Marius Weyers) to his knees. And me playing Tituba (I think I was the last 'whitey' to 'black up'), standing in the wings looking at the stage hands, and feeling very embarrassed.

I also remember one of Barney's improvs for Tituba and the girls. All of us going to some woody area (can't think where that could have been!) and dancing around in various stages of 'being under a spell'. I have a vague recollection of chicken blood being present. (Did we drink it?)

Barney's improvs in "Marat/Sade" – drooling around for hours on end. Bess Finney communicating with an animal skull, and Barney being so proud that he'd lured Eddie Calvert into playing an inmate. Music and Barney – big thing. He'd encourage me to sing beautiful, simple jazz songs. Each word, word for word, he'd sing quietly. Beautifully. He loved melodies. He loved a good melody and he loved good food!

Late one night he came around to my flat to talk about the music for "Hedda Gabler". He sat in my rocking chair, went into a semi-meditation, and said, 'I want it to be music, but not to sound like music. Do you know what I mean?' '... Er... ja?...' (I lit candles and incense.) 'Play the top end of the piano and think very delicately about the fragility of Hedda. Let it come from your soul.' Right there, one time, I composed the theme music. It was beautiful working with Barney like that, and a few days later, with him sitting in The Market Theatre auditorium, beaming up at me on stage, we recorded it.

Barney taught me how to work slowly on a text. How to rid the mind of preconceived patterns. To speak each word carefully, with equal value and space, allowing, not forcing, a truth to emerge.

Opposite – Michele Maxwell at home in Yeoville, July 1980.
Photograph by Ruphin Coudyzer.

Jana Cilliers

'Before you're a pope, you're a human being...'

In "Marat/Sade" I immediately knew he wasn't somebody for the external. Jacqui Singer and I, I suppose, moved well. He said, 'Well I'm not interested in how well you move. You must show me who you are.' That's Barney! And some time later our paths crossed again. I was a young mother. My children were two and four years old. I loved being a mother. But then there comes a time when you want to sort of rip your child from your bosom, buy a packet of cigarettes, kind of abandon yourself to the creativity of the arts again.

I remember going into the office at The Market Theatre. He was sitting there very relaxed. There was this wonderful ambience that he created. He was eating a roti. And to this day my love of rotis has not gone away because he was enjoying it so much. As far as I can recall, Aletta Bezuidenhout was with me. These two women waltzed into his space. I was quite desperate. I started speaking, saying to him, 'Should I go about getting a job, being creative?' And he chewed at his roti and looked at me and said, 'But Jana, don't you have children?' I said, 'Yes, and now I want to move on.' But he said, 'You've borne two children.' And he proceeded to lecture me very subtly, saying, 'You are in a very, very creative space now. Please recognise that. Please enjoy that and please keep at it. Don't allow the confusion to come in that you are not being creative and therefore you need to go and rush off and do theatre.' That day he put theatre in perspective for me. I've never ever forgotten that. And he was right. I am in a way an extremely fulfilled human being and not a frustrated actress in these difficult times.

While doing "The American Popess" I said to Barney that I found it very difficult to play something which is so foreign to me. But he had that wonderful way of bringing you back to basics, to the origin, to where the birth of all happens. Which is the fact that you're a human being. 'Before you're a pope, you're a human being, Jana'. I remember very well, that sense of using the ordinary platform in order to kick-start a process that feels way beyond you. I was well into the run and thinking I'm doing a great job. When Barney came to see me, he sat in the lighting box. He came to me afterwards and said, 'I didn't see the human being, Jana. And I'm not interested in following the pope's story.' He had this wonderful way of dealing with the truth and being hard with it.

Opposite – Jana Cilliers in "The American Popess", May 1985.
Photograph by Ruphin Coudyzer.

Bruce Koch

'Director, lighting designer, stage manager, writer...'

(Interviewed by Vanessa Cooke)

When I joined The Market Theatre in 1980, I didn't know Barney's work. I knew Athol. That's why I went to The Market. Barney made me look at a photo and asked me what I thought of it. It was just a woman in a hut with a baby.

What was coming your way?

I just laughed at it. That was the first time I met him. I didn't know who this guy, Barney, was. I only clocked later that he was sort of behind the whole Market.

What was the first show you worked with him on?

Well, I was assistant stage manager on "Cold Stone Jug".

Do you remember anything about it?

Yes, he told me I must be more authoritative with the actors because they were very intimidating. I was very green.

Do you remember how he gave notes?

His notes were a very unusual angle. They weren't what you would call the theatre note. They were very penetrating, and probably sometimes could clear up a lot of mess and leave the actor very focused into the function of the character, and themselves, at the same time. He always was encouraging, and I do not think I totally understood. I don't think I realised how much Barney was opening me up. Yeah, it's true. Barney had a way inside if you allowed him. He confused you so that you would have to re-think. Which is a good thing. Then out of that confusion you could come to another plateau of understanding... Not only with performers – technicians, production managers – everything. I think if you allowed him in then he did a lot of work, like real dentists [laughs]. I was actually extremely quiet when I started at The Market Theatre. Confidence-wise, with Barney I was not only comfortable but I could feel like I was letting my parents go, in a way, moving onto something bigger, and vast.

There is a dilemma in the theatre. A lot of actors don't think that stage managers should give them notes. There is a tradition in other theatres where the technicians are kept very separate from the performers. I remember that Barney encouraged you to give notes, which got you into trouble with some actors. How did he give you that confidence?

By asking me what I thought at very, very strange times. He started giving me a voice and then letting me explore my own voice. And then, as the plateau of trust went on I was allowed to give the cast notes. I learnt good notes and bad notes, what notes are and what they can do, and perhaps how to give them. That is actually the best part about it, because that is the structure of growth. I have worked with a lot of technicians who do not feel they have a right, and even don't want, to have an artistic input. So they do not grow or develop although they are good at what they do. When he was getting Fats into his character, I think he took him back into an area of his childhood, an area of recognition, into that kind of focus again, so that Fats would feel safe. It was done with such care. Generally his notes were... I suppose some performers would say they were cruel, but they weren't actually cruel because there was a humility about them.

Barney had always been caring and friendly with his technicians. He always had a sort of off-stage relationship with them. Even sceptical technicians came up with a broader outlook. Barney said to me once, 'You can give an actor three things.' But I was such a prat. I didn't ask him what they are. I do remember him saying the show is like a train, one carriage pulls the other, pulls the other, pulls the other, until the whole train is in motion. He had an interview on the TV and they asked him what life was like living in South Africa, and he said that if he wanted to have a little piece of chocolate cake, he would have to live the life of a cockroach and only come out when the lights were off.

When Barney died we were touring overseas, we got to Lisbon. Moira Forgas came to see the show. She just desperately needed to talk to someone about Barney. So I went to her for breakfast the next morning. She had all these pictures, and she had a cry, and she told me Barney and she were still trying to get their film together. When they were in Lisbon the whole city was burning. Barney would not let her go out and watch her city burn because she must stay home and write [laughs].

I was thinking of Barney giving director's notes when he was artistic director of The Market. He was brilliant. He came and he watched the shows. I remember he gave Clare Stopford notes in "The Last Trek". She herself, and not the cast. He always made a point of that. He got up and clambered all over the stage, showing her the various different ways she could inhabit the stage. And I heard her years later giving the same notes to another director. It is like passing the flame along.

Michael Maxwell

'On their toes'

You had to jump in at the deep end when you worked with Barney because little was known, nothing was certain. All that was known was that Barney had a new story to tell and his production team had to be on their toes and ready to move into action. Not a lot of pre-production possible here! Barney was on a quest for truth and searching for truth demands the kind of exploration that doesn't always obey the dictates of time. The fact that his products, whether "Woza", "Cincinatti" or "The Suit", were works of such delicacy and richness seems astonishing, given that he created whole new works in four weeks.

Janet Suzman

'A sort of gnome-like charm would persuade you to attempt all manner of things, both poetical and plain'

I think it's true to say that my dealings with Barney were more as a friend than an actor/director. Although I had the pleasure of being guided by him on two occasions. The first was a poetry and prose anthology programme that I toured with in South Africa, and which Barney got his teeth into to help make it better. It was under the auspices of the late Ian Bernhardt.

I have a clear picture of Barney giving me a note about the speech of Cleopatra's we were working on. Eyes twinkling above the beard, a smile urging me to capture the image he was trying to convey with his hands – stretched out to describe the line of an endless far horizon shimmering between sand and sky. He wanted me to reach for a sense of eternal space, a distancing from the mundane. He wanted me to reach for a sense of infinity, I suppose. A tall order, but I tried. One would try anything for Barney. A sort of gnome-like charm would persuade you to attempt all manner of things, both poetical and plain, which I think sums up his ethos best. He was always searching for poetry in so-called 'mundanity', which of course is what all the best artists want, I believe. Athol was the best at writing that seeming antithesis. And Barney was best at trying to interpret it actively. He had a good understanding of what an actor might be capable of, and worked within those perceived limits.

He once sent me out on an exercise in Johannesburg Station – this was just before I was about to return to London to play Hester in Athol Fugard's "Hello and Goodbye". So this was about 1973. He made me dress up as a hooker and see if I could pick anyone up. I won't go into what sort of time I had on that rather unsavoury concourse, but I remember Barney's delight at dropping me off there at 5pm, and his wicked grin when he came back for me at midnight. The debriefing session was unnecessary. He saw that I had learnt what I needed to learn, limited though it was, I must hasten to say.

Another time he took me to a play by Credo Mutwa in Alex. He had an avid fascination with African legends and stories, matching the allegorical wisdom of his own ancient people, perhaps. His delight in the acting process stemmed mainly from his delight in body-language, especially the particular genius of black actors whose way of interpreting character is so much more instinctively physically freer than the often more diffident white actor. I sensed, though, that he harboured a certain distrust of high language and consequently he found my classical background intermittently fascinating. We would have long talks about imagery in blank verse and the like. I was weaned into acting with the Royal Shakespeare Company's work in the '60s.

Barney was, at the bottom, very Jewish and had an endless fund of family stories and old wives' tales. Talmudic stories with a sting in the tail. A kind of sadness, an amused grief at the comedy of the human condition, was very much a part of Barney's make-up. The stories always made him chuckle and they always had some bearing on the point he was trying to make. He always used to watch old films – he had an amazing collection of videos at home – Charlie Chaplin, Buster Keaton, the Marx brothers, et al. He found them inspirational and one could often see that as source material in his directing. He was never quite satisfied with what he came up with and was famous for giving notes well after the first night. Funny stories abound of Barney hiding behind props and furniture on the stage and giving notes in performance, which may or may not be apocryphal, but is charming.

Busi Zokufa

'A director, mentor, father and friend...'

I was married to Stompie Mavi who was already working on my nerves at the time. Our marriage was destroyed by professional jealousy. I told Barney everything, for he was also a great listener and adviser. I told him how frustrated I was and that I was planning to leave my husband. Then I came home from rehearsals of "Starbrites" and found him gone with all his belongings. This shattered me. I went to work the following day and during that rehearsal I just broke into tears. Barney took me aside and asked me what was wrong. I related the story to him and he said, 'But, isn't this what you've wanted all the time?'

I wiped my face immediately and looked him straight in the eye and said, 'Yes, you're right.' And he said, 'Then, let's go on with this scene.' We continued working like nothing had happened. From that day I never cried again for my husband.

I was doing a showcase at the Lab when Barney noticed me. I had no lines in this play. I just had to move around on a beach dressed in a swimsuit with a towel around my waist. He had also seen me in a play I did earlier on called "So Where To?" Barney said he liked me and that I was daring... that I am the kind of actress he'd like to work with. So he told Handspring about me and when they teamed up to do "Starbrites" in 1990 I got the singing part, and I gained a director, mentor, father and friend in him.

Motshabi Tyelele

'Same language'

Knowledge is not what you learn from books. Barney had a way with people, respect for people, and for me. Irrespective of whether I spoke English, you know, we spoke the same language.

When some director talks to somebody you can tell that he thinks he is now talking to a black person, or a dumb person... I was very comfortable in Barney's company. He would respect the background that I came from. Barney knew a number of things about me. He knew that my father had died. He knew little things that not many directors want to know. They don't care a shit about where you come from, who you are. I will give you an example. I worked on a production one year. I refused to perform on June 16th. I saw the schedule a month before the show and I said, 'By the way, on the 16th I shall not be performing.' The director said, 'Okay, listen, you can come and sleep at my house.' I said: 'Why didn't you offer that before, because people have been killing each other every day in Soweto and I have been having to drive back every night. Did anybody care to ask me the following morning how did you get home? Are you okay? Or just to care to phone after an hour to check if I got home safely? No! But now, because of your bloody production, suddenly you can offer me your bed on the 16th. Now what happens on the 17th?' Then they shut up.

Those are the kind of things that Barney would have known, and actually even beforehand said, 'Do you think it is safe to go home? Do you think we should arrange something?' That's the type of man he was.

Sheila Fugard

'He came every night to hold our hands and keep the faith'

Barney first came into our lives after we had staged "Nongogo" at the Darragh Hall. The meeting took place backstage. He responded so warmly to the play which had received terrible notices – the theme of homosexuality on the mines was a little heavy for the Jo'burg of those days. We had a regrettable gala first night when I peeped through a hole in the curtains and saw Harry Oppenheimer yawning at the action on stage. Our audience average was about twenty a night. Barney's support was magnificent. He came every night to hold our hands and keep the faith.

He was then a man with one foot in the business world and the other one in theatre. Our friendship was immediate. One funny little coincidence in the friendship was that both Barney and Athol applied for the same job as copy writer with a Johannesburg advertising agent. Barney got the job and Athol, to his great relief, did not. Barney earned good money and never hesitated to share his good fortune with us. A few years later Athol and Barney were a wonderful team in The Rehearsal Room at Dorkay House where they tried out their new work. Barney's "Anna" and Athol's "Blood Knot".

Typical of Barney's generosity was the occasion when our baby daughter grabbed an electrical live wire on a heater and needed serious plastic surgery to her hand. Without a moment's hesitation Barney helped us with the hospital bills. Our lives changed when Athol, Lisa and I bought a little seaside shack and settled in Port Elizabeth. Athol had become absorbed in his own writing and replaced his practical involvement in The Rehearsal Room with his Serpent Players in Port Elizabeth. "Siswe Banzi" and "The Island" came out of that situation.

Athol's and Barney's separate successes eventually revealed a competitive element in the relationship. Each of them felt let down by the other. Reasons advanced by both were niggling, petty and without justification. But the respect that they had for each other, and the work done, was never compromised, or diminished. I believe they had a great love for each other.

Kate Edwards

'Text is the great God'

My strongest image of him as a director is somebody with infinite time and who was performer-centred rather than text-centred. Now in London most directors are completely concerned with text, or pretend that they are. And text is the great God. We are here to serve the text. Barney just absolutely wasn't that at all.

I'll give you an example. The play that I worked with him on was "Flight" by David Lan. The published play I read was not the play we performed. Barney had made a number of alterations. And they were all made in order to help the performer.

Gina Benjamin

'Makes you weep'

I remember Barney giving us notes on a Pieter Toerien production, privately. He just said, 'But isn't the sand hot?' That was my note and I knew exactly what he meant. The whole play happened on the beach and I came in holding my sandals, and he was dead right. It was not real for that moment, but it was not just that, it was about the character. She was a straight woman in a gay community, just had a broken up marriage and falls in love with a woman. It defined for me exactly what to do. It is the kind of thing that makes you weep. I felt so ashamed that I hadn't worked that out myself.

Megan Kruskal

'Discovery'

When Barney died I was living in New York and a couple of months pregnant with my son Benjamin Simon. Dealing with my grief in New York was very isolating and difficult. However, in the first few years of my children's life, as they experienced things for the first time, I couldn't stop thinking of Barney and how he would try to get us to experience things as actors, the discovery of the tongue, the toes, language, the commitment and focus at each step, a child learning to walk, a rehearsal process. Never has a person affected me so deeply as a friend and an actor. Life is not the same without Barney and I try to incorporate his words, 'Keep doing the work as honestly as you can.'

Christo Leach

'He once said that he was in the nutrition business. He gave me enough nourishment for a lifetime'

The first time I met Barney was around 1984. I wrote "Die Spinner", which was a short story based on what was told to me by a friend of mine, Jan du Toit. He was a parabat soldier who had jumped about thirteen times over Angola. I just wrote down these stories and they became a one-man play with Gys de Villiers.

I'd been to The Market Theatre once before to see a production which Barney directed. It was Athol Fugard's "Statements After an Arrest Under the Immorality Act", with Wilma Stockenström and Vivien Solomons, who died shortly afterwards. I came from a very traditional Afrikaner Christian Nationalist family, and it was basically my first contact with that kind of work. I was still at school.

Wilma Stockenström was a brilliant Afrikaans poet who had won all the major prizes for poetry, and I never knew she acted. It was astounding to see her work. I didn't even know who Barney Simon was. But I saw this production and obviously it showed black and white relationships. What they did blew my mind. Up to then I never really had to think about black and white. I was in a very white environment and a very white school. The production was quite astounding.

Why was it astounding?

The intensity of it. The emotions. The absolute reality. I didn't imagine relationships like that happened. The way he did the police arriving, the arrests, the pain that was shown, the injustice. I'd never had to think about something like that before in my life.

"Die Spinner" was the first time Barney started interfering in my vision. Everybody else was raving about it. Barney was the only one who came and said something like, 'No, I don't like this, I don't like that. That was interesting to me.' "Die Spinner" was about the army. It was about being an Afrikaner. It was about being victimised. It was about telling the other side of the story. I had begun to understand the divisions. It was the first piece of work that dealt with the Border War from the Afrikaner side. After Border Literature. "Die Spinner" opened the way for debate, which I was happy about. Barney asked me to bring Jan, the guy who told me the story, to meet him. We were very young and hip and doing drugs, and running all over town. We went. Barney asked me to come and stay at his house while he was in America working. Jannie started hanging out there. When Barney came back he started interviewing Jannie, asking him to retell stories that he had told me. Jannie was a master storyteller. He could just sit nights through and tell these beautiful stories. At the time they were doing "Black Dog", so Barney used Jan's stories to help redirect Neil McCarthy's character.

He started taking me to rehearsals for the previews of "Black Dog" in the Upstairs Theatre. He'd take me to the lighting box with him. He'd be questioning me extensively about what I, as an Afrikaner boy out of the laager, was feeling about what was going on in the country. What did the future hold? How did I see everything. I remember the first preview he took me to. We were sitting upstairs in the lighting box. About half an hour into the play I had an extremely emotional reaction – completely hysterical because I saw the country I lived in for the first time in my life, through that production on stage. Marie Human's story about her ouma and growing up on the farm was basically my story. John Ledwaba – I'd never seen the comrades. I have never had contact with that part of life. Kurt Egelhof, Neil McCarthy. It was a vision of the country I was living in. I never knew I lived in this country. I was absolutely devastated. I could not stop crying. I just stayed in the lighting box. I was still there about half an hour after the play because I just couldn't digest this vision.

My entire life changed that night. After that I started a company with John Ledwaba called Mamu Players. That was the night I saw John Ledwaba, and I believe that performance was probably the best performance I have seen by a male actor in this country. John played his own story. Neil's story was not his own, it was Jannie's. Marie's story was close, it was her biography. John's was his. I could sense that from his performance. I think that night I understood what Barney's about, what his gift was. He had been telling me all the time that you should only deal with what you know.

Barney was angry with the Jewish community at the time – because of this country and the role that a lot of Jewish people played. He had friends like Joe Slovo and people like that. Once Barney took me into his study outside his house at 130 Muller Street; he lifted up the carpet in the middle of the floor and opened up a trapdoor showing me a bed, water, food and a torch – a place to hide a comrade on the run.

I had some Afrikaner uncles and aunts I could look up to, people like Breyten Breytenbach, but very few. During all this time Barney used to speak about his relationship with Ruth First and Joe Slovo. He'd come back from a visit to them in Mozambique and tell me stories. He said he slept in Joe's bedroom, and he woke up in the night and the cupboard door was open. There was an AK47 lying there and he just realised what danger Joe was living under. And fear. He'd go for the weekend to Mozambique and he'd come back and say things like, 'Joe Slovo said, the Afrikaner regime is like an over-cooked chicken.' I remember those words. 'It's ready to fall off the bones.' It was political education. I saw my country for the first time through "Black Dog". I saw a horrible place. And I saw all this pain. I saw all these atrocities. I saw that my whole history had become a lie. I always thought there were certain things that the Afrikaner taught which held water. Barney always spoke about the onion with layers being stripped away. Being with him year after year, the time we spent, it was like seeing more and more than just little bits of information: Joe Slovo was a monster... a communist KGB demon who wanted to kill us all. Then here is Barney, friendly with Joe. Joe became a person. I hear about Ruth. Ruth First becomes a person. In '86 with "The Dybbuk" I was beginning to understand Barney's journey. What I learnt about that amazing process was that Barney was searching for connections. Searching for some kind of reality to go back to. Some kind of clarity about the religion he was born into. The life he was born into. So it was very beautiful for me to watch. The Songs of Solomon, all the great Jewish writings. And watching him work with Dawid Minnaar and Megan Kruskal was extraordinary – how he created "The Dybbuk" with them. There were one or two other rehearsals when he didn't want to allow me to be with them on it. He took them alone and he worked. I saw enough, before and after, and understood how he created the union, making them work with breath. He once said that he was in the nutrition business. He gave me enough nourishment for a lifetime.

Chapter 14. Legacy

Barney Simon left us a legacy. Whether in his approach to health-care education or to any creative endeavour, Barney's lessons remain significant. His work in the field with nurses related completely to his work in the theatre.

Another project that Barney initiated was The Market Theatre Laboratory. A speech Mark Fleishman gave for the 10th birthday of The Market Laboratory outlines what the Lab is about. Finally, Ariel Dorfman pays tribute to his friend Barney Simon.

Opposite – Barney Simon.
Photograph courtesy of NELM.

Mark Fleishman

'Deeply passionate workings and re-workings of ideas and the thoughts behind them'

It was in the middle of 1989 that Barney first began to appear in the kitchen of my home in Yeoville with a plan he had been developing with John Kani for a space at The Market where time would be allowed for the development of new theatrical ideas, including ideas emerging from the surrounding communities.

Funds had been raised from the Rockefeller Foundation and he wanted me to be the first administrator of the Laboratory as he called it. Those of you who knew Barney would understand that these were not simple brief discussions but deeply passionate workings and re-workings of ideas and the thoughts behind them, which continued late into the night. Barney didn't want me just to say 'yes' or 'no' to his offer – he wanted to be 100% convinced that I understood implicitly what the philosophy was behind the venture, and by the time the year had come to an end we had developed the following plan.

That the Lab would:

- provide space for the development of new work through project residencies during which a small group of people would be given support to work on a daily basis on a new idea in workshop, and through play readings of new plays by aspirant writers;
- assist and support theatre work already happening in the communities around The Market when support had been requested by the community through fieldwork;
- provide ongoing training for professional actors on a daily basis.

There was no space in The Market precinct for the Lab in those early days so new premises needed to be found. It was early in 1990 that we first ventured under the bridge in Pim Street to look at what was to become the first home of The Market Laboratory, a large warehouse attached to a Chinese food supplies wholesaler. It had been used as a storeroom but was now not needed by our landlord, an elderly Chinese gentleman who remained constantly bewildered by our activities and who, if my memory serves me correctly, never came in person to see what was happening next door. Instead he sent his son in a large black Mercedes Benz with tinted windows every time he needed to make a complaint.

The space was very dirty. The toilets were not working. And the floor was concrete and covered in a thick layer of dust which seeped in under the heavy metal roller door. Undeterred we set to work and with the help of Lucas, Oupa and Matthew, an office was built in one corner, the toilets were returned to working order, the space was cleaned (up to a point, we never did quite manage to defeat the creeping dust coming in under the door) and a new floor covering was laid. We scavenged some old furniture from The Market and brought in my old computer from home and installed it in the office.

We set up an advisory board including Barney, John, Vanessa and Gcina Mhlope and a fieldwork committee co-ordinated by James Mthoba which included Tale Motsepe, Mickey Dube, Gladwin Marumo, Dan Robbertse, Doreen Mazibuko, Arthur Molepo, Robert Colman and Irene Stephanou amongst others. And then we opened our doors for business. I think the first person who entered our new space was Master trying to sell us one of his endless supply of Pirates or Chiefs team posters and he became a permanent fixture at the Lab during that first year. I understand from Vanessa that he has never really left. We organised a press conference in our new space to launch the Lab, to which only one journalist, Adrienne Sichel, turned up and we were thoroughly depressed. But we needn't have worried. From the moment we opened the Lab we were swamped with requests for help and our field workers could hardly keep up with the demand. Our Sunday afternoon showcases were held regularly, showcasing a huge range of new work, and drew good houses and lively discussion. Our classes for professional actors were full for the first week, half full in the second week and tailed off almost to nothing in the third week. However, by this time a strong group of youths from the townships, particularly from the Vaal Triangle townships where violence was intense at the time, came to the Lab searching for drama activities to occupy their time. The classes shifted their emphasis from ongoing training for professionals to introductory sessions for beginners, and the full-time laboratory training programme, which has grown so much and has become so successful over the past ten years, was born.

There were many highlights of that first year. The creation of "Starbrites" by Barney and the Handspring Puppet Company, play readings of new plays by Nhlanhla Sicelo and Barry Berk, our first Shakespeare project designed to be taken into township schools. But the Lab was also a meeting place for people and a lot of other things happened there which didn't fit the immediate terms of reference. I recall vividly all of us standing around the radio listening incredulously to FW in his speech at the opening of parliament that year when he unbanned the ANC, PAC and SACP and committed himself to negotiations and the releasing of Nelson Mandela. And the state of hushed uncertainty that filled the space for a long while after the end of the speech. It was in the Lab that many of the first meetings of the interim executive committee of the new union PAWE were held, and for a while the office of the Lab doubled as the PAWE office.

From there we went into battle against Louis Bezuidenhout and the management of PACT on more than one occasion. And then I remember being visited by the critic of the Guardian newspaper in London, Michael Billington, and taking him into Soweto on an extremely cold and wet evening when I was working with Jackie Semela and the Soweto Dance Theatre on their play "Children of the Ghetto". By the time we were halfway through Fordsburg the rain was lashing against the windscreen and the wipers on my Citi Golf were fighting a losing battle. I happened to glance down to my left and noticed that the floor in front of the passenger seat was about one foot under water which was seeping in through the air vents, and Mr Billington, not wanting to impose, was chatting away cheerily in an attempt to pretend that his shoes, socks and the lower reaches of his trousers were not soaked. We pulled into a garage just long

enough to bale out the water and for Mr Billington to squeeze out the moisture from his socks and then we were off again. Later, he was to write in a book published by the Guardian entitled "An Altered State" about what he had witnessed at the Lab and on that fieldwork trip, and he ended with the following words: 'On a wet, gloomy night in Soweto, I felt that rarest of all sensations in South Africa, a sudden charge of optimism.'

Since those first days the Lab has moved twice and is now housed in swish new premises right here in the precinct. The optimism Michael Billington felt ten years ago has been proved right. Not only have we moved forward unbelievably as a country from those uncertain and difficult days but the Lab has grown and prospered and now rightly occupies a very central and hugely important place at the heart of The Market and the theatre industry in South Africa as a whole. But, to borrow a metaphor, the road ahead is still long and the work the Lab was founded to do remains as important now as it did when Barney first dreamt it up. Long may The Market Lab continue to prosper...

Interval at The Market Theatre Lab Foyer, 1985.
Photograph by Rodney Barnett / South Photos.

Ariel Dorfman

'He always made everyone he met feel himself, herself, to be the dignified centre of the universe'

I first met Barney in early July of 1991 in London. He was in town with a production from The Market Theatre, as part of the same LIFT programme which had selected "Death and the Maiden" for its world premiere at the Royal Upstairs, so I felt that, even though he would probably have not the slightest idea of who I was, I had a good chance that this legendary director from South Africa might spare a few minutes to meet me.

It turned out, of course, surprisingly easy to reach him, and he immediately proposed dinner at small Indian restaurant. The dinner lasted for hours and then our conversation continued endlessly in assorted pubs and then along the stumbling darkened streets of London, almost till dawn – because, of course, that first night we had to make up for the obvious mistake or sad joke of destiny that had foolishly kept us apart for the first half century of our lives.

I was to discover later that Barney had a similar communion with many others – but the discovery only came later because he made me feel that I was special, that this immediate deep understanding between us was due to something in me and not to his marvellous rambling camaraderie. He always made everyone he met feel himself, herself, to be the dignified centre of the universe. Though I have to admit that besides our interest in so many shared topics, what glued us together was also the twisted proximity of Chile and South Africa, one more case, as with Nadine Gordimer, as with André Brink, as with Achmat Dangor and Wally Serote, as with Sue and Allister Sparks (and I could go on and on), where the parallel courses of our unfortunate lands and the connected dilemmas of the transition we were facing, helped to create a common ground of experience and hopes and pain and quests which made it all the easier for perfect strangers from our two sad countries to feel as if they were twins separated at birth.

Even so, Barney was... well, unique. There was – what can I call it? – a well of wisdom that came flowing out of him, but obliquely, almost mystically, and yet so down to earth, so concrete, so ultimately pragmatic and funny. We said good-bye swearing eternal friendship, but Barney saw eternity between friends as projects, things you did together, minute by minute, and two days later he called me up. 'That play of yours,' he said. 'I saw it. It's about South Africa. It's what we need in Jo'burg. If you'd let me, I'd like to do it at The Market. If you don't mind.'

If I didn't mind. As if he were somebody unknown, as if The Market Theatre in Johannesburg were not one of the greatest stages in World Theatre. He recognised my play. Before any reviews, before it was bound for the Oliviers and Broadway, before it was destined to be directed by Roman Polanski. And as he spoke to me about what he discerned in "Death and the Maiden", I realised that he did not only consider its immediate political repercussions, but was interested in its perversity, its exploration of how men and women love and betray one another, its search for the uncertain longitude of memory. He was, as a human being and a future director, opening the play up to me, adding to it, making it his and therefore more mine.

It was to be like this between us always. We met three or four more times in different places around the world, getting close on each occasion. But more crucially, I began to call him in South Africa every week or so, just to talk, just to consult him, as if he were an elder brother who could guide me in the labyrinth of traps and temptations that surrounded my sudden success. And also, of course, to discuss the staging of the play and the newest work I was writing, "Reader", which he also agreed to direct at The Market (a project that was never to be).

I remember particularly his plans for the set design of "Death and the Maiden", how he turned the lack of resources of his theatre ('a mirror is really too expensive, you know, Ariel') into a positive development. ('I've put the stage in the middle of the theatre and curtains will be billowing in the wind, half hiding the actors from view, just like they're hiding from each other, until at the end the curtains will be drawn and half the audience will see the other half. I want to put the National Party on one side and the ANC on the other one, just have them staring at each other across the stage as if they were seeing themselves in a distorted mirror.') I remember the day he called and told me that they had been forced to suspend the performance one evening because the black actor who played Gerardo had been jailed the previous day and Barney had tried, without success, to get him out of prison in time.

And Barney became, of course, a friend of the family. He told my wife, Angelica, with whom he instantly communed as soon as they met, what she should do with a project she had doubts about. He spoke to my sons as if they were his own children. He took my friends under his wings. And always, whenever we gathered and whenever we talked, the same melody and the same song. 'When are you coming to visit me? This house is much too big for me. I have to fill it up with you and yours.' Including the last time we were together in Holland, where the Ro Theatre had organised a homage to my work and asked me to name the one person I wanted to attend and I had asked them to fly Barney in from South Africa. How was I to know (or did I know, did I suspect?) that those four, five days were to be our last together, and that's why we spent all the time we could find talking, planning, drinking, eating, celebrating.

The news of his death came to us when "Reader" was about to open at the Traverse for the Edinburgh Festival – in the middle of the summer. His death came to us precisely a few days before I was going to call him from Scotland to tell him that the play was ready for him, that he should come and get it, or maybe the time had come for me to take it to him there.

Why in the hell didn't you wait for us to come to South Africa, Barney?

But let me tell you something, hermano mio. I finally made it to your land, the land you loved and demanded so much of. And though you weren't there with your smile and waving wand of your hands and that slow enigmatic ripple of words that wove together strands from here and there to form a real tapestry of meaning, even if you were not there to take me around and hug me and sit down for hours to explore God and justice and ambivalence and madness, well, you were everywhere, Barney. Everybody I met remembered you, had another wild and outrageous and warm anecdote (many of them must be in this book). It was as if some deity had scattered your ashes over the land and covered every tongue and every eye and you had been breathed in and out of so many lungs, and I didn't mind, all of a sudden, that you hadn't waited for the visit we had so minutely charted so many times, I didn't reproach myself for not having taken the plane while you were still alive. Because now I could mourn you among your people, the ones who missed you even more.

One more thing I need to tell you, I still can't believe you're not around. Even now, when I've got a problem or an idea or a project, I find my hand reaching for the phone, and then I realise that you won't answer, there, on the other side of the line. I realise that I'm going to have to figure this one out by myself.

I'm going to have to figure your absence out by myself.

The Foyer of The Market Theatre.
Photograph courtesy of The Market Theatre.

Epilogue

by Hilary Hamburger

Barney and I didn't work together, but we talked enough about his work during a friendship that spanned the whole of our adult lives, only to be cut short by his sudden disappearance.

His death was a big shock to everyone. There were so many obituaries and interviews with well-known and articulate people who spoke eloquently about the importance and significance of his work. Some people said negative things about him, but I dismissed those on his behalf because I knew, and he would have known, that they didn't understand. I did understand, so I felt that my irritations and impatience with him at times were permissible.

I was astonished though at how many people loved and valued him, and I found myself mumbling to him under my breath, 'I didn't know you were so famous,' and he answering me with a shake of his finger and a nod of his head: 'Vell now you know.' (I couldn't do his Yiddish accent but I heard it.) I laughed out loud, and then my amusement turned to grief as I remembered that morning only two weeks after his operation. He was convalescing at my house and doing well until he woke that Wednesday feeling really ill. I recall my bossy insistence on driving him back to hospital. When the doctor arrived to examine him, I left him in the ward, kissing him hurriedly and promising that I would be back in the morning. I didn't know that he was going to die on us that night. Now seven and a half years later I still miss him greatly, even though he remains forever alive in my internal world. I suppose it's quite understandable when you think of how much we had shared.

We became friends when he returned from London in 1957, an experienced man of the world to my 21-year-old eyes. He told me how he had noticed me walking to school when I was thirteen because he thought I looked a bit like Ingrid Bergman. I knew about him long before, from my mother who knew his mother because they were on the Benevolent Society Committee together. My mother had a picture of his mother in her scrapbook, which she had cut out of the Outspan Magazine. Perhaps he had arranged for his mother to model for that Mazawattee tea advert through his advertising connections. I remember how unfulfilling he found his copy-writing job with J Walter Thompson, even though he was so good at it. He spoke constantly about wanting to quit and become a full-time director, but to my shame, I tried to discourage him from behaving in so irresponsible and unrealistic a manner!

In any event, not having ever seen anything which he had directed, I thought that he should stick to creative writing, and that in his spare time. To my credit, though, I changed my mind when I saw his first production, "Of Mice and Men" at Dorkay House with Fats Dibeco and Corney Mabaso. His talent for directing an American play and making it so relevant to our lives in South Africa just bowled me over. I decided that it didn't matter if he was going to be a poor and struggling artist for the rest of his life! After that, I don't think I missed a single play that he directed or worked on since the Dorkay House days, and through the years I always saw evidence of his gift as a director.

By the way, it may have nothing to do with directing, but I don't think I ever got around to thanking him for pushing me to write my first psychology exam. I had decided that I wasn't going to write it. The night before I was due to write it, he was having family supper with us. He questioned me about it and I explained that it was too late and the task of going back to study at that late stage in my life was too onerous. He challenged me to go into the exam room and risk handing in a blank page because I was so unprepared. What I thought would be making a fool of myself, he thought would be a show of courage. I let him persuade me, and passing that exam set me on the road to becoming a psychotherapist.

So fixed in my mind was the image of him as a struggling artist that when he died leaving a sizeable estate to his American family, I was astonished once again. Their decision to create the Barney Simon Memorial Trust was testimony to their love and admiration for his work and their wish to perpetuate not only his memory but also his creative vision. It is the Trust which has helped to sponsor this book, which I hope will give some insight into the way he was able to harness the energy of his actors to create a vision and a body of work which held up a mirror to those painful and extraordinary years of our history.

Something that saddened me was that the fierce integrity of purpose which so illuminated his work also exhausted him, and I tried to encourage him in later years to do more work abroad, where the demands on him would be less stressful. So right near the end, when he couldn't go to London for his production of "The Suit", I thought it a positive thing that he was being forced to pay attention to himself. I'll never forget how, on the opening night of its London run at the Tricycle Theatre, they phoned at the end of the play. He took the call from his bed and listened to the applause that went on for ages. But his post-operative fragility dimmed the sound of the ovation. He had heard it before. His work was done.

Woza Barney!

Barney Simon died on the 30th June 1995 at the age of sixty-three.

Epitaph to Joe Slovo by Barney Simon

Joe was my friend and I was his. What made us that had little to do with politics or theatre. We spent little time discussing either. In fact, because of exile, life and work, we spent very little time together. All I know is that our best times were rare and quiet and alone, when we shared the comfort of our trust in each other. I found Joe through Ruth, and I found her in the Rivonia days, her time of greatest fragility and transformation, when, with Joe in exile, she was isolated by bannings and restrictions and ravaged by her 117 days of solitary confinement. When she joined Joe in exile, I visited them whenever I passed through London. My earliest memory of those times seems more fantastic than real. A glorious Sunday morning. In London that's fantasy already. Joe and Ruth bare-shouldered in bed, surrounded by newspapers, coffee and toast, which they invited me to join. Not even a shared dream less than a year before. In contrast, a few years later, I witnessed their bitter arguments over Czechoslovakia and Joe's stubborn defence of the Russian invasion. I remember equally vividly during those days the times that he and I spent wandering on the Heath, and his yearning questions about our country and the people and the places that he had loved and left behind. It was here that our bonding began. To this day, when I think of Hampstead Heath, more essential than the Houses of Parliament, I don't think of England, I think of Joe.

In 1982, weeks after Ruth's assassination, I remember Joe's enveloping embrace at the Riverside studios when we dedicated the opening night of "Woza Albert!" to her and added her name to our list of heroes. And I also remember the next day and the coffee-bar we abandoned to walk and weep together on the Heath. Our next meeting was in Mozambique, after the Nkomati Accord. Joe was subdued. He had lost light. I had never before seen him so despondent, so truly hurt. He had been instructed to leave Mozambique with the rest of the A.N.C. and he was moved from the safety of his home in the Government Compound to the unguarded danger of an ordinary suburban house. He was fetching me for a lunch that he had prepared around a precious piece of pork. When we climbed into his parked car I found an envelope, type-addressed to him, lying on my seat. A clear bull's-eye for any of the many who wanted to make him a target. We had the only argument that I can recall. At least, I argued. Joe just shrugged and smiled and mumbled something I didn't care to hear. It was a very hot and humid day, and the pork, as precious as it was, lay heavily within us, particularly me, the visitor to Mozambique. I was offered a rest in the only air-conditioned space, his bedroom upstairs. I lay down on his bed, and as I turned to doze I faced into his open wardrobe and the AK-47 that leaned in waiting among the shadows of his clothes. There is a Chassidic saying that God created man because He loves to listen to stories. If that's the case, then, despite himself, Joe had to be one of the Lord's favourites. He could spin a yarn and tell a joke with the cream of us down here below. In fact, I made Joe a proposition. We would film him telling 365 jokes and replace the daily religious programme on T.V. with a daily Joke with Joe. I thought it would do wonders for our country. But he wouldn't take me up on it. I suspect that he didn't know 365 jokes. It's not that I'm pushing God, I have my doubts about Him myself; but I suspect that Joe's life, as varied and difficult as it was, was always punctuated by miracles. The clearest one was Joe himself, and his extraordinary faith in the life that is always in the now. His genius in pragmatic transformation. His capacity for astonishment. I remember in 1990, when he first came home, trying to get him to come into my garage studio to see my greatest treasure, my Jackson Hlungwane throne. He was immoveable on my backyard stairs, staring at the sky. it was dove-grey and imprinted with two perfect rainbows. 'Gee, Barney,' he said, 'Look at that! Can you believe it! Just look at that.' I was ashamed of even trying to move him on. The other miracle was Helena. She had to be some kind of divine assignation. He was granted a woman who was his best friend, his challenge, his lover and his wife. She brought blessings to his days, and through the courage and joy that she engendered in him, brought blessings to our country. Miracles can be cruel too. The last that I will mention, and it is one that I am still struggling to respect, was the assignation of Joe's death. I have learnt through my witnessing of him in these last three years, that death is not simply the enemy of life but can also be its friend. I have learnt that if we can find the courage, and love is the greatest source of that, the knowledge that our years are limited can illuminate our every day and help us enrich what surrounds us. Maimonides wrote, in "The Guide for the Perplexed", 'When the blessed man is near death, his knowledge increases mightily, and his love for the object of his knowledge becomes more intense, and it is in this great delight that his soul separates from his body.'
Hamba kahle Joe.

Barney Simon's written epitaph to Joe Slovo, found amidst his desk papers. Joe Slovo was an anti-apartheid activist, one of the founders of Umkhonto we Sizwe, the armed wing of the ANC. He was the General Secretary of the Communist Party during the 1980s. He was the husband of Ruth First, and Minister of Housing for the Government of National Unity, until his death in January 1995, six months before Barney died.

Opposite – Joe Slovo.
Photograph courtesy of The Sunday Times.

Appendices

Barney Simon Chronology

13 April 1932	Barney Simon was born
Education	Jeppe Hebrew School Jeppe Boys High Architects draftmanship – Natal University Works in father's cap and hat factory in the assembly line
1953	Goes to Britain and works backstage for Joan Littlewood at the Theatre Royal
1953	Returns to South Africa aged 24
1959 – 1960	Sees Athol Fugard's "No Good Friday" Meets Fugard after a performance of "Nongogo" written by Athol Fugard
1961	Works as a junior copywriter in Johannesburg Works at the Rehearsal Room, Dorkay House – "The Blood Knot" written by Athol Fugard Directs "Krapps Last Tape" written by Samuel Beckett Writes and directs "Anna" Holds writers and directors workshops at Dorkay House
1964 Directs	"The Maids" written by Jean Genet "End Game" written by Samuel Beckett "Happy Days" written by Samuel Beckett
1965 Directs	World premier of Athol Fugard's "Hello and Goodbye" at The Library Theatre "An Evening of Brecht's Poetry" written by Bertolt Brecht, performed by Athol Fugard "Of Mice and Men" – with an all black cast, written by John Steinbeck Opens theatre in Parktown – "Fedora" – advertised 'free theatre for all races' Joint editor of The Classic Magazine with Casey Motsisi Dugmore Boetie comes to a writers workshop at the request of Nat Nakasa and Motsisi
1966 – 1968	Writes "Familiarity is the kingdom of the lost" with Dugmore Boetie
1968	Visits USA Directs "The Blood Knot" written by Athol Fugard for a theatre company in Boston Attends Joseph Chaikin and Jerzy Grotowski workshops Works with Puerto Rican Young Lords – equivalent of Black Panthers Associate Editor of the New American Review Directs "Hello and Goodbye", written by Athol Fugard, in New York Writes for The Village Voice – Parables of South Africa Works as an editor of The Literary Review Works on a screenplay about Raymond Krohl who resisted the Vietnam draft Adapts Isaac Bashevis Singer's novel "Enemies" for a screenplay

1970	Barney's father dies, Barney returns to South Africa Devises and runs health education projects with nurses in missionary hospitals in the Transkei, Winterveld and KwaZzulu-Natal. These were called 'Sensitivity Training'
1971	Starts Mirror One – a theatre company that could perform any where... 'in a backyard so that a person under house arrest could watch'
1971 – 1973 *Directs*	"Cayenne Pepper" written by Diobaldi "Phiri" adapted by Barney Simon from Ben Johnson's "Volpone" "The Death of Bessie Smith" written by Edward Albee "Black and Blue" written by Barney Simon and Corney Mabaso *Uses the following venues:* Dorkey House, The Old Arena, a shop front in Orange Grove, The Chelsea hotel in Hillbrow, The Blue Fox at the Oxford Hotel in Rosebank and the Nunnery and The Box Theatre at the University of the Witwatersrand Conducts workshops with actors, writers and directors at Dorkay House called Workshop 71
1973 Directs	"Begeerte" – Afrikaans adaptation of "Desire Under the Elms" written by Eugene O'Neil performed at The Old Arena "Hey Listen 2" – written by Barney Simon and cast consisting of a triple bill – "Miss South Africa (6)", "Men Should Cry More Often" and "Joburg, Sis!" performed at The Old Arena "The Maids' written by Jean Genet performed at The Old Arena "Six Characters In Search of an Author" written by Luigi Pirandello performed at The Old Arena "People" written by Barney Simon performed at The Old Arena "Woyzeck" written by Georg Büchner performed at The Old Arena
1974 Directs	"Lysistrata" written by Aristophanes performed at The Old Arena "Hey Listen 2" written by Barney Simon and cast performed at The Old Arena "Hello and Goodbye" written by Athol Fugard performed at The Blue Fox "Storytime" written by Barney Simon and cast performed at The Village in Orange Grove "Show Me Yours" written by Barney Simon and cast performed at The Blue Fox Begins The Company
1975 Directs	"Antigone" written by Sophocles performed at The Blue Fox "People Too" written by Barney Simon and cast performed at The Nunnery "Fortune and Men's Eyes" written by John Herbert (first play to rehearse at The Market) performed at The Nunnery "The Crucible" written by Arthur Miller performed at PACT
1976	Directs "Pleasure and Repentance" written by Barney Simon and cast performed in The Market upstairs foyer The Company moves into The Market Theatre

1976 Directs	"The Seagull" written by Anton Chekhov "Marat/Sade" written by Peter Weiss "Mother Courage" by Bertolt Brecht
1977 Directs	"Luv" written by Murray Schisgal "Vroue van Troje" written by Euripides (Afrikaans translation) "People are Living There" written by Athol Fugard
1978 Directs	"East" written by Stephen Berkoff "The Death of Bessie Smith" written by Edward Albee "Rosenkrantz and Guildenstern are Dead" written by Tom Stoppard "Play it Again Sam" written by Woody Allen
1979 Directs	"Cincinatti – Scenes from City Life" written by Barney Simon and cast "Statements After An Arrest Under The Immorality Act" written by Athol Fugard "Long Days Journey Into Night" written by Eugene O'Neill "Call Me Woman" written by Barney Simon and cast "Savage Love" written by Sam Shephard and Joseph Chaikin
1980 Directs	"Cat on a Hot Tin Roof" written by Tennessee Williams "Oedipus" written by Euripides "Cold Stone Jug" written by Stephen Gray and Barney Simon from the novel by HC Bosman "Brecht on Brecht" written by Bertolt Brecht
1981 Directs	"Woza, Albert!" written by Percy Mtwa, Mbongeni Ngema and Barney Simon "Marico, Moonshine and Mampoer" written by HC Bosman
1983 Directs	"Night Mother" written by Marsha Norman "Still Life" by Emily Mann
1984 Directs	"Black Dog Inj'emnyama" written by Barney Simon and cast Assisted Peter Brook in re- staging "Woza, Albert!" for France
1985 Directs	"Born in the RSA" written by Barney Simon and cast
1986 Directs	"Outers" written by Barney Simon and Nicky Rebelo "The Dybbuk" adapted by Barney Simon from the play "Yiddish" by S Ansky "Klaaglied vir Koos" written by Barney Simon and Christo Leach "Woza, Albert!" revival directed by Dixon Malele with help from Barney Simon
1987 Directs	"Eden and Other Places" written by Barney Simon and cast
1988 Directs	"Flight" written by David Lan "The Blood Knot" written by Athol Fugard
1989 Directs	"Score Me the Ages" by Barney Simon and cast "Inyanga" written by Barney Simon and cast "Born in the RSA" written by Barney Simon and cast, redirected in Chicago

1990	Directs "Starbrites" written by the Handspring Puppet Theatre, Barney Simon and cast Co-founder and Co-director of The Market Theatre Laboratory
1991 Directs	"So Whats' New?" written by Fatima Dike
1992 Directs	"Singing the Times" written by Barney Simon and cast "Death and the Maiden" written by Ariel Dorfman "The Lion and the Lamb" written by Barney Simon and John Kani
1993 Directs	"Silent Movie" written by Barney Simon and cast "The Suit" written by Barney Simon, Mothobi Mutloatse based on the short story by Can Themba
1994 Directs	"Hedda Gabler" written by Henrik Ibsen "The Fourth Day of Christmas" written by Barney Simon Participates in international workshops organised by Peter Brook in Ireland
1995	Directs "East" written by Stephen Berkoff Receives Jujamcyn Award Re-stages "Jozi Jozi" written by John Ledwaba – LIFT and tours to Stockholm Re-stages "The Suit" for London International Festival of Theatre (LIFT) Tricycle Theatre
30 June 1995	*Barney Simon dies after a heart bypass operation in Johannesburg at the age of 63.*

Goal-orientated theatre in the Winterveld, 1979

Barney said: 'In the early 1970s I started doing health work. When writer Dugmore Boetie was dying I took him to a mission hospital in Zululand. I began to do little jobs around the hospital. I became aware of the problems of communication. I began to read the problems and started doing workshops with the nurses, getting them to talk as black women, not as trained nurses, about their patients. In turn I sent them into the villages incognito to study what people felt they needed. And then bit-by-bit we began to find a vocabulary.'

Hilary Blecher's report on a workshop held at the De Wildt Catholic Mission from 26 November 1979, culminating in a performance at the Roman Catholic Church at Klipgat on Sunday 2 December 1979, documents Barney Simon's workshops in the Winterveld. Although the work in Bophuthatswana cannot strictly be regarded as 'theatre', it involved a very similar procedure to the rehearsal of a play for performance.

Published plays by Barney Simon

Simon, Barney, "Storytime" (1976) The Yellow Star Quarry, Johannesburg.

Simon, Barney, "Cold Stone Jug" (1982) Human and Rousseau, Cape Town (adapted from Stephen Gray's play "Cold Stone Jug", based on Herman Charles Bosman's book of the same name).

Simon, Barney, Percy Mtwa and Mbongeni Ngema, "Woza, Albert!" (1983) Methuen, London.

Simon, Barney, "Cincinatti – Scenes from City Life" (1984), in "South African Theatre", T. Hauptfleisch and I. Steadman (eds.) HAUM Educational Publishers, Johannesburg.

Simon, Barney, "Born in the RSA" (1986), in "Woza Afrika!", Duma Ka Ndlovu (ed.) Braziller, New York and (1994), in "More Market Plays", John Kani (ed.) AD. Donker, Johannesburg.

Simon, Barney, "Hey, Listen" (1986), in "Market Plays", Stephen Gray (ed.) A.D. Donker, Johannesburg.

Simon, Barney, "Black Dog Inj'emnyama", "Outers", "Born in the RSA" and "Score Me the Ages" (1997), in "Four Workshopped Plays", Pat Schwartz (ed.) Witwatersrand University Press, Johannesburg.

Published Fiction/Short Story Anthologies by Barney Simon

Boetie, D. with Barney Simon, "Familiarity is the Kingdom of the Lost" (1969) Barrie and Rockliff: The Cresset Press, London.

Simon, Barney, "Joburg, Sis!" (1974) Bataleur Press, Johannesburg.

Books on Barney Simon and South African Theatre

Benson, M., "Athol Fugard and Barney Simon: Bare Stage, a Few Props, Great Theatre" (1997) Ravan Press, Johannesburg.

Coplan, D., "In Township Tonight!: South Africa's Black City Music and Theatre" (1985) Longman, London.

Crow, B. with Chris Banfield, "An Introduction to Post-Colonial Theatre" (1996) Cambridge University Press, Cambridge.

Davis, G.V. and A. Fuchs (eds.), "Theatre and Change in South Africa" (1996) Harwood Academic, Amsterdam.

Fuchs, A., "Playing the Market: The Market Theatre, Johannesburg" (Revised/Updated edition) (2002) B.V. Rodopi, Amsterdam.

Hauptfleisch, T. and I. Steadman (eds.), "South African Theatre" (1984) HAUM Educational Publishers, Pretoria.

Hauptfleisch, T., "Theatre and Society in South Africa: Some Reflections in a Fractured Mirror" (1997) Van Schaik, Pretoria.

Kavanagh, R.M., "Making People's Theatre" (1997) Witwatersrand University Press, Johannesburg.

Kavanagh, R.M., "Theatre and Cultural Struggle in South Africa" (1985) Zed Books, London.

Kruger, L., "Post-imperial Brecht: Politics and Performance, East and South" (2004) Cambridge University Press, Cambridge.

Kruger, L., "The Drama of South Africa: Plays, Pageants and Publics since 1910" (1999) Routledge, London.

Orkin, M., "Drama and the South African State" (1991) Manchester University Press, Manchester, and Witwatersrand University Press, Johannesburg.

Schwartz, P., "The Best of Company: The Story of Johannesburg's Market Theatre" (1988) A.D. Donker, Johannesburg.

Select list of the references used in this book

Benson, M., "Athol Fugard and Barney Simon: Bare Stage, a Few Props, Great Theatre" (1997) Ravan Press, Johannesburg.

Boal, Augusto, "Theatre of the Oppressed" (1982) Routledge Press, New York.

Brecht, B., "Brecht on Theatre: the Development of an Aesthetic" (1964) Hill and Wang, New York.

Delgado, M. and P. Heritage, "In Contact with the Gods" (1996) Manchester University Press, Manchester.

Grotowski, Jerzy, "Towards a Poor Theatre" (1968) Methuen, London.

Hauptfleisch, T. and I. Steadman, "South African Theatre" (1983) HAUM Educational Publishers, Pretoria.

Herber, Avril (ed.), "Conversations" (1979) Bateleur Press, Johannesburg.

Schwartz, P., "The Best Of Company: The story of Johannesburg's Market Theatre" (1988) A.D. Donker, Johannesburg.

Suttner, Immanuel (ed.), "Cutting Through The Mountain: Interviews with Jewish Activists" (1997) Viking Press, London.

Tucker, Percy, "Just The Ticket!" (1997) Jonathan Ball, Johannesburg.

The Authors

Leila Henriques

Irene Stephanou

Irene Stephanou graduated with a BA (Dramatic Arts) Honours from Wits University. She is an award-winning actor writer, performer and teacher in Johannesburg. She has co-written and performed three one-woman shows, which have toured South Africa and abroad. All her new work has been staged at The Market Theatre. She developed a course under the supervision of Barney Simon, called Theatre and Life, which she still runs at The Market Theatre Laboratory. She organises development workshops in Johannesburg and is currently involved in the staging of her latest play, "Acropolis Cafe", at The Market Theatre.

Leila Henriques is an award-winning actor who grew up in Johannesburg. After leaving school, she trained at the Oxford School of Drama, and spent two years working at various locations in London, including the Tabard Theatre, which specialised in new writing. On returning to South Africa she joined the innovative Loft Theatre Company in Durban. But it was at The Market Theatre in Johannesburg where she did some of her most challenging and exciting work. She was directed by Barney Simon in "Silent Movie" and "Hedda Gabler". Leila lives in Johannesburg, where in addition to being an actor, she is a teacher, writer and mother.

Photograph by Sue Pam Grant.

Acknowledgements

The Publisher's Acknowledgements:

The Publisher would like to thank The French Institute of South Africa, the French Embassy to South Africa and the Dibuka-Information Centre on Contemporary France. Thank you also to Vanessa Cooke, Bénédicte Alliot, Jérôme Bessière, Xavier Person, Hilary Hamburger, Fiona Ramsay, Professor Willie Kgotsitsile and Matthew Krouse. This book would not have been possible without the imaginations of Julia Raynham and Rita Potenza. For that, we thank them deeply.

The Authors' Acknowledgements:

This book would not have been possible without the generosity and care of all the actors and artists that worked with Barney. Equally the Barney Simon Trust, who gave us financial support and who guided us in our choices. Vanessa Cooke, Geoff Sifrin, Hilary Hamburger and Matthew Krouse gave us their time listening and advising. Tony Stephanou, Jean Power and Nick Warren shared their computers and computer skills and made our journey smoother. We thank Rita Potenza our photographic collator for her generosity of spirit and enthusiasm and the National Arts Council for funding. Thank you to Pippa Stein for her consultation regarding the bibliography. We thank Adrienne Sichel for her invaluable, insightful contribution, and for bringing a fresh perspective to the material. Finally, we thank our publisher Maggie Davey, who always believed in the project and stuck with us through everything.

Printed by CTP Book Printers

Cover Design – Julia Raynham

Design and Layout – Julia Raynham, SIGNAL pan african ARTS

Picture Researcher and Picture Editor – Rita Potenza

Front Cover – photograph of Barney Simon by Ruphin Coudyzer
(contact for Ruphin Coudyzer FPPSA – www.ruphin.com)

Front and Back End Pages – photograph of Johannesburg Skyline by David Goldblatt

First published in the U.S. in 2006 by Seven Stories Press
140 Watts Street
New York, NY 10013
www.sevenstories.com

Originally published in South Africa in 2005 by Jacana Media (Pty) Ltd.

ISBN 1-58322-711-3